WHATEVER HAPPENED
TO TRIXIE SKYRME?

JENNIFER GREEN

BASED ON THE LIFE OF
THE MOST SKILFUL AND UNSCRUPULOUS
ADVENTURESS SCOTLAND YARD EVER
SET OUT TO CAPTURE

First published in 2011
by
Green Grass Enterprises
Copyright© Jennifer Green.

* * * * * * * *

Editor: Alison Grange

* * * * * * * *

Cover Picture
News of the World (1927)

Cover design and layout.
Pauline Vincent: Gillian Mayle: Roger Tansley.

* * * * * * * *

ISBN 978-09537534-1-3

Printed in England by
Orphans Press Ltd.
Enterprise Park : Leominster : Herefordshire : HR6 OLD.
T. 01568 612460 : E. info@orphanspress.co.uk

FOR PV WITH LOVE

Much thanks to:-

Sarah Boston
Jenni Braithwaite
Anita Corbin-O'Grady
Edward Fletcher
Alison Grange
John and Penny Green
Wilma Hayes
Nigel Heins
Murat Gunay Karpat
Gillian Mayle
Rob Ramshaw
Joan Roberts
Gill Tew
Roger Tansley
Keith Thompson
Ann Winn
The Blue Note Brigade
and the
The Vincent Three
Pauline : Wendy : Diane

For their continued support, friendship, patience and laughter.

Jen also thanks:-
Computer Knowledge: One Stop Print Shop: Orphans Press Ltd.
in Leominster, for their invaluable, technical help and assistance.

EARLY REVIEWS

"An enthralling read. Jennifer Green tells the extraordinary life story of Trixie Skyrme framed by a rich backdrop of period detail."

Sarah Boston - Writer and Film Maker

"A delightful read from start to finish, bringing the colourful character of Trixie very much to life. A heart-warming story revealing how this charismatic woman had such a dramatic influence on everyone who met her.

Alison Grange - Journalist

"My first response is that the book is already very cinematic, visual, atmospheric and evocative. The dialogue is great."

Jane Hawksley - International Screenwriter

Jennifer (Jen) Green was born in Hampshire in 1938. After a basic secondary education, she worked for Boots the Chemist before joining the Women's Royal Naval Service attached to the Fleet Air Arm. From then, she progressed through mechanical engineering into senior posts in university administration and later into executive management at the Family Planning Association.

Eventually, she took the opportunity to set up a major arts complex in the Home Counties resulting in six months researching theatre and arts in New Zealand.

In 1976, she saw a gravestone in the churchyard of a small town in Mid-Wales and became a writer publishing her first book in 1987 and again in 1990; it was later optioned and developed into a screenplay. An experienced freelance journalist, feature writer and occasional broadcaster, she remains a popular after dinner and public speaker for all occasions working out of Leominster in Herefordshire. If she ever gets the time Jen can be found watching cricket, at the cinema or putting the world to rights in the Blue Note Café Bar in Leominster.

January 2011.

PROLOGUE

There was nothing going on in Mayfair. The Festival of Britain on the South Bank had poached most of the summer tourists leaving London's West End to its daily self. The Wednesday morning traffic tooted its way around Marble Arch, the ear-piercing ring of the distant ambulance bell going unnoticed by the steady flow of window-gazing shoppers promenading the pavements of Oxford Street.

In nearby Bond Street, coffee hour was at its peak, the newly painted coffee houses playing host to weary shoppers flopped out on bentwood chairs. Fired by confidence boosting recommendations from fashionable friends, the women of suburbia refreshed themselves with copious cups of French-style coffee before popping back to Fenwick to check out a little black number for Saturday night's do at the golf club.

Conversation centred upon the health of the King, Winston Churchill's election prospects and Basil Spence's prize-winning design for Coventry Cathedral. Part hidden behind the potted plants, minor conspirators were more concerned with newspaper headlines alleging that the missing diplomats, Guy Burgess and Donald Maclean, were Soviet spies and homosexual to boot.

In the foyers of the Ritz and Claridge's discreet, Jaeger-clad mistresses lightly dipped in Chanel No.5, awaited adulterous captains of industry keen for an afternoon's diversion before departing for the family home in leafy Surrey, after a busy day at the office!

Amid the hustle and bustle of late morning in Mayfair, Big Ben struck 11.00am and life went on - or did it? Nobody heard or cared about the speeding ambulance cutting its way through South Audley Street or the ear-shattering bell warning other drivers to move over and make way. It turned into Curzon Street, and then left into Queen's Street before slowing down as it approached Chesterfield Gardens.

The driver cancelled the bell and halted outside a block of smart mansion flats; a dapper gentleman in his late middle years was standing in the doorway.

He beckoned to the attendants and, after a few words, they quickly lifted a folded stretcher from the rear of the ambulance and between them manoeuvred it through the doorway and into the building. The senior attendant paused to make enquiries and the group moved awkwardly into the waiting lift.

In the spacious entrance hall of a large apartment on the first floor, Dr. Creighton, a local general practitioner, sat at a writing table. He looked up when he heard the whine of the lift motor. Quickly completing his medical notes, he slipped them into a manila envelope and then picked up a small brown bottle emptied of its prescribed contents and carefully studied the label. The sudden metallic clang of the lift doors made him jump up nervously and he hurriedly slipped the bottle inside the same package.

The dapper man calmly ushered the medical attendants past the doctor, now standing in the hallway, into a bedroom where the unconscious body of a middle-aged woman lay on a large double bed. She was wearing stylish cream silk pyjamas partly covered by matching cream silk sheets; the small group silently looked at her and then at each other. The doctor nodded and, under his watchful eye, the woman, wrapped in a rough, red blanket, was gently carried from the room. Pausing in the hallway, the stretcher party waited long enough for Dr. Creighton to drop the manila envelope onto the red blanket and, for a brief moment, saw tension in the ashen face of the occupier of the apartment as he silently stared down on the lifeless form of the unconscious woman.

Breaking the silence, the attendant informed him they would take her to St. George's Hospital as fast as possible and invited him to ride with her in the ambulance but he declined, preferring to follow on later, and escorted them to the lift. When he returned to the apartment, he had one hand suspiciously in his pocket; it went unnoticed by Dr. Creighton and, for a short while, the GP paced the hallway quietly muttering he had done all he could and offered to take the shocked man with him to St. George's Hospital.

Clearly shaken by events, he said he would visit later when he hoped to see an improvement in her condition but Creighton warned him that, in his opinion, the patient was beyond help and questioned as to why he had not called him in sooner. The older man's reasons seemed plausible enough; he thought she was sleeping heavily after a night out but added that she had drunk no more than her usual quota.

Shaking his head in disbelief, Dr. Creighton announced that, despite being her physician for a very long time, she had never struck him as a likely suicide and, should she not recover, her stomach content could provide further evidence. As the two men walked to the door, the gentleman nervously cleared his throat and enquired whether the woman would pull through. The doctor advised him to prepare for the worst and to contact any family.

He quickly agreed to contact her sister in Mortlake and the two men shook hands in the doorway; before the doctor entered the lift, the concerned man quietly suggested his position at work might require some discretion regarding the unfortunate incident. Creighton told him that, in the case of sudden death, all matters relating to the incident are passed to the Coroner's Office for investigation and inquest.

Returning to his apartment, the quiet man went to the kitchen, made himself a strong coffee, added a dash of brandy for good measure and carried it into the fashionable drawing room furnished entirely by Heal's. He sat down at an occasional table and, after a while, lifted the telephone and asked the operator for a West London number. The call was unemotional and straight to the point, formally telling the listener that her sister was on her way to St. George's Hospital and there was little hope of recovery.

Stressing his shock at finding her, he explained he was taking a brandy with his coffee and after a few minutes of detailed conversation, they agreed to meet up at St. George's and he would pray her sister would pull through. Replacing the phone, he picked up his coffee cup and went into the empty bedroom.

Seated at the dressing table, he studied the room as if he had never seen it before. Large, stylish and tastefully decorated, it carried an air of class that betrayed the rest of the apartment. Artistically, it more than hinted at flair and quality, the fashionable, contemporary furniture and fittings mixing easily with the selective paintings, antiques and memorabilia that one day might tell a tale or two. Signed photographs of famous personalities from the past lined the cream walls and a wooden model of a racing car, cleverly converted into a table lamp, illuminated a corner of the room.

A colourful sequined jacket casually tossed onto the back of a chair hinted at a life of glamour and, on the top of the wardrobe, covered by a light layer of household dust, a khaki pith helmet trimmed with an Indian silk scarf sat alongside a riding crop.

Well-thumbed outdated society magazines littered the bedside tables and the man wearily picked one up; fingers trembling he flicked through the pages until he spotted a framed picture of an attractive young woman in riding habit. His eyes glazed over as they rested on the familiar features and he all but sobbed as he struggled to hold back his tears.

The dressing table was a muddle of jewellery, perfume bottles and cosmetics; otherwise, the room was quite neat and tidy. The weary man leaned forward and stared at himself in the triple mirror but, after a brief moment, he aggressively threw the magazine at his reflection. As he stooped to retrieve it, he spotted a silver framed, hand-tinted photograph lying face down on the floor. It was inscribed 50th Birthday Party, Claridge's March 1949. Lifting it carefully, he confronted the portrait of a strikingly handsome woman in her middle years, her eyes and the lines around them recording a well-lived but troubled life. The once dark hair was peppered grey and she was sipping champagne from a cut glass flute. The dress she wore was definitely designer and the jewellery very expensive - apart, that is, from a cheap-looking silver locket around her neck.

The ring of the telephone on the bedside table startled him. He quickly picked it up and, as he listened, what colour there was drained slowly from his face. It was Dr. Creighton reporting that the woman was dead on arrival at the hospital, her sister had not yet arrived and would he please come and make a formal identification for the police.

He tried to stand up but could not and sat down again; the photo frame slipped from his grasp and smashed into pieces as it struck the edge of the bedside table. Shaking from head to toe he struggled to his feet and tried to stay calm but the room suddenly felt very cold and he trembled as he tried to contain the fear surging through his ageing veins. Smoothing the ruffled bed linen that had covered the unconscious woman, he softly touched the pillow before taking a final look around the room. It was a room he had hardly ever entered, accept by invitation, yet he knew many of the secrets hidden between the four walls. He was about to leave when something or someone jogged his memory. For a few moments, he rummaged among the jewellery scattered on top of the dressing table until he found what he was looking for, a silver locket on a silver chain. It had dulled with age and did not stand out among the rest of the pieces but he clasped it as if it were solid gold.

Opening it, he revealed two small portraits featuring an attractive young woman and a good-looking man each dressed in Edwardian style; quickly snapping it shut he slipped it into his pocket and hesitantly moved towards the door. Pausing in the doorway, he turned to bow his head in final farewell to the departed woman and as he did so sensed the heady aroma of Chanel No.5 filtering through the room. Closing the door behind him, he thought he heard a familiar voice whisper goodbye and his body began to shake.

Deeply shocked, he hurried into his own room, changed his tie to black, brushed what hair he had and covered it with a stylish, hand-made trilby; carefully locking the front door behind him, he left the apartment and called up the lift. The hum of the winding gear echoed through the marbled landings as the metal cage carried the tired man to the ground floor. On the doorstep, he gulped in the fresh air, composed himself, looked about him and marched 'Sergeant Major like' towards Hyde Park Corner.

CHAPTER ONE

Herefordshire in May is a stunning patchwork of colour. Red earth, green meadows, and eager young hop shoots winding through a maze of twine and wooden poles proving the point. In the small, black and white villages dotted about the countryside, life appeared relatively untouched by the gathering clouds of war in Europe.

In the hop yards around Wellington, local youths bantered bawdy comments as they competed for the attentions of the village girls and when it came to favours, Trixie Skyrme, a plain country girl with plaited hair and a best dress for Sundays allowed them just enough rope to dangle on and they loved it. On the dry, stonewall separating village from fields, the post pubescent local lads observed silent worship as 15-year-old Trixie strolled past. Flouting her sexuality with a candour that belied her years, she casually looked them over before waving to her sister Fanny, handicapped since birth by a clubbed foot.

Trixie, short for Theresa, was born in the shadow of the magpie on 8th January 1899 at Holmer Cottage in Wellington, a black and white village halfway between Hereford city and Leominster. The youngest of six children, her father, John Skyrme, an itinerant general labourer, pilfered his way across the county seeking work for himself and his sons and quickly losing it under suspicion of theft. His world-weary wife Mary struggled to bring up the family in whatever tied or rented accommodation came with the job, forcing young Trixie into a variety of schools including a Catholic Convent school near to Hereford.

Fanny and Trixie were the youngest in the family and very close to their mother. Their three older brothers had left home as soon as they could but George, a chip off his father's block, stayed at home. The small, family income came and went between bouts of heavy cider drinking and the three women regularly suffered at the hands - and fists - of the remaining men-folk. Like father like son, their brother George Skyrme was also a violent, moody, drunken misogynist.

What happened to Mary Skyrme usually occurred behind the closed doors of the bedroom and, although not seen, it relayed through the walls of Holmer cottage. Fanny generally took the brunt of the verbal and physical assaults but Trixie managed to escape a walloping, her strong will and strength of character enabling her to stand up to her violent father. Nevertheless, the regular beatings and abuse she witnessed left a deeply etched scar upon her young memory. Despite her limited education, Trixie made the most of school life. Considered a bright girl and a keen learner, when the occasion demanded she could speak like a Girton Girl but in moments of anger and passion she was let down by a lack of grammar. As she grew up she attracted the boys like bees around a honeypot; they yearned for her attentions and it soon became obvious that Trixie's sharp mind, promising looks and out-going personality had a lot to offer but little did she realise then what life would offer her in return.

It all began on a warm, late afternoon in Wellington. It was May Fair week in Hereford and payday for the farmer's boys and she was out to enjoy herself as she flirtatiously paraded the local hop yards for admirers keen to take her to town. Acutely aware of the effect her swishing petticoat was having on the young men waiting on the wall, she suggestively brushed past them prompting a scruffy lad, not long out of short pants, to shout: 'Show us yer knickers Trix.'

His pals took up the theme. 'No, you don't wanna' show him nothing, Trix. He don't even know what he's lookin' for. Come in the fields with me girl, I'll show yer and don't bother bringin' yer knickers.'

Behind the hand, sniggers broke into smutty laughter and Trixie turned sharply. Hitching up her frock to knicker leg height she provocatively invited a second look but this time she was unable to avoid the outstretched arms that reached down and lifted her onto the wall. Catching her breath, she joined in the laughter until she realised that the same scruffy lad was trying to slip his grubby hand up her skirt. She spun round, slapped his face hard and he recoiled in fear and embarrassment.

'Keep your mucky 'ands to yerself,' she yelled. 'Now clear off.'

She pulled her skirt over her knees and announced in a warning to the others: 'He ain't comin' out with us tonight and that's final and if any of you wants to try it, it'll be a slap in the face for you too.'

Tom Evans, her most ardent admirer, leaned across Trixie and pushed the offending yob backwards; to loud jeers, he fell over the wall and landed on a very soft cowpat.

'Sod off home and take that cow shit with yer,' Tom Evans advised him, and everyone laughed as he got up and walked away, the cowpat firmly stuck to his pants.

Tom waited for the coarse laugher to die down before asking: 'Are yer coming to the May Fair then, Trix?'

'I might...if it's you askin' Tom Evans,' and winked at him. The rest of the lads, including Sid Hoskins, noticed it.

'Your lucky night then Tom?' he said and pointed at him.

'He'll be burstin' through his buttons if 'er big eyes linger on his pants for much longer.'

'Shut yer piggy mouth,' Trixie warned. 'One thing you can be sure of nitty head, I won't be goin' anywhere with the likes of you, ever.'

'Yeah Sid, you can go out with clod hoppin' Fanny and 'er big foot.'

Billy Little laughed too soon; he had taken a big risk attacking Fanny in front of her sister. In a flash of anger, Trixie grabbed him by his shirt collar.

'You'll get my big foot on yer tiddler if yer carry on talking about my sister like that.'

Knocked off balance, Billy slid off the wall just as Trixie's anger spilled over and she lashed at his groin with her foot. The collective gasp as her pointed shoe narrowly missed his crotch was warning enough that you do not meddle with Trixie Skyrme.

The lads froze as she looked at each one of them in turn. 'You'd best remember this, all of you. If I ever hears any of you slaggin' off my sister, it will be flashing lights and blinding pain when my boot hits your balls. Now get off to the pigsty you call home Billy Little and don't come back.'

Realising that this was not the time to be fooling around, Tom Evans took a chance and cautiously broached the subject of Fanny. Jumping off the wall, he took a decisive step backwards before asking: 'You weren't planning to bring Fanny with us were yer Trix? I mean it's May Fair night. She ain't comin' is she?' he pleaded.

She stared at him and he visibly paled; the others on the wall lowered their eyes and fidgeted. Exercising the power she held over them, Trixie did not answer straightaway and each one dropped their eyes to avoid her steady gaze.

In a moment her sunshine mood had returned and, in a voice that mischievously hinted at the sexual promise to come, she replied: 'Not if you're takin' me, Tom Evans. I does like a bit of privacy when I'm courting.'

Blushing from the neck upwards, he lifted her off the wall and, to the wide-eyed amazement of the eager watchers, he gripped his dream girl against his muscular body for just a mite too long. She quickly wriggled free, adjusted her skirts and called out to her sister sitting on the grass bank across the road.

'Get off home now our Fanny. Tell Ma I'm off to the May Fair, I might be late home.'

'But Trixie you promised to help with me readin' tonight,' she replied.

Trixie sensed her disappointment. 'Tomorrow Fan, I promise, we'll do a proper job then.'

Still within hearing distance, Sid Hoskins picked up the banter and chanced his arm again.

'And Tom Evans will do a proper job on you tonight if you drop yer drawers before bedtime.'

Nobody dared laugh as Trixie calmly turned on him: 'Yes Sid Hoskins, he might well, but it's somethin' you'll never manage in a month of Sundays not without your Ma holding it for yer.'

Laughter flooded the quiet lane as Sid Hoskins, finally put in his place, sloped off to loud jeers from his pals. The verbal encounter with Trixie almost caused him to collide with the cider-bus to Hereford.

'Bus is here,' Tom yelled. 'Are we goin' to the May Fair or not?'

He grabbed Trixie's hand and they ran towards the wagon waving their arms for the driver to stop. Fanny lay on the grassy bank and watched the bus as it disappeared towards Hereford, then awkwardly stood up and limped home praying that this was not going to be another Friday night when her father and brother came home drunk.

At the turn of the 20th century, Hereford's May Fair was a not-to-be-missed annual event; packed with attractions and amusements it provided a pleasure ground for all classes. Cheek by jowl, people elbowed their way through the crowded city bumping into each other at every twist and turn to be first in the queue for the latest rides.

At its height, the ragtime music pumped out of colourful steam organs and the hymns and tambourines of the Salvation Army created a roistering fun of the fair atmosphere.

Flashy showmen and mouthy barkers pushed pay-night punters into spending all their wages on freak shows, the latest fairground challenges and new-to-the-scene attractions like prize-fighting, fire-eaters and the tiniest crowded pullers, the performing fleas.

Mr. Studt's great circular switchback, known as the 'mountain climber', made its debut in the city and soon became a magnet for daring lads and lasses keen to be whirled round and round, prompting terrified girls to cling onto brave boys, just in case. The more timid preferred Mr. Studt's elaborately decorated roundabouts which moved up and down imitating horses at the gallop. These were so popular that when the fair opened people swarmed to mount the horses in what was known locally as 'the Zulu Rush'. To add to the atmosphere a unique contraption dispensed ozone into the crowds to bring a touch of a seaside outing to Borth on a breezy day.

For three pence, a girl could buy a brooch with a fake diamond bigger than the famous Koh-I-Noor but Trixie Skyrme had better things than a cheap fake on her mind as she clambered down from the bus.

It was her first proper visit to the fair without her mother and sister in tow and she was over-excited at the thought of being out alone for the first time.

Chased by Tom Evans and the rest of the village lads, she dashed into High Town and quickly disappeared into the crowd. Weaving her way past courting couples, she hid behind bushy sticks of candyfloss and laughed at sticky faced children pleading with parents to part with more money than they could afford. High above her she waved to the gaudy roundabout riders and screamed at the switchback as it careered towards her.

Almost breathless, she paused to watch sweethearts and lovers oblivious of the approaching war, canoodling under the noses of eagle-eyed recruiting sergeants prowling the fairgrounds for fit, young fighting men. She cared little for their plight.

Trixie finally let the boys catch up with her but time and cash was fast running low for the farmer's Wellington boys; most of their wage packets had gone on winning a glittering prize at the hoopla stall for their best girl. Well aware of her restless nature, Tom desperately wanted to win a keepsake for the love of his life too, but he was also aware of the flirtatious glances she was giving passing admirers. Scared that a quiet nod, a wink or tip of a cap might instantly attract her attention away from him, he possessively clung onto her arm as they made their way through the fair ground. At the hoopla, the persuasive barker beckoned the small group over for a fourth time.

'Over 'ere lads,' he called out hopefully. 'Come on, win a prize for the little lady and walk her home tonight.' He winked at Tom.

Sid Hoskins, undeterred by the earlier threats from Trixie, had followed the group into town. Still unable to keep out of trouble he yelled back: 'That's what we've been tryin' to do on your nitty 'oopla stall. I reckon it's fixed.'

'Nothing fixed about my hoopla mate. You just ain't got the knack, that's all.'

Trixie smiled at the barker's backchat.

'He ain't got the knack for anythin' have yer Sid, but his Ma still let's him out.'

The others sniggered. 'Shut yer mouth tart face,' Sid snapped back but, before he could finish, Tom Evans had him by the shirtfront. 'Just watch your dirty gob Hoskins or I'll shove your teeth down yer throat.'

The barker leaned over his stall and pulled them apart. 'Break it up lads, women ain't worth fighting over.'

'Maybe not at your age mate, but I'll break him into pieces if he mouths off my girl again,' Tom threatened.

'Now Tom Evans, I'm no-one's girl yet. Not until someone wins me a prize I'm not,' Trixie announced.

'Well we ain't got any more money for prizes have we Tom?' Sid said.

'Then shove off and let those who has 'ave a go,' the barker replied.

They shuffled off and stood a few feet away from the stall. One by one they turned out their pockets until Tom Evans found a penny piece.

'Let's toss for it,' he said. 'You do it Trix, winner takes all. Okay lads?'

As they formed a small closed circle for the toss-up, Tom failed to notice George Davis, a flashy young man, watching them closely from behind the awning of a nearby stall.

Captivated by Trixie, he moved in closer and watched her as she tossed the coin high in the air and waited for it to fall into her waiting hand. Before she could catch it, Davis stepped forward, snatched at it and held it in the palm of his own hand. Mouths open, the small gang watched the unwanted intruder take Trixie's arm and lead her to the hoopla stall.

'How many guv?' the barker asked.

'Three will do it,' Davis replied and turned to smile at Trixie. 'Well little lady, what's the prize to be apart from you?'

Trixie flushed with excitement, she looked over her shoulder at her flabbergasted companions. Pointing to the hoopla prizes, she smiled and said: 'The locket would suit me nicely mister,' and grinned at her friends.

The barker handed Davis the three rings. 'Good luck to yer sir.'

He looked at the young girl at his side and quietly commented: 'I think I've already got it.'

The dejected lads moved protectively towards Trixie as Davis, taking precise aim, tossed the first ring and missed, the lads laughed and he aimed again. The second throw hit the locket but did not circle it. Tom Evans sighed in relief.

Davis paused, looked at Trixie and crossed his fingers. He arrogantly flexed his muscles and launched the final ring and, to the amazement of the gathering, the ring dropped neatly over the wooden plinth and settled around the locket.

'Shit,' Sid Hoskins gasped. His mates nodded in silent disbelief. The barker was about to hand the prize to Trixie but Davis leaned across and took it from him.

Disappointed, she confronted her new admirer but he gently turned her round, lifted her hair above her neckline and carefully fixed the chain in place. Smiling broadly, she paraded it in triumph before her friends who grudgingly admired it. Pink with pleasure, she looked over her shoulder towards Davis, but he was not there.

'He buggered off sharpish Trix,' Sid said. 'It's back to the farmer's boys for you girl.'

Trixie shrugged her shoulders and took Tom's waiting arm. 'Farmer's boy! Sid Hoskins. It ain't your lucky day either nitty 'ead.'

Out of pocket and with nothing to show from their weekly earnings, the small group strolled through the busy fairground towards the waiting buses. Sid grabbed a stick or two of candyfloss from an unattended stall and they all ran off laughing.

From the window of the Market Tavern, George Davis watched their every move and grinned to himself. The girl had taken his fancy and she knew it, but for now he had decided to play it safe until she was ready to step into a criminal way of life.

CHAPTER TWO

It was more than a year later when Trixie saw George Davis again; she was on her way home from visiting her uncle and aunt in Ivington and her wicker basket was full of fresh produce from their market garden. Dressed in her Sunday best and wearing her prized silver locket, she had tied her hair back with a ribbon to show it off. Walking into the breeze, she kept a steady pace and sang to herself as she trailed through the long grass beside the road. It was still a good mile to the footpath across the meadows leading to Wellington and she was glad that Fanny had decided to stay at home. She was fond of her big sister but Fanny's crippled leg always slowed them down and, sometimes, she liked to walk alone at a faster pace.

Trixie had matured since her brief adventure at the hoopla stall and she no longer mixed with the village boys, her once girlish looks had all but disappeared and she was turning into an attractive young woman. Strong willed and more positive than ever, and engrossed in her dreams of a better life for herself, her mother and her sister, she did not hear the approaching car until the horn sounded. Trying to avoid it, she stumbled into the hedge, spilling the contents of her basket onto the carriageway.

'Sod off,' she yelled at the driver and shook her fist until the vehicle slowed down and stopped a few yards ahead. It was a flashy, open-top two-seater bordering on the sporty and at first Trixie did not recognise George Davis. She was carefully re-packing her basket when he reversed back, leaned out of the car and spoke to her.

'Well, well if it isn't Miss Hoopla 1914. It's been a long time.'

Looking around he asked: 'Where are all the boyfriends today?'

Trixie put the basket down, brushed the grass from her dress and carefully checked her hair. He laughed at her efforts.

She glared at him: 'What's it to you road hog, and what yer laughing at? This is my best dress.'

Still laughing he said: 'If I'm a road-hog, you must be a hedgehog!'

'This ain't any laughing matter Mister. Folks aren't safe with toffs like you muckin' up the lanes with your smelly machines.'

'Motor car young lady, this is a motor car, now, can I give you a lift home. Wellington is it?'

'How do you know that?'

Pointing to the signpost: 'Because that's the way you're going. Don't you remember me?'

'Yeah! Yeah! Course I do.' She walked towards the car and leaned over the door. 'What I want to know is why you nipped off like that after the May Fair?'

'I didn't want to upset the boyfriends,' he replied mischievously. She snapped back at him: 'They weren't my boyfriends, just boys.'

Swinging the basket onto the car bonnet, she jumped up beside it and, using the cloth that covered the food, polished the big wing mirror and peered into it.

Slightly amused, Davis watched her carefully: 'Like what you see, do you? I do.'

'I like the car, that's all. It's nice.'

'Then let me drive you home? Get in. It's on my way.'

'To where?' she asked. 'Wherever you're going,' he replied.

Trixie handed him the basket and he tucked it into the small space behind the seats. As she slid off the bonnet, he opened the passenger door. 'In you get little lady.'

Unexpectedly hesitating, she defiantly challenged: 'Ma wouldn't like me to go car riding with strange men.'

'Then don't,' he replied sharply and revved up the engine, stretched across the passenger seat and tried to close the door but she stopped him with her foot. Hitching up her dress to expose her trim legs, she cheekily replied: 'But as I knows yer mister, I trusts yer to behave like a gent - in a gent's car that is.'

George Davis smiled and waited for her to make herself comfortable on the soft leather seat.

'Really nice car,' she cooed. 'I bet you can give a girl a good time?'

Davis smiled again: 'Depends on the girl and how much time she's got.'

He reached over and touched her neck. 'I see you're wearing it then?' She blushed as he ran his finger around the chain on her neck.

'Yeah, well can't leave it hanging around at home. Given half the chance me rotten brother would have sold it for cider by now. It's safer where it is and it's staying there.'

George took his arm away and drove off, at the crossroads he turned left and cruised along the lane towards Wellington.

Trixie untied the ribbon holding back her hair and let it fly in the wind. Davis remained silent, his head was in a whirl but he managed to keep his eyes on the road.

Lying back in her comfortable seat Trixie asked him again: 'How did you know where I lived when I don't even know who you are?' He gave her a serious look: 'A good reporter never reveals his sources.'

'You really work for the papers then?' 'Among other things,' he replied.

'So what's yer name then. Is it in the paper or what?'

'Sometimes it is and sometimes I write under a different one.'

'You must earn a lot of money to drive a car like this. Can I toot the horn?'

'Toot away,' he invited. She leaned across him and pressed the rubber bulb at the end of the brass horn.

Excited by the unexpected encounter she unintentionally put her free hand on his knee and felt the shockwave that surged through him. 'Whatever next,' she exclaimed.

'Whatever next indeed,' he said, yet instantly knew that with a bit of coaxing and coaching she was just what he had been waiting for.

He dropped her off at the edge of the village and, as she turned to walk away, he suddenly announced: 'I'm George Davis. It has been a pleasure.'

She stopped and, with just a touch of the Girton Girl in her voice, she quickly replied: 'Really, thanks for the ride. I'm Theresa Skyrme, Trixie to my friends,' and with a brief wave, she turned and walked away.

'I already know who you are,' he shouted. She stopped again, turned back a pace or two and laughed at him.

'Oh you do, do you. I suppose you have your sources for that too. Be seeing you.'

'Indeed you will, Miss Skyrme, and sooner than you think,' he muttered to himself and watched her disappear round the bend in the lane. Looking at his pocket at his watch, he set off for Hereford.

George Davis, three years older than Trixie, was born into a 'respectable' Hereford family living at Coningsby Street; his parents sent George and his brothers to be educated at the Lord Scudamore School. Good looking with a sharp mind, he later claimed to be a freelance reporter working for the 'Hereford Times' and various regional newspapers. He carried the air and sartorial bearing of a well off young man about town and sailed to close to the wind when it came to bending the law.

Popular with women, he looked and presented beyond his years: he had been eighteen when he bumped into Trixie Skyrme at the May Fair. Despite the three-year age gap, from the very first moment he saw her among the crowds in High Town, he was smitten. Throughout the evening he had tracked the small group as they strolled through the fairground and was immediately impressed with the way she used her body language to extract money from the wage packets of the farmer's boys. It was obvious that she favoured one, more than she favoured the others and he had felt an unexpected pang of jealousy.

At the time, he was dodging conscription but recruiting officers were about town looking for eager candidates to send to foreign fields and he was intent on keeping a low profile. There were plenty of faces in uniform and he would soon be recognised if he stayed in one place for too long but he had things to do before the inevitable call-up papers caught up with him.

A clever and smooth operator with a good many strings to his bow, he practised his considerable skills as a forger to make money, but now the time was ripe to recruit a gullible, pretty woman assistant to front his plans. Chatty, challenging and well groomed, apart from her age, young Trixie Skyrme looked the likely candidate and in the hands of an expert like himself, she had the potential for almost anything. Since their second meeting on the road to Wellington, George Davis had secretly dogged her footsteps, carefully noting what she wore and how she presented herself when out on her own. Now and again he contrived to bump into her and, without giving too much away, he carefully guided the young girl Trixie towards 'the good' life she dreamed of, quietly taught her the tricks of his shady trade and broadened her mind to the ways of the world. Quick to learn, she absorbed it all but when George asked for bedroom 'favours', she was hard to crack. Trixie had discovered early that certain favours needed to be held back, just in case.

Twelve months after their second meeting, George launched his young prodigy into the delights of Hereford's teatime society; Trixie had matured beyond her years and was looking good. To help provide extra income for her hard-pressed mother, now and again she occasionally took on domestic duties for the local gentry. Working below stairs in large country houses brought her many opportunities to check out the upstairs way of life and learn a few new tricks. The 'rainy day' bonus came from the petty criminal activities her new consort introduced her to which she often practised, without his knowledge, on her own.

The Herefordian accent had all but disappeared, she was amusing, sharp-witted and quietly seductive and, before long, she was working with George in a variety of dubious activities, making her much more than she could have expected.

When George felt she was ready, he took her for afternoon tea at the Veranda Tea Rooms, in Leominster. The waitress brought a dish of fancy cakes to the table and, much to the annoyance of the impatient server, Trixie had difficulty in making a choice.

'I can't make up my mind, they all look so tasty,' she said. 'Perhaps I'll have the pink one...no the chocolate looks nicer.' She looked at the waitress and then her partner and suggested: 'George, why don't you choose?'

The waitress was irritated and sighed heavily.

'If it's too much trouble,' George enquired.

'It's our busy time sir,' she replied.

'Then leave them all please,' George replied. The first hint of his short temper was beginning to show.

The waitress pressed on regardless: 'We are rationed sir.'

'Then I shall pay for them all,' he said and tossed more than a few shillings onto the table. 'This will pay for them, yours as well I shouldn't wonder. Consider it a tip.'

The surly waitress smiled sweetly: 'Certainly sir,' and placed the dish of cakes in front of a smug-faced Trixie and walked away.

'All for me?' Trixie asked.

'Of course,' George replied: 'All for you and much more if you stick with me girl.'

He took her manicured hand in his but she pulled it away. Much to the distaste of the waitress, by now deep in conversation with the cashier in the kiosk, Trixie waved a finger over the confections like a magic wand.

'Eenie meeni minee mo, which will be the first to go?' and kept on waving it over the dish until it rested on a pink cake.

'That one,' she cried out in glee and, nodding politely to nearby customers, she lifted it onto her plate and in an exaggerated posh accent offered the dish to Davis. 'Confections Mr. Davis?'

He followed her mischievous mood: 'Most kind Miss Skyrme. The Victoria sponge looks quite delicious. Do you want to try it?'

'Just a nibble,' she replied and accepted a bite from George's slice?

'I must say it is not as nice as mother makes. It's the jam you know, she much prefers to spread raspberry inside.'

George bit into his cake: 'Yes so do, I my dear. So light with her touch your mother. In my opinion, hers is quite simply the best in the borders. But there is a war you know.'

They laughed so loud that heads turned and, for a few moments, they silently concentrated on tea. George changed the subject.

'You've worked hard on your accent Trixie. It's good, very good.'

'I have to hide it at home but Ma has noticed and wants me to teach our Fanny.' George lowered his voice and took her hand again.

'It's time to move on, Trixie.'

She looked puzzled: 'Have a heart George I haven't finished my tea yet.'

'I mean, leave home. It's time for my fledgling to fly the nest.'

'Move from Wellington. I can't leave Ma and Fanny. They need me?'

'Look Trix. If we are going to con the world together, we can't do it from Wellington. We've had the practice and now it's time to let you loose on a punter or two.'

'You think I'm ready then?'

'As you'll ever be at this stage. There's still a lot to learn from the master, but I think we can put you under starter's orders.'

'Meaning?' she asked.

He carefully studied the cake stand.

'Meaning that you should find a place of your own. Are you going to eat those cakes? They have cost me a tidy packet,' he said as he pushed the dish towards her.

The suggestion of a move alarmed her.

'Look George, I can't leave them now, it's me bringing the money in these days but I will take the cakes home for Ma and Fanny.'

'After we've bounced a few cheques around the county you will earn enough cash to rent a place for the three of you and provide a base for us.'

Trixie shook her head in amazement. 'You've planned this haven't you, George? I've been wondering why you've spent so much time teaching me the tricks of your trade. Well well, so I'm going to be rich am I?'

Looking at her in mock admiration, he laughed and said: 'You can be anything you want to be Trix. Good looks and a quick mind are rare in a woman and at your age too. Well, let me tell you, the world's your oyster girl. I have never known anyone pick up things so quickly and not just purses from pockets. I tell you Trix, with my brains and your looks and cunning we're a winning team.'

Sitting back, he whistled through his teeth before suggesting: 'Before long I will change that cheap silver locket you wear for solid gold.'

Twisting the chain round her neck, Trixie leaned forward. 'Not likely, it's my talisman and you won it for me fair and square but you have taught me a lot George, I'll give you that but I did get us out of some bad moments. You could have landed in clink without me watching yer back and I have come up with a few good scams myself.'

'Granted Trix, but it's the 'big ones' that bring the dosh in and I'm working on a few new tricks, so let's find you a house and take it from there. There is a decent sized place to rent in Barton Road; I know the agent and I can get a good deal on it. So let's go and look.'

Trixie was quick to respond: 'What, go and see it now George, with you? I'm not so sure about that!'

Wisely, George took a mental step back and played his cards carefully.

'Lord no,' he exclaimed. 'Best I keep a low profile on the home front, remember I'm trying to dodge the trenches, no permanent base for me just yet Trix. Let's get the bill and go home.'

Beckoning to the waitress, a surprised Trixie whispered: 'Oh! Are you going to pay for this one George? Not slipping off to the gents while I nip off to the ladies cloakroom.'

'Always remember one thing Trix, the golden rule of a good confidence trickster is, never mess about on your own door step. Next time we'll have tea at De Grey's.'

'What! All the way to lovely Ludlow! Lucky me,' she said sarcastically.

'For now yes. One day it might even be the Ritz,' he replied with some conviction.

Trixie pretended to faint. 'The Ritz! Well now yer talking George Davis. Afternoon tea at the London Ritz! What more can a country girl ask for?'

'I told you girl, stick with Georgie Boy and you're on the up. I will pay on the way out. Oh yes and don't forget to ask the waitress to wrap up the cakes. Don't go stuffing them up your knicker leg; I shall pay up front, in cash, no bouncers today. Give me ten minutes to pick up the car and I'll be back in a flash.'

He tweaked her nose, and she grinned at him, but through gritted teeth, she muttered: 'Clever bastard, one day George Davis...one day!'

She waited for a little while and then wrapped up the remaining cakes in a linen napkin. As she fumbled under the table, she spotted Davis watching her through the window.

'Old habits die hard,' she mouthed at him and he sauntered down the street without a care in the world until he saw the local plod and dodged into Drapers Lane.

Carefully adjusting her skirt, Trixie stood up and carefully made her way to the door. At the kiosk, she paused to interrupt the conspiratorial conversation between the middle-aged cashier and the impatient young waitress. Patting her waistline, she said: 'Delicious cakes, thank you so much. I'm so full, I can hardly move.' With that she wiggled her way to the exit.

CHAPTER THREE

The domestic upheaval at Wellington unexpectedly came to a head on the following Sunday when Trixie's mother and sister were setting the table for lunch. Sunday roast was a must in the Skyrme household; where it came from was rarely questioned although for a farm labourer a joint of beef, a hand of pork or a leg of lamb was generally considered a 'perk of the job'.

However, for the Skyrme family it came by way of the local poacher at the alehouse. Nevertheless, Jack Skyrme brought it home, his wife roasted it and sometimes he arrived home from the pub in time to eat it.

It was ritual in the Skyrme home and if it did not happen it was the cue for domestic violence.

The small labourer's cottage was basic and sparsely furnished with only the bare necessities for day-to-day living. Mary did her best to keep it neat and tidy and despite his foul domestic habits, Jack Skyrme managed the adjacent vegetable garden well enough to produce a regular seasonal supply.

Apart from the matrimonial bedroom, the two sisters shared the attic room while George, when he was at home, slept on a plump horsehair sofa on the lower landing.

Dinnertime was almost over when the door flew open and the two men almost fell into the room. Supported by his son, Jack Skyrme staggered to his chair at the table and demanded his dinner. They had both been at the drink since noon and it showed, they reeked of rough cider and could hardly string a sentence together.

They were later than usual; dinnertime was almost over and Mary and Fanny had made a start on the clearing up, Trixie had disappeared upstairs. The Sabbath Day peace awaited the usual onslaught and it came to an unusual extent.

Jack aggressively brought his fist down on the table and demanded: 'Where's the dinner mother?'

His son joined in: 'Yeah! Where's the bloody dinner woman?'

'Don't speak to your mother like that?' his father challenged.

Prompted by the effects of the rough cider, George boldly replied: 'You do, so why not me?'

In one swift movement, his father struck him hard across the face. 'Well I can 'cos I shag the old bag,' he replied.

Unmoved by her husband's violent action, Mary muttered: 'And all the tarts in town.' Jack stared at his wife. 'What yer on about woman. You don't know nothin', now fetch me bleedin' dinner our Fanny, all that ale has sharpened me appetite.'

Fanny cowed and clumped off to the stove.

'And pick yer bloody feet up girl, yer scuffing the boards with that bloody boot.'

'Leave 'er be Jack,' Mary said just as Fanny returned with two plates covered with saucepan lids and placed them on the table. George snatched off the covers.

'What we got 'ere then mother. Not scraggy end again?'

'No George,' she said sarcastically. 'Its prime 'ereford beef. There's a war on and we ain't got any money for best beef. What few shillings we do have you two splash against the walls of half the public houses in the county. Anyway it's the pork your father got at the farm, so make the most of it.' The two men shovelled food into gaping mouths until Mr Skyrme demanded: 'Fetch us that jug of scrumpy from the sill Fanny and don't fall over yer foot and spill it.'

George laughed. 'She'd fall over the dog's dick given half a chance.'

Hiding her tears, Fanny unexpectedly yelled back at him: 'Get it yerself',' and ran into the kitchen.

In the doorway, she bumped into Trixie dressed up in her Sunday best. 'Why don't you leave her alone you bully, pickin' on 'er all the time. Just leave 'er be, George.'

Jack Skyrme pushed back his empty plate and banged the table again, this time with his cider mug. 'Will someone fetch that bloody jug?'

'I'm going outside for a piss,' George told them. 'It best be 'ere when I gets back.'

Trixie turned on him sharply: 'If you want it George, you can fetch it.'

Jack Skyrme grunted a swift reply: 'He can't stand up never mind bloody walk to the privy, he'll pee himself before he gets there. Can't hold his ale, not our George. Not like his old man.'

Exasperated, Mary walked to the windowsill, took the cider jug from the cool ledge and poured it out. Jack took a long drink, burped and grinned drunkenly at Trixie.

'I suppose yer off with your fancy man. What he sees in you girl God only knows.'

Trixie ignored him but George, returning from the garden snarled back: 'You mean that bloody crook Davis? It's about time he got called to the bloody regiment; he's been dodging long enough.'

'Just like you,' Trixie said.

'I'm exempt, farm labourer like the old man.'

'Pity really,' his mother replied. 'With you two in the trenches we'd 'ave finished off the Kaiser by now!'

George puffed his chest out proudly: 'Yer reckon so Ma? Hear that dad; Ma reckons that they'd have won the war by now with us two fightin' up front.'

Jack looked quizzically at his wife: 'How do yer make that out mother?'

'All those cider fumes swillin' around the Somme and you two fartin' like pigs, the white flag would be up in no time.'

The sound of Fanny laughing upset George. 'Shut up you stupid bitch,' he yelled. 'You'll be laughing on yer backside when I kick yer bloody foot from under.'

Trixie had just about enough of her drunken brother and responded angrily: 'Drink or no drink George, I've told yer to leave our Fanny alone or...'

'And who asked you to be judge and bloody jury Miss Fancy Pants?' her father said. 'You look more like an auctioneer's mistress every time yer goes out with him.'

'Davis's bloody mistress yer mean dad, he wants lockin' up he does. Bent as a bleedin' corkscrew. I don't know what 'er sees in him.'

'That ain't any business of ours,' his mother warned.

'Whatever 'er does, it fills our pantry and don't you two drunkards forget it. Our Trixie pays more than her fair share in this household and if yer don't like it, start payin' yerself instead of handin' your wages over to the landlord at the New Inn.'

Mary looked her daughter up and down: 'Mind you that outfit looks a bit posh for a picnic with our kin at Canon Pyon?'

'To her mother's surprise she announced: 'It's me last Sunday visit Ma, after today I shan't be goin' no more.'

'Why ever not girl, your aunty loves seein' yer?'

'I know Ma, so it's a good time to break the habit.'

George sniggered: 'Yer mean you're sloping off with yer fancy man on Sunday afternoons.'

'Shut yer mouth George?'

'Or Davis will shut it for me will he?' he challenged.

'No. I'll just tell him to tip off the 'Hereford Journal' about you and him.' She pointed to her father. 'The pair of 'em was up before the bench last week for a breach of the peace.'

Mary looked shocked. 'What breach of the bloody peace Jack? You never told me about it?'

'No need woman,' Jack muttered. 'It was nothin' to bother you with.'

'It wasn't bloody nothing, Ma,' Trixie said. 'The pair of 'em was so drunk they were fartin' at the Morris Dancers in High Town and upset two posh old girls. Instead of saying, sorry, thick head George grabbed the nearest pair of tits just as the constable arrived. I did try to persuade my journalist friend Mr. Davis not to report it.'

'So what,' her drunken brother replied sheepishly. Trixie paused and quietly suggested: 'So if you don't stop goin' on at our Fanny, I might change my mind.'

Jack Skyrme watched his daughter very carefully and commented: 'So what girl, we ain't afeared of the law, anyway the copper went off and left us alone.'

Casting all caution to the wind, Trixie took the bit between the teeth and let rip.

'I'll tell you what dad. If yer boss finds out that the pair of yer were up to no good again, you can say goodbye to yer bloody jobs, that's what. You George Skyrme will get yer marching orders and be up to yer arse in mud and bullets before yer can shout Lord bloody Kitchener.'

The silence was more threatening than all the shouting and Trixie knew she had finally overstepped the mark. The motionless response from her father disturbed her and she inwardly set her self-defences into action. She stood quietly beside her mother and prepared for the expected physical response but a loud fart suddenly interrupted the long silence.

'For God's sake, Jack,' Mary said in mock disgust.

Jack Skyrme picked up his plate and threw it at his wife.

'Shut yer ugly face or I'll fix yer face again.'

Fanny instinctively rushed to Trixie but, before she could reach her, her father kicked over his chair and grabbed her by the neck. Mary Skyrme reached out to protect her disabled daughter.

'Leave her be, Jack,' she muttered nervously.

'Don't tell me what to do you stupid mare,' and raised his fist to strike Fanny.

' Don't hit 'er Jack,' his wife pleaded. 'She's had enough of your fists lately.'

The drunken man could hardly wait to show his strength. Purple with anger, he began to unbuckle the heavy leather belt holding up his pants.

'Had enough as 'er. I'll show 'er what enough is.' He tried to grab her again.

George watched in silence as his terrified sister clung on to her mother.

'Don't let him belt me, Trix,' she sobbed as her father attempted to drag her towards him. 'Stop yer bloody cryin' and come 'ere. You've been asking for the belt and this time no-one is going to stop me.'

Trixie yelled 'enough is enough' and pulled her sister away from her mother just as her bullying father raised the belt buckle. As he turned to bring it down across Fanny's back, his wife struck him with a plate.

'You stupid cow, you'll pay for that.' With his anger well out of control, he tossed Fanny to one side and punched his wife full in the face. Wide eyed, Trixie and Fanny watched the blood pour from her nose and splatter the once white tablecloth. It was a shocking moment even for George, and he laughed nervously.

'Two to one the old man,' he offered through half clenched teeth.

Terrified, Fanny rushed from the room and hid behind the scullery door while Trixie angrily pushed her father out of the way and attended to her injured mother.

'You bleedin' bully,' she screamed at her father. He whipped round and struck her hard across the face, snatched the locket from her neck and dropped it on the table.

Smirking at his sister, George drunkenly picked up the locket and slurring announced: 'I always thought Davis was a bloody cheapskate Pa, it won't even stretch to a pint of cider.'

A small trickle of blood drained from the corner of Trixie's mouth, she wiped it away with her hand and defiantly stared at her father, he did not move.

George knew better than to interfere and backed out of the firing line. His sister picked up the wooden chair he had been sitting on. It was heavy, but Trixie found enough strength to lift it shoulder high and smash it over her father's head. He fell across the table and slid to the floor without a sound, watched by his ashen-faced, bully of a son. She carefully touched her bruised and swollen lip and announced to her mother and sister: 'That's the last time he'll strike any of us again. We're moving out of this hellhole.'

Ignoring her own injuries, she placed her arm about her mother and tenderly wiped the blood from her face with the corner of the tablecloth. Mary Skyrme was terrified, her face was a mess but her concerned daughter gently calmed her down.

'Don't worry Ma, I've found us a new place to live and you and Fanny are coming with me.'

Fanny peered out from behind the door just as Trixie steamed in on George.

'Pick him up and get him out of 'ere and you can go with him. You can start payin' yer own way from next week.'

George half lifted his semi-conscious father from the floor and dragged him upstairs. Fanny cautiously came into the room and put her arms round her sister. 'Take care of Ma our Fanny,' Trixie said. 'I'll clear up the mess and then we'd best be off to your aunty for tea.'

Mary looked a lot better after Fanny had carefully cleaned up her badly bruised and split nose. She sat back in the chair and sighed: 'He's done a proper job this time our Trixie, I can't go out like this. What will I tell your aunty?'

'Course you can Ma, you ain't done nothing to be ashamed of. It's about time the family knew what you've had to put up with all these years.'

'Yer a good girl our Trixie, always was, right from a little 'un.'

'Don't be soft Ma, I've been planning a move for some time and takin' you and Fan with me. I'll find a nice place for us in the City and I've put a bit of money by for emergencies. We're all we have, me you and Fanny.'

She realised that her sudden aggression had shocked herself as well as everyone else and tried to hide the emotion in her voice. If ever she needed her keen sense of humour, she needed it now. Just as Fanny was about to cry, she announced:

'We three are family now and what do families do, our Fanny?' Her sister beamed broadly, as she recognised her sister's familiar comment: 'Sticks together.'

Trixie took hold of her mother's hand, helped her up from the chair and then reached for her sister. 'We sticks together like what?' she asked. 'Like glue,' they replied and hugged each other tight, despite everything, they were happy again.

Mary Skyrme tried to smile through her swollen face. 'We best count our blessings and get on with it I suppose. I've had worse.' She dabbed at her bulging nose and went into the scullery. 'But you're not going to have any more Ma,' Fanny shouted. 'Not with our Trix to look out for us.'

'We're really goin' then?' her mother replied.

'Yeah Ma. We're leavin' this dump and those two upstairs once and for all. I've a few loose ends to tie up which might take a bit of time but we'll be out of here as fast as a fiddlers elbow.'

Unaware of the plotting, the snoring from upstairs droned on as the two men slept off pints of rough cider.

'You could have killed him Trixie,' Fanny whispered.

'That's right Fanny I could have done, but he was lucky this time. Next time who knows? Now let's get sorted and be off to Ivington before all the cakes have gone.'

Four weeks later the Skyrme women arrived at Barton Manor, a large brick-built villa- to start a new life. Close to the city, it was not long before whispered gossip over the regular 'carryings on' in Barton Road establishment declared it the most discussed house in the neighbourhood. Under the expert tutorage of George Davis, by now an established conman with an increasingly shady reputation, it did not take long to gain a notorious reputation.

The country girl from Wellington had developed from novice into a skilled con woman and by the time she was seventeen Trixie was earning a good living as George's accomplice in a wide range of petty criminal activities.

Within six months of moving house, her passion for money increased, her greed became an obsession and she thought and spoke of little else. What she wanted most was adventure and her dream of riches to come true. To this end, she had been secretly working alone, putting the extra earnings aside for that 'rainy day'. Her so-called mentor had no idea of her extra-curricular activities, only her mother and sister knew these and her secret was safe with them. They of course benefited considerably from Trixie's private income and, despite local gossip, she did all they could to maintain a respectable household.

By now Trixie was on a swiftly moving learning curve. Using George to establish her credentials, she grew into a highly confident young woman with a thirst for knowledge, albeit criminal. Well able to support herself, her sister and her mother in comfortable style, she was, she thought, well and truly on the road to fame and possibly fortune. Free from the threat of domestic violence, Mary Skyrme settled into the roll of housekeeper at Barton Manor and happily accepted that her daughter provided, without question, all the family needs.

Safe from the threat of abuse and beatings, Fanny happily pottered about carrying out assorted household tasks and was more content than she had ever been in her life. The rented furnished house was comfortable and, like her mother, she had her own room and regular supply of 'hand me down' clothes from her sister. Trixie provided all the little extras that made up for the bad times; neither Fanny nor her mother cared how and where the money came from, preferring to close their eyes to any 'goings on'.

It was Christmas Day and the three women spent it together exchanging gifts, which they never dared expect a year ago. They left the seasonal festivities until the evening when, for the very first time, Trixie invited George Davis and a few new friends to supper.

In the festively decorated dining room, supper was almost over and Trixie was holding court at the head of the table. Some of the guests had overdressed for the occasion, particularly the women who had heavily applied their make-up in a fashion similar to that of bit part actresses.

Seated at either end of the long table, Mary and Fanny were listening intently to cross table conversations and Fanny was giggling hysterically.

'And then what happened?' Doris asked.

Her partner Dennis, eager to embellish the original story, cut in. 'I'll tell you what bleedin' happened,' he said, but Trixie stopped him with sharp warning.

'Shut up Dennis this is my story and I'll tell it straight from the horse's mouth.

'I grabbed the pearls, turned to walk away but...' she paused and tried to stifle a laugh. 'But the catch snagged her hair.'

'Then what?' Phyllis asked. Trixie caught her sister's eye and together they laughed aloud.

'I gave it a tug and hoped for the best. The silly cow screamed, I hangs onto the pearls, nips round a corner and stuffed them down me drawers.'

The laughter died down as the listeners hung onto her every word. Davis sat back and smiled to himself.

'For God's sake Trixie get on with it and toss 'em the punch line. Your sister is about to pee herself.'

Fanny usually enjoyed the teasing but not in front of visitors. She blushed lightly and reprimanded him.

'Stop it George, that's not nice when we've got company.'

'Company, what company?' he replied sarcastically. 'This lot are the best of the criminal fringe of Hereford, you won't find better outside Soho. Not usually keen on socialising this lot were more used to thieving and lying.'

'More than likely on their arse for some other woman's man,' Mary muttered under her breath.

Trixie sighed impatiently; she enjoyed being the centre of attention and wanted to tell the story her way. 'Do you want me to go on or shall we call it a night?'

'For gawd's sake give her a poxy break. You lot might have 'eard this before but we haven't, have we May?'

May nodded and loudly suggested: 'You carry on Trixie, and we're all ears. Take no notice of George, he don't know when he's well off, having a girl like you!'

Trixie stared at George and quietly asked: 'If it's alright with you Mr Davis I'll carry on regardless?'

Fanny quietly smiled at her mother; they had both felt the veiled threat in Trixie's tone.

'As I was saying. I was stuffin' the row of pearls down my drawers when I heard the police whistle. I staggered to the bathhouse at the back of the auctioneer's office, tucked up me skirts and did a swift walk towards George's car. The specials hadn't spotted me and I couldn't see him behind the wheel. The bloody coward had ducked out of sight just in case.'

'What did you do that for George?' May asked.

'Rule number one,' George said. 'Always keep your head down when the 'rozzers' are around and you won't get caught. Anyway, I was watching out for her and what a sight she was. Rushing towards me, skirts up around her arse when this hairy thing falls from her privates.'

Doris and May screamed in unison before Doris asked: 'What 'airy thing for gawd's sake.'

'Yeah,' May said, 'what the bleedin' hell was it and where did it come from?'

'The posh bint's bloomin' wig that's what. It got caught up on the clasp of the bloody pearls and when I stuffed it up me knicker leg it was left dangling between me legs.'

The quiet chuckling suddenly built into raucous laughter and Doris and May wiped their tear-filled eyes on the soiled napkins.

It was a wonderful moment; Trixie enjoyed telling tales of her escapades, each one was funnier than the last, but George always had to spoil it all.

He waited until the fun had died down and then arrogantly said: 'Mind you, although I say so myself, I've moulded this girl and taught her everything she needed to know. Petty thieving is one thing, but thanks to me she can hustle with the best and work a sting better than most.'

Trixie was not amused, her eyes narrowed as she addressed her partner-in-crime.

'You have, have you George Davis. Well now, let's get down to it and tell us just how and why you think that.'

Fearing her rising temper Dennis tried to change the subject. 'What about a bit of music. Give us a tune Trixie.'

He immediately regretted his interference the moment Fanny looked at her mother and raised her eyes to heaven.

'Shut it Dennis,' her sister yelled without taking her eyes off Davis. 'This is between George and me. Now what is it you're saying George that I can't work alone? Is that it or is there something else?'

'Well...yes I suppose there is,' he replied cautiously.

'What you need is a man around...with brains and you've got mine at your entire disposal.' He tilted his chair back and smirked at everyone.

'After all, I am the best in the business.'

Fanny nudged her mother and whispered: 'Hang on to yer hat Ma, the way he's goin' he won't see Boxing Day.'

Trixie drew in a deep breath. Davis eased his chair into the upright position and waited for the anticipated onslaught. The four guests had already sensed the antagonistic atmosphere and hardly dared to move, Trixie's temper was notorious but they had not yet been on the end of it. They were not disappointed.

Her dark eyes narrowed as she homed in on her self-styled patron and he visibly blanched. The charming hostess had become the deadly inquisitor.

'You are, are you George? Then let me tell you something. You might think that you're bleedin' Svengali but I am not yer bloody Trilby.'

Ignoring Dennis's silent warning to keep quiet, George tried to make a joke of it. 'I quite agree Miss Skyrme you're definitely not a Trilby, more my very own saucy Easter Bonnet.'

He waited for the laughter but it never came. The joke fell flat and he was about to fall with it as Trixie went on the attack.

'Without me hanging on to your coat tails George Davis you would have come seriously unstuck on a couple of scams this last six months.'

'When?' he asked arrogantly.

'You know when,' she quickly replied. 'But if you want me to spell it out for everyone, I will. We could have gone down for that mistake you made at Ledbury.'

George suddenly looked very sheepish. 'Oh that! It was just a small error of judgement, that's all. Given a bit of time I could have talked us out of it.'

Determined to show him up in front of his associates Trixie went for the kill.

'You couldn't have talked your way out of the gents.'

She looked at the others. 'You don't know the half of it, if I hadn't used my wits we'd both be shacked up in Gloucester jail.'

Nobody dared say a word; they just listened as a slowly deflating Davis waited to be exposed. Fanny and her mother were not amused, they realised that Trixie had come of age and sensed that her relationship with George had changed.

Her temper under control, the actress in Trixie took over and she smiled before exposing the failings of her working partner.

'He might have taught me how to use me wiles when bouncing dud cheques, but as for brains, he met his match when he met me.'

Without a hint of uncertainty, Trixie publicly challenged her mentor and suggested: 'Go on then, if you're so bleedin' clever George Davis, carry on without me and let's see how yer gets on. Believe me, I can manage without you, but can you manage without me?'

The arrogant grin on George's face had long since gone and he looked around for support; none came. Pupil had turned on the Master and he knew when he was beaten. Trixie had blown his plans right out of the window and he had more to salvage than just his reputation.

No doubt about it, young as she was, they were a clever and practised team ready to go big time but she was right, without her deviously sharp mind, and convincing persona, he wouldn't go far. She was the tasty jam on his not so fresh bread. Alone he was nothing but a parochial petty crook with a skill for forging signatures and a knack for a good con. He didn't want to lose 'his girl', it was time to acknowledge her real worth, and he should have given her full credit long before this.

In the uncomfortable silence that followed, George noticed that everyone was looking at the table apart from Fanny who had caught her sister's eye and gave a little grimace. Trixie laughed, clapped her hands and everyone relaxed. As far as she was concerned, the row was over.

'We know where we stand now George don't we? Less said soonest mended so let's get on with Christmas.'

She leapt from the chair and smiled broadly. 'Right Ma, you and Fanny clear up and then we'll all go into the sitting room.'

She affectionately hugged George's arm for effect and said to her guests: 'You go on through and make yourselves comfortable. George will fetch the liqueurs and I'll bring the sweetmeats.'

Fanny and Mary gathered up a few dishes and quickly left for the kitchen.

George released himself from Trixie's grip, smiled and cockily strolled to the sideboard to collect the liqueurs and glasses but, before he could finish arranging them on the tray, Trixie gestured him to sit down again.

She waited for the others to leave the room and looked long and hard at him, his natural, confident poise suddenly slipped and he prepared for the worst. He backed towards the nearest chair and Trixie positioned herself on the edge of the dining table and stared down onto him.

'Don't you ever speak to me like that in company again George,' she said.

'What do you mean?' he replied defensively. 'We're supposed to be a team, Trix.'

'Are we indeed, well it don't look like that to me or to that lot in there,' she said directing an upturned thumb towards the sitting room. George stood up and tried to put his arms around her half-turned shoulders. She angrily shrugged him off but he persisted.

'Come on girl, it was just a bit of fun. You know you're the best.'

Her clenched fist hit the table with a bang; a surprised George jumped an inch or two into the air.

'And don't you ever forget it,' she yelled. 'I've got the measure of you George Davis. If you think you can manage without me that is your first big mistake; your second is takin' me for granted. Now bring that tray and let's get this party goin' again. It's the first time Ma and Fanny has had a proper Christmas and we ain't going to spoil it for them... are we?'

His usual charming smile wobbled as he gingerly crossed to the sideboard. Trixie remained seated on the table, her newly discovered power racing through her veins, the same power she felt when she accidentally brushed his thigh at their second meeting. It was not sexual, came, and went like the breeze, but this time it was gale force and George Davis, for all his worldliness, knew he had met his match.

Tray in hand, he turned to admire her. She was going on sixteen when he first met her, just a slip of a girl snapping at his heels and he had nothing to lose.

She took his fancy and ever since he first saw her, he tried every trick in his young man's book in his desire to bed her. The girl was definitely flighty enough, mature enough even, but she always closed her door at just the right moment for her and the wrong one for him, but two years on, despite his desires, he didn't dare push it open.

As he passed the table he half smiled at her, she stopped him, lightly kissed him on the mouth and beckoned him to go on ahead. Grabbing the dish of sweetmeats, she went out of the room and paused in the hallway. Still amused at the outcome, she smiled to herself as she listened to the animated conversation between her mother and sister coming from behind the kitchen door.

'Er's told him then?' Mary said.

'Aye,' her daughter replied. 'And it won't be the last time. Our Trix knows what she wants and, the way she's going, she'll soon get it.'

'And men don't play no part in her plans,' her mother added.

'What makes yer say that our Ma?'

'Intuition girl, and I'll tell yer somethin' else. No bloody man is goin' to put our Trixie 'up the duff' and knock her about like yer father did.'

Fanny laughed uneasily. 'If he does, he'll need half the British army on 'is side.' Mary nodded. 'And he'll still end up the loser against my girl.'

Prompted by their laughter, Trixie without warning, flung back the door.

'Too right there Ma. No man is goin' to get to me, not without paying a price. I didn't drag us out of Wellington for no good reason, George Davis or no bloody George Davis we three are goin' places.'

Trixie laughed again and dramatically popped a sweetmeat into her mouth. 'Leave the dishes, it's still Christmas Day; we'll do it together in the morning.'

Assuming her Girton accent, she announced: 'So dry your hands please ladies, we must join our guests in the parlour.'

Fanny threw her drying up towel into the air and mimicked her sister's accent. 'Hear that mother dear, our Trixie's gone posh again.'

The atmosphere in the sitting room was seasonal jollity as Davis, despite the austerity of war, dispensed yet another round of brandy and liqueurs.

Gaudy decorations and winter greenery littered every available space and a surprising number of greeting cards stood proudly on side tables, window ledges and the piano top. Candlelight supplemented the fixed gas mantles that mysteriously hissed and caused strange shadows to flicker on ceiling and walls. By now and more than slightly intoxicated, May and Doris tried to outdo the men at joke telling and the conversation became more and more ribald until Trixie, determined to uphold her position as hostess, unwrapped another present. It was an attractive beaded necklace, a gift from Dennis.

'Thanks Dennis, it's really lovely. Where did you lift it?' she asked with just a touch of admiration. Everyone laughed. 'Charlie Chadds, where else,' he replied with a grin. 'Nothin' but the best for you girl.'

Trixie passed it around for the others to admire and they nodded their appreciation at its quality. When it reached Doris, she set about teasing George.

'He picked it out special just for her, didn't yer Dennis?' she screeched. 'Said he was fed up seein' her wearin' that bloody so-called silver locket all the time.'

'Where did you pick that one up Trixie?' May asked. 'A tart's Christmas cracker?'

Trixie smiled and fingered the silver locket loosely fixed about her neck. 'Best the May Fair could supply,' she said.

'May Fair. What does it have to do with the bleeding' fair?' May commented. 'That's for me to know and if you two are so bleedin' interested it's for you to find out!' she replied, looking at Davis.

'Best you don't stick yer big nose in too far though, it might get nipped off'. Now how about a singsong? Come on Albert you tinkle the keys while I tickle me tonsils.'

Albert stood up, bowed and offered her his arm and together they walked to the piano in the corner of the room.

Trixie lifted the seat of the stool and rifled through a pile of music.

'This will do for starters Albert,' she said and tossed him a folded sheet. He peered at it, smiled and sat down at the keyboard. After stretching his arms and making a show of flexing his muscles, he let his fingers dally with a few notes. Much to the surprise of his friends and with the assurance of an up and coming concert pianist, he ran up and down a few scales. The spontaneous applause brought Mary and Fanny rushing from the kitchen where they had gone to get a few snacks to soak up the alcohol.

'If our Trixie's goin' to sing then we best set the chairs back,' an excited Fanny said. Surprised, George looked around, shrugged his shoulders at the others and stayed where he was.

'Come on George and you Dennis, get cracking and clear the room,' Mary said.

'Our Trixie won't sing if 'er can't move about a bit so we had best move the chairs back to the wall.'

'Right oh,' Dennis said enthusiastically. 'Give us a hand George, this could be worth hearing.'

The excited chattering ceased when, to the opening bars of a Maria Lloyd song, Trixie, in a provocatively revealing dress strutted onto a hastily arranged stage. It was a moment of sudden awareness for George Davis and he gasped more times than a beached goldfish. He had long since accepted that when it came to looks his rising star on the criminal stage was not a natural beauty, but this was someone else. Still only in her late teens, Trixie had matured into a boyishly handsome rather than a lovely young woman and what she lacked in beauty she clearly made up for in personality and body language. Poised, polished, and pursued by just about every man about town; she carried herself well in company and young as she was, in the workplace of the con woman, she very rarely faltered.

His desperation for her sole attentions irked him; it often got in the way of a good working relationship and troubled him far more than he cared to let on. Her rampant sexuality played on his mind at the most inopportune moments and caused him, at times, to make stupid mistakes. She gave nothing away, to anyone, and although he had known her more than a year or two, he knew little of what went on in her head. Any light, physical overture he made was verbally swatted away like a persistent bee lusting after a much sought after honey pot and Christmas night or not, goodwill was off the seasonal menu for George Davis. There was no special package to unwrap that might ease his lusting, no kindly words to warm his heart, nothing but the occasional bright smile that indicated 'Stick with me Georgie boy, you ain't seen nothin' yet' - and he hadn't.

Dennis struck the keys of the old piano with exceptional gusto and in a voice and style that would have surprised the originator let alone the small gathering at Barton Manor; Trixie Skyrme became Miss Maria Lloyd. Her rendition of 'When I Takes My Morning Promenade' was impressive enough for George, a connoisseur of the Music Hall, to gasp in genuine admiration.

'Ain't she just wonderful George?' Fanny sighed as he silently rose up from his seat and stared in amazement until Trixie ended her party piece. She bowed at the enthusiastic applause from her friends, embraced Albert and winked at Fanny.

George Davis was bewitched. His sheer admiration shone like a beacon and he managed to utter: 'I didn't know you could sing like that Trix?'

He moved forward to kiss her as she glided past, but the stunning songstress avoided his embrace and said: 'There's a lot yer don't know about me George,' and blew him a kiss before parking herself on Albert's lap.

'Our Trixie could always sing, couldn't she Ma?' Fanny announced proudly.

Mary smiled fondly at her talented daughter. 'Got it from my mother, she often took us to the matinees at the Garrick music 'all when I was a child. Mind you, I could sing a bit myself in me day,' she added shyly.

'Yer still can Ma,' Trixie replied with affection, 'especially when you were picking the hops in the yards. You took us with yer and we stayed in the hop-shed with the other kids until the end of yer shift. We could hear her singing at the top of her voice in the yards.'

Dennis, May and Doris sat back and clapped in heartily.

'That was bleedin' good Trixie. How about another one?' Dennis requested.

'Go on with yer Dennis, that's yer lot for tonight. I only does it at Christmas so if you want to hear me repertoires you best come back next year.'

'Please Trix?' George asked and started clapping, 'just one more to send them on their way.'

'Another time perhaps. Always leave 'em wantin' more George,' she teased. 'It's called using yer brains.'

Above the laughter, the mantle clock struck midnight and Marie Lloyd reverted to Trixie Skyrme.

'Is that the time? I think we best call it a day folks.' She put her arms around her mother and sister. 'Ma looks tired, the pair of you have worked hard all day.'

Nodding in agreement, the guests got up and stretched their legs.

'It's been lovely dear,' Doris said. 'Nicest Christmas day we've for years, ain't it May?' May beamed and patted her full figure hard.

'Very nice indeed, so much food and drink I shall waddle back home to Harold Street, 'appy as Larry. It makes a change to be off me back for twenty four hours.'

Amid the hoots of laughter, Dennis never missed the chance to top the joke.

'Well,' he chortled. 'That won't last long, the rent's due next week.'

The laughter rolled on until Albert said: 'For gawd's sake don't get him started again or we'll never get him over Wye Bridge before milk-oh. Thank you kindly everyone, most enjoyable. Coats outside are they?'

'In the hall,' Trixie advised and the well-oiled guests slipped out into the hall, donned their outer-ware, tottered up the garden path and ambled merrily along Barton Road.

George watched them disappear out of view and then took Trixie's arm as she paused in the doorway. 'There will be a lot of soft touches over New Year and it's time we made plans.'

Trixie stayed quiet for a moment before answering: 'I've been thinkin' about that. There is the Boxing Day hunt at Leominster tomorrow. Sure to be a few toffs about with fat wallet's ripe for the lifting.'

George smiled broadly. 'Good thinking girl, I'll pick you up about ten and we'll hang around the Talbot until the punters arrive. If they catch the poor bloody fox, they will be well into their cups by lunchtime. We'll make a killing.'

Ever the opportunist, he tried to kiss her on the mouth but she offered him her cheek.

'Goodnight George, it's been a good Christmas in so many ways. See you tomorrow.'

She closed and locked the door, leaned back against it and sighed. From the hallway she watched Fanny awkwardly climb upstairs dragging her disabled foot behind her. Silently Mary Skyrme came and stood beside her and Trixie wrapped her arms about her mother. 'I promise you Ma,' she said, 'if money could put that right, come hell or high water I'd get it from somewhere.'

'I know yer would and so does our Fanny,' her mother replied. Well aware of the effects of drink they had consumed, mother and daughter propelled each other into the sitting room for a nightcap.

Trixie poured out two large brandies and the happy pair kicked off their shoes and flopped onto the sofa.

'It's been a grand day ma,' Trixie announced happily.

'Best ever Christmas of me life girl,' her mother said with a wry smile. 'It's the first time I haven't had me block knocked off on Christmas Day.'

Trixie hugged her tight. 'Never again Ma. Christmas will never be the same again for any of us.'

From the top of the stairs, Fanny shouted: 'That was a proper job our Trixie, a real proper job.'

At that moment, a limp paper chain fell slowly from the ceiling and draped across Trixie and her mother. They smiled affectionately at each other and raised their glasses to the fairy on top of the floor-to-ceiling Christmas tree.

CHAPTER FOUR

The Hereford Spring Fat stock sales in 1916 were busy in spite of the war. It was business as usual for the farming community. Market day was an outing for most of the agricultural workers and their families and they poured into town to examine the prized sheep and cattle going under the auctioneer's hammer.

After government requirements had been met, farmers' wives and daughters laid out their stalls with as much locally produced food as they could muster, fresh fruit and vegetables, meat and bread was quickly snapped up by eager customers keen to stockpile what they could now that the war in Europe had well and truly set in.

Sellers and buyers shared conversations with townies and rural invaders from across the Welsh Border but for the pickpockets and petty criminals market day was a three-ring circus and with plenty of local rogues to share the spoils. George Davis was the perfect ringmaster.

Trixie watched him make contact with Dennis to casually hand over a bulging wallet, lifted from a tipsy punter on his way from the auctioneer's office. Beckoning to her, he directed her to the Market Tavern, their usual meeting place on market days.

The two men chatted as they ambled along. 'Nice picking's today George. I ordered three hot pots earlier.'

George nodded. 'Yeah! Sun brings the punters out. Trix is on her way, we can have a bite to eat, divide the takings and skedaddle.'

They walked through the swing doors and pushed their way towards a table where Trixie was chatting to a couple of elderly farmers. The farmers moved away when George sat down and Dennis went over to the bar.

'I've ordered a jug and three,' Trixie said and waved to the bartender to bring the tray to the table.

'What were you saying to the two woolybacks?' Davis asked as the waiter put the drinks onto the table.

'Thanks Eddie,' she said. 'Usual farmer's complaint, moaning on about money, good labour lost to the trenches. You know, the old story, nothing to spare but plenty in the bank for a rainy day. Is Dennis fetching us the hot platter?'

'Yes, he ordered earlier to avoid the rush.'

George took a good look around the large bar. 'Quiet in here for a market day. You and the girls had a good morning Trix?'

'Better than most. A few drovers from Brecon came for the sellin' and made a large profit on the spring lambs. Doris and May did well beddin' 'em and liftin' the wallets.'

Davis looked a bit anxious but she soon reassured him.

'Don't worry Georgie-boy, I've taken my percentage and made a bit on the side.'

Shocked by her comments, George suggested: 'You don't mean?'

'For God's sake,' she interrupted. 'It's not what you're thinking....You know that's not my game. I use me 'ead, not me arse. How's Dennis done?'

'Very nicely. Plenty of wallets, a fair bit of loose cash and wait for it, a chequebook. All in all, not a bad morning's work.'

'I should say so, don't often get a chequebook. What bank?'

'National Provincial.'

'Hereford?' Trixie enquired.

'Worcester.'

'Off our regular patch, that's useful. Where's Albert Marriot today?'

George grinned. 'You mean the brave Captain Marriot? Brushing up his new image on some unsuspecting good lady.'

'Since when?'

'Since he decided a military title in war time plus a slight limp might help his chances of a good scam or two.' George paused and looked long and hard at Trixie before continuing. 'On the subject of the war...'

Trixie looked serious for a moment. 'What's happened George? Come on out with it?'

'Nothing...yet,' he ventured, 'but it won't be long before they catch up with me.'

'Who! The rozzers, you ain't slipped up again have yer George? Come on, spit it out for gawd's sake. We've been doing alright and I don't need this.'

'Nothing like that girl, it's getting more difficult dodging the recruiters, and my conscription papers are long overdue. They'll have me soon.'

'How long yer got?'

'About a couple of months or so,' George said.

Trixie was aghast. 'Bloody hell George! What yer going to do?'

'Yeah! Well, I've been thinking about that...and you.'

'What's it got to do with me?' a horrified Trixie asked. 'They're not sending for us women as well?'

'No. Not unless you want to run a field hospital and I can't see you in a V.A.D. uniform.'

'What's that? I hope it ain't some dirty disease yer catch down below?'

George laughed and she whacked him on the shoulder. 'It's not funny George?'

He laughed again. 'Pack it in girl. It means Voluntary Aid Detachment, a sort of regiment of nice, upper-class women who volunteer to do their bit for King and Country.'

Trixie laughed with him. 'May and Doris do that all the time but not in uniform. Mind you George, there's not a lot of difference when yer drawers are round yer ankles.'

George changed the mood. 'Be serious for a minute Trix, it's me for the trenches if I am conscripted, and you on your own to fend for yerself.'

'So!' Trixie responded defiantly. 'Now where the hell has Dennis got to with the grub, I'm getting a bit peckish.'

'He's waiting for the order; he'll be here in a minute. Before he comes though, just listen to what I am saying. When they catch up with me how will you manage? You're going to need some help.'

'Don't fret yourself George, I'll cope.' In a gesture of genuine affection, Trixie took his face in her hands. 'Dennis will still be around, for some reason he doesn't have to go, good old Captain Marriot will have worked his ticket somehow. All you have to do George is take care that you don't get shell shocked and come back daft as a brush.'

She smiled at him. 'We can all work together and look after each other 'til you come home. Anyhow I've got a few tricks up me sleeve sure to earn me a bob or two.'

'Like what?' George exclaimed anxiously and unexpectedly blurted out. 'To be on the safe side, I'll stay at the Manor with you until I get my papers. I can help you polish up your skills... and your accent.'

'Look George,' she stressed. 'Me skills are polished bright as a button thanks and my accent is awfully good and frightfully cut glass, indeed the vicar and I challenge anyone to think otherwise Mr. Davis,' she mocked.

Just as easily, she switched back into her rural accent. 'Don't worry George, I really can look out for myself, I've had a good teacher and lots of practice. You can come and stay with me anyway, at least until the bugle calls.'

Davis relaxed and looked more than hopeful.

'But not in my bed,' Trixie confirmed sharply. 'You can lodge with us at Barton Road but you has to pay yer way.'

George had hoped that a little intimate activity would be on offer to a departing hero who might not return. Bitter disappointment for George might have set in had not Dennis arrived with the food and placed the hot dishes on the table.

'Thank gawd Dennis, I'm starvin'. It took you long enough, where did yer go for this Welsh lamb, Abba bleedin' gavenny?' she added.

Dennis laughed. 'Cooked to order luv. I'll nip and get the tools.'

A dejected George looked into the distance as he tried to come to terms with Trixie's growing confidence. Aware of his change of mood she tried to jolly him along and leaned across him to give his cheek an affectionate squeeze.

'Come on, eat your hot pot luvvie and give us a smile. It's not the end of the world, that is, unless yer off to the Dardanelles.'

She grinned mischievously at Dennis who had caught the end of the conversation.

'She's only teasin' yer George,' he said. 'Don't worry old chap, we'll keep an eye on her while you're diggin' in.'

Trixie giggled and tucked into her hot pot but George watched her and wondered about his future now and after the war; that is if he had one.

Eight weeks later, his call-up papers arrived and he was on his way to the front line.

Early morning Hereford was an autumnal joy at most times but today it was extra special. Despite a soft mist floating above the River Wye, just enough in places to mask the distant Cathedral, nevertheless there was promise of a bright, sunny start to the day.

The red brick railway station at the bottom end of Commercial Road was alive with activity. The cider harvest was reaching its peak; the light railway trains that circumnavigated Herefordshire's orchards were filled with bumper crops of apples for Mr. Bulmer's processing factory in Ryelands Street.

Inside the crowded station, the mood was less optimistic. Overloaded troop-trains packed to the gunnels with young men, waited for the green flag and the long ride to the channel ports for a sea journey to God knows where.

On the platform, pale-faced families grouped together in silent farewell to fathers, sons and brothers, not knowing when or where they will see again. Forced smiles and stuttered last goodbyes were painfully interrupted by the final blast of the guard's whistle, a hiss of steam and the echoing announcement that the first train out was about to move off.

On board the train, officers belted out 'orders of the day', along the carriages for the keen and not-so-keen recruits and a ripple of cheers, hand clapping and shouts of 'good luck lads' accompanied the train out of the station until it had crossed the bridge over the River Wye. For a short while, the station was quiet again allowing families to silently pray for a safe return of loved ones.

Through the door from the booking hall, a cheerfully dressed Trixie escorted her partner-in-crime onto the platform. Clad in a khaki uniform highlighted by colourful regimental flashes, George Davis carried a well-stuffed kit bag over his shoulder, a gas mask and a great coat carefully folded over his arm.

In contrast, Trixie, sporting a saucy hat with a union jack pinned to the band was loyally clinging to his arm as they walked along the platform to the next train out. Pausing beside the large metal sign emblazoned with the name of the station, George dumped his kit at the base. Leaning Trixie against it, he did his best to summon up his flagging spirits. He managed a cheery grin.

'Well Trix, snared at last. It's time for me to join the big boys up the front.'

'Yes! And we are all very proud of you,' she encouraged.

'I know but I'm not looking forward to it. The old man is proud enough, but mother is breaking her heart.'

'Course she is George, many mothers are. War is a bad time for all of us. You'll be alright though; you always could look out for yourself.'

He put his arms around her. 'It's you I'm worried about girl. What are you, your Ma and Fanny going to do while I'm away?'

'Look luvvie, I've told you there's nothing for you to worry about here, you'll have enough to do fighting on the front. I shall take care of things while you're away, you can count on that and so can me family.'

Unnoticed by George, she glanced over his shoulder and nodded to a man standing in the shadows by the gents lavatory.

'I'll miss you Trixie, I really will,' George said quietly.

Sensitive to his mood she offered the answer he wanted. 'And I'll miss you too George. It won't be the same around the city without you, and Barton Manor will be lonely without our big boy.'

'You will think of me won't you, Trix?' he asked anxiously, 'and write to me when you can?'

'Course I will, and so will our Fanny now that she's learned to write. Do your best to let us know where you are, if you can? You mean a lot to us all and we want to know when you'll be home again so we can organise a bit of a welcome home party.'

The laboured conversation was interrupted by the loud hiss of released steam as the next train gave notice that it was ready for the off and Trixie was grateful when the Transport Officer called final boarding. Fond farewells were quickly wound up apart from George who tried to stretch his out a bit longer.

The Regimental Sergeant Major slapped George across the back

'Time to move out son,' he demanded. 'Kiss the little lady goodbye and let's be on our way.'

'Does a departing soldier get a kiss, Trixie?' George asked.

She smiled up at him. 'What! Let a Tommy slope off to the trenches without so much of a kiss from his special girl!'

She kissed him so vigorously on the mouth that she felt him tremble as he hugged her tightly.

'There you are son,' the Sergeant said. 'With her big heart hanging on yer khaki sleeve, Jerry ain't going to see you off is he? Now, can we get this show on the rails?'

George picked up his kit bag and coat, stood back and smiled. 'Will I do girl?'

'You look fair handsome George Davis, I'll give you that,' she said.

More in hope than judgement George asked: 'Anything else to give me?'

She looked at him for longer than necessary and then unexpectedly removed the silver locket that nestled around her neck and dropped it into the top pocket of his battle dress.

'Don't come home without it soldier boy, I want it back, you with it and in one piece. Now get on that bleedin' train before that nice Sergeant turns nasty and bursts a blood vessel'.

George approached the train in silence, looked back at her and smiled. He tossed his tack into the carriage, clambered up behind it and opened the window. Leaning out, he took Trixie's waiting hand.

'Keep up the good work old girl and keep my bed warm at Barton Street. I'll be back before you know it, I promise.'

'I know yer will. It will take more than the Kaiser to stop a Herefordian in his tracks. As our Fanny always says, do a proper job George.'

With a single, loud blast from the Station Master's whistle, the engine driver eased the crowded train out of the siding onto the main track accompanied by tears and cheers from anxious families and friends, loyally waving union jacks. Trixie freed her hand as the train gathered speed and watched it disappear round the wide bend across the River Wye. The platform quickly cleared and she walked to the bookstall to purchase a glossy society magazine. Flicking through the pages, she made her way to the booking hall. Removing the red white and blue ribbon pinned to her hat, she tossed it into a waste bucket along with her union jack and left the station.

Waiting for her in the station forecourt, comfortably seated in his brand new car, a smiling Captain Marriot leaped from his leather seat as Trixie approached the car.

'May I assume all went well on the departure front, Miss Skyrme?'

'Very well indeed Albert, now tell me, what have you got planned for the next stage of my education?'

He laughed as he helped her into the passenger seat. 'A few weeks personal tutorage at my college for clever scams and the world, well, at least the Welsh Marches and the Border Counties, will be your oyster. Not that you need much teaching, just a broader practical experience in the right quarter and a bit of detailed market research will do you nicely. Where to now my lady, the Market Tavern?'

Trixie preened herself in the driving mirror and announced in her well-rehearsed new accent:

'Not today Albert, perhaps it's time to up the stakes and take lunch at the Angel in Ledbury. Care to join me old chap?'

With a light touch on the accelerator, Captain Marriot circled the station approach, turned left over the railway bridge and headed out of the city.

Albert Marriot was no Captain; nevertheless, he could become anyone he wanted to be if it was in the best interest of a good scam. Thanks to his father, a much-respected resident of Hereford, he gained a good education and met George Davis during his school days. A clever and active petty criminal, he had teamed up with him and became a main player in his gang of miscreants and together practised their criminal activities across the three counties.

He briefly met Trixie when Davis introduced her to the gang and for such a young girl, he admired her quick thinking and skills. Albert was also attracted to her and with his partner in crime off to war it felt a duty to take her under his wing on both counts. Under the close guidance of her obliging tutor, Trixie learned so many ropes that she was never quite sure which one to pull next.

Forging cheques, training young pickpockets, organising call girls and working up her own clever swindles; it was the education she needed to qualify for a life of crime.

Throughout the duration of the latter years of the war Albert and Trixie played the punters for all they were worth, netting a substantial, personal income, which Trixie continued to stash away for the rainy day that was destined to be on the horizon. Her favourite and most lucrative fraud was setting up a bogus employment agency in Leominster supplying domestic staff for the gentry and selling on insider information to organised gangs of burglars from the West Midlands.

However, her major launch into the big wide world of grifting came almost at the end of the war years. No-one had heard from George Davis, he had not returned home and rumours hinted that he was dead. Albert decided that it was now or never time for the polished professional Trixie had become, to go it alone. For her first outing, she had planned her own scam with Albert Marriot and her adrenaline was pumped up.

CHAPTER FIVE

It was late afternoon on the last day of the local race meeting in Gloucester; in the shadow of Gloucester Cathedral, Trixie was setting out her stall close to the precincts. Her experience and practice at the Hereford racecourse had shown her that successful punters drifted into the town to spend their winnings before catching the last train back to Birmingham and beyond.

She chose Gloucester for her debut because it was far enough from her own patch to avoid recognition. Decked out in red, white and blue she was wearing a broad sash across her upper body; the bold slogan written in large letters simply said 'For our Brave Boys'.

She had made herself up to look older than she was and used a soapbox to give her height. A colourful, overhead banner matched her outfit and a large matching bucket containing a good handful of mixed coins rested at her feet; smartly uniformed Captain Marriot, leaning heavily on a walking stick, stood guard over the money. Attracted by the striking young woman, a biggish crowd had already gathered and in a cut glass accent touched with a hint of sadness, Trixie addressed the growing assembly: 'I stand before you all a humble, widow woman. I also stand here with all my limbs, faculties and endowments, intact.'

'Not so sure about your faculties luv,' a heckler commented. His companions sniggered but Trixie ignored them and carried on regardless.

'Today, in Gloucester, we are free from the horrors of the battlefields, and why? I will tell you why, because brave young men have given their lives to save you, me and our children from the evil and despicable Hun.'

She paused and scanned the listening faces; some were already nodding in agreement. 'Like many women of all ages and classes, my late departed husband, the dear colonel, laid down his life for his country leaving our child fatherless.'

She paused just long enough for a young woman to throw in her pennyworth.

'Yeah, mine are fatherless as well lady and he departed sharpish too when I told him I was 'up the duff'.'

Trixie calmly waited for the ripple of laughter to die down before lowering her eyes at Albert. Raising his voice, he pleasantly dispersed the rising laughter. Adjusting his gammy leg, he tapped it with his cane.

'Please ladies and gents, let Her Ladyship speak. I too have suffered at the hands of the enemy and I almost lost my lungs in a gas attack. Let me tell you good people of Gloucester, mustard gas was everywhere, clogging up your innards, burning your skin and leaving you unable to breathe. I can only implore you, if you haven't been to the front and experienced these horrors then keep quiet and please listen to the dear lady on the platform.'

He finished in a frenzy of coughing; enough to bring Trixie down from her soapbox to help him.

'There, there gallant Captain,' and she comforted him for a moment or two before continuing.

'Here stands a brave soldier who lives to tell his tragic tale, please let us give him his dues.' Sporadic applause broke out as Albert, still choking on his breath, struggled to help Trixie up to her soapbox.

'Thank you Captain, thank you and I impress upon you today that there are many like him, brave men indeed, who did not return to the waiting bosom of the family.'

Grasping a large handkerchief from under her sleeve, Trixie blew her nose and dabbed at her eyes. 'But where are they now?'

She let the silence wash over the subdued crowd and in a voice rising with emotion she stepped up the patter and tearfully told her captive audience...

'Let me tell you where they are. They sleep the long sleep of the glorious dead below the red poppies in Flanders, buried in the deep mud of the trenches in water-logged graves dug by their comrades in arms.'

The crowd, unable to keep silent any longer, again burst into sympathetic applause and Trixie knew she was onto a winner. Captain Marriot looked up at her and marvelled at her eloquence.

Cathedral Close was filling up as more and more people came to hear her moving sermon. High on her own success and without referring to notes, she continued to project her vivid and moving speech.

'Others fell before the enemy guns, caught in the onslaught of bullets and shrapnel and shattered into pieces, others fell but did not die on the battlefield, they have since been returned home, blinded, deaf and crippled. Some are even now slowly dying from the effects of the dastardly mustard gas that has seeped into their young lungs, destroying every breath they take. Many are so severely shell shocked that they are now lunatic in behaviour and unable to live normal lives, they are a danger even to their loved ones, as well as themselves.'

Albert's quiet acknowledgement of approval encouraged her to a rousing finale and she did not let him down.

'These men are returning home in droves and they need our help.' The applause was gathering momentum. 'They need it now! And I for one intend to make sure that they get it.'

The cheers rose louder than ever. 'The brave boys from our three counties Gloucestershire, Herefordshire and Worcestershire will be arriving home soon to be cared for in our hospitals and the special institutions currently being made ready to receive them. They shall not return forgotten heroes, we shall see to that.'

The big build-up was coming. 'And we shall do it together. With your help and contributions, I intend to establish, with the help of God and the good Bishop, The Three Counties Military Rehabilitation Centre for the War Wounded, at a country house near Dursley.'

A purple-clad clergyman stepped up to more applause and stood beside his patron on the makeshift platform. Captain Marriott limped forward and in a most moving gesture grasped the hands of Trixie and the smiling Bishop. After a tearful moment, he turned, calmed the noisy gathering and humbly addressed the people.

'On behalf of our returning war wounded, I thank, from the bottom of my heart, His Grace the Bishop and this truly wonderful woman. With the Bishop's faith and hope and Her Ladyship's generous charity, I know that with the Good Lord on our side we shall not be found wanting and our brave, injured soldiers will be provided with a place truly fit for heroes. I intend to start the ball rolling with ten pounds, rehabilitation money given to me by a Great Aunt. Today I have been convinced that their need is greater than mine.' Trixie joyfully responded: 'Thank you, thank you gallant Captain, the Lord truly does move in a mysterious way, but whatever your kind thoughts and generous donations might be we must never forget what our boys have done to save us from the forces of evil.'

A large part of he crowd chanted 'Hear! Hear!' which almost caused Trixie to laugh and give the game away. Taking a grip on herself, she again appealed for a quiet moment and to the utter amazement of Albert Marriot and His Grace, she unexpectedly addressed the Bishop.

'Perhaps we could ask you, my dear Bishop, to offer a short prayer of thanksgiving for the kindness and generosity we are about to receive.'

A puzzled expression spread across the Bishop's face as he struggled to find suitable words for the occasion; Albert Marriot saved the day by handing him a pre-written card containing a suitable religious text. Bowing his head and reading aloud in a steady, calm voice the Bishop's prayer clearly implied 'tis better to give than to receive' and the wounded Captain held out the collection. Moved by the prayer, the people came forward in droves to shake hands with Trixie and make their donations; the Bishop blessed them and before long, the bucket was full to the brim with coins and paper money. After an hour or so the crowd had dispersed and, apart from a tattered banner and a torn sash, there was little to show of the makeshift platform.

The Bishop had made a hasty exit, Albert Marriot had slipped away to find the car and, cool as a cucumber, Trixie, her colourful outfit covered by a simple coat, was heading for the docks, carrying a large Gladstone bag in both hands.

Up ahead a smart car slowed to a stop and Albert, dressed in civilian clothes and minus his stick and exaggerated limp, hopped out, took the bag from her and laid it on the back seat.

She grinned broadly, as he settled her in the passenger seat and drove off. A few minutes later, he pulled up alongside a lone figure casually strolling along the pavement and Trixie beckoned to him. Leaning into the car, he grinned and said:

'Very neat job Miss Skyrme if I might say so, please stay in touch.'

'Thank you Bishop, better get your prayers sorted out next time.'

Patting his pockets, the old actor from the local theatre, did a little skip and continued on his travels.

Trixie turned to Albert. 'Proper job I think old boy.'

'Couldn't agree more old girl,' he replied. 'Must be a good few hundred pounds in the kitty, not bad for your first run out.'

'We'll do the share-out when we stop off at Newent,' Trixie suggested. 'I'm ready for a good dinner tonight, how about you?'

He put his arm around her. 'You're the boss now Trixie, you've passed with flying colours.'

She smiled to herself. 'Yes and in red, white and blue too. Now Albert, let's be on our way and don't spare the horsepower.'

It was almost two years since George Davis left had for the battlefields and Trixie's life had changed beyond her wildest dreams. She had spread her wings across the three counties and become a clever, well-practised confidence trickster able to compete with the best; her working partnership with Albert had prospered without too many hiccups and the 'rainy day' fund was overflowing.

Family lifestyle had also improved, well enough for her mother and sister to give up the domestic work needed to cover the loss of George's board and lodging; Fanny in particular was looking very well and life at Barton Manor was more than comfortable.

However, on the downside it had become the source for local rumours circling the neighbourhood that, since the arrival of the Skyrme women with their decidedly downmarket retinue, the area had sunk to an all-time low.

Amused at the allegations, Trixie and her associates dismissed them out of hand, nevertheless local residents were shocked by the reported 'unsavoury and doubtful goings on' at Barton Road. Most residents in the area believed it to be a house of ill repute and the base for a wide range of criminal and immoral activities, but were unable to prove it, but change was in the air.

Hostilities in Europe were almost at an end and the armistice was about to be signed; Trixie had been celebrating out of all proportion with the officers at the local barracks and was sleeping in after a long night.

Fanny was making breakfast for her mother when she heard the rattle of the letterbox.

'Postman's late today, Ma, I'll fetch it.'

She limped off and came back with a brown envelope, placed it on the table and sat down to finish her coffee.

'What is it, Fanny?' her mother asked.

'A package for our Trixie! I'll take it up to her.'

Mary stopped her. 'She will still be asleep, another late night I suppose, can't fathom what's she's up to these days.'

'Been out celebrating at the barracks again I expect,' Fanny said. 'Papers say the war is almost over.'

'Good thing too. Mind you, with all that money to spend, our Trixie will celebrate anything these days.'

Fanny was very protective of her sister's social whirl. 'She earns it Ma and deserves her fun, after all she keeps this house goin' for us and we want for nothing.'

'Aye, I know 'er does Fanny but where's it all going to end? We live well on 'er earnings but sometimes, life has a funny way of turning out. I don't grudge her nothing, but...well... I don't know. She is looking tired these days and she definitely has things on 'er mind.'

'What sort of things Ma?'

'George Davis must be on 'is way home soon, he'll see a big change in our Trixie and she'll be bothered that he might have found out about 'er working with Albert.'

Picking up the envelope, Fanny said: 'You mean Albert working for 'er? I'll take this up to her now Ma, she might be awake.'

'Stay here Fan and let her lie a while. She won't thank you for disturbing her before 'ers ready. She'll be up soon enough; she's got 'er meeting.'

'Oh gawd! I'd forgotten that, it comes round so quick. Best make a start on the sandwiches. I'll make a fresh brew and take it up.'

Shaking the packet, she asked her mother: 'I wonder who this is from?'

'You'll soon find out when she opens it. Go on up Lady Nosey Parker, you're dying to find out, so am I. I'll bring the tea.'

Trixie was half asleep and she could hear her sister clumping up the stairs followed by a few light squeaks on the landing outside her bedroom door. She waited for the familiar double knock.

'It's only me, Trix,' her sister announced cheerfully.

'Oh, it's you fairy light foot, as if I didn't know, but what is that squeaking on the landing?'

Fanny crossed the room to pull the curtains back. 'Me calliper, the new one you got for me. It needs a bit of oil or something.'   Trixie got back under the covers. 'Then get some and quick about it, you'll drive me crackers if it goes on like that.'

Hiding her eyes under the covers, she yelled: 'And don't pull those curtains Fanny.'

'Why? It's a lovely day out there.'

'Yes, it might well be, but lovely or not Fanny, I could go blind from the dazzle.'

'Oh come out from under the blankets, Trix. Ma's on her way up with a fresh cup of tea and I've got a letter for you.' She waved it under her sister's nose.

'What's that?' demanded Trixie.

'It came just now and it's for your eyes only.'

'Show me what it is; I can't see a dammed thing.'

Fanny pranced across the bedroom to the windows, laughed and swished the curtains back. 'Now we can see what we're doing.'

Trixie yelled and shaded her eyes from the strong sunlight. 'I'll swing for you one day our Fanny now give it 'ere.'

As she became more animated Trixie slipped in to her Herefordian accent, which only served to encourage Fanny to tease her further.

'Do you want me to read it to you, Trix; it might be a love letter from one of the officers.'

'No I bleedin' don't. I can cope with me own correspondence thanks Fan, now give it 'ere or I'll cuff you one.'

Fanny threw the letter on the bed just as Mary came in with the tea.

'Here's yer tea girl.' Mary said, staring at her younger daughter.

'You must have sunk a few these past nights, yer lookin' very pasty to say the least.'

Trixie pulled a face at her mother. 'Thanks very much, Ma,' she said sarcastically. 'What a night though! Everyone was talking about the war ending soon and Albert was flashing the cash around like a good 'un.'

'Not yours I hope girl?' her mother questioned.

Trixie was affronted at the suggestion. 'You most be joking, Ma. I'm tucking it away for a rainy day and it will have to pee down before I flash it around. Besides, it is all spoken for in me plans.'

Fanny and Mary raised their eyebrows and sat down on the bed while Trixie opened her package. The colour drained from her face as the familiar locket dropped out and nestled in the folds of the crumpled bedding.

'What's up girl? You looks like you've seen a ghost? It's only your locket,' her mother said. 'I thought you told us it was lost.'

'Any message with it?' Fanny asked.

Her sister sat back against the brass bed head and tried to contain her emotions. She had expected something like this but it was still a bit of a shock.

'It's a message all right, our Fanny! George is back.'

'What! Our George? Mary said. 'I thought he'd gone off to Shropshire lookin' for work with your father.'

'Not our George Ma... George Davis, our short stay lodger and so-called creator of my destiny. Bloody 'ell ! I thought he weren't comin' back.'

The three women sat and stared at the wall until Fanny spoke. 'They said he was missin' presumed....'

'Dead. Yes that's what we all thought, that's what his old man told Albert. Not a word for two years and now this. Blimey it's bad timing, for all of us.'

'But how do yer know he is back Trix. I don't see a message, just the locket.'

'That is the message Fanny. I gave it to him at the station when he left. I told him to come back safe and bring it with him.'

Sitting bolt upright and almost dazed by the news, Mary muttered: 'He's done that alright. What yer goin' to do now luv?'

'A lot of thinkin' Ma, a lot of bloody thinkin' and he mustn't know about me nest egg.'

She threw back the blankets, leaped out of bed and opened the window. Breathing in the fresh air, she announced:

'I need a clear head to do this amount of thinking. I wonder if Albert knows he is back. If he has been seen around town he ain't told me.'

A sharp ring on the doorbell caused the three women to freeze on the spot. Trixie began to panic.

'Who the hell is that? You go Ma; you're faster on yer feet than Fanny. If it's George I'm out.'

Surprisingly nimble for her years, Mary dashed downstairs to answer the door and Fanny reminded her sister about the meeting.

'It won't be him, Trix, they'll all be arriving for the meeting just now.'

'Hell's teeth, I forgot the damn meeting. We'll have to cancel it Fanny. Go and tell them I'm not too well... unless it's Albert, give him a cup of tea and a sandwich while I get dressed and do not tell him about the locket. I will be down in a bit. Now get downstairs and don't let Ma open her mouth to Albert, we need to stay calm until I sort this out.'

Her sister nodded in agreement and then giggled hysterically before suggesting:

'Look Trix, if George is back, it's best to sort yer secrets out too, and the profits or you will be for the high jump. You'll be pleased to see him though?'

'I suppose so. But there's no denying things have changed and I'm in the driving seat now.'

'But you still needs him though, Trixie?' her sister insisted.

'In some ways I suppose we will need each other for a while, but I'm no longer a mug where George is concerned. I've learned a lot these past two years, grown up too and know me place.'

Fanny laughed. 'And where's that, as Gran used to say, on the ladder of life?'

Trixie joined in the family joke and laughed heartily before replying:

'Three rungs up and rising and this is only the start our Fanny. You don't get a second chance at living your life and I'm goin' to do a proper job first time round.'

She turned and looked out of the window and for a brief moment, she was deadly serious. 'You're right Fanny. I'll tidy up a few secrets first, make myself respectable and then come downstairs to face the world.'

She walked to the doorway and hugged her sister. 'Come here hop along,' she said affectionately. 'What would I do without you?'

'What would we do without you, yer mean?' Fanny quietly replied. 'We'd have no home, not like this we wouldn't.'

'You'll always have a home with me, I'd be lost without Ma and you Fan, I mean it. If I could get rid of that gammy-leg for you, I would do it whatever it cost.'

'I know yer would Trix. I told yer, you won't ever have to do without me, we're stuck together.'

Trixie broke into a soft smile and Fanny knew what was coming. 'Whatever 'appens?'

'Whatever 'appens,' Fanny echoed.

'Like glue,' Trixie added.

'Like glue our Trixie, just like glue.'

As Fanny made her way downstairs, Trixie smiled and muttered 'and get that bloody calliper oiled' before shutting the bedroom door.

Alone in the room, Trixie removed a suitcase from the large wardrobe, fished about inside the lining and extracted a large quantity of five pound notes. Flicking through them with apparent pleasure, she took them to a corner of the room where she carefully moved a small oak chest and dragged it clear of the wall. With a slight tug, she pulled back the carpet and exposed a loose floorboard, lifted it clear and took out a large tin chocolate box filled with paper cash of various denominations. She carefully smoothed them out before adding the new bundle to the pile already there. Pushing back the floorboards, she replaced the tin, tapped down the boards, pressed down the carpet and dragged the chest back over it. She stowed the suitcase away in the bottom of the wardrobe and locked it.

Stripped of her nightclothes, she admired herself in the mirror and then carefully slipped into an attractive and expensive silk dressing gown before brushing her thick hair. Collecting a few toiletries, she opened the door and shouted downstairs without a hint of her Herefordian accent:

'I am taking a bath now Mother, I will be down shortly for the meeting. A light lunch would be very nice, after which I shall be ready for anyone.'

CHAPTER SIX

The London train slowed down as it approached the signal box on the Wye Bridge and shunted to a halt. The journey from Southampton to Waterloo was routed through Basingstoke, which meant a long wait at Reading for the connection to Hereford, embarkation from France had been even worse and George was glad of the extra time to reflect on his homecoming. For the umpteenth time he tried to rub the dirt from the carriage window, this time hoping for a glimpse of the Cathedral rising above the city he knew so well.

Back in the trenches, his visual memories of home had kept him going when it got tough. In his worse moments, he thought he could hear the Cathedral organ pumping out an Elgar anthem as the shells whizzed over his head. It reminded him of his mother's Sunday morning visit to the Lady Chapel to offer up prayers for his safe return.

As the steam driven engine chuffed into life again, he caught his first glimpse of the Cathedral tower he had taken so much for granted and was relieved to see it was still there to welcome him home.

Stretching his legs, he reached for his battered kit bag stowed in the overhead luggage rack; the engine hissed into life and puffed its way across the bridge into the grubby railway station he left over two years ago. It seemed a lifetime away.

George knew that nobody would be waiting to greet him. After all, only he knew if he was dead or alive. Since the final surrender, it had been total confusion and in the mad rush to get home, it was officers up front instead of leading from the rear as they did in the trenches! However, when it came to 'Tommy's turn' casualties apart; it was every man for himself. Nevertheless, he was thankful to have dodged the bullets and gas and fortunate not to have been laid low by the influenza epidemic that had killed off so many of his comrades on the way home.

The noisy engine eased into the gloomy station spewing passengers in all directions. George pushed his way through them, headed for the gents, relieved himself and checked his appearance in the cracked half mirror.

War had taken its toll. He looked older than his twenty-one years but well enough to convince, other than his closest family and friends, that he had somehow survived his tour of duty despite the death and destruction in the trenches. Nevertheless, his sunken, bloodshot eyes and rough part shaven face could not hide the desperate need for peace, quiet and a long, long sleep.

For the sake of his own emotional and physical well-being, the returning soldier intended to keep a very low profile for a couple of weeks. He needed to clear his head of the bloodshed and devastation that had so shocked and disturbed him and he needed to do it in private. It was too deep for tears, too personal to share and he had to ease them out in his own good time but, despite his inner feelings, he was determined to pick up where he left off and dreamed of earning real money again.

After a quick wash and brush-up, he smoothed out his uniform, polished his boots on the back of his gaiters, adjusted his cap to a jaunty angle and smiled at himself in mock approval. Outside, the crowded platform had all but emptied and he made a swift dash through the booking hall and into the station forecourt. Thankfully no-one was around to recognise him as he part marched up Commercial Road towards Coningsby Street.

Unexpectedly, the welcome sight of his native city emotionally gripped him and he had the urge to whistle, just as he once did on his way home from school. As he turned the corner and walked towards the family villa, he spotted his mother gazing nostalgically into the distance from behind the curtain of the bay window. She suddenly saw him too and buried her prematurely grey-haired head into her hands. After a brief moment of disbelief, she called out to his father:

'It's George, George is back. Come and see for yourself.'

Flushed with a mixture of excitement and relief, they rushed to the door to receive their son, his mother shedding tears of joy as he fell into her waiting arms; his father, not knowing quite what to do, pumped his arm a little too enthusiastically. Parents and son walked into the sitting room together and, casting his glazed eyes over the familiar walls, apart from the collection of embroidered silk postcards propped up on the mantelpiece, little had changed.

Looking at them, George had not realised just how many special messages he had sent from the front. He had little faith in the battlefield postal services and was pleased to see how many had eventually reached Hereford.

Seated in his father's club chair, the returning warrior studied the 'No Place like Home' sampler hanging over the fireplace. Worked in needlepoint during the second Boer War by his grandmother for George, it was a meaningless message. He would not be staying at home for long, he had another 'home and family' to call on, that is if they were still living at Barton Manor.

Despite the short-term generosity of his father, two weeks in the bosom of the family was long enough for the restless George but he had to admit that the rest had done him good. Mindful of bumping into old friends and associates, he had kept a very low profile but maintained a watchful eye on Trixie. He was not surprised that she appeared more confident than ever and, to a returning soldier with two years at the front, she was a wonderful and welcome sight. Dug into the deep trenches of the Somme, covered in mud, shit, blood and gore, he comforted his wounded comrades with tales of his girl - his Trixie.

It eased their final moments before death and helped George survive the dogs of war by convincing his departing comrades in arms that his lovely girl was with them in spirit during their final journey.

Since arriving home, he had dogged her footsteps back and forth across the city; he had to know how she was doing and what she had been up to in his absence and when the time was right he sent her a note and included the silver locket he had clung to in moments of utter despair.

It was mid-afternoon when he slipped into Barton Road and sat for a while on a garden wall. There was little traffic and encouraged by the warmth of a late summer, a few scruffy lads were seriously engaged in a cricket match. Keen to impress the silent observer, a small boy stoically protected his dustbin wicket before facing up to a lanky bowler. He furiously hit out at a loose delivery and surprised by his own skill and strength he watched, open-mouthed, as the battered leather ball soared over the head of extra cover watched by the equally stunned bowler.

Wide-eyed, the astonished fielders followed the flight until it bounced off a lime tree, dropped onto the wall a few feet from the silent watcher and fell to the ground. Rolling towards the highly polished shoes of George Davis, picking it up, he rubbed it on his jacket sleeve and, without a word, walked the short distance to the bowler's end. Giving the ball an extra rub he looked long and hard at the little batsman who fearlessly stared back, shrugged his shoulders and 'took guard' for the second time.

Extravagantly loosening up, George paced out his run-up and mockingly turned his arm over two or three times; you could hear a pin drop as the tension grew between man and boys. The heavy thud of booted feet on the rough road surface gave notice of impending delivery but the boy at the wicket never flinched. He played at the ball, missed it completely and it struck the metal dustbin with a resounding clang, moving the bin a good few inches off its original mark.

'Howzat?' yelled Davis as if the Ashes depended on it. The scruffy little batsman looked hard at the makeshift wicket and then at the bowler. Gripping his bat tighter, he silently appealed to the fielders and waited for the collective shout.

'No ball,' they yelled and the verdict echoed along the length of Barton Road. The batsman grinned wickedly at George.

'Who'd yer think you are Mister, Maurice Tate?'

'If I was I'd have hit you and not the wicket, now walk, like any good English batsman would.'

The kids made faces at him and, as he walked away, he laughed at them until the oldest of the group caught his arm.

'Eh! Mister, you feelin' better after doin' that to a tiddler like him?' George put his arm around the youngster. 'When you are sent to war and find yourself stuck in some filthy trench, up to your eyes in mud, shit and bullets, all you need to be reminded of home is a game of street cricket played fair. That was home for me son and if you ever have to go through what I've been through these past two years, and I really hope not, it's what you will dream of too. Thanks for the game lads, now I'm off to find the girl I left behind.'

He strolled towards the gate into Barton Manor followed by the admiring gazes of the boy cricketers. Stopping outside the place he called home, he paused and looked up and down the street; unbuttoning his jacket, he hitched up his trousers and vaulted over the garden gate. Genuinely amused, the young cricketers cheered as he lightly landed on the other side. He grinned back at them, bowed from the waist and raised his hands above his head like a victorious boxer. On the doorstep, he paused again, this time to straighten his tie and re-button his jacket. Two years of hell in the trenches had matured his handsome features and, thanks to his mother's home cooking, he looked and felt reasonably fit and well. The two or three weeks of rest had helped him readjust but those who knew him could not fail to notice his experiences had aged him inwardly and outwardly.

Nervously, he knocked his familiar knock on the front door of Barton Manor. Inside Trixie was relaxing and enjoying tea with her mother and sister and when she heard it, her heart shipped a beat or two, and a sudden rush of adrenalin swamped her body. She had heard rumours of George's homecoming but she discarded them until he identified himself in his old familiar way.

'This is it, Ma!' she said. 'He's back and we have to keep calm. Let's be our usual selves but make sure we don't give anything away.'

The knock came again, this time with just a hint of impatience and Fanny went to the window and peeped out from behind the net curtains.

'Heck! It is George,' she said breathlessly. 'You know Trix, George Davis.'

'I know who George is Fanny,' she said tersely. 'Now like I said, just keep calm and answer the door. Ma you brew a fresh pot while I go upstairs.'

As she passed her sister, she whispered: 'Call me in five minutes Fan and look pleased to see him, both of you.'

Dumbstruck, Fanny pulled herself together and smiled broadly before opening the door. George looked her up and down taking careful note of her stylish appearance, yet he sensed her moment of foreboding.

'Well now, if it's not Miss Fanny Skyrme. My you have grown up and tidy with it!' he said and kissed her on the cheek.

'Who is it, Fanny?' her mother called out from the kitchen.

'It's George, Ma, George Davis back from the war.'
Mary stepped out of the kitchen looking genuinely pleased to see him.

'My Lord, it is you George Davis, we've been so worried. It is good to see you home safe and sound. Your Ma must be pleased to have yer back.'

'Aye, she is,' he said and hugged Mary in a warm embrace.

'And where's your other lovely daughter?' he enquired as he looked around the hallway. 'Not at home these days?'

'She's upstairs resting after a late night.' Mary nervously replied.

'Been gadding about while I've been away, 'as she?'

'At the music hall with some friends, yer know how she likes to sing. I best tell her you are here.' She went to the bottom of the stairs

'Are you awake our Trixie? Someone here to see you.'

Fanny smiled secretly at George and nodded to her mother.

Mrs. Skyrme cheerfully invited him into the parlour. 'Kettle's on George, so set yourself down. She'll be down in a minute or two and I'll make a fresh pot of tea.'

As she moved across the hallway, Trixie's head appeared over the stairwell. In mock surprise, she called out:

'George bloomin' Davis, I don't believe it. I thought the bloody Germans had knocked your block off.'

Half skipping down the staircase, she allowed him to sweep her off the bottom step but carefully avoided the expected kiss. Holding her tight, George swung her round until she was almost dizzy.

'Not even the bloody Kaiser could keep me from my girl,' he said as he finally got his kiss in.

'I really am pleased to see you George. It's been so long since we had any news, the last we heard was that you had been killed in action.'

'Almost,' he replied quietly. 'I was lucky. My lot copped a gas attack and most of them went down, I just missed it.'

'How come?' Trixie queried. 'Skiving again I suppose.'

'Not quite. The Captain sent me on a courier run to headquarters but when I got back, it was all over, Captain and all. Corpses everywhere and blokes coughing their guts up, believe me, it was bleedin' rough.'

For a moment, he did not speak and it was obvious to Trixie that he was upset in a way she would never have expected.

'That bad was it, George?' she said, stroking his hand as she spoke.

'Lost my best mate, Nobby, a Worcestershire bloke from Tenbury Wells. He lived at the back of the old Pump Rooms and I met him on basic training. Nothing in common except the war but we got on well enough, he died in my arms, Trix, and I couldn't hack it. We'd been through a hell of lot together. He had a wife and three kids to feed back home. I promised to look out for them if I didn't cop it too and that's why I'm a bit late back. The Company Commander had a whip round and I had to go to Tenbury first, someone had to tell his family how brave he was and all that stuff.'

Trixie kept silent and waited for him to go on. He was clearly upset and he needed to talk it out of his system.

'What I didn't tell them, Trix, is that he didn't have time to be brave; none of them did.' There was a long pause before he was able to speak again. 'I tell you Trixie, I almost lost my head. I was so bloody angry at what was happening to us, and the few of us left wanted to go after the German bastards but we could do bugger all.'

By now, Fanny and her mother had come out of the kitchen with the tea and were listening to the conversation. Mary Skyrme was almost in tears as she carried the tray to the table, Fanny put an arm around George and then followed her mother into the parlour while Trixie gently pushed on with her questioning.

'Couldn't your officers do something?' she asked.

'What! That yellow livered lot always kept a safe distance and scarpered without any warning whenever it got heavy. Honestly Trix there was nothing we could do, none of us, except go after them and then we would have been shot at dawn for cowardice.'

Mary, on her way back to the kitchen, overheard the last part of the conversation. 'It's sickening that is. Yer mean Hereford boys ran away? I can't believe that.'

'The Hereford and Worcester lads stood their ground and died, Mary, the officers came from posh Home Counties regiments and were scared shitless when it came to a fight,' and he began to sob.

Trixie had never seen this side of George and she sensitively tried to console him. She stood up and cheerfully tried to lighten the atmosphere.

'It's all over now George, you're back home, and we are very glad to see you back, safe and sound. Never mind the tea Ma, fetch some glasses and a bottle from the sideboard, it's time to celebrate the return of our hero.'

George visibly bucked up when Fanny smiled and asked him: 'Did yer get a medal George?'

He gave her a big hug. 'Coming home to you is the best medal I could have Fan, they can keep all the others. Never mind the glasses. What I fancy is a cup of Mary's tea, a slice of her Victoria sponge and a chinwag with my girls. We've got plans to make.'

Fanny and Trixie exchanged dubious glances, left the room and, refreshments over and done with, Trixie and George sat alone at the table deep in conversation.

'I'll need my room again, Trix,' he told her.

'I know you will George, but what about your family. Don't you think you ought to spend more time with them, after all you've been through they need to talk to you too?'

'I have been staying there for a couple of weeks but you know what it's like at home, Trix. Yes, I had a good rest but I'm restless and need to get active again. The sooner I do it the better I shall be, I want things to be like I've never been gone.'

After carefully considering the situation at Barton Manor, Trixie explained the domestic arrangements:

'We had to let your room out, George. Since you've been away, money has been short but if you give me a couple of days to arrange something I'll be sure to get it all sorted by the weekend.' George perked up. 'No need to worry about money old girl, now that I'm back in charge it's you and me kid, we can start where we left off. Some of those toffee-nosed officers are going to cop it when I get started. We're on equal terms now, no pips or crowns to hide behind; you and me girl are going to take them for every penny we can snatch.'

'How?' Trixie asked. 'You said they were from London somewhere.'

'So they are but that won't stop us.'

'How come?'

'I helped myself to a few dog tags, pocket books, identity cards, letters left on the bodies in the trenches.'

George looked carefully for her reaction and he got it. For all her bravado, Trixie was shocked. Grave robbing was another matter and, not keen to show her true feelings, she played her cards carefully.

'That's awful George. How could you?'

'How could I what?' he replied sheepishly.

'How could you take stuff from dead bodies?'

'Easy! They were all scavenging around for trinkets and souvenirs. It's everyone for themselves in the trenches love and I knew they would come in handy and I have a stack of addresses and next-of-kin details to go with them. A nice little package or two more useful to a couple of grifters like us than buried in the Belgian mud, Trix. Starting next week, we are back in business so hang onto my coat tails Trixie, George is home and heading for the big time. Are you with me lovely girl?'

'Right with you George, at least for now,' she said with just a hint of impatience.

George looked surprised. 'What do you mean, for now?'

'Not a lot at the moment George, let's just say I'm more alongside than behind you these days.'

He looked puzzled and was about to pursue the matter when Fanny interrupted with a tray set for tea.

'Ma's brewed another pot and we've got the cake out. Want some George?'

'Yes please Fan. You timed that nicely,' and smiled suspiciously at Trixie.

Mary brought in the Victoria sponge and Fanny laid out the best china on the table.

'Tea, George?' Mary asked, 'or have you lost your taste for it?'

'Never. I have to get used to drinking from a china cup and saucer again Mary. Your tea is wonderful compared to tea sweetened with sticky milk and drunk from a tin can. Not an acquired taste for a gent?'

He carefully studied the china on the table. 'Bit swanky this, going up in the world are we Trix?'

Fanny hastily changed the subject. 'Try the Victoria sponge George, I made it myself.'

'Did you now and when did you take to baking cakes for tea?' George smiled wickedly at Trixie. 'Just like her mother makes 'eh Trix?

'Just like our Fanny makes 'em this time George. A bit too heavy on the flour and light on the jam.'

Fanny dropped her smile but George just laughed. 'She's only kidding Fan, it's delicious, just like yer Ma's.'

Ignoring the teasing Trixie asked: 'Now, what are we going to do celebrate your return George?'

'We're all off to the Garrick music hall tonight to celebrate the victory, I have booked us a box and it's best bib and tucker, interval drinks and a late supper at the Market Tavern afterwards. How's that for starters?'

Fanny screamed in delight and swung her mother round and round. 'You always knew how to treat a girl, George.' Mary said.

'Only when they are my girls,' he replied with a grin and gleefully kicked Fanny's booted foot with his very shiny shoe.

'Now young Fanny have you won the hundred yards since I've been away?'

She giggled and with an exaggerated limp, she quickly cleared the tea table and disappeared into the kitchen. George leaned back in his seat, stretched and looked around the room.

'It's good to be back, Trix, it really is.'

'It's good to have you back, George. We've all missed you these past two years.'

Smiling at her he suggested: 'I expect you've been a bit lost without me. I hope you've been practicing a few of my skills?'

'One or two,' she replied convincingly. 'I had to; we needed a few bob to keep the house-keeping ticking over.'

'I trust Albert Marriot kept a weather eye out for you like he promised me he would,' he asked cautiously.

'He's been very kind and most helpful in so many ways. Now, if I'm to look me best for you tonight I'll need a bit of tarting up time. Will you be collecting us?'

'Of course, the old man has kept the car well and truly oiled and watered so I had best be on my way, if you want me back in good time.'

Trixie walked him to the front door but he stopped her in her tracks.

'I've thought of you such a lot girl. It was hell at Ypres and it was only the thought of seeing you again that kept me going. I even thought about doing a runner, I was so scared. You were in my head day and night.'

'Good,' Trixie replied. 'Now you're back safe and sound, you did your duty and we're all very proud of you. Now put it behind you and let's get on.'

'I have big plans, Trix, and you're part of them.'

'So I should be. I have kept it all ticking over, just in case.'

'I know but I'm back in the saddle. Now, where's the locket? It never once left my pocket, and if you look at it closely you'll see where it got nicked by a stray bullet when I left it hanging with me gun in the bunker.'

Pulling back the top of her dress, Trixie laughed. 'Round me neck, where else? It won't go round me arse. See you tonight soldier, seven sharp or you'll be for the high jump. Us Skyrme women don't like being kept waiting.'

'Seven sharp it is,' George confirmed.

'And we'll be scrubbed up, ready and waiting. Bye for now George,' and she brushed his cheek with a kiss.

Closing the door behind, she leaned back against it and called for her mother and sister. They came rushing into the hall and waited for instructions.

'Right. Now listen carefully, I want George's old room ready for the weekend, Doris and May know the score and will be out in a day or two. Give the room a good clean and we'll buy fresh bedding tomorrow.'

'We're due rent from them,' Mary said.

'Let them off it. Goodwill and all that and it won't effect us that much. Anyway we'll be in the real money again soon but both of you remember, George must not be told a thing about our business activities.'

'But what about Albert Marriot, will he say anything to George? After all they are supposed to be friends.'

'Water under the bridge, Ma,' Trixie insisted. 'Albert plays with the side that butters his bread. We work well together and he knows that too, he ain't going to cut off his nose to spite his face, believe me.'

Mary nodded. 'We know that, don't we Fanny? You make a right clever pair, you with the brains and his disguises. That nursing home set-up was a real money-spinner and it's still coming in. But won't he miss working with you Trixie?'

'Don't worry Ma, he'll still be around. He's a good friend and partner in crime and I don't plan on cutting him out of any deal unless George puts his oar in. Now you two, not a dickey bird to George, especially where the money is coming from.'

Fanny and Mary tapped their noses and Trixie winked at them.

Giggling to herself, Fanny said: 'Oh our Trixie, just good friends is it, well I've 'eard it all now.'

Trixie nodded. 'It's true I suppose he has been very kind and looked out for us but he never got more than I offered.'

'But you had him on a promise,' her mother replied.

'A promise is one thing, Ma, keepin' it is another.'

Slipping into her posh voice, she suggested: 'Now mother dear more tea and a slice of Victoria sponge before we prepare for the theatre.'

Gently teasing her sister, she added: 'As for you my girl polish up your boot or you'll be barred from the Market Tavern. If all he can manage is the bleedin' Market Tavern then he will have to change his ways. I've traded up a bit since he's been gone, it's The Half Crown now but a real proper job would be The Green Dragon.'

Jauntily flicking up her leg from beneath her skirts, she grinned and dashed upstairs.

CHAPTER SEVEN

During George's long absence, Trixie had practised hard to become a polished performer in her own right. She liked to work on her own but for George's sake she sometimes worked with his gang, but whenever she got the chance, she worked a few smart frauds of her own to help build up her 'rainy day' fund. However, with George back in the driving seat again things could get difficult.

There's no denying it was easy money all the way, too easy though for George who since his return was fast becoming a skilled forger but without the guile and cunning of his partner in crime, he might well have 'gone down' for a few more years. Nevertheless, they needed to package what they had learned together and go upmarket instead of playing in the lower divisions of the criminal fraternity.

Trixie needed little convincing that she was ready for anything and eager to go upmarket. Fair play, George had prepared her well for the important trial run at The Green Dragon and she was both nervous and excited when he collected her for the big night out. She paused at the top of the stairs and smiled.

'Mother, Fanny, this is my entrance into the county set. Do I look the part?'

Lost in the magic of the moment, Mary Skyrme stared at her youngest daughter as she confidently carried the stunning, fashionable evening wear with the poise and ease of the catwalk model. Fanny silently took it all in.

Her escort, clad in black tie and tails, took a sharp intake of breath before taking her hand and guiding her down the last few steps.

'Who'd have thought it?' Mary said. 'She's a sight for sore eyes and fit for the King of England.'

George checked the time on his recently acquired gold pocket watch and opened the front door.

'We're under starters orders Trix, let's show 'em what we are really made of.'

Outside, the September air was warm; the intoxicating aroma of fermenting apples from Bulmer's cider plant filtering through the Hereford streets gave George a heady moment or two as he escorted a most glamorous Trixie to the garden gate and carefully seated her in the chauffeur-driven Rolls Royce. Smiling broadly, she waved a regal goodbye to her awestruck mother and sister. It was also a moment to remember for the girl from Wellington.

After a short drive to Broad Street, the chauffeur stopped outside The Green Dragon, the most prestigious hotel in the county. The doorkeeper saluted, his gloved hand shaking slightly as he opened the door. Dazzled by the glamorous young woman, he accompanied the couple through the foyer to the cloakrooms.

Handing her elegant evening cloak to the waiting receptionist, she careful noted the expensive fur coats hanging in rows, took her cloakroom ticket, preened into the full-length mirror, smiled and left the room to wait for George.

At the entrance to the dining room, the Maître de Hotel, aware of the sudden interest in the handsome couple, escorted them across the extravagantly furnished room already full of affluent guests. Heads turned automatically as the unidentifiable young couple arrived at the pre-booked table in the window. They had heard the whispered asides of admiration as they passed the other diners and waiters. Trixie smiled graciously and politely, acknowledging their appraisal.

On a raised platform, a string quartet played light music and the couple, fully aware of the envious glances from their fellow diners, made a game of settling at their table.

The supercilious headwaiter, keen to check out their credentials, handed out large menus written up in French and watched for a reaction. It did not come. Impressed by the hint of conversational French quietly delivered by the young woman, he beckoned to a subordinate to bring the wine list. George brushed it away insisting only a bottle of the very best French champagne would do while they studied the menu. It came in an ice-filled bucket chilled to perfection and poured into delicate flutes by the wine waiter.

Watched over by the headwaiter, the handsome couple raised their glasses and silently toasted each other.

'First round to us,' Trixie whispered from behind her starched napkin.

'No. Checking us out for the size of the tip, that's all. Choose what you want to eat, relax and enjoy yourself but whatever you do stick to the plan.'

Keeping up the pretence, Trixie ordered the food in French. Served up in style by a retinue of waiters, it was thoroughly enjoyed without complaint. The scene was set, the evening going well and it was soon time to put into practice the months and weeks of training.

It was game on for Trixie but as usual, she could see the funny side of the situation and could not resist a little tomfoolery; George was up for it too. In cultured tones he announced: 'How were the snails my dear?'

'Quite delicious if a little slippery, although I must say I've seen better in our garden at Wellington.'

His partner giggled hysterically and George had to kick her under the table.

'Sorry George, this place is a bit like the convent school I went to but without all the trappings? I always wanted to giggle when the nuns came in for silent prayer; they looked like a pack of penguins when they shuffled into chapel.'

George reminded her: 'Compared to the places we're going to be seen in, this one is ordinary. We are simply using it as the launching pad to our future and if we can pull it off tonight, Trix, we are on our way to the big time. All eyes are on us and the chap's captivated by you.'

Trixie laughed again. 'It's my magnetic charm and good looks George, that's all.'

'I don't care what it is. Even the women are hooked. Whatever it is, it's working wonders, all you need to do is turn, nod, smile and watch 'em fall apart....'

Surprised by his comments, Trixie queried: 'What do you mean George, you seem quite excited?'

'It's the women, Trix; they can't stop looking at you either.'

'It's you they are admiring George, not me.'.

Unaware of her attraction, he stared at his partner in astonishment.

'No. They are looking at you, not me. Can't you feel it. I'm just the lucky escort.'

Knocked out by her lack of worldliness, he grasped her hand tightly. 'Sexuality is powerful and used well, very, very useful.'

'Are you telling me that the women fancy me too? Now there's a funny thing if ever I heard it. All the men might want me George but wanting is not having as well you know but I don't know about the women.'

'Mark my words, you will one day, Trix, I can guarantee that.' Her infectious laughter brought a sudden lull in the buzz of table talk and she almost gave the game away when she said:

'Tasty bit of lamb this George, nice gravy and veg too.'

'For Heaven's sake Trixie, keep your voice down, anyway it's not gravy, it's sauce, redcurrant and port sauce. Just remember that we are here to enjoy haute cuisine not the Market Tavern hot pot.'

Trixie lowered her voice and angrily retorted: 'I know what it is you pompous arse, and don't talk to me like that. Anyway, I have finished, thank you.'

Carefully placing her knife and fork across the empty plate, she silently waited for George to finish his meal.

As if by magic, the waiter appeared and asked 'madam' if she had enjoyed the meal.

'Madam has,' she replied. 'Absolutely delicious and so tantalizing on the taste buds, thank you so much waiter.'

Struggling to avert his eyes from her cleavage, he cleared the dishes and called for the dessert trolley.

'Would Madam care for dessert?' he enquired.

George replied on her behalf: 'No thank you, just coffee and brandy.'

The waiter moved off but Trixie, put out by George's attitude, snapped back at him:

'Why do you do that George? I can decide for myself.'

'You rarely take dessert and you always have brandy with your coffee,' he told her.

'I know, but please stop making decisions for me, it's becoming very boring. Now, what's this big adventure you have got planned for us?'

The waiter interrupted them with the coffee and poured the brandy into warmed brandy bowls.

George relaxed for a moment and when the waiter departed spoke quietly to his partner:

'Look Trix once this dummy run is over with we're going upmarket and staying there. I have planned a six-week spree around the Shires and we'll make a killing. Albert is coming with us.'

'Albert. Since when?' Trixie asked in surprise.

The waiter interrupted again. 'More brandy and coffee sir?'

'Yes please for both of us,' and muttered his thanks.

Whispering quietly he told her: 'Since this afternoon, he's a natural grifter and we both know how good he can be at planting the seeds for a good scam. We can send him ahead to set things up and if this comes off we can all make mint.'

She gave George a warning look cautioning him that he was heading towards dangerous ground.

'What's up now, Trixie? It's all arranged.'

'So it seems but you should have asked me first,' and kicked him hard on the shin.

Rubbing his leg hard, he asked: 'What's that all about?'

'Albert tagging along. I hope this is not a three-way split, I won't be best pleased if it is?'

Anxious not to foul up the entire evening, George tried to pacify her.

'Of course not, he is on a percentage and expenses that is all. You know him well enough by now, he looked after you girls while I was away, didn't he? Got a soft spot for you, admires the way you work.'

Trixie blushed and tried to shrug it off. 'That was ages ago, I've changed a lot since then but you are right George, he could be useful. He can come this time but next time, ask me first.'

'Duly noted old girl. We can tie up the arrangements this week and send Albert ahead to open the dodgy bank accounts and book the hotels. Believe me Miss Skyrme, it's money for old rope.'

Trixie laughed. 'You mean for the odd forged cheque or two.'

'Or three, or even one hundred if we plan it right.'

Excited at the thought of making a large profit, she raised her glass to George and sipped a second brandy.

Clearly impressed by their good looks and easy banter, fellow diners enjoyed the charade until it was time to leave.

George took a moment or two to finish his cigar, prompting Trixie's next cue. Pushing her chair back, she gazed at the row of waiters waiting her next move and lightly touching George's arm, she pointed to them and announced.

'Well, George. Time to pay the bill while I powder my nose. It has been a wonderful evening and I bet you a pound to a penny the chap with the fair moustache gets to me first. He's been panting for me all bloomin' evening.'

Giving her a lopsided grin, George stood up. Three waiters dashed forward to take Trixie's chair and, as she had forecast, the fair one led the way. Winking at George, she deliberately stumbled against him and the young man blushed as she took his arm; to the envy of most of the men in the room, he escorted her to the exit.

'Class act,' George muttered to himself as he sat down again and smiled proudly as he watched his partner disappear into the foyer.

Calling for a final brandy and the bill, he waited for the headwaiter to pour out the brandy and warm the glass over the candle flame before pointedly placing the bill in front of him for payment by cheque.

With an extravagant flourish of his gold pen, George signed it in the name of Sir Clive Dimwoody and left his card with full details of his banking account.

Accepting George's substantial tip, the headwaiter swiftly pocketed the cash, glanced at the business card and picked up the cheque. After a suitable interval, George left the dining room.

In the ladies cloakroom room two or three women were waiting to collect their coats. Trixie came out of the WC cubicle and watched closely as the pleasant attendant sorted out their tickets before handing them their expensive coats and hats.

Studying the rails of fashionable clothing, Trixie spotted a very expensive velvet coat and waited for the other women to leave before searching through her handbag.

Embarrassed, she smiled awkwardly at the friendly attendant, shuffled through her handbag and carefully tipped the contents onto the counter top.

'I am so sorry to keep you waiting. I seem to have mislaid my cloakroom ticket. Dear me, I'm sure it was in my purse. What on earth have I done with it?'

'No hurry Madam,' the middle-aged woman said helpfully. 'Which coat was yours?'

Without looking up Trixie replied: 'The blue velvet evening coat with a diamond clasp or did I wear my cream mink? Do you know I have such a fashionable wardrobe to choose from, I simply can't remember?'

'There's a very nice blue velvet on the right-hand rail, the one with the high collar. Is that yours?' the woman suggested.

Feigning surprise Trixie said: 'So clever of you to spot it and how kind of you to admire it. Look my dear, I think I must have given the ticket to my husband. Oh, dash it! I expect he has gone for the car.'

Placing a pound note on the counter Trixie pleaded: 'It's awfully late. I don't suppose you could oblige me?'

Hesitating briefly, the attendant picked up the money.

'I shouldn't really miss but I suppose yer know yer own coat when you see it,' and laid it on the counter.

With remarkable aplomb, Trixie confidently threw it around her shoulders.

'Thank you so much. You have been most kind. Do have this for your trouble,' and pushed another pound note into her hand.

Giving the attendant her warmest 'you're a mug' smile, Trixie picked up her handbag and left the cloakroom.

George was chatting to the door attendant and when he saw Trixie coming through the swing doors, he did a double take. Full of confidence she walked towards him and took his arm just as the hire car drew up. Helping her into the vehicle, the door attendant touched his cap, saluted and said: 'Goodnight Madam, goodnight sir.' Davis tipped him well.

The hire car drove off quickly catching the couple off guard. George directed the driver to the railway station.

Trixie whispered: 'Why the railway station, George?'

He stroked the velvet coat. 'This is worth a good few bob, well done old girl; we don't want to get caught out do we. So we make a short detour my dear, just to be on the safe side.'

Smoothing the velvet sleeves, she suggested: 'It will pay for the dinner ten times over and with change to spare.'

'You can say that again, Trix, it's a right royal coat and suits an up and coming woman of distinction but forget about the bill for dinner, I have taken care of that.'

'And whose picking up that tab?' she asked.

'Sir Clive Dimwoody, he's on holiday in the area with his mistress.'

Trixie chuckled. 'His mistress was she. Not by any chance his good lady?'

'Good woman, yes, lady, who knows...? You have done well Trix, with a bit more practice, you will soon be up to scratch.'

'Who needs practice Mr. Davis I'm word bleedin' perfect these days.'

'Indeed you are my dear but running before you can walk can trip us both up.'

'Not me George. I have been under starters orders for far too long.'

CHAPTER EIGHT

For the next twelve months, George and Trixie worked hard, honing their unlawful skills and establishing their dishonest credentials. Working 'off the patch' in and around the Three Counties, forging cheques, cheating race goers, outsmarting the banks and picking a ripe pocket became daily habits. With plenty of cash to spare and using false names, they stayed in the best hotels and enjoyed the very best money can buy.

As their criminal and social status increased so did the hangers on and before long, they had a following of amateur and professional thieves and fraudsters keen to cash in on the swindles. One in particular carefully dogged their every move.

After a successful day at Worcester races, Trixie and George were enjoying a drink with Albert Marriot and a small group of associates, at The King's Head. The day's takings had been excellent, thanks to 'insider information' on the runners and riders, which, sold on to the eager and gullible punters in the grandstand, netted more than expected. However, when it came to racing certainties, Trixie trusted her own instincts and pulled in a couple of very good winners. Sipping champagne and dallying over a plate of canapés she was aware that George was chatting intently to a late arrival. Elated by the day's outcome Trixie ignored him, preferring to converse with her old associate Albert Marriot.

'Good day's work, Albert. The suckers just kept coming back for more.'

'And who wouldn't with the insider tips you were turning out at a fiver a time. Who's that chap with George?'

'Haven't a clue. He's been around for a while, said he's an old friend.'

Before Albert could take a second look, the middle-aged man turned away from George, butted into the conversation between Trixie and Albert and laughingly enquired: 'Now don't tell me young lady that all those winners you were selling had come straight from the horse's mouth?'

Trixie grinned. 'More like the horse's arse.'

Her comment drew loud laughter from the company around the table.

'Why's that then?' the casual inquisitor asked.

George replied for her: 'Because old boy, it was all a load of horse shit and nothing to do with her grand aunt being a mistress of the Aga Khan.'

'So she makes it all up and the punters pay out good money for a winning tip. Very clever.'

Flattered, Trixie preened at the comment and smiled.

'Exactly. If they want to pay a fiver a throw for the secrets of a top trainer's private notes, who am I to stop 'em splashing out on my special little envelopes?'

'Well, well, well! Now that is a clever bit of criminal deception if ever I heard it. How do you get away with it?'

Keen to show her deceptive mind, Trixie boasted: 'Well! It's not a game of marbles is it?'

They all laughed again but failed to notice the quizzical look on the face of the chatty intruder. The laughter died down but the champagne continued to loosen tongues.

'We must have taken a good pot today, Trix?' Albert suggested.

'About two hundred quid from the fake tips alone, plus the pickings from a good few pockets and there were plenty of toffs around for the taking.'

The stranger butted in. 'You were picking pockets as well?'

'I was doing the dipping,' Marriot told him. 'While the toffs were concentrating on the lovely Trixie, I whipped out the wallets from their back pockets.'

Not wanting to miss any praise George boasted: 'While my associates were working the punters, I was bouncing cheques at the cashier's office in the betting hall and the bars.'

Trixie laughed. 'After all the hard work we have to eat and drink and that's what we are doing here.'

Her voice suddenly trailed off. She stopped talking, looked at the stranger in their midst and her mood quickly changed. Prodding him in the chest she said: 'You've been hanging around us asking questions long enough. Just who are you anyway?'

She looked at George first and then at the others. 'Come on George, is he with you?'

The others stopped talking, looked directly at the interloper and then at each other. The man shrugged his shoulders, stood up and excused himself. 'Off to the gents. I'll get a round in on the way back.'

Puzzled, George watched him for a moment or two before asking the others: 'How long has he been with us, Albert?'

'I don't know, George. I thought he was with you and Trix.'

Staring hard at the group, Trixie whispered: 'Who the hell does know him then; if he's not with us which one of you brought him along?'

Confusion shadowed their faces; it quickly dawned that nobody knew their unidentified drinking companion.

George looked sick, Trixie quickly seized the moment.

'Albert go to the gents and check him out,' she ordered.

'Don't flap, Trixie, he must be alright, he's been tagging along for a week or two now,' George said.

'Yes and not one of us knows who he is. For God's sake George! Come to think, he's been watching us like a bloody hawk and always asking the same bloody questions where ever we are.'

A shocked Albert re-joined them at the table. 'Any news, Albert. Who is he and more to the point, where is he now?'

'Scarpered, it seems old girl.'

'What do you mean scarpered?'

'Gone, no sign of him anywhere Trix, disappeared into thin air it seems.'

'Are you sure Albert?' George said.

Trixie snapped back: 'Gone George, Albert said he's bloody vanished.'

'But he was buying the next round,' George replied.

'Sod the next round, George; we could be in big trouble if we hang about here. Best we split up and leave now, just in case.'

'Just in case of what, Trix?' George asked pompously.

'In case he's the bloody law.'

She watched George and Albert visibly panic and then calmly took control.

'Now it's your turn not to flap George,' she said sarcastically. 'Move your arse, go and pay up what we owe and we will leave together normally.'

'What a bloody mess Albert. We could be in real trouble now.'

'But I honestly thought he was with the others,' he pleaded.

'So it seems,' she said.

George, who had caught the end of the conversation, added: 'He seemed a decent chap; I really thought he was with us.'

'And we three George, the leaders of the bleedin' pack, thought he was with each other. Bloody hell, he could be 'old bill'.'

The penny suddenly dropped and after a stunned silence, a troubled Trixie suggested: 'And then again he couldn't be...could he?'

'Best not to wait around to find out. We need to shift ourselves and fast,' George suggested.

Casually drifting towards the main exit, they waved to the landlord, Trixie cheerfully calling out: 'Goodnight Henry, see you next race day.'

Outside on the forecourt two gents in bowler hats mingled with the passers by. When the trio appeared in the doorway they immediately identified themselves with warrant cards. Trixie took one pace back leaving George and Albert to front up and face the music.

The younger of the two police officers placed a hand on George's shoulder. 'We don't want any fuss sir. I am Detective Sergeant Gough, Worcester Police and this is Detective Inspector Tanner from Hereford City.'

George went white, stood still and looked nervously back at Trixie and Albert.

'Yes Sergeant and what can we do for you?'

Before George could say anything more, the Inspector pronounced: 'Theresa Agnes Skyrme and William George Davis, I have a warrant for your arrest.'

Albert took a swift sideways step away from his companions. Outwardly calm and fighting back his shock and surprise George sobered up enough to ask: 'On what grounds officer?'

'On suspicion of uttering forged cheques and criminal deception. I must caution you and the young lady that you need not say anything, but anything you do say may be written down and used in evidence against you?'

Trixie was stunned. Badly shaken by events, all her bravado drained from her young face; Albert put his arm around her to comfort her but the overly keen police officer brushed it aside. By now passers by had stopped promenading, preferring to stand and watch the arrest; Henry the publican, followed by a loyal band of tipsy customers, drifted out of the public house to see what all the fuss was. Standing his ground, George confidently looked the arresting officer straight in the eye before gesturing to Albert who spoke quickly to Trixie.

Regaining her composure, she quietly asked: 'Where are you taking us officer?'

'Worcester police station for now miss and then onto Hereford pending further enquiries,' the Inspector replied.

To steady herself, Trixie gripped Albert's arm; George went to her, smiled confidently and beckoned to Henry in the doorway of the pub.

'Landlord, could you bring a glass of water for the lady please. Is that alright with you Inspector?'

The officer nodded and the willing proprietor returned with a glass of water. George tried to speak with him but was prevented from doing do by the officious police sergeant reminding him of his right to contact his solicitor. Stepping back, Inspector Tanner allowed George to hand a card to Henry.

'Please be good enough to give this to my senior associate and ask him to kindly call on my solicitor at his Worcester office and bring him to the police station.'

Addressing the arresting officer, he added: 'We shall, of course, remain silent until he arrives.'

The Inspector smiled knowingly and escorted Trixie into the first vehicle; the second contained the stranger who had so easily befriended them after the races.

Bundled in beside him, she quickly realised he must have been an undercover police officer used to trap them.

Closely watched by a group of independent observers, the convoy drove off; in the distance, Albert Marriot was dutifully heading for the city office of George's solicitor.

Bailed to appear seven days later at Hereford Magistrates Court, the forenoon session was almost at an end when the Stipendiary Magistrate agreed to an extension to enable the defending solicitor to present legal argument concerning the arrest. Up in the public gallery Mary, Fanny and Albert sat with a few former associates of the accused in the dock. Confident of an acquittal, George and Trixie smiled at their friends and listened intently as their solicitor addressed the bench.

Bringing his case to a climax the defending solicitor explained: 'And so your Worships, it is obvious to this court, let alone the collective intelligence of the Bench, that this entire prosecution hinges on the sole evidence of a police officer acting as agent provocateur in a deliberate ploy to entrap my clients. Clients, whom I might add, have no previous convictions.'

Pausing long enough for his words to sink in, he waved in the direction of the dock.

'Therefore I ask that all charges against the defendants be dropped and my clients released from custody forthwith,' and with a final challenging look at the police prosecutor, he sat down, assured of the response.

The Chairman leaned forward to converse with the Clerk of the Court and then retired with him to deliberate on a point of law.

From the dock, Trixie caught her sister's eye and smiled at her mother. In the press box, the reporter from the 'Hereford Times' winked at George; he responded with a 'thumbs up'.

After a short interval, the door to the Magistrates' retiring room opened and the anxious gathering stood up and sat down again.

'Will the defendants please rise,' the Clerk uttered in customary fashion. Ever the gentleman, George stood up at once and helped his co-defendant to her feet. Inwardly scared to death at the possible outcome, Trixie gripped the dock rail. As they waited for the verdict, George confidently patted her shaking hand. 'Theresa Agnes Skyrme, William George Davis, the Court finds that the prosecution evidence against you has been obtained in a manner contrary to the Police and Criminal Justice Act and therefore technically flawed.'

Looking hard and long at the Prosecuting Officer, the Magistrate delivered a sharp reprimand to everyone involved.

'It worries this court that the actions of the police in this matter should besmirch the name of justice in this grubby way and I shall be making a report to the Chief Constable. However, in dismissing the defendants, I would be failing in my duty if I did not warn you both that your shady way of life leaves much to be desired.'

Re-adjusting his spectacles, he turned his attention to Trixie.

'As for you young woman, it seems that the police officers involved in your goings on were astounded at your audacity and courage when arrested. Although you leave this court without a stain on your character, I must caution you to reject your notorious and unsavoury way of life and use your obvious talents in a less profligate manner. My colleagues and I sincerely hope never to see you before us again. Case dismissed!'

He brought his hammer down with such a short, sharp knock that the entire court responded to the Clerk's formal request to rise, before he had time to say it.

The collective sigh from the public gallery was clearly audible and the beaming defendants hugged each other. In the foyer of the courthouse, family and friends greeted the released couple with warm handshakes. Wrapping her arms around her mother and sister, she whispered: 'Never again, Ma, never.'

Police and prosecutors watched the defendants, their solicitor and friends fight their way to the exit but before they reached the main door, a court official, accompanied, by Inspector Tanner stopped them.

'William George Davis I have here a warrant for your arrest.'

George stood his ground. 'Good God man, not again, this is becoming a habit.'

Ignoring him, the officer continued: 'You need not say anything but anything you do say may be written down and used in evidence. Please come with me.'

There was instant silence in the foyer. The smiles of success faded from the smug faces of Trixie and her party of supporters. Police and prosecutors looked on with satisfaction when Trixie pulled at Inspector Tanner's arm and yelled: 'You can't do this we've been cleared. It's all a big mistake, we got off.'

'It's no mistake, please let go of my arm miss, otherwise I shall have to arrest you for obstruction,' Tanner said.

Surprised and angry George Davis snapped at his solicitor: 'Ask to see the bloody warrant or something. It's what I pay you to do.'

'Take it easy George, all in good time, as I have already told you, I am your legal representative. Now Inspector, can I see the arrest warrant.'

The officer handed it over and, reading it carefully, the solicitor told his clients: 'It's a new charge Miss Skyrme, against George, not you. You must go with them George, I shall catch up with you at the police station. Not a word until I get there.'

As the arresting officer accompanied him to the waiting police car, Trixie shouted: 'You stupid man George Davis, you bloody stupid man.'

Albert tried to calm her down. 'Steady Trix, let the solicitor sort it out down at the station.'

'But what now Albert, what bloody happens now?' she pleaded. 'What's he bleedin' done this time?'

'I have no idea. Let's have a spot of lunch and then I will liaise with the solicitor, by then he will know what the charge is. Come on little Fanny and you Mary, Doris and Phyllis can come as well. Will the Market Tavern do?'

'Very kind Albert, it will be like old times again. I expect the boys will be there already,' Doris said.

Trixie was not impressed. 'Who wants bleedin' old times. We need to move on not back; with him inside life's going to be one bloody great bore.'

Mary put her arm around her dejected daughter.

'Life's what yer make it girl, and you've done a proper job so far, hasn't she our Fanny?

'Trixie always does a proper job. Now let's be off and get some dinner.'

The little gathering crossed High Town watched by a patrolling constable and his Sergeant; they had been in court all morning.

'Got him this time son and that little beauty won't be short of takers with him on a stretch inside,' the Sergeant said with more than a hint of lust in his middle-aged voice.

'I wouldn't mind a taste of it myself Sarge, but we're well out of that cunning little vixen's league. I bet you a ten bob note that Marriot will have his polished boots well under the table by the time Davis comes out...if he ever does.'

'Oh he'll be out again, that smarmy legal bastard from Worcester will see to that. That's what he pays him good money for, mind you there's a list of charges as long as me arm waiting to be answered.'

'So I might give 'er a tap when I next see 'er about town,' the keen young constable replied with a snigger.

His superior laughed. 'And pigs might fly sonny Jim. Half the city will be after her favours, knobs and all, if she stays in town. She is an ambitious little madam and you can bet that she will be long gone by the time Davis comes out. Now back to the station, we've got paperwork to do before we go off shift.'

Some months later, a restless Trixie was playing cards with Mary and Fanny at Barton Manor, when out of the blue she smashed a clenched fist onto the table.

Albert lifted his head out of the daily paper.

'What's up Trixie, did your Ma deal you a rotten hand? Come on buck up, it's only a game.'

'That's all it ever is to you lot, a bloody game. What I need is more excitement and I ain't getting it here.'

The others knew when to stay silent; the expected outburst had been on the cards since George's arrest. Angry at his betrayal and frustrated by his absence, the cracks had been showing for some weeks. The volcano was just about ready to pump out hell fire and damnation and her mother and sister were ready for it.

Albert was not. Trixie's black moments had not touched him so far and he was unprepared for the onslaught to come. She stood up, swept the playing cards from the table and paced the room.

'This is a pig of a town, nothing ever happens now that George is inside; what the hell was he thinking of going it alone behind my back? If the stupid bastard expects me to wait around for him to get out he's got another thing coming. I wait for no man, not ever and it won't bother me if he rots in his bleedin' cell.'

Her mother tried to pacify her. 'He won't do the full time and he'll soon be out.'

Trixie yelled back at her: 'No, he bloody won't Ma, he'll do at least two years despite what that clever sod from Worcester promised. God knows what else he has been up to without tellin' us?'

Albert finally put his paper down and got up.

'Come on girl, don't be so hard on him; his solicitor put up a damned good defence but the odds were stacked against him. We all knew George had been sailing close to the wind for a good while and keeping you in the dark.'

Mary and Fanny tried to leave the room but he stopped them. 'Best you hear all the facts.'

'What facts, Albert?' Trixie snapped.

'Since he's been home from the war, he's been into all sorts of dodgy deals; CID had his card marked the moment he set foot in the city again. He may be the best forger for many a mile but he gets cocky and careless at times; he was bound to get caught with or without us.'

Shaken at the news, Trixie sat down. 'But we worked as a team Albert, all of us.'

'Only when it suited him. You were useful, a good cover for his own fiddles but believe me he made more money for himself on our escapades that you and I ever did on our own.'

Mary looked up.

'Yeah, and he hung onto it too. Come to think of it, he hardly ever coughed up for his board and lodgings 'ere. Kept all his money to himself and lived off our Trixie. Well he can stay inside for all I care.'

Trixie could hardly believe what she had heard; she needed someone to attack and turned on her mother.

'And what did you cough up, Ma? All you ever chipped in was from a couple of hours standin' in for Doris and her tart-faced friend after closin' time on a Saturday night.'

Fanny was upset. 'Don't say that about our Ma, she did her best for us.'

Trixie calmed down a bit when she realised how nasty she had been and put her arm around her sister.

'Well, she didn't exactly break the bank at bleedin' Monte Carlo did she Fanny? Anyway, who needs Mr. William George Davis? For all I damn well care Gloucester jail is welcome to him. It's time I struck out on my own, Albert.'

'At last you're thinking straight. We make a good team Trix and we can manage without him. We did rather well from the employment agency scam in Leominster and we can try it again somewhere else.'

Trixie laughed. 'Why not Albert. I can manage without him all right, we all can. I might look strapped for cash but I've always managed to put a good bit aside for me 'rainy day' fund.'

The glint in her eye was back and the moment had come for announcing the plans she had been hatching for some time. Back to her old self, she fell into the nearest armchair and announced: 'George was only the brawn, I was the brains. Whenever it went wrong, it was down to me to get us out of trouble, me who spotted that the bloke in Worcester might be a rozzer. Crikey Albert, he asked George enough bloody questions and he didn't even twig.'

Her excitement was building but not enough to give away her game plan too soon but Fanny pushed her for more information.

'What have yer got planned then, Trix, come on, give us a clue.'

Tapping her nose, Trixie answered: 'Ask no questions our Fanny and yer won't hear any lies. I am planning big time and that is all you lot need to know, for now. Now, who's for cocoa before our gallant captain goes home, it's the races tomorrow and we can't keep the suckers waiting.'

Within a month, the household at Barton Manor was on the move. Stripped of all the quality furnishings and fittings, apart from an assortment of baggage and boxes stacked up in the hall, it was almost bare. Mary Skyrme was pacing the hallway and Fanny, trying to come to terms with what was happening, was sobbing in the kitchen when Trixie came down the stairs. She was carrying a large quality suitcase, a battered Gladstone bag and a neat, matching handbag which she stacked by the front door. She also had a stylish carrier bag labelled Chadds of Hereford containing a new hat and coat.

Accompanied by her mother and a still sobbing sister she took one last walk through the house they had shared through the good and bad times.

'Please don't go, Trix. Tell 'er Ma; tell 'er not to leave us,' Fanny pleaded.

She hugged her tightly. 'Ma doesn't need to tell me anything Fanny; it's going to be alright. I promised yer didn't I. I can't stay in this one horse town any longer, there's no fun, no adventure any more and I need that Fanny, I need it to get me going again.'

'But what about George? He'll soon be out won't he?' Mary said.

'No Ma. Not this time, the cops are lining up warrants like hot cross buns on Good Friday and they'll be waiting for him the moment he steps out of Gloucester jail.'

'How do yer know that Trixie. Who told you?' Fanny said.

'That young copper in High Town. He keeps me well informed in return for a smile and a promise, he's so gone on me he'd arrest the King if I told him to.'

They laughed together for one last time.

'Believe me Ma, George has made a bleedin' pig's ear of everything, I was lucky I didn't go down with him after the mess he made of the Worcester job. If I'm ever going to leave this trap he has shut round me, I've got to get shot of him for good, I need a brand new start and it's best I do it away from Hereford.'

The doorknocker brought them back to reality.

'That will be Albert,' Trixie said. 'I'll tell him to take your baggage to the car.'

Captain Marriot doffed his peaked cap in his usual jaunty manner. 'Good morning to you dear ladies, Withington first stop.'

He swept up the bags and boxes belonging to Mary and Fanny and carried them to the car; Trixie put her arms around her mother and sister. 'I paid Aunt

Hetty six months board and lodging up front and she's more than happy, if I haven't sent for the two of you by then, I'll send her some more.'

Tearfully Fanny asked. 'What if we don't 'ear nothin' from yer ever again?'

Trixie was finding the fond goodbye unexpectedly difficult but she had to show her strength of character.

'Don't go on so Fanny, I'm upset too. This is not easy for me you know, leaving you and Ma behind like this but it has to be, for the short term at least. Just remember, we sticks together like glue.'

To comfort her, Mary took hold of Fanny more tightly than ever.

'Come on me duck, Trixie is right, she won't let us down, I know it in me water. Now give her a smile before we go.'

'Thanks Ma. I know she will but I'm going to miss her so much.'

Trixie was quiet for a minute or two before assuring her mother that all will turn out well.

'Don't worry Ma I've arranged for Albert to keep an eye on you both, just let him know if you need anything and he'll get it for you. Here's the cash from the furniture and the other odd bits I sold off plus a bit more, that will keep you in treats our Fanny and you in sherry Ma.'

'But I thought most of all that belonged with the house, Trixie.'

'Well it doesn't anymore Ma and I'm not leaving a forwarding address so keep it by for emergencies. I have plenty of cash for my needs and a nice bit stashed away. Whatever happens I will send for you.'

She turned to her sister and joked: 'As for you and that bloody great boot I shall have to warn the Life Guards that you'll soon be clumping round the Palace Yard. Now give us a kiss and let's get out of this place, my taxi cab's on the way.'

The three women tearfully hugged each other for the last time and walked out to the waiting car. Trixie settled them in and then said goodbye to Albert.

'Goodbye old girl and chin up. You're doing the right thing and I'll be standing by for a recall into your service any time.' He gave her a mock salute, which she returned with a kiss on the cheek. 'Take good care of them, Albert.'

'I will and you take care too. Watch out for those pavements of gold and grab what you can,' he added with his usual optimistic outlook on life.

'Thanks Albert and I promise to save you a slab or two of the best pavements.'

She waved them off and watched sadly, as the car drove away but her sadness lifted the moment a taxi cab drew up and her natural enthusiasm flooded back.

'The bags are just inside the door cabbie, I can manage the vanity case and the small Gladstone bag so will you take the large one please?'

He picked it up muttering: 'What yer got in 'ere girl, swag from a bank robbery?'

'You never know these days,' she said and shamelessly grinned.

The street was almost empty as she closed the door to Barton Manor for the last time and posted the key through the letterbox. The sleek ginger cat on the garden wall rubbed up against her and she stopped to stroke him.

'So long big Ginger. It's my turn to go hunting now so wish me luck?'

Fingering the silver locket around her neck, she looked up and down the street. The dustbin wicket was about to become a Test match ground again for the local lads and for a moment Trixie thought she could see the ghostly figure of George Davis picking up the ball and bowling at the imaginary wicket.

'Come on now,' the Cabbie encouraged. 'The London train is always on time and waits for no-one, not even a polished young lady like you, Miss.'

Trixie shrugged her shoulders and stuck two gloved fingers in the air, leaving the taxi driver shocked at the unladylike gesture but she laughed at him.

'Not you cabbie, I'm saying my own farewell to this dead end city, its rainy day time at last and I'm free, at least from the bloody bells on Sundays.'

Leaving her Hereford accent behind her, she clambered into the back seat and ordered: 'The railway station cabbie, if you please,' and waved goodbye to Ginger and all in Barton Road.

At the station a porter wheeled her luggage from the taxi cab into the booking hall where she bought a first class single ticket to Paddington and made her way to the 'Ladies Only' waiting room. Changing her unfashionable, day-to-day clothes for a comfortable, stylish coat and matching hat, she stuffed her old clothes into the now empty carrier bag, she checked her appearance in the mirror and picked up her hand luggage.

Outside on the platform she waited by the bookstall with her luggage giving her time to select a batch of magazines to read on the journey.

The London train was already approaching the platform and taking a final look at the county of her birth, as the train slowed to a steamy halt the porter escorted her to a reserved seat in the first class carriages. Lifting her large suitcase onto the rack, he attempted to do the same with the smaller ones.

'Leave those please, I may need them for the journey.'

'Yes Miss,' he replied and placed them on the seat beside her. Tipping him well, he wished her a good journey and respectfully touched the peak of his uniform cap. Pleased to have the compartment to herself, she stared blissfully out of the window until the train moved off.

When it paused at the red signal on the Wye Bridge, she stood up, lowered the window, and threw the carrier bag out of the open window; it caught on the wind and hitting the river with some force, it burst open on impact.

With a smile of satisfaction, Trixie watched her former life float away downstream and after a while settled down to enjoy the long journey to London.

Opening the Gladstone bag on the seat beside her, she took out a small nightdress case and removed a substantial package of high denomination bank notes, wrapped in a pink silk nightdress. Flicking through them, she selected enough to see her through the day, tucked them into her handbag and returned the rest to the larger bag. Before closing it, she removed a silver locket from an inner pocket.

Determined to throw it out of the window with the rest of her past, she looked at the photos framed inside, hesitated and unexpectedly thought of George. Instead of tossing it away, she dropped it back into its hiding place, closed the window and sat back for a final farewell look at the familiar Cathedral until it disappeared from view. Hoisting up her skirts and kicking off her new shoes, she stretched out her legs and settled down to read her society magazines. By the time she reached Oxford, she had memorised the interests and habits of just about every society hostess in Mayfair.

CHAPTER NINE

A fifteen-minute wait for a signal change at West Ealing delayed the arrival into Paddington but Trixie was unconcerned. The short break allowed her to spruce up and brush out the creases in her fashionable outfit; a new adventure was about to begin.

Despite the long journey, she did not feel tired and the adrenalin was still pumping; she had arranged for a porter to meet her off the train, collect her luggage and escort her to the nearby taxi rank. He was a chirpy young lad and she welcomed his friendly chatter.

'Nice day, Miss. Come far have you, staying in the big city for long?'

His inquisitive patter reminded her of the farmer's boys back home, always rabbiting on and asking niggling questions. Determined not to give herself away, she shut him up with a suitable tip.

'Where to, Miss?' the cabbie asked as she settled in the back seat of the taxi and, flicking through the pages of her well-thumbed magazine, she replied: 'The Savoy Hotel please and take the scenic route, I'd like to see the sights before dark.'

About an hour later, the taxi cab trundled along The Strand and turned into the main entrance of the famous hotel. The tail-coated door attendant doffed his topper, helped her out and called for the bell-boy to collect the bags. Paying the driver and thanking him for the guided tour, she rewarded him with an unusually large tip.

Trixie was awestruck by the huge building; the pictures in her glossy magazine did not do it justice, the opulence hit her straight between the eyes and she instantly knew she was about start on the adventure of her life.

Following the doorman into the reception area, the Duty Manager, a corpulent, middle-aged gent in a gold trimmed tailcoat and fancy waistcoat, graciously welcomed her to the hotel.

He looked her up and down two or three times before inviting her to register.

'Good afternoon, Madam, do we have reservation.'

'No we have not, neither have I and for future reference, it is Miss not Madam,' she replied sarcastically.

Taken aback by her confident response and polished voice, the manager respectfully stepped back a pace.

'I am so sorry, Miss, what am I thinking?'

'Indeed, I was about to ask you the same question although you need not answer that, at least not at present. I may ask you again at a later date.'

Trixie had clearly done her research. 'Now, have you a room with plenty of space and a river view?'

'For how long, Miss?'

Heaving an impatient sigh. 'O'Dare, Miss Josephine O'Dare and I shall require a suite for as long as needs be. My cabin trunk is being sent on from Southampton and should be here in a few days.'

Opening her handbag wide enough to hint money would be no problem, the Duty Manager took note of her expensive jewels, much of them accrued from her criminal activities, handed her a key with an extravagant flourish and ordered the bellboy to take her luggage to her rooms.

'As requested Miss O'Dare, it is one of our finest penthouse suites overlooking our beautiful River Thames. It has every thing you will need for an enjoyable stay and should you require our services at anytime, please inform reception.'

Behind her back she heard him mutter to his reception staff: 'And it will cost you an arm and a leg dear.'

She was about to rebuke him but, not wanting a showdown so early in her visit, she made a mental note of his caustic comment, just in case.

As the young bellboy unlocked the ornate door to her suite, little did he know that the turn of a golden key into a posh hotel door lock meant Trixie Skyrme, farm labourer's daughter from Herefordshire, is no more? Josephine O'Dare, woman of substance, was about to cast her net in pursuit of a lifestyle beyond her wildest imaginings.

The rooms on the third floor were indeed spacious. The large balcony running the length of the sitting room justified the promised panoramic view of the river and she shivered as she gazed into the dark waters below. Dazed by the effects of such luxury, Josephine strolled through the spacious suite of rooms as if she were born to it. The two large, blue, soft leather sofas with matching cushions dominated one end of the sitting room, with vases of fresh flowers and bowls of mixed fruits arranged on occasional tables. What luggage she had was neatly stacked beside the wardrobe in the bedroom; the adjoining bathroom featured a wide range of toiletries and cosmetics.

She had almost forgotten the bellboy was still in the room; he was balancing an ice bucket with a bottle of champagne and a fine, cut glass flute. Picking up the bottle, she read the label, nodded her approval and returned it to the ice bucket.

'Compliments of the management, Miss. If you need anything at all, pull the bell cord and the floor maid will come immediately.'

'Thank you young man, I think that will be all.'

Before leaving the room, he coughed politely.

'Good gracious, what am I thinking of?' and she handed him a few coins from her purse.

Impressed at the size of the tip, he confirmed: 'Dinner is served from 7.00pm in the brassiere and any of the main dining rooms but if you prefer it can be sent up. Use the intercom on the table, ask for room service and I will personally see to it.'

'Thank you, young man'.

'It's James, Miss,' he said with a cheeky grin.

'Yes, well thank you again James, you have been most helpful.'

As the door closed behind him, she muttered to herself: 'There goes a bright boy, keep in with the rich ladies, James, and you'll go far.'

Lifting the Moet & Chandon from the ice bucket, she wrapped it in a white napkin and carefully loosening the cork she let the bubbles rise to the surface, just enough for the liquid to trickle over the edge into the waiting flute.
She carried it to the balcony just as Big Ben struck the hour. Taking a sip, she loudly whispered: 'Please God not more bloody bells.'

It took a week or two for Josie O'Dare to familiarise herself with her luxurious surroundings but she slipped comfortably into her new identity as if to the manor born.

Key staff, constant in their attentions, had taken a genuine shine to her and, before long, she had skilfully fed them her new persona.

Her cabin trunk, cleverly disguised in oriental style by Albert Marriot, arrived in her suite the following day. Sent by rail from Hereford to Southampton and delivered to the Savoy by a bogus carrier, it caught the eye of all and sundry. The contents, obtained under false pretences from the salon of a well-known designer based in Cheltenham, had been chosen before she left Herefordshire. For good measure, she had included a few silk kimonos and embroidered slippers, a gift from a Birmingham importer she had met at the Hereford races.

The large, wooden trunk emblazoned with her initials, three matching suitcases and a number of hatboxes confirmed her status and background. It did much to improve her standing among the staff and regular guests.

She had also noted that since her arrival at The Savoy, a well-to-do, middle-aged woman had been quietly observing her from a table in an alcove adjacent to the afternoon tea terrace. It reminded her of George when they first dined at the Green Dragon.

'It's not just the men that find you attractive,' he had told her. 'Women do as well, so use it.'

Now and again Josie sauntered confidently past the woman, caught her eye and half smiled at her. The woman responded with an appreciative look delivered from beneath the brow of a fashionable trilby style, soft felt hat. At times, it was almost a semi-intimate appraisal of Josie, a look usually associated with a member of the opposite sex.

To enhance her prospects on the social scene, she used her first weeks in London to look, learn and carefully study the social pattern and mannerisms of the society classes and practise them in the privacy of her rooms. She shopped in elegant salons, high-class department stores and at fashion shows and for cultural improvement visited museums and art galleries.

Evening entertainment usually centred on concerts at Wigmore Hall, popular theatre and the Savoy operas of Gilbert and Sullivan performed

102

nightly by the D'Oyly Carte company in the auditorium next door; regulars and staff at The Savoy noting each visit was usually unaccompanied.

Growing in self-assurance, within a matter of weeks rather than months she had self-educated enough to finally bid goodbye to Trixie Skyrme, country girl, erase her from her memory and say hello to Josephine O'Dare, woman about town and society adventuress. The time was right to be seen and heard in the right places and prepare for a new life of money-making adventures.

Although the suite was a major expense, her 'rainy-day' fund was holding up well. She was less than halfway through her planned one-year stay and her budget was intact. She also had plenty of jewels to sell if needs be but that seemed highly unlikely; it was clear to Josie, and everyone at The Savoy, that scores of rich young men were falling over themselves to wine and dine her and older men thought her the mistress to die for. If she was to become a much sought-after woman of romantic importance, she needed to make a few subtle overtures.

Some weeks later Josie unexpectedly met the mysterious woman who had been watching her since her arrival. She was about fifty years old and enjoying a late morning coffee in the tea room. Carrying more than a hint of wealth and social standing, for some time Josie had admired the woman's fashionable Eton cropped hair and designer clothes. Nevertheless, she had felt uneasy on the two or three occasions they had passed the time of day and, apart from staff gossip, Josie had no idea who she was. Deciding it was time to take the plunge, she paused at the partly concealed table and took the liberty of inviting the woman to join her for afternoon tea.

Taken aback at the unexpected intrusion, the woman raised an eyebrow. 'How fortunate to be meeting you like this, I had been planning to ask you to take tea with me. If you happen to be free today, perhaps we could meet up on the terrace later. The tea lounge can often become over-crowded in the afternoon but I have my own table. Shall we say three-thirty my dear; I shall look forward to it.'

Josie was delighted if not slightly surprised by the invitation and accepted with pleasure and the woman walked to reception and hit the bell hard. The Duty Manager responded with military precision.

'Now Wells, some arrangements to make if you will be so good to attend to them.'

'Certainly, Your Grace,' he replied with a perfect nod of his well-greased head.

Constance Radcliff, an only child, was definitely more than 'nouveau riche'; wherever she went, she oozed wealth and was not ashamed to use or show it. Born in India where her late father owned and managed a number of tea plantations, his only child was tutored by an English governess brought out to educate her in the social graces. Her parents had not wanted to send their daughter to be educated in England, preferring to wait until they could return home as a family. A Swiss finishing school did the rest and, in her twenties, she shared her adult years with a woman companion until her worried father suggested marriage.

Constance first met her 'chosen' husband Sir Henry, later to inherit a Dukedom, when he was commanding a Regiment of Dragoons sent to boost the Indian Army after the terrible uprising in Calcutta. Despite the substantial age gap, a marriage of convenience was arranged, her parents providing a substantial dowry and Henry the 'blue blood' line of the English nobility.

On his recall to England, the couple married in the Guards Chapel at Windsor.

After dutifully delivering a son and heir, much to the relief of both parties, intimate relations ceased and the couple carried on with their own lives until the death of Henry's father. Henry inherited the title, estates to go with it and certain Royal duties.

Well received in court circles, the Duke and Duchess attended royal functions, their family estates in Northumberland and Hampshire providing first-class sporting facilities for shooting parties and sailing weekends at Cowes.

On the board of a number of city banks, Henry liked to play the stock market and, like his father before him, he was a member of the Marylebone Cricket Club.

Throughout the cricket season, he spent his days at the Oval or at Lords, usually staying at his Pall Mall club. This suited Constance who much preferred, apart from the two weeks at Wimbledon for the All England Ladies

Championship, to spend her time with her female companions at her Kensington apartment.

The unexpected death of their son Crispin at Ypres, brought his father much grief, Constance overcame hers by fundraising for suitable charities and supporting the Women's Suffrage campaign. Her friendship with the Pankhursts raised an eyebrow or two in royal circles but as a woman of independent means, she cared less about idle gossip and used the Savoy like a personal club.

From the moment she spotted Josie in the foyer, Constance was instantly attracted to the young woman's confident approach and handsome good looks but experience told her that she needed a polish or two when it came to presentation. Quietly determined to help her in any way she could, today she was more excited rather than delighted to see Josie waiting for her on the terrace and had a feeling she was in for an intriguing hour or two.

The Palm Court Tea Lounge was busy, the chatter of conversation fighting against a light quartet merrily meandering through a selection of musical highlights. The afternoon tea dance was about to start and Josie, seated at a table overlooking the river, had exchanged her walking out clothes for a designer day dress in a shade of blue.

Impressed by her companion's well-positioned table, she trembled slightly as she watched Wells escort her hostess across the room.

She stood up to greet her as Wells pompously pulled back her chair and announced: 'Your Grace, Miss Josephine O'Dare, your guest for afternoon tea.'

'Thank you, Wells,' the Duchess said and sat down.

'So pleased to meet you formally at last Miss O'Dare. Do sit down.'

'Likewise,' Josie replied, and waited for Wells to adjust her seat.

'Delighted you could come my dear, and on time too. Kindly leave the menu for a moment or two Wells and then send the waiter over.'

Carefully removing her gloves, she placed her hand over Josie's and said: 'Josephine, my dear girl, thank you for taking tea with me, it is a must for discovering new friends.'

Apart from idle gossip gleaned from the well-informed James and her daily maid, Josie knew very little about her companion. However, although she was aware Constance had an older husband in tow, she had little idea who she was until Wells referred to her as Duchess.

'Thank you, for inviting me, Your Grace. I am delighted to be taking tea with you. I have been watching the barges chugging up and down the river and I'm simply amazed how busy the river is at this time of day.'

Constance removed her hand and smiled. 'We can drop the title my dear and the small talk. It is time to cement our passing acquaintance and get to know each other.'

Wells interrupted the conversation: 'Your usual afternoon tea, Your Grace?'

'Please Wells, unless you plan to tango with Miss O'Dare?'

Josie laughed and teasing told him: 'It's alright I have already ordered, I am aware of her Ladyship's likes and dislikes. Is your husband with you?'

'Not today my dear but he will be pleased that we have finally made time for a long chat. I have spoken of you to him and he would indeed like to meet you.'

'Is he at business today?' Josie enquired.

'Heavens above no, he leaves all that to his brokers. You'll find him at Lords or the Oval at this time of year.'

Josie was puzzled, she had little knowledge of sporting activities.

'Lords my dear, an English gentleman's summer Mecca. It is a crucial Test Match against Australia and God only knows why he puts himself through it. Same old story I'm afraid, we are up against it again and I just don't know why we bother. Now tell me Josephine, I may call you that, I trust, you are getting out and about in the right circles?'

'Yes, I am but I'm a little tired and somewhat bored, I'm afraid. London life is quite a culture shock from where I have come from and now everyone seems to be off to watch cricket.'

'And where would that be?' Constance asked.

Before Josie could reply, the tea arrived.

Removing the lid from the teapot she exclaimed: 'My goodness, Darjeeling! Indeed you have been finding out my tastes. Thank you for being so thoughtful.'

Suitably impressed, Constance settled back in the chair, poured tea for her companion and tucked into afternoon tea, giving Josie time to think before her companion persisted with the conversation.

'Now where were we before we were interrupted, you were about to tell me how and why you suddenly arrived from surely not some exotic, faraway place?'

'Actually yes. My father unexpectedly died and I have just returned to England from the Far East.'

'I am so very sorry to hear that. Was he on holiday, a cruise perhaps?'

'No, he was working for the family shipping business in China which he inherited from his father, my grandfather an Irish peer. The title passed onto Daddy and I was actually born in Shanghai. Sadly, my mother died in a riding accident when I was four; I never really knew her but my aunt, Daddy's sister, came over from Ireland to take care of us. I had a tutor until I was old enough to be educated at a convent school in Dublin until, for unknown reasons, it was forced to close. I lived with my aunt until she died and after a while I returned to Shanghai to teach English at the company's school for the children of local employees.'

Constance was mesmerised. 'How perfectly fascinating, please, do go on. How and when did your father pass on?'

Josie paused to gather her thoughts.

'Just over three months ago, a heart attack it seems; he was a heavy smoker and liked to live the high life. After the funeral, I stayed on until his associates sorted out his large estate and my inheritance. I know very little of his business dealings but I think it was to do with developing and exporting poppies for medical purposes. Whatever it was, supplies were shipped all over the world and the business made him a fortune. He has left me very well provided for and I do miss him.'

Constance reassuringly took her hand again.

'He must have done my dear if you are able to stay here for weeks on end. I assume you sailed home?'

'Yes. We scattered his ashes in the poppy fields and soon after, I left China for good. His executors insisted P&O First Class all the way to Southampton where I stayed for a few days to sign some papers for his Irish partners. Now I am completely alone in the world and trying to find my place in society.'

Clearly taken in by her story, Constance persisted.

'Orphaned. How very sad for you Josephine but not for much longer, dear girl. I shall become your sponsor and ensure you are well looked after, not necessarily financially of course, your dear father has seen to that, however, I shall introduce to the right people and the right places.'

'You're very kind and I would value any help and introductions you can give me.'

Constance thought for a moment. 'We're off to the races this weekend, that's if I can tear Henry away from the cricket. I simply cannot understand what they see in it. All those men in white flannels and shirts hitting a ball to score as many runs as possibly until they are out and then another one does the same and so on. It's so frightfully boring, everyone sits in silence as English wickets topple and then travel home in misery. It's much more fun at the races. Have you ever been?'

Continuing her charade and lying through her teeth Trixie began to lay the foundations for success.

'Unfortunately not, but you appear to be well informed on the subject of cricket. Have you been to a cricket match?' Josie said with a hint of mockery.

'Oh yes. I have been to Lords a few times and the Kennington Oval, usually when Henry officially accompanies the King. Did you know at Lords, according to some damn silly rule, women have to sit separately, well away from the pavilion?'

Josie laughed. 'You are so amusing Constance, it's so much fun being with you. Perhaps you should have taken the Pankhursts with you; it would surely have set the cat among the pigeons.'

Constance shared her laughter. 'What fun you are and such a pleasure too, I shall be more than happy to launch you into Home Counties society. Consider me your patron. I happen to have many friends in high places, and rest assured my friends will he happy to meet such a promising young woman.'

She smiled at Josie and was about to continue the conversation but was interrupted by the hovering waiter.

'I'm so sorry to disturb you ladies but His Grace has arrived, he's in the bar.'

'He damn well would be, England must have had a bad day with the bat and that's all I need today.'

Looking at her watch she added: 'How time flies in enjoyable company. Thank you young man, please inform His Grace that I shall join him shortly.'

Leaning across the table Constance gently touched Josie's cheek.

'Dear girl, how lovely our little sojourn has been, we must meet again and very, very soon.'

The handsome older woman kissed her young guest on both cheeks commenting: 'Your skin may be pale but it is as soft as the finest of oriental silks. Indeed you are the most endearing young woman Josephine, you really are and I am much tempted to stay but needs must when the Duke calls.'

Surprised at the warm gesture, Josie smiled. 'Thank you, Your Grace. I shall look forward to it.'

'Enjoy the rest of your tea, it will be Henry's treat, you my dear girl are mine. Please think about the weekend and I shall include you in our party for a day's racing at Sandown Park.'

She was about to walk away when Josie, knowing the likely response, tested the waters.

'You are wearing such a lovely jacket, Your Grace.'

' I am so pleased you like it Josephine. I shall have my designer call you.' Josie smiled her best smile. 'Yet another treat, I shall soon feel utterly spoiled.'

Touching Josie's hair, Constance caught a glimpse of the silver locket around her neck.

'Sometimes dear girl it's preferable to wear no jewellery at all than something rather cheap,' and swept purposefully out of the room. Thrown by the unexpected caustic comment, Josie muttered 'snobby cow' under her breath. The hovering Wells noted the comment.

Sitting back in a more relaxed position, she pondered for a while until the waiter brought a tray of sumptuous fancy cakes, selected by her hostess. After completing a leisurely tea, Josie delved into her handbag, brought out a silk covered notebook and with a silver pencil began to write a few comments on the afternoon diversions.

The tea dancing was well under way when she noticed a smooth looking, presentable man in his forties hovering behind her. Smiling at him, he invited her to dance and much to his surprise, she gracefully accepted. It was the perfect moment to show off her social skills and graces.

He was a good dancing partner, not unlike George Davis, with whom she had attended various legitimate social events in Hereford. Today she was the centre of attention as she quickstepped her way across the dance floor, watched by a clutch of admirers including a somewhat envious Duchess. She had paused to admire the dancing couple through the glass screen separating the Palm Court Bar from the tearoom where her husband was propping up the bar with a cricketing chum.

Both men wore the traditional red and yellow striped blazer and matching tie, confirming prized membership of the Marylebone Cricket Club. Constance approached them and smiled.

'There you are Henry and how are you Charles?'

'Hello old girl, how's the delicious Miss O'Dare?' her husband enquired.

'Delightful, interesting and most charming and I am hopeful of persuading her to join us at Sandown Park on Saturday. Margot not with you Charles?'

'Not seen her since I dropped her at Harrods. I think she must be stuck in the lift.'

'More like weighed down with packages and parcels in a taxi cab and on her way here. I must say Henry the more I see of that young woman the more I enjoy her companionship but be warned, I intend to present her at Court.'

'Pity you didn't bring her to Lords, she would have been better company than the Australian Ambassador gloating his bloody arse orf,' Charles suggested.

'Bad day was it Henry dear?'

He almost exploded. 'A bloody eight wicket humiliation and that's putting it mildly. Two pink gins barman, if you please old chap. By George we missed Hobbs today didn't we Charles. Charlie reckons he'll miss the whole series, don't you Charlie?' His chum nodded his agreement.

'Now my dear how was your tea party? They still seem to be dancing.'

'Who is Henry?'

'Your little prodigy and the odious Hetherington-Jones.'

'That bloody loathsome creep, Henry, twice her age and definitely not blood stock is he Charles?'

'Definitely not. Wouldn't touch him at the MCC and blackballed out of Browns. Mind you he has the money, money talks and Miss O'Dare is a very attractive young girl Constance.'

'So I am told but if I'm to take her under my wing he has to go.'

'Another little beauty on the list is she my dear?' her husband asked.

'This one's a bit special Henry and if I'm to chaperone her towards a good marriage and groom her for presentation at Court, it is essential she is seen in the right places. I shall expect you to pull a string or two for Royal Ascot in June.'

The joint spluttering between Henry and Charles caused something of a stir in the bar.

'You mean the Royal enclosure! What next old girl, polo at Windsor, the palace garden party, Trooping the Colour! Are you sure she's up for it?'

'By the time I have finished with her, yes. I can assure you she will sail through the season,' Constance challenged.

'Not with her current dancing partner, I hope?

'Certainly not, I shall soon put a stop to that. The dear girl has lived in China for so long she has been cheated out of her rightful place in society and I intend to make up for it.'

'China! What has it to do with China?'

'It's a long story Henry and I can't wait to tell you all about it.'

Josie and her wealthy partner commanded the dance floor for most of the afternoon bringing much applause from her admirers.

The following months brought great change for Josie's new life. Thanks to her mentor, she made unforgettable appearances at the right events and enjoyed meeting and flirting with well off young men wherever she went.

More important, thanks to the patronage and generosity from the Duke and Duchess, her increasingly stunning entrances confirmed her credentials as the rising star of London and Home Counties society. Carefully watched over by a smitten Constance, the country girl with an eye for the main chance was emerging from her Herefordshire cocoon into a social butterfly ready to take on anyone rich and gullible enough to fall for her charms. Before long, she was the talk of the town, never shirking the opportunity to build up the Josephine O'Dare dossier of possible targets for future scams.

Keeping notes on social do's and don'ts, her sharp memory recorded upper class mannerisms, behaviour patterns and fashions; using her sexuality to attract both men and women of means, she created close relationships on false promises on her way to a lucrative future. She was, of course, very much aware that Constance was completely infatuated with her but as with her relationship with George Davis, arms length coupled with close, but not too close affection, was the way forward until she could float alone.

Accompanied by her Duchess, Josie was wined and dined in a social whirl of celebrity dinner parties and balls and escorted to theatres and musical events by a variety of well-heeled young men, her weekends spent in the country or at the races.

CHAPTER TEN

It was on her third visit to Sandown Park. The course was filling up with afternoon punters intent on picking a winner and making a few pounds. The amount of traffic coming out of central London had slowed down the arrival of the upmarket racing community leaving the member's dining room barely full. Outside on the rails, there was an air of anticipation as the bookmakers, tipsters and tic-tac men shouted the latest odds on the runners and riders. In the member's dining room, lunch was almost over and a fashionably dressed Josie was watching the familiar scene from a table on the veranda hosted by the Duke and Duchess.

The colourful scene below had brought back many memories of the 'working' trips to Hereford and Ludlow races with George, Albert and the rest of the Davis gang where she honed her petty criminal trade.

She muttered to herself 'if they could see me now' and smiled. Thinking it was for him, the elderly man on her left noticed the smile and she quickly engaged him in light conversation.

'Is this your first visit to Sandown Park, Mr. Docker?'

'Not at all young lady, when I come to London on business Henry kindly invites me to join his party.'

'But you do like racing, Mr. Docker?'

'I try to go when I can, usually to meetings nearer home.'

'And where is nearer home?' she gently prodded.

Without hesitation, Mr. Docker replied: 'My main business is in Solihull and I like to visit the local courses, Lichfield, Stratford, Worcester and sometimes Hereford.'

Josie's sudden intake of breath almost caused her to choke at his words. 'Are you alright Miss ...?'

Quickly recovering her composure, she told him 'O'Dare, Miss Josephine O'Dare.'

'From London?' he asked.

Catching the pause in their conversation, Constance came to the rescue and cut in.

'Not quite, Edwin. She has recently returned from China and is taking time to adjust to London society, under my wing of course. Her late father was an Irish peer and brought his daughter up in the Orient.'

Instantly taken with her, Mr. Docker persisted with the conversation.

'Really! Where are you and your mother residing now?'

Josie smiled sadly before answering: 'My mother died in a riding accident when I was very young and I was brought up in Shanghai by a maiden aunt on my father's side. Later I travelled to Ireland with my aunt and was educated at a convent school in Dublin. I rejoined Daddy two years ago to help in the family business but, after his premature death some months ago, I sailed for Southampton and came to London where I was fortunate to meet the Duke and Duchess. Now I am staying in rooms kindly provided by them until my trustees release my inheritance. It seems to be taking so long,' she sighed.

Constance cut in again. 'I first met Josephine at the Savoy; she was staying there for a few months and looked a little lost; I felt she needed a motherly eye to look out for her.'

'How very fortunate indeed for you Miss O'Dare and how kind of Constance, and Henry, to help.'

He turned to Josie and took her hand. 'If I can be of service in any way at all please do call on me.' Taking a calling card from a silver holder in his waistcoat pocket, he handed it to her.

Josie read it. 'You work for a firm of solicitors?'

'He is the legal firm my dear,' Constance told her. 'Indeed the best firm outside of London. The Dockers have represented my family for years and I wouldn't attempt a legal move without him.'

'We do our best,' Mr. Docker replied modestly. 'My son runs the legal chambers these days. At my age I tend to take a back seat but if you need my help at any time please feel free to call me.'

'Come, come Mr. Docker,' Josie replied flirtatiously. 'You are still a very handsome and not at all old. I'd be delighted to have your advice...whatever the cost.'

'No charge my dear, certainly not for a lovely young woman like you. If there is anything I can do please don't hesitate.'

Constance interrupted again. 'Of course she will need help, particularly getting her funds out of Shanghai or arranging a letter of intent from her trustees. After all, our young friend is looking to lease a suitable suite of rooms for her launch into society; Henry and I have agreed to sponsor her debut.'

Edwin Docker was memorised by her frailty and charm. 'That I can arrange, that's if we could talk, in private of course.'

Josie seized the moment. 'Well, I don't know... It is most kind of you Mr. Docker but will that be appropriate?'

'Have you engaged solicitors, Miss O'Dare?' Docker asked.

'Of course she hasn't, Edwin; she doesn't know where to start. Henry's offered to help but....'

'But you have done so much for me already Your Grace,' she suggested.

'Then allow me to be of service,' Edwin offered. 'Why don't we take coffee in the lounge, if that's agreeable to you and Henry? It is your party.'

'Of course it is and as we want to watch the first race. We will be taking coffee in our box but do join us for the three thirty, Henry has a runner, if you can call it that.'

Constance laughed. 'Now don't keep her too long Edwin, you know what a pretty face does to you...especially one as pretty as this.'

She touched Josie's hand. 'Use this time well dear girl, Edwin has considerable experience in financial matters. I'll have the coffee sent over to you.'

The elderly solicitor stumbled a little as he got to his feet. Josie took his arm and smiled.

'Whoops-a-daisy Mr. Docker, steady the buffs,' and they both laughed. Escorting her to a corner table in the lounge, he playfully patted her bottom before she sat down.

An hour or so later, they joined the Duke in his grandstand box where there were twenty or so guests, eagerly waiting for the three-thirty race to come under starter's orders. Happily sipping champagne. Henry and Constance waved to them.

'Come along you two. They're off in ten minutes so you need get a bet on before the odds drop.'

Josie quickly released Edwin's arm. 'You place the bets while I powder my nose and then we had better join the others. We will meet again soon, more privately perhaps.'

'I can come to London at the drop of a hat; now off you go and not a word to Henry or Constance. We must keep our little secret to ourselves.'

'Of course we will, you have my word Edwin. You've been very kind and more than helpful.'

'Delighted to do so, we can iron out details later.'

Henry was becoming impatient insisting: 'Do get a move on, you will miss my donkey.'

'I'll join you in a moment or two Henry, please excuse me, I'm off to the ladies powder room,' Josie replied.

Henry took his old friend's arm, helped him to a comfortable chair and sent a flunkey to place his bet. Constance handed him pair of field glasses and tucked a tartan rug around his legs.

'I hope you enjoyed meeting Miss O'Dare; I am sure she will appreciate any help you can give her.'

'Indeed I did. She's a pretty little filly and I am sure we can come to some sort of arrangement,' he said with a twinkle in his ageing eyes.

Constance chuckled. 'It's a bit chilly on the balcony so wrap up in the rug and keep warm. You are getting on a bit Edwin and you must take care of yourself. We don't want you to catch a chill at your time of life; your son will never forgive us.'

In the privacy of the powder room, Josie opened her handbag and took out a Coutts Bank cheque for £3,000 payable in cash to Miss Josephine O'Dare. It was signed Edwin Docker - personal account and if it wasn't for the other women in the room she would have whooped out loud.

It's like taking sweets from a baby, she told herself, and smiling broadly she almost skipped to the grandstand box. However there was a shock in store.

Pausing to look down on the crowds below the grandstand, she spotted George, her one time partner in crime, placing a bet with an on course bookmaker. He looked up but before he could catch her eye she stepped back and hid behind a large potted plant. Heart beating fast, she pulled herself together, slipped out of view and headed for the empty seat next to Constance. She had just returned from the parade enclosure and, before she could sense Josie's panic, the runners and riders came under starters orders. Cheers went up and the three thirty at Sandown was under way.

The brief encounter with George Davis had unsettled Josie. She wasn't sure if he had seen her so, claiming to be suffering from an attack of the vapours, she stayed quietly in her rooms. Keen to get her prodigy up and about, Constance attended to her needs, feeding her nourishing soups and tasty titbits and called in most days for afternoon tea.

'As soon as you feel up to it we shall go the country and put some colour into those pale cheeks. Henry has planned a house party at the family pile in Hampshire. It's the annual point-to-point and country fair, an all-day jolly with Morris dancing, games. We provide a running buffet for the estate workers, tenants and villagers. You will be able to ride and I shall find you a few interesting people to chat with. It's all in a good cause and it will also do you good.'

Excusing herself, Josie explained: 'Father never wanted me to ride especially after mother's accident but my aunt suggested I went to riding school. Since his death, well... I've always tried to respect his memory.'

'I do understand my dear but it is time to get you back in the saddle again. We have a good stable at White Water and I promise to take good care of you. Besides, my friends are intrigued to meet the daughter of an aristocratic Irish peer from Shanghai. Think about it, Josephine. Now, shall I be mother? English tea I'm afraid, if that suits you of course.'

'Perfectly, I never really took to Lapsang or Jasmine, I much prefer English blends.'

Josie was aware Constance was staring at her.

'Has anyone ever told you that you have wonderfully high cheek bones? Quite lovely. Please come for the weekend, if only to allow me to show you off.'

Josie paused: 'It's the riding; it's been such a long time but I will give it some thought.'

'But I hear you've been having refreshers in Hyde Park with the Horse Guards and doing awfully well too.'

'Yes, I have, on Sunday mornings. May I think about it, I could do with getting out of town for a few days? Living here can be somewhat stifling.'

'Of course, we all need a blast of country air now and again so let's concentrate on getting some colour into those lovely cheeks of yours. Before long, with a touch of grooming, we'll have you in the Royal Enclosure at Ascot, Henry's owed a favour or two.'

Josie laughed. 'Little me! In the Royal Enclosure at Ascot. Father would be so proud.'

'Believe me, rich young men will fall at your feet Josephine, as I do of course. More tea?'

'Yes please, to all three,' she relied flirtatiously. 'Afternoon tea, rich young men and your affectionate friendship. What more could I want? You have done so much for me since I came to London. Sometimes I wonder how I can ever repay you.'

Constance responded in mock delight. 'Tut tut, Josephine. Tea I can accept but surely you place me before the rich young men of London?'

Josie blushed. 'Of course I do but the rich young men that lounge around racecourses and polo grounds are very attractive in many ways.'

'My dear Josephine, Ascot week is rather special. For being seen in the right places at the right time, forget the racing. Ascot is one of the most prestigious events on the sporting calendar and I have persuaded Henry to include you in our party. Now other than Sandown Park, have you been racing before?'

Once more Josie's mind flashed back to George and the gang picking pockets at Hereford racecourse.

'Yes, now and again in Shanghai, not England, and it was quite entertaining as well as profitable.'

'So you can pick a winner or two?'

'Yes I've picked a good few and usually did quite well. My father owned a thoroughbred horse and it is under training in Ireland. I don't know what the situation is now but I expect my trustees will be dealing with it.'

'Well let us hope it is a potential winner and you must join us again at Sandown Park. Henry is taking his usual party of punters, but first you must come to White Water at the weekend.'

Having convinced the Duchess and her retinue that she was born into purple with the blood of medieval aristocracy running through her veins, Josie spent many subsequent weekends in Hampshire enjoying country living on the White Water Estate. She played tennis and croquet, polished up her credentials and charmed influential guests into including her in their social diaries. In the run-up to her first Christmas in London, she enjoyed society gatherings, private parties and various nightspots.

Scheming her way towards financial security became a priority for Josie. Rich businessmen saw her as the ideal mistress, their sons wanted to marry her, nevertheless Josie preferred to keep her distance until she was ready and able to call the tune.

Her one close and trusted intimate was Francine, the only daughter of a retired Church of England Bishop. They had met during a weekend at White Water when the Duke opened a garden party and fete at the Bishop's Palace. Since the death of her mother, some years before, Francine had kept house for her father and older brother Peter, a Cambridge Don in the Theology department. It was an interesting meeting and Josie delighted in the company of her new friend. Over the weeks, they became partners on the tennis court, shared time in the library reading, and took long quiet walks across the meadows. Eager to learn,   Francine led her companion on a pathway to literary knowledge and friendship, Josie wisely keeping the closeness of the relationship from Constance.

After almost a year of intense social acceptability, Constance announced her prodigy was ready for presentation at Court. Of all the daring things Josie had dreamed of accomplishing was to curtsey before the King and Queen at Buckingham Palace and she almost pulled it off.

In certain circles, rumours circulated that the dark-eyed, fascinating, young woman, fatal to impressionable men and women was not quite the innocent she claimed to be. It had been noted in some quarters that when 'in drink' or in moments of passion and anger, Josie slipped into her natural Herefordian accent and the occasional indiscretion. Word eventually reached the Duke that Miss O'Dare was not up to the mark and, to be on the safe side, he insisted his wife should quietly drop her.

Shaken and angry that she had very nearly brought a thief to Buckingham Palace, she confronted Josie and sadly suggested it was time to move on and form her own circle of younger friends. There was no mention of the rumours and hearsay and no explanation given for the sudden dismissal from Constance's exclusive group of friends, leaving Josie feeling betrayed and angry. During a heated quarrel with Constance, Josie vigorously defended herself but after the Duke agreed to pay off her half-yearly account at the Savoy and top it up with a few thousand for an apartment of her own, Josie went quietly with fake farewells and three trunks of the most expensive clothes from her broken hearted mentor. Thus began the revenge of Josephine O'Dare.

Undeterred by her failure, she remained on such friendly terms with her many admirers she was determined to use her substantial monetary gifts to set up her own home and place herself at the heart of London's society. Little was said of the sudden parting between her and the Duchess and everyone assumed her trust fund was finally settled and she was now a woman of independent means well able to stand alone.

Her bank account was by now rock solid and with advice and help from her constant admirer Edwin Docker, she took out a lease on a substantial, stylishly furnished apartment at 27 Park Mansions in Knightsbridge, and settled down to take stock of her new life. Thankfully, Edwin lived far enough away to be an infrequent visitor although she was happy to spend the occasional evening with him on his business trips to the capital. More important, he knew little of her of her darker side and Josie was grateful her split with Constance and Henry was amicable and not common knowledge.

The Birmingham solicitor was vital to her future and she hesitated before keeping her promise to bring her mother and sister to London until she was ready. Fanny kept in touch by letter and although her correspondence was generally jolly, between the lines it was clear to Josie that despite the money she regularly sent them, she feared her mother and sister were losing hope that they may never see their Trixie again.

Although family was important to her, Josie continued to rely on the friendships and contacts she had made under the guidance of Constance. The valuable experiences had opened a good many doors to high living but she still needed time and space to extend her catchment area. She also needed to surround herself with a team of low-life, petty criminals she could trust, control and knock into shape.

She had thought about pulling in a few of the Hereford crew but she was worried George would track her down. However, she had toyed with bringing Albert Marriot on board to help set up a few scams but despite his loyalty she later discovered that he and George had been up before the bench on a number of fraud charges and had recently gone down for two years.

CHAPTER ELEVEN

It took a few weeks to settle in to her rented home in Knightsbridge. Good luck letters, flowers and calling cards from old and new admirers filled her sitting room. One in particular, a sort of religious tract from Francine, pleased her more than most but there was nothing from Constance and Henry.

Internal decorations completed, soft furnishings arranged and fitted, 27 Park Mansions was ready to receive visitors.

Josie was keen to organise a house-warming party and needing reliable domestic help it was time for Mary and Fanny to leave for London. Keeping her promise, she wrote to tell them they could come and live with her as housekeeper and cook, making it clear that they must not tell a soul they were leaving for London. She also sent money to buy new clothes for the journey and, apart from a few possessions and mementoes, all else was to be destroyed and on their arrival in London she would take them shopping for new clothes and anything else they might need.

Paddington Station was very busy. Josie had hired a chauffeur-driven car to meet the train from Hereford; it waited with the taxi cabs alongside the arrivals platform.

It had taken a few weeks to finalise arrangements. Albert had kept his word not to tell anyone, particularly George, she was in London and, before arranging for Mary and Fanny to join her, she received assurances George had been convicted yet again.

Josie had not seen her family for many months and, despite her relief that George was behind bars in the West Midlands, she waited nervously in the back of the car wondering what to expect. When the echoing announcement told her the morning train from Hereford was about to arrive she pulled herself together, her eyes pricked with tears as she spotted Fanny struggling along the platform with her mother. Leaving the car, she excitedly ran towards them. Looking tired after the long journey, the moment Mary saw her daughter her face lit up in a familiar smile. Over-excited at seeing her sister again Fanny bounded towards her yelling: 'Its Trixie, Ma, our Trixie at last,' and leaped into her sister's arms before dragging her towards her waiting mother.

Making sure the chauffeur was far enough away not to hear, she whispered: 'I'm Josie now, Josephine O'Dare to be precise, you can't call me Trixie any more, except in private. I'll explain later, meanwhile your car is waiting.'

Fanny was agog at all the people and could not wait to climb into the posh car. The chauffeur strapped what luggage they had into the box seat and then helped her mother and sister into the back. Josie sat in the front.

'Knightsbridge and take the slow route. My guests have not been to London before and I want to point out the sights.'

She looked over her shoulder to see her mother and sister sharing a giggle or two and smiled. After a short tour of central London, the car arrived in Knightsbridge. Mary had dropped off to sleep but not Fanny; she was captivated by all the sights and overwhelmed by what she had seen. Josie had provided a commentary from Paddington Station, past the Marble Arch and around Hyde Park, pointing out the Dorchester Hotel, the Albert Hall and Kensington Gardens before stopping at the apartment block where Josie lived. The impressive looking doorkeeper touched his cap and a young boot boy escorted them across the wide, marbled hall to the ground floor apartment where Josie lived. Fanny was amazed at the size of her sister's London home.

Settling her mother and sister into the spacious and comfortable shared bedroom cum sitting room, Josie prepared a rather late lunch after which her mother rested and Fanny had a brief tour of the apartment, ending up in the large kitchen.

'Here we are, Fanny, home sweet home at last, at least for now. What do you think, are we on our way or not?'

'Blimey, our Trix, I never expected all this. It must cost you a fair few pounds in rent, let alone all this posh furniture and stuff.'

'It took me a while to get it together, a bit longer than I had hoped but now you and Ma are here and it's going to be the adventure of our lives. Mind you there are a few ground rules before we go out shopping. Ma needs to recover from the journey first and I need to explain a few things before I let you both loose in Kensington High Street. I once promised you the very best cobbler to make you a brand new surgical boot, at the very least, one without a bloody squeak.'

Reminded of a particular moment at Barton Manor, Fanny giggled and said: 'Thank God there ain't no stairs in this place, I'll be driving you potty again with my squeaking and you'll have me on the next train to Hereford.'

'I'll never do that. You and Ma have been battered enough to last a lifetime. Now tell me, did Pa and our brother try to track you down after I left?'

'I saw them once or twice drunk as skunks in High Town but they never saw me. Good riddance, I say. I once saw George and Albert up to a few tricks in the cattle market and George kept pestering me about where you were and what you were up to but I kept me mouth zipped. Just before you sent for us, I heard he was going down for a two year stretch in Birmingham.'

'What about Albert, was he involved as well? I hope not, he is much too clever to get involved in George's petty frauds. Anyway, he has been a good friend and stood by us when we did the flit. Did he keep an eye out for you like he promised?'

'Oh! He did that all right, he always looked out for us when we came into town and never breathed a word to anyone. Petty frauds or not Trixie, if George could see you now, living it up in this swanky place, he'd be so jealous.'

Josie quickly got a firm grip. 'Yes and the rest; if he knew where I was, before you can say Market Tavern, it will be the fast train to Paddington but don't worry our Fanny he won't be tied to my coat tails ever again. The only way for us now is up and by the time George gets out of jail we will be out of this place and into the big time. Meanwhile get mother up and we will make plans for a shopping spree.'

'What sort of plans, Trixie?'

'I told you not to call me that, or refer to me as your sister and that goes for Ma too. For now, you and Ma will keep house and I have asked a close friend to be my companion and her mother my cook. Her brother is also keen to get in on the act but if I know his game he will dashing about town splashing my cash around.

'They will be living in a couple of furnished rooms in the basement and see how it goes. To be on the safe side Fan, you will be my confidante and always act as greeter for any visitors and to help you I have arranged a few lessons in diction, elocution and polite manners.'

'So I'll be able to speak posh like you when I open the front door and that?' Fanny suggested.

'Exactly because from now on wherever I live you and Ma will live in warm, comfortable surroundings and at all times hear no evil, speak no evil and more importantly you will see no evil. Play along with me and we are all in the money.'

After the shopping spree in Kensington, it was immediately clear to Fanny that her sister had plenty of cash to throw around and she knew her sister well enough not to ask where she got it. Her sister's usual response was 'never you mind, there is plenty more where that came from' and that was that.

As well as shopping, outings to parks and local attractions, on special occasions the three women went for a matinee at the theatre followed by afternoon tea at the famous Rumpelmayer's tearoom, St James Street; dressed in her red georgette frock and matching picture hat, she was always the centre of attention. The outings became occasions of social learning for Fanny and, although her mother sometimes joined them, it was more for company than learning. Because of her advancing years, Josie felt Mary was too set in her Herefordshire ways to be socially plausible in Knightsbridge and she encouraged her to keep to her room unless called upon to help with Fanny's day-to-day duties.

Set up in her new apartment with her family and new associates to surround her, Josie embarked on the next stage of her criminal career. Very shady people began to call on her day and night, including a once wealthy man who, due to heavy gambling debts, had hit rock bottom. He ended up a dubious, low-level moneylender's tout, a position considered the lowest of the low in the criminal fraternity. Josie met him by chance at a local hotel bar and after learning about his financial disaster, believing she could learn from it, she took a very keen interest in his new career.

She arranged a second meeting, checked him out and he was so taken with her, he offered to educate her into his specialist and notorious calling. Josie cottoned on fast; with quick money to be had, very soon she was lending money to vulnerable people at very high rates of interest and using unscrupulous means to force bad debtors to pay up.

Her sharp and devious mind absorbed his clever skills until, like her early days with George Davis, the pupil became more fluent than the teacher and he was cast aside. Like Davis, he was simply a means to an end. However, when he tried bullying tactics to persuade her to share her spoils with him, she threatened to expose him to the authorities and he left London for Manchester with a few pounds in his pocket to help him on his way.

By the time she was twenty-two, Josie was a professional moneylender with her own business. Cleverly weaving her way through a maze of well-heeled young men, she was wined, dined and bejewelled before she inevitably took them for all they had.

Not exactly beautiful, Josie had grown into a handsome, dark-eyed and innocent looking young woman fatal to impressionable young men. Using her strong personality and remarkable self-possession, she planted herself in the centre of the most exclusive circles in London.

Scores of single men wanted marriage, and happily married men were ready to leave home and family just to be with her. However, armed with experience, she was always very circumspect and played her cards very carefully. The ace in her pack was always money. The more she earned, the more she wanted to spend but always careful to set aside a proportion for whatever the future had in store and trusted her sister to hide it away. As her ambitions grew, so did her nerve and when the right opportunity came along she was confident enough to go it alone.

Opportunity opened up when she met her first wealthy punter in a hotel lift. The son of a very important and prosperous government contractor, he was well ripe for a financial fraud and was crazy about her. He became her persistent admirer spending untold amounts of money wining and dining her in the right places and lavishing her with expensive gifts. Totally convinced she loved him as much as he loved her, he promised her the world and later installed her as his 'wife' in a fashionable block of flats in Piccadilly.

Fanny took it all in her stride; while Josie was away she and her mother stayed on at Park Mansions informing shady callers that Miss O'Dare had been ill and was recuperating in Bath.

The marriage of convenience lasted no more than two months; two months of spend, spend, spend before the unsuspecting suitor discovered his 'wife' had bled him dry. Financially crippled and with nothing else to give, Josie heartlessly ditched him and refused to return the expensive jewels and gifts he had given her, but that wasn't the end of her cunning. In a very clever financial scam, she spun him a yarn which helped him secure a high interest loan to tide him over until he got back on his feet and took commission from both parties for arranging the deal.

Returning to her flat in Knightsbridge Josie realised the benefits of the money lending business and began thinking in thousands rather than hundreds of pounds. Her reputation as a successful moneylender grew and it was clear among her peers that she was on the way up. Holding an entourage of financially ruined young men in the palm of her hand, she was able to skim off thousands of pounds from old and new clients.

Undeterred by Fanny's warnings to be careful and despite her rumoured record for parting well off young men from their cash, they still kept coming for more.

It almost came unstuck when a stranger, claiming to be desperately in love with Josie, appeared at the flat. Ignoring Fanny's pleadings to go away he refused to leave, like all the rest he felt his feelings for Josie were reciprocated and offered her his worldly possessions - two thousand pounds worth of government stock - for her to invest for him.

Jumping onto her financial bandwagon, Josie coaxed him into selling the bonds and giving her the cash to invest and he lost the lot; all he had left in the world was his love for Josie. Tossing him aside, she told him she had never had feelings for him and that he was a fool to trust her.

Her unkind words and devious dealings almost drove him mad; in a tormented rage he turned up at Park Mansions, kicked up a mighty disturbance with the other residents and refused to leave until he could speak to Josie. It was a difficult situation; fearing an unwanted public display, Fanny and the doorman took him inside to see her. Calming him down with false promises, she persuaded him to stay for a week or two before dispatching him broken hearted and broke into the night; the same way as the others she had ripped off.

Despite her growing concerns, Fanny kept her own counsel and, whatever her sister did, loyally looked out for her and watched as wealthy men and women fawned at her sister's feet in return for her special favours, whatever they were. The common denominator was always money.

Josie's rising status attracted considerable celebrity attention. Her circle of well-heeled associates and friends increased to the next level of London Society and her sister wisely counselled her not to let her guard down.

Whatever she knew, Fanny kept to herself. She also kept her secrets and savings safe and topped up the 'rainy day' fund; after all she and her mother enjoyed the benefits of the good life Josie had provided since their arrival in London. Fanny was already benefiting from two expensive, supportive boots recommended by a foot specialist in Wigmore Street to help improve her mobility. One was for everyday use, the other a smarter, squeak-free version, for special occasions.

The ageing Mrs. Skyrme preferred to stay in her room surrounded by magazines, chocolates and pastries from Harrods until it was time for her daily stroll in Kensington Gardens. Fanny educated herself in the nearby museums and, on one occasion, took her mother to see the Changing of the Guard at Buckingham Palace and they both waved to the King. It was a whole new world for the Skyrme women and they made the most of it. Back in Wellington, Josie had promised them a dream life in London and she kept her word; Fanny and Mary enjoyed a comfortable lifestyle and never once referred to Herefordshire in company.

Josie's sun was at its meridian and nothing was going to stop the rise and rise of Josephine O'Dare. Lords, Ladies and wealthy businessmen and women were more than keen to entertain her, yet she continued to hold back until the time was right to move her playground to Belgravia.

The Ritz, Prince's and Claridge's had become her hunting grounds, her boisterous behaviour at private parties attracting attention and it wasn't long before any of the fashionable nightspots banned her. They knew from experience that an appearance by Josephine O'Dare and her hangers on meant an evening of excessive drinking, horseplay and the occasional free fight but, fair play, she always left one hundred pounds with the cashier to cover any damages. It was her marketplace and she knew how to play it.

Dressed in the latest fashions with just a hint of frailty in her demeanour, wealthy men, including members of the House of Lords, demand to be her protector and, in their eyes, she could do no wrong. What they did not know was, at Park Mansions by day and in a certain low haunt off Piccadilly by night, more burglaries and hold-ups were planned by Josie and staged by her shady associates, than Scotland Yard could ever imagine. When it wasn't burglary, it was blackmail or fraud; the money had to come from somewhere and she took it all, never paying her gang more than twenty per cent of the take. They didn't like her rules and abused her in violent terms calling her 'Shylock' but they never received a penny more. Whatever the dispute, she never failed to remind each and everyone of them it was her brain that devised and planned every job.

Although she was earning good money she was spending more than she was bringing in, with bills piling up it wasn't all plain sailing. Staff had to be paid, and everyone had to be fed, including her gang of thieves below stairs in the cellar. Her companion's family, more users than helpers, were also a drain on the household expenses, yet she still avoided her sister's frequent warnings to be careful until she got her first real scare.

During an evening with friends at Kettners, she was introduced to a former military officer. The recent death of his father had forced him to resign his commission to take care of his younger sister. Completely smitten with Josie, he flirted with her over dinner and before he knew it she had coaxed him into confiding he and his sister had inherited substantial funds from his late parents and he was looking for a good investment.

Always on the look-out for the next big swindle, Josie kept her head and teasingly invited him to dinner at the Ritz. He jumped at the chance and, over a sumptuous dinner which he insisted on paying for, she cunningly convinced him into backing an invention in which she also had a big financial interest. Moreover, she also persuaded him that he should become a guest at her house paying thirty pounds per week for the pleasure. Totally besotted with the persuasive young woman, he instantly accepted and agreed to pay up and invest in the project. It was to be the first of a series of clever frauds. The non-existent invention was claimed a financial disaster and the captain lost all his money. Little did he know that Josie had taken it to cover her own growing personal debts and liabilities?

With the family inheritance gone, both he and his sister were ruined, worse still the poor fellow was no longer able to pay Josie for his room and board but agreed she should try to find a creditor to make him bankrupt. Shortly after, desperate, broke and homeless, he disappeared leaving his personal belongings and a letter to his sister in his room; he was seen on Westminster Bridge staring into the dark waters of the Thames.

Badly shaken by events, it had never occurred to Josie that her cunning and devious behaviour could lead a man to suicide and his sister to poverty. It played on her mind and, despite the concerns of her mother and sister, she took to occasionally sniffing cocaine provided for her at cost by one of her shady associates. It proved to be very expensive and she needed to keep her eyes and ears open for the right opportunity to make big money. Not only to feed the growing habit but also to bring in enough cash to mount even bigger frauds and swindles.

Out of the blue, an opportunity arrived during a private lunch party at the Dorchester. It was a mixed gathering with guests arriving from the county set, business and the House of Lords keen to be seen raising funds in support of the pensioners at The Royal Hospital in Chelsea. During a conversation at her table, a guest unknowingly told Josie the tragic story of a neighbour, a rich but feeble-minded old man who, that very morning, had been carted off to a home for the mentally frail, in Worthing. As far as anyone knew, he had no family or friends to care or speak for him and Josie asked what might happen to him. The adrenalin was racing again. This was her moment, her main chance to acquire the riches she had always yearned for and Josie listened sympathetically and without comment.

She went home to think about what she could do with the information and invited the anonymous guest to a similar good cause lunch she was organising at the Ritz and asked her for her address.

It didn't take long to trace the old man and, two days later, she was on her way to Worthing with an associate, to convince doctors at the mental home that she alone was his great niece and his only living relative, recently arrived from Shanghai. Declaring her good intentions, she wanted him released into her care at her new home in Bath where experienced carers would look after him. Hopeful of a large share of his fortune, she negotiated his release and promised the trustees a substantial donation. She would contribute to the upkeep of the care home the moment her accounts had been transferred from her bank in China.

It was a very convincing performance but, just when Josie looked like bringing off her most daring scheme yet, one of her associates blundered, inadvertently gave the game away and the plot was exposed! Consumed with anger, she never forgave the man who made the false move and banished him from ever working for her again.

The unexpected failure nettled her; she felt cheated of legitimate spoils and swore to get even by carrying out a campaign of polite plunder. It was a life-changing moment; selecting her victims with regard only to their assets and means, she determined to get even with London society.

CHAPTER TWELVE

A month later, Mayfair was beckoning. Tipped off by an associate, a slightly dodgy property agent, that an exceptional property in Belgravia had come on the market and if she were interested, he would arrange a viewing, a long lease and a reduction in the rent. Well positioned in Park Street, it was the perfect place for phase three of Josie's London adventure. It was expensive to rent and maintain but if the apartment in Knightsbridge was a spacious example of comfortable, society living, then how much more would the stunning home overlooking Hyde Park be.

It was a grand residence with countless rooms for entertaining and plenty of accommodation for her failing mother and hard-working sister. Her domestic staff had agreed to stay on in comfortable quarters below stairs, the move was agreed and the household settled into the smartest area in London. To show off her status as a woman of substance, she upgraded her motor car to a superb Daimler and employed a convicted thief and brothel keeper as her chauffeur.

The bait laid, Josie planned lavish parties with syncopated bands, hosted countless mannequin parades in luxurious surroundings and set her sights on celebrity status.

Yet something was lacking; she missed the warmth and closeness of an intimate relationship and her thoughts drifted back to the country weekends with Francine at White Water Hall.

Francine had little knowledge of Josie's true self or her exclusion from the Henry and Constance set. Nevertheless, Josie was keen to see her again and persuaded to come to London. However, if gossip over Josie's lifestyle reached Hampshire, it would be a hard task. Some weeks after the move, she chanced her arm.

In an exchange of letters, Francine agreed to meet her in the gardens at Lambeth Palace during one of her father's regular meetings of Synod. Excited at renewing a once-enjoyed relationship, Josie suggested she became her social secretary with an office at Park Street but Francine was unsure about leaving her widowed father for too long.

Eventually she agreed to come to London for three or four days a week and return home at weekends, at least until her father completed his memoirs. It was an amicable arrangement and Josie showered her longed-for companion with care and affection like no other, bringing more than a touch of jealousy from the cook's daughter, now relegated to the servants' quarters. After some discussion, she moved on with her family, clutching a cash settlement and muttering hints of revenge.

Despite her affection for her Francine, it was vital Josie maintained her relationships with her male consorts; they were her bread and butter and lodged in storage rooms off the kitchen and lived on the charity of the woman who cheated them out of every penny they owned. A sad conclave of dispirited men sharing common misery and humiliation, no longer rivals in love but broken and discarded suitors kept on a string by a devious woman.

When Josie was not entertaining her society friends, she occasionally invited them into the upstairs drawing room but always kept a tight rein on their pleadings of love and devotion and curbing their tempers with threats of eviction. But they knew their place; the ill-lit rooms in the basement, and forced to pay board and lodging for the privilege. Among them quietly plotting his future, was the infamous George Davis.

Still very much attracted to Josie, he was determined to track her down and cash in on her spoils and, instead of returning to Hereford after his release from custody in Birmingham, he had joined up with a couple of ex-cons on the South London criminal fringe. Unbeknown to his former partner, he had been successfully bouncing cheques in and around the Home Counties for some months; so much so that Scotland Yard paid him the compliment of being 'the most perfect forger in the Kingdom' when he was finally arrested in Blackheath. Failing to answer the charge, he disappeared into London's underworld and eventually tracked Josie. Smiling to himself, he first spotted her portrait in the pages of a number of illustrated society magazines; dressed in riding habit, she had bluffed a gullible public into believing that 'somewhere in Ireland' she was training a thoroughbred racehorse to win the 1925 Derby for her. To confirm her credentials she christened the horse 'The O'Dare' and hired a hack in Hyde Park so that the photographers on Rotten Row could show the nation what an accomplished horsewoman she was and knew what she was talking about. It was a clever ruse; for a cash donation, she willingly gave the bookies and the punters so-called insider information on the form and the latest odds on the non-existent racehorse and made a large profit. The resulting publicity made it easy for George to find his way to 27 Park Street but it was a chance meeting with Fanny in Hyde Park which brought him to the imposing home of his Hereford girl.

Surprised yet genuinely glad to see him, Josie quickly accepted how valuable he would be; she had plans in the pipeline and, subject to certain conditions, offered him a place of safety in the basement and explained the ground rules. It was a double-edged offer; for as much as he needed her, she also needed him, if only to be on standby to help make even more money. It was a strange decision; money was her God, not George, and she was not bothered how she got it and it was the sole reason for bringing him back into the fold.

It was the turning point in both their lives.

By now Josie had become a female Jekyll and Hyde; on the surface, she was the indolent, carefree, money-to-burn woman about town and was seen in all the right places. In the evening she raced around with the smart set and spent what was left of her nights with Francine. Little did George or indeed anyone else know that she was the devious, clever and successful leader of a villainous gang of crooks, scheming her way to thousands of pounds.

George kept to his end of the bargain not to intrude into her daily life unless invited but, with her permission, he practised his forger's skills while Josie focused on building her income and reputation. Her Sunday mornings were dedicated to riding through Rotten Row, blowing kisses at her high-ranking admirer, the Earl of March, heir to the Duke of Richmond and Gordon. He was her most loyal protector and utterly devoted to her but the elderly Edwin Docker was top of her rich list.

Besotted with his darling girl, it was common gossip he was completely under her spell and showering her with flowers and expensive gifts. They met as often as possible, usually at the races or over quiet lunches in the countryside and he was always on hand with cash whenever she asked for it.

Despite his continual generosity, Josie's restless brain was shaping her next moneymaking ideas. They came to fruition over lunch in Edwin's private box at the June flat race meeting at Ascot. Bursting into tears of frustration, she told him the tale of a non-existent Captain Montague, a man she claimed owed her money. Admitting she was fond of him, she had lent him all her available cash, £1700 but he let her down and refused to repay it and she was now facing a costly court hearing and social ruin.

Edwin was both furious and confused. Josephine had often entertained him at some wonderful dinners and tête-à-tête luncheons and believed her funds unlimited at any Belgravia hotel or store but, as usual, he promised to help her out, this time with two conditions. Firstly, that she told him everything there was to know about the scoundrel captain and agree to prosecute when the evidence was complete.

In an effort to make fiction become fact, she had already persuaded an associate to take on the persona of her imagined Captain Montague and move to Sussex from where a bogus solicitor would post a succession of letters demanding repayment of the initial £1700 plus interest and costs. The impostor then took the demands to a genuine local solicitor who, in an exchange of letters, told her his client had agreed to see what he could do to pay back the debt. Thoroughly convinced that Josephine was telling the truth, Edwin again fronted up and agreed to advance her £2000 in return for an interest in the £1700. She told him he was 'too wonderful, too splendid and too generous for words' and readily signed the agreement.

Josie got her money all right but the trusting Mr. Docker did not. The elusive Captain scarpered and was never seen again. Well paid for his loyalty, her associate returned to the criminal fold in Mayfair and used her ill-gotten gains to rent a magnificent old mansion in Worplesdon, near Guilford. She invited all her friends, including Edwin, to join her for Christmas and New Year at her country seat.

Edwin continued to visit her at Worplesdon, particularly at weekends where it was always open house for the rich set, but Josie soon tired of the countryside. She missed the buzz and excitement of London and the scope it gave her for making money; she also missed her mother and sister and, at times, her gang of scoundrels. Boredom took over and in March she returned to London to oversee the final renovations and decoration at Park Street.

Creating her bogus beginnings, she had opted for an oriental design, black, red and gold dominating just about every room. Her friends marvelled at the overstated changes and whispered among themselves that the cost of the transformation must have been excessive. Little did they know that Josie was not bothered about the cost, Edwin was happy to foot the bill.

Fanny was delighted to see her home again. Happy to play the part of servant at Worplesdon Manor during the Christmas period, she had missed catching up with her sister's escapades and needed to bring her up-to-date on the domestic situation. Unpaid bills were piling up and her ailing mother needed more care and attention; yet it was vital Josie kept up appearances. Keen to show off her stunning, refurbished home, when she heard that a Bond Street fashion house wanted to organise mannequin parades for the rich and famous, Josie jumped at it.

It was perhaps, the perfect event for a strapped-for-cash society hostess and, never one to shirk a risk, she offered Park Street for a glamorous fashion show but almost came a cropper. Prior to the opening, debt collectors arrived asking for money. Her suitably dressed, overly-sized butler persuaded them to leave the matter until later, except for one who refused to be threatened. He was an officer of the High Court with a warrant for her arrest for contempt of a judgment order for £35. Prison was the very last place she wanted to be; the event had been widely advertised and she could not afford to lose face with her friends and associates so, reluctantly, she paid up.

The fashion show was a huge success; wealthy men from across London arrived in style not only to indulge their wives and mistresses but also for the opportunity to see the palatial setting of the venue. Josie spent well on afternoon tea and cakes but refused to provide whisky for men paying the bills for designer gowns and furs.

When a well-known sporting Lord was offered a cup of tea, he told the flunky what he could do with his 'Chinese beverage', picked up his hat and left the gathering.

Giddy with success and the publicity the show had brought her, before long she was the envy of the smart set and riding a wave of society popularity.

Determined to make it work for her, she flirted outrageously with older men in high positions with substantial assets to match, regardless of age or marital status. To this end, she set her cap at a venerable Earl unable to get about without assistance. An uneasy character with a very difficult temperament, his friends labelled him 'bloody awkward'.

Josie could do almost as she liked with the elderly nobleman; if she saw him in the park, she would stop her car and call him to her side, blatantly addressing him by his Christian name when people with a higher claim for friendship referred to him as My Lord or Sir.

Smitten with her, he sent her effusive, affectionate letters, sometimes two or three a day, and she responded in a similar way but when the time came to broach the subject of money the old boy knocked her back explaining: 'Money, what use is my money to me. It's been locked up, every last penny of it, by my family and I cannot get to it.'

Undeterred, she delicately mentioned she knew of a moneylender who could help him out with ready cash and she charmed him into discussing it further. The Earl half-heartedly agreed to give it more thought but, persistent as ever, Josie jumped the gun again.

Taking the arrangement as read and without referring back to the old gent, Josie persuaded a seedy moneylender's tout to pressure him into borrowing cash on the strength of his estate. It was a case of more haste, less speed; the tout telephoned the Earl, wrote letters of intent to him and eventually called on him at his home. It was Josie's undoing; her target became suspicious and, after making a few enquiries, flatly refused to sign up for a high interest loan of £10,000, intended to net Josie a couple of thousand pounds. It was back to square one for the incorrigible chancer. Despite all her efforts, the slippery slope was approaching and she had to think fast.

The blow came with the bankruptcy petition; all household credit ceased and a meeting of all staff, the rejected lovers in the kitchen and the shady lodgers below stairs called to discuss the situation. After much argument, Fanny agreed to oversee household finances and sign all outgoing cheques and correspondence. To avoid the expected summons, Josie bought a set of fine Italian furniture for £133 at an auction sale and paid for it with a dud cheque.

Using a false name, the following day she sold it on for £350 which, she hoped, would temporarily halt proceedings, but it did not work. The hearing took place and the bailiffs stripped her Park Street home of everything personally belonging to her but, as usual, her luck still held.

Introduced at a dinner party to the Managing Director of a substantial paint and varnish business in the city, it was clear to Josie that he was up to his eyes in drugs. He seemed a safe bet for easy money and the financial bleeding began the moment she installed him in her apartment. She got more than she had bargained for; like all the rest he was crazy about her but this time it was a craziness bordering on obsession and jealousy. She could not answer the telephone without her demented 'lover' in tow; he listened in to her conversations and watched every move she made in or out of the apartment. It played on her nerves, but she held on for the sake of his money. In moments of respite, she conceived ways of increasing her income and one evening booked a room in a downmarket London club for an illegal chemin de fer party. Inviting shady cardsharps, gamblers and petty crooks to play the tables, she planned to make a quick killing on the door, take a percentage of the winnings and disappear; but trouble was brewing in Mayfair. Determined to know what his 'lady' was up to, the dope-crazed businessman locked a screaming Josie in her bedroom and threatened Fanny with violence if she dared to interfere. The screaming went on and on until she told him her plan; he left for the club in a rage and Fanny called for a couple of heavies from below stairs to break the door down. Consumed with jealousy and determined to maintain power over her, the angry suitor found the club, aggressively ordered the doorman to make sure that everyone was out by midnight and threatened the management with the vice squad for running an illegal gambling den. Released from her room, Josie followed him to the club and unable to keep her temper, the Girton accent slipped into foul-mouthed Herefordian, stopping the chaos in its tracks. It was to be one of Josie's colossal failures, the first convincing debit against her many successes.

As her mounting troubles piled up, she used her valuable relationship with Edwin Docker and remained well positioned as the rich old man's darling. Despite his advancing years, Edwin was still a level-headed, shrewd and strong-willed man of the world yet, when it came to money, he was putty in her hands. Easily persuaded to meet her domestic bills and store accounts, writing them off as losses at the races, Josie was worried when he broke the news of his retirement. On what was to be their final visit to the races, he explained that he had lately become frail and somewhat confused and, following advice from his doctors and his family, he decided to close his London business interests and live quietly in Leamington Spa.

Feigning concern for his wellbeing, Josie wiped her eyes, told him how much she would miss his companionship and would never forget his kindness. In return, he assured her he would make changes to his will in her favour and handed her £3000 in cash to help with domestic expenses.

Delighted with the unexpected windfall, when a retired Naval Commander and his lady friend invited her to a gambling spree in Monte Carlo, she jumped at the chance. She had never been to the Cote d'Azure and she saw it as a trip with the dual motive of pleasure and money. The boat-train journey was long but exciting for the girl from Herefordshire and she used the time to plan. As the engine steamed into Monte Carlo station, her adrenalin was pumping at the thought of cashing in at the casino. As she stepped off the train, little did she know that she was also stepping into an orgy of drink, dope and dubious parties.

Bluffing her way into the right places, Josie mixed and matched with the rich and famous including the dangerous and exciting motor racing set, particularly the Bugatti Queens. The dashing and daring female racing car drivers were up for anything on wheels and Josie was particularly attracted to a well-known woman driver. Ignoring the collective 'tut-tut' of the English gentry strolling along the seafront, Josie roared through the streets wearing leathers, helmet, boots and goggles. However, it wasn't all fun and high living.

Regardless of her wide-ranging experience in the criminal world, Josie had very little knowledge of serious gambling and, believing that Commander Allen was the expert, she soon came unstuck. The dodgy tourists ended up with heavy losses at the tables, and caught up in one of the liveliest scandals Monte Carlo has ever known and for days the trio were the talk of the Cote d'Azure.

It was the same old story. The Commander had imagined he was in love with Josie, she claimed to feel the same way about him, the common denominator, cash. Each thought the other had the money but those who knew the Commander well recalled a wealthy, titled woman of means, living in retirement at Antibes, who financed the cunning 'old salt'. Informed by the

French newspapers of the sleazy goings on the Cote d'Azure, she demanded her chauffeur take to her to Monte Carlo for a fiery confrontation with her lover and his tart.

The sudden arrival of Her Ladyship put an end to the drinking orgies, drug taking and all-night parties and she firmly refused to pay his debts. A few days later, he woke up without a penny to his name and a substantial hotel account on the dressing table he could not meet. The management promptly seized all his belongings and clothes, some of which belonged to Josie, and all three were at a loss as to what to do next. They had not bargained for Josie's resourcefulness and daring.

Disappearing for an hour, she returned with a wallet and chequebook picked from the pocket of a tipsy punter in the casino bar, signed a cheque and presented it to the hotel cashier to cover the hotel and bar bills and a few other debts. She generously tipped the staff with francs from the wallet and the jubilant trio left Monte Carlo for Mayfair, shaken but unscathed.

For a while, the Commander continued to live at Park Street with Josie, each still thinking that the other had money but, unknown to her, the Commander was a kept man. For many years, he had been living a comfortable quiet life in Whitney with his mistress, the wife of the Governor of HM Prison, Broadmoor. After a few weeks of riotous living with Josie and her dubious retinue, he packed his bags and returned to Whitney, much the poorer for having succumbed to Josie's charms.

Meanwhile, George Davis, by now bored with his exile to the kitchens, had kept himself amused in prison by writing scandalous newspaper articles about the lifestyle of his former partner. In the name of Captain Hellier, he auctioned the rights and sold them to the highest bidder, 'Reynolds Illustrated News'. The articles suggested he had been introduced to Josephine O'Dare on board a ship in American waters shortly after the war but these were not taken seriously; Josie left Hereford in 1921 when George was serving time in Gloucester prison.

A year after publication, George appeared at the Central Criminal Court charged in the name of Hellier, with stealing and forging cheques with Guy Hart, also known as Albert Marriot; he was sentenced to fifteen months imprisonment.

Fanny continued to keep house but Josie's mother, now seriously infirm and confused, was moved into a small flat in Westbourne Park and cared for by a live-in nurse. This left Josie with two homes to support and the debts were mounting up.

Determined to keep up appearances, she remained one of the smartest young women in London with an impressive social diary. In the afternoons she entertained noble and aristocratic paramours in the salubrious drawing room of her 'little palace' in Mayfair but not all of her relationships were fruitful. One such relationship swiftly became common gossip; Andrew Carlisle, an intimate of the Kaiser, seemed genuinely fond of Josie and she him. He was older than her and it showed but his connections with the Kaiser tended to make him a bit of a traitor in some eyes. Nevertheless his wealth bought him respectability and, known to be an astute observer of people, he was so impressed by Josie's bright, outgoing personality. The fun-loving couple were never short of invitations.

Once again, Josie was in her element; her friends were optimistic for a relationship, which promised much but in the end delivered little. Andrew Carlisle began doubting her motives and, during a high society dinner party, he pointed at her and, to the surprise of the other guests, asked: 'What do you think of the little lady? Is there not some mystery about her?'

A few eyebrows, including Josie's, raised at his unexpected rudeness; her hopes and dreams were knocked back and expectations of further financial rewards quickly disappeared. He had already gifted her a few thousand pounds in expensive jewellery and trusted her with the occasional bundle of cash from dubious business deals in Germany. When he unexpectedly died, she was not mentioned in his £70,000 estate and crushed at receiving nothing.

Approaching her late twenties, her fast and furious lifestyle was beginning to show; her body was telling her to rest but, as usual, her head and not her heart dictated her.

More important, her relationship with Francine was floundering as doubt and suspicion crept in and, after a few niggling rows over the company she was keeping, Francine returned broken-hearted to the comfort and security of White Water. Her father had completed his memoirs and missed his daughter's care and companionship.

Josie missed her too; she missed the warmth and affection of her gentle companion and the loving conversations in the quiet moments of the early hours of the morning when she usually arrived home. It was a gap she could not fill and, refusing to admit that she was sometimes depressed at the way her life was heading, she turned again to cocaine; this time sniffing with characteristic enthusiasm.

When her despairing doctor begged her to take a six-month cure at an out-of-town private clinic she meekly consented but only managed six weeks. Bribing an attendant to assist her escape, she took two women patients with her and, for a short time, installed them as maids at her house.

Never a quitter, whatever the circumstances, Josie pushed ahead with her life of crime and deceit; her extravagances grew to such an extent that bankruptcy hearings against her were piling up and, with summonses flying around like confetti, she feigned ill-health and flatly refused to show up at court. There was much concern for her well-being; an anonymous donor cleared the debts and claims against her were withdrawn at the last minute.

Meanwhile the failing Edwin Docker, said to be in a confused state, had been moved into a nursing home in Leamington Spa. Reminded of her mounting unpaid bills, she made it her business to send a message of sympathy, arranged for a daily delivery of fruit and flowers to his room and eventually mustered up the courage to visit him. However, his family had given written notice to the nursing staff that on no account must Miss O'Dare be allowed to see or speak to Mr. Docker, but money has a habit of talking and Josie refused to be beaten. Tracking down an unscrupulous carer ready and willing to take a few pounds, she arranged a clandestine visit to see the old man. He was nearing the end of his days and, unaware she was barred from seeing him, was sitting in a comfortable chair and delighted to see her. Disregarding his frailty, they chatted about their visits to Sandown Park and Ascot and, after some gentle coaxing, the old solicitor grasped her hand, drew her towards him and confidentially whispered: 'You are still my lovely girl and well provided for in my will. I have arranged for a small legacy of £15,000 to spend and enjoy.'

She took his hand in both of hers and replied equally fondly: 'Dearest Edwin, how very generous and most kind. I hope to put it to good use later rather sooner.'

With that, she gratefully kissed him on his forehead and, having already secured a further covert visit, she assured him of her devoted affection and promised to see him again soon. The hovering attendant noted her cunning smile and audible sigh of relief. On the strength of his failing health and the promise of a large inheritance, Josie raised £1350 to help settle her affairs in Carey Street. What she failed to notice was that, for some time, she was being shadowed.

CHAPTER THIRTEEN

Waiting for Edwin Docker to die took longer than expected. Josie's debts had built up again and the only way out was to join up with George. By now his reputation for forgery and fraud had forced the Metropolitan Police to consider him the 'most skilful imitator of signatures in all England' and it was time to use his skills. With his unmatched reputation for forgery and deception and a thieves' kitchen waiting in the wings, she was back in business again.

In a clever financial coup, the gang successfully targeted banks and department stores in and around South London and Surrey using bogus cheques and forged documents to bring in the much-needed cash. After a week or two, they returned to Mayfair to share out the spoils, but Josie failed to keep her end of the bargain. Instead of using George's skills, she asked a former associate to forge a cheque or two for her own use, just in case everything went down. She might never have been caught out had she used her own valuable experience but it all went wrong.

To keep her head above water, she continued to dash between Edwin's nursing home, her solicitor and the bankruptcy court building. When the nursing home eventually discovered her identity, her cover was blown and the O'Dare criminal dynasty and everyone associated with it was about to come down with a resounding crash.

Fanny was frantic; her sister had briefed her on the situation and suggested started packing up her fashionable clothing, expensive jewellery and personal effects before the bailiffs moved in and pawn the rest but not the silver locket and chain which she wanted to keep. The fine furnishings and fittings which had come with the apartment would be offered in a free-for-all to the residents below stairs; the leftovers would keep the bailiffs quiet.

When word of the flit reached the below stairs brigade, the steady flow of traffic to and from the battered vans parked outside the tradesmen entrance, was chaotic but, once the confusion had died down, Fanny and Josie waited for George to arrive with a team of bogus removal men and a suitable stolen vehicle. Boxes of clothes, jewellery and gifts were piled into the large removal van together with small pieces of oriental furnishings and fittings destined for the cellar in Westbourne Park. With everything loaded up, Josie called for a taxi cab to take Fanny and the secure boxes, including the 'rainy-day' fund, to Mary Skyrme's apartment. In a smart piece of forward planning, her kindly nurse carer had agreed to go, leaving Fanny to care for her mother.

Josie stayed put in Park Street until she could find alterative accommodation. She tried all the smart hotels in the West End but her shocking and seedy reputation was out of the bag and not one had room for the 'notorious Josephine O'Dare'. However, thanks to a mysterious backer, she took rooms at a high-class hotel, just off Piccadilly Circus, registered as Miss Joan Dean and warned close associates to always ask for her in that name.

To celebrate her change of address she arranged a party for her criminal consorts; it turned out to be a rum do, yet with just a few shillings between them, they drank the bar dry. The final account included costs for the damage caused by their raucous behaviour but Josie was unable to pay it. Aware of whom she was and with little chance of getting a penny out of her, the management quietly allowed the matter to drop and she returned to her family in Westbourne Park. Chances are that Josie did have the cash but, knowing she was due in court the following day, she needed it for her counsel fees.

With most of her magnificent wardrobe seized by the bailiffs and her Park Street house finally lost, the woman who boasted never having descended to a bus, tube or train in her entire life and always used taxi cabs was glad enough to ride in anything now! She no longer had a penny to her name apart that is, from the well-stocked pension pot and 'rainy day' fund she was shrewd enough to set aside over the years, now in the safe hands of her devoted sister. Nonetheless, she was hanging by her manicured fingernails at the end of a tight, financial rope and hated living a monotonous life in Westbourne Terrace.

It was that or a prison cell. In one final attempt to save herself from the debtor's prison, she bullied her nervous associates into a last money-making scheme involving flooding London with £100,000 worth of forged bank and treasury notes.

Discussions went as far as arranging for a dodgy print shop off Peckham High Road to engrave and print the plates but, after a tip-off that Scotland Yard was continuing to watch her every move, she announced it was too dangerous and pulled out.

With all the police attention, Josie was forced to moved out of Westbourne Terrace, leaving loyal Fanny to care for their mother. She took a fifty pound a week room in an exclusive hotel in the West End, claiming she was heading towards a physical and mental breakdown. When her creditors and associates heard they were most sympathetic, cancelled the bankruptcy hearings and paid for a nursing home. The end was nigh when she slipped out of the nursing home to meet George for a final flurry of forgery. A sharp-eyed police officer followed her into a fashionable couturiers in Piccadilly, arrested her and charged her with deception.

Waiting outside, George realised that the game was up and quietly walked away but she had a final ace in her fading pack: Edwin Docker's last will and testament.

The time had come for a final gamble she had been planning with George since his elevation to the drawing room at Park Street and desperate times needed desperate measures.

The elderly solicitor from Birmingham had outlasted Josie's expectations. All the same, he was clearly very confused and just about on his last legs. Some weeks had passed since she visited Leamington Spa and, fortunately, the corrupt care nurse was still around and she was able to arrange a time for the final goodbye.

Propped up by pillows and prevented from falling out of bed by adjustable bars, Edwin appeared pleased to see her and pointed to a drawer in his locker. Unable to understand his actions, she openly showered him with her usual affection and asked his nurse to bring tea. Quietly reminding Edwin of his a promise to leave her £15,000 in his will and convinced of her affection, he flung his arms about and pointed noisily at the locker. Inside she discovered his will and arrangements for his funeral.

Discarding the latter, she waited until the nurse returned with the tea tray and, when Edwin slept for a while, read and pocketed the will. Satisfied that George could easily forge it, she patiently waited Edwin's return, helped settle him into his bed and affectionately hugged him. Profusely thanking the nurse for her kindness and care, she slipped her a five-pound note and made her way to a side entrance at the end of a long corridor.

Outside, she took a deep gulp of fresh air, jauntily walked to the main road where George was anxiously waiting in a stolen car. When she eventually showed him the will, the self-assured forger grinned, confirmed he could easily doctor the figures and suggested he made a full copy adding a further £10,000 to her supposed legacy. On the journey home, the conniving couple talked through plans to use the promised inheritance as collateral for their next scam and cast around for a 'pigeon' to front it.

He appeared in the shape of Lord Curzon, an extremely opulent man. He walked into her 'hired for the day' hotel suite like a fly into a spider's web, instantly fell under her spell and believed her heart-breaking story of bad luck and misfortune. Convincing him she was to be the recipient of a substantial inheritance and in consideration of her expectations he offered her a cash loan of £700 in cash; he later learned too late that it was a bluff!

Although subsequent correspondence confirmed enough evidence for a fraud conviction, Lord Curzon chose to lose the money rather than face up to public embarrassment and the ridicule of friends and associates.

Nevertheless, Josie was up and running again. While George kept a low profile, she used the £700 to reform her criminal team and, with the reliable Albert Marriot, organised a systematic swindle of many banks in London and the Home Counties. The cash was coming in, her lifestyle was on the up and she was able to pay the rent for her mother and sister's home in Westbourne Terrace. The rest was stacking up in the 'rainy day' fund but the crunch was coming!

She was twenty-seven when she received news from her informant at the Leamington Spa nursing home that the old solicitor had eventually passed away quietly in his sleep. Head spinning, she considered her forged inheritance but was floored when she heard the family solicitor and business partner, Sebastian Hosegood, contested the will. Convinced it was a forgery, he informed the police and, after extensive investigations, Inspector Yelland from Scotland Yard, arrested and charged Josie with deception, uttering forged cheques and obtaining money by false pretences.

On April 13th, she appeared before the bench at Marlborough Street Police Court and, on the advice of her solicitors Messrs. Cooper and Wright, a reputable firm in Chancery Lane, pleaded guilty to the charge. All other charges and misdemeanours were dropped and she was remanded in custody at Holloway prison pending sentence at the Central Criminal Court (Old Bailey).

When news of her arrest reached George, he did his usual vanishing trick; he quit London and, with Albert Marriot in tow, returned to Hereford, leaving Josie to take the rap.

It soon became obvious to her close associates that she had agreed to some sort of deal with Scotland Yard and, after an anonymous 'tip off', George was arrested by a sharp-eyed police officer in High Town, Hereford, and returned to London under police escort. The following day. George and Albert appeared at Marlborough Street Police Court, charged with 'conspiring between January and May 1926 with Josephine O'Hare, to forge and utter a document, purporting to be the will of the late Edwin Docker, with intent to defraud'.

Davis faced further charges of forging various bankers' drafts, including one in the name of Lord Curzon, for £600; the same 'wealthy pigeon' that had loaned Josie £700 on the strength of her likely inheritance.

When she arrived from Holloway Prison, an army of news reporters and photographers eager to record her fall from grace, treated her as a celebrity; inside the courtroom former associates, enemies and one or two socialites filled the public gallery. The atmosphere buzzed with rumour and hearsay as the courtroom patiently waited for the curtain to go up on what turned out to be a touch of the theatricals.

Fanny smiled nervously when her sister joined her co-defendants in the dock. It was Josie's second appearance at Marlborough Street but this time she was not alone; to the amazement and anger of her co-defendants, she confirmed guilty. Cheering and applause exploded from the public gallery and she responded with a wave and a smile, followed by a sharp reprimand from the Bench. The Clerk called the first witness, Birmingham solicitor Sebastian Hosegood, the late Edwin Docker's business partner.

Under oath he explained: 'I knew my partner's handwriting very well indeed and after examining the alleged will I have no hesitation in confirming not one word of it, including the signature, is Edwin Docker's handwriting.

'My late partner always wrote in a great hurry and never finished his letters off. The forged will is neatly written with purpose and with great care and deliberation.'

Questioned over the absence of an attestation clause on behalf of Miss O'Dare, Mr. Hosegood insisted: 'Mr. Docker could not possibly have forgotten to put it in because he was very experienced and particular when it came to formulating wills.'

During cross examination by Counsel for George Davis, Josie denied under oath that she had been the mistress of his client adding: 'I have known the accused for seven years but never physically cohabited with him although, for a short time, we did live under the same roof. Since the unfortunate matter of Mr. Docker's will, I have not seen or heard of him, due perhaps to his being in jail. I tracked him down through newspaper articles about me he had written for the 'Glasgow Weekly Record' and 'Reynolds Illustrated News'. These were absolute lies and I eventually traced him to Highbury and went to see him to complain about the articles.'

Denying that George was no longer on friendly terms with her, she told the court: 'He had not the foggiest idea who Edwin Docker was but he definitely forged the will and received no payment.'

Put to her that her evidence against George Davis was a tissue of lies from start to finish told in spite because he wanted nothing more to do with her, she calmly answered: 'Not at all. I do not see why I should lie against him.'

Cross examined over her relationship with Edwin Docker, Josie admitted: 'I was very fond of him and regularly received quarterly gifts of cash from him out of kindness. Despite having a car and entertaining quite a lot, I did not use the gifts to live a life of luxury.'

Taking advice from his own Counsel, George pleaded not guilty to all charges and the case was set for trial at the Central Criminal Court. An application for bail from Davis and Marriot was refused, Josie returned to Holloway to await sentencing.

CHAPTER FOURTEEN

A Black Maria, more commonly known as a Paddy wagon, was waiting for her. The secure motorised vehicle contained seven wooden booths in a single row, each booth locked with a separate turnkey; prisoners perched on solid box seats with leather restraining straps and watched over by a uniformed wardress. When the exterior doors were shut, there was hardly room to swing a cat and little chance of escape; apart from the communal piss-pot for emergencies, there were few facilities, not even drinking water for the journey.

For prisoners lucky enough to be in the first batch of daily offenders, the interior generally stank of strong disinfectant but, by the end of a busy court, the stench of stale piss and escaping bodily functions was sickening. A medicated scarf protected the nose and mouth of the duty wardress but, stoical as ever, Josie fronted up, gritted her teeth and told her whinging companions to shut up.

The Central Criminal Court was barely ten miles from Holloway Prison but in the intimidating Black Maria, it was a nerve-racking ride, particularly for a woman who, since her arrival in London, had travelled only in taxi cabs, private hire cars or a chauffeur-driven Bentley.

The constant moans, groans and menacing threats from her enforced travelling companions was bad enough but the suffocating reek of assorted bodies had almost brought her to vomiting point and reminded her of the stink from the muck-spreading around Leominster on a hot steamy day. If the bouncing vehicle had not slowed down, she might have thrown up.

When the vehicle stopped outside the Gatehouse, the duty escort produced a loud sigh of relief. She stepped from the wagon, stretched her legs and announced to the gatekeeper: 'Cor blimey. Thank gawd I'm off the rota after this delivery. It's bad enough in there now and unless it's hosed down at the turn round, the next trip will stink like a bloody pig sty.'

Experience told him not to venture too near the suspect van and, gripping his clipboard, he shouted the regulation roll call from a safe distance.

'What we got today then, Mavis?' he asked.

'Two or three remands, a couple of lifers, a possible for the swing and the usual bunch of 'I'll never do it again, me Lord' and a couple of recidivists up for a couple of weeks bed and board. Oh yes and some posh bint on a guilty plea for fraud, remanded until the spring sessions for sentencing.'

The Paddy wagon driver leaned out of the window for his usual chat with the gatekeeper and two more warders arrived to escort the prisoners to the reception centre.

Situated at the junction of Parkhurst Road with Camden Road, Holloway Prison, designed and built by J.B. Bunning in 1849, is a dark, depressing building which took three years to complete. The gothic-looking Gatehouse, a replica of the one at Warwick Castle, has houses either side for the Governor and the Prison Chaplain; two iron doors open into an archway leading to the main prison complex.

Until 1902, Holloway housed both male and female offenders in dark and filthy conditions, a year later it was updated and designated a women-only prison with a maximum population of nine hundred remand and convicted prisoners. These ranged from petty thieves, prostitutes and swindlers to debtors, society fraudsters and embezzlers and murderers awaiting execution.

Josie said little during transportation from Holloway; she used the time in the van to work out some sort of survival strategy but, standing before the awesome exterior of the gloomy building, the shadow of fear hovered over her.

Convicted prisoners were processed through a secure reception area into the main building; prisoners on remand awaiting trial had separate quarters with a less secure entrance. They were able to pay for a bigger cell, have food delivered from outside the prison and allowed daily visits and to wear their own clothes until sentenced.

Josie preferred to keep her own stylish outfits for court appearances and elected to wear prison 'haute couture' as she liked to call it, which gave her the opportunity to sort out the rough from the smooth when it came to who was who on the prison list.

Helped by a more than friendly wardress, she was stripped of her posh togs and handed the dour grey uniform of the unconvicted. Afterwards she was taken to the clothing store and given a coat hanger, covered with a dustsheet, for her best (court) clothes, which she hung on a rail. While the officer carefully tagged them with her name and number, Josie checked the rest of the clothes on the same the rail.

Noticing her interest, the official said sarcastically: 'We generally store the top quality clothes of our better class of guests in here to air; the rough, low-life stuff goes for burning in the boiler house. Can't leave mucky, smelly clothes to rub against the smart clobber, can we?' and laughed at her smart remark.

Josie's first meeting with the Rev. Seymour-King, the Prison Chaplain, gave her much food for thought. He, like the rest of the men she meets, was charmed and she easily convinced him she was 'an ill-judged, grievously wronged woman' and keen to help others to adjust to prison life. The kind-hearted gent gave her the benefit of the doubt and a few days later took her to the privacy of his chapel for a chat.

'A woman of your education might like to befriend our vulnerable and lonely first-time inmates and help them through their ordeal.

'I can attach you with one of our prison visitors and you can keep her informed of conditions in here, cleanliness, food and the like.'

'You mean be a sort of honorary grass, Vicar?' she said with a wry smile and chuckled quietly under her breath.

'Oh! Dear me no, Miss O'Dare, not at all, not at all,' he blustered. 'I want you to help others less fortunate than you.'

'Only joking, Reverend. I have been thinking about helping out where I can and if the good Lord can point me in the right direction I am a willing soul.'

After a few meetings with him, he eventually introduced her to Lady Carter, a kindly, understanding woman with a wealth of experience in the prison system.

However, it did not match Josie's skills; the plausible, well-spoken con-woman was able to persuade her Ladyship to arrange a more private and comfortable cell where she could offer tea and sympathy to troubled remand and long-term offenders and those waiting. It worked a treat.

Remand accommodation at Holloway was a 10.5 feet x 7 feet cell complete with water closet, copper washbasin, bed, fold-down table and a corner cupboard with shelves for crockery, cutlery, toiletries and cleaning materials. A further shelf was set aside for books, including the obligatory prayer book, Bible and rulebooks. Josie's new cell was one of two attached to the hospital wing and adjacent to the condemned cell. The rooms were kept for prison staff on execution watch and more spacious and comfortable than a standard cell and had a small kitchen for providing food and hot drinks. In common with all the cells, hot air from an outlet over the door kept inmates warm during the winter and a small barred window let in the daylight.

Making the most of her new environment, she mixed with all comers during recreation periods, entertaining them with light-hearted tales of her society exploits and promising to keep in touch when they left prison.

Unaware she was a 'grass', when a group of hardened miscreants jested that a 'swindler' could go down for a possible ten years, Josie laughed nervously and told them she had friends in high places and paid good money for the best legal team in London to defend her.

Over the following months, she concentrated on keeping up appearances, sticking to her promise to help when required and liaising with her prison visitor.

In return, she received extra visits from her sister to keep her in touch with her bedridden mother.

She also befriended Kristy Potts, a young woman from Bethnal Green awaiting trial for attacking her father with a chair.

In a quiet moment with Josie, she told her: 'It was awful; I was only trying to protect our mother. He came home from the alehouse full of beer and hard liquor and started cursin' and swearin' at us. He went for mother with his leather strap; I managed to drag him off but this time he went too far and almost strangled her. Too scared to help, my brothers stood by and watched him bash her about and I had to stop him before he killed her. I didn't hit him hard but, as he fell to the floor, he whacked his 'ead on our heavy sideboard and went down like sack of spuds, bleedin' like a pig.'

Josie wrapped her arms round the young girl. 'What are you doing in here then? Surely it's self defence?'

'Yea, that's what it was, but when we got him to the hospital in Whitechapel, the rozzers were already there. I was in a terrible state; my lily-livered brothers sided with father and told them I had tried to kill him. Despite what Ma had to say they took me before the bench on a GBH charge.'

'But didn't anyone speak up for you in court?' Josie asked.

'Only at my committal when the public defender was brought in. I play tambourine in the Sally Army band and they found me a good 'wig and gown' man for me trial. Ma is speaking up for me, so is the next-door neighbour who had seen it all before. My brief said it is provocation and I might get a lighter sentence.'

Realising how close she had been to the same charge if she had stayed in Wellington, Josie warmed to the girl.

'What will you do and where will you stay if you are discharged? It's a big bad world out there if you can't go home.'

'Don't worry about that. The Sally Army is looking out for Ma while I'm inside and when I do get out we've been promised rooms in a hostel next to the training college in Denmark Hill. I am still in the band and God willing we will be all right, Josie, honest.'

Almost in tears Josie replied: 'I know you will. I shall arrange for my sister to send a donation when you get out. I shall miss our little chats and, whatever happens, we must keep in touch.'

'I will Josie and if you do get off and you come back here, try to keep an eye on Rose. It's very sad; she murdered her employer years ago and was sentenced to hang but, thanks to the suffragists, at the last minute she was given life. I don't know all the story but she has been in here since she was twenty-one and she is forty-five now, with a lump the size of an orange in her, you know, boobs. They say she doesn't have long to live and keeps to herself in her own room in the infirmary corridor. I'll tell her about you, she could do with a good friend.'

'And so will I if I find myself back here banged up with the convicted lot despite pleading guilty.'

As the weeks went by, as well as the Chaplain and welfare visitors, a steady stream of regular oddballs dropped into Josie's cell, but Josie and Kristy relied on each other for idle chitchat. As the Docker fraud trial drew near it played on Josie's mind. She was, after all, the main prosecution witness in what promised to be a long, drawn-out case and at times was distracted.

'It's the waiting about Kristy. The endless chats with my legal team wind me up like a spring. Whatever happens, I just want to get it over with and done with.'

Lowering her voice to a whisper, she added: 'Between you and me, my brief has suggested I could help the police out a bit and get a reduced sentence, otherwise I could find myself doing hard labour somewhere out in the sticks. Thinking about it is a bloody nightmare; if I am going down for a stretch I want to stay here where I know my way around and my sister can visit me.

My mother is getting on a bit, her brain has gone and she's on the downhill run.'

'What about your sister, won't she take care of her?'

'Oh yes. Our Fanny's a little gem at taking care of Ma but it is tough at times. I know she's older than me and even though I'm in this hellhole I feel responsible for her too. My hands are tied and I am beginning to doubt if I shall ever see her again, except in a coffin.'

She let out a deep sign which would have succumbed to a sob had not Kristy been with her but the unexpected gloomy moment soon passed, she pulled herself together and gave her young friend a brief hug.

'Don't mind me, Kristy, being in this place can trigger the emotions and cooped up in this place I tend to ramble on a bit. Now let's get back on the cheerful bus and think positive. It's Judge and Jury for you next week and, before you know it, you and your Ma will be settled in the Sally Army hostel and rattling your tambourine up and down Denmark Hill.'

Kristy laughed. 'I'm going to miss you something awful. You reckon I'll be okay then, Josie?'

'Of course you will. When they hear your story, not even a hard-hearted jury could send you down. It will be self-defence, not guilty and Bob's your uncle. Believe me I know what it's like. I had a couple of bullyboy brothers to cope with and a father who regularly beat up my mother. However, we won't go into that. Now off to the kitchen and make us a pot of tea, mine's Earl Grey.'

Turning to the friendly wardress seated outside the open cell door, she grinned and said: 'What about you, Miss, fancy a cup yourself?'
Josie's bravado was up and running again and she was going to need it. A week later the Holloway grapevine rippled with news that the jury had found Kristy not guilty on the grounds of self-defence. Her father and brothers cursed the Jury and were removed from the public gallery, Kristy slipped quietly out of court via the rear entrance and was taken to a place of safety at Denmark Hill. At the nearby hostel, she met up with her relieved mother and the happy pair settled in to their new surroundings.

Back in Holloway, Josie's whoops of delight echoed around the remand wing followed by spontaneous applause from offenders and staff alike but time was running out for Josephine O'Dare. The March Sessions at the Central Criminal Court were beckoning and the scene set for the performance of her life.

CHAPTER FIFTEEN

By the early 20th century, the Old Bailey had served the capital for around 400 years. Periodically remodelled to suit the needs of the times, it takes its name from the street on which it stands, some 200 yards from St Paul's Cathedral and follows the line of the original fortified wall, (bailey) of the City of London.

Faced in Portland stone, the interior lobbies, staircase and floors, crafted from Sicilian Marble, encourage a natural echo and figurative paintings, representing Labour, Art, Wisdom, and Truth, decorate the walls. The spacious oak- panelled courtrooms provided ample room for attending solicitors, barristers, court reporters and viewing galleries for spectators. Male and female witnesses had separate rooms leading from the central lobby, some reserved for 'the better class' of witness. Barristers and solicitors had private interviewing rooms, to prevent malpractices and touting for business among prisoners and their associates; the clerks shared glass-fronted offices. In keeping with the past, Judges retired to lavishly-appointed accommodation with serviced dining rooms.

Number one court, like all the others at the Bailey, has a partially enclosed dock and staircase leading to the holding cells below; for first-time offenders the impressive surroundings could be unnerving.

That was then, this is now and, although buildings and procedure may have changed, crime and punishment remained the same and Josie had to face the music.

Four weeks into the March sessions, news was out that the notorious and cunning society host Josephine O'Dare will be giving evidence at the trial of her former criminal associates George Davis and Albert Marriot. It was the moment editors of national newspapers had been waiting for. Front-page, banner headlines announcing, 'scandalous and outrageous goings on at Mayfair home of society hostess and thieves' kitchen discovered below stairs at Park Street Mansions' encouraged mass curiosity and intense public interest. Within three days, the queue for the public gallery in Court Number One was buzzing with rumour and expectancy rarely seen at the Old Bailey.

Never before had London society knowingly mingled so closely with the lower end of the criminal fraternity, however, this was mischievously challenged by the downmarket press keen to prove that there was not much to choose between the lot of them. While over-eager journalists jostled for prime position in the press box, the long-in-the-tooth reporter from the 'Hereford Times' had pipped them to the post. Travelling by rail overnight, he camped out in the waiting room at Paddington Station until the buses were running. His good lady wife had packed a satchel with best Herefordshire beef sandwiches, home-made cake from the local Women's Institute and a flask of tea to see him through the day's proceedings; he also carried a change of underwear, should he need to lodge with relatives in Kilburn. A dedicated angler, he had strapped a folding canvas stool, more suited to the banks of the River Wye, to his suitcase.

In dawn's early light, he parked it on the courthouse steps and refused to budge until the doors were open.

The case against Davis and Marriot was set before London Recorder Sir Ernest Wilde and was listed to last until June; J.B. Cassel KC and Sir Travers Humphries led for the prosecution, Henry Peregrine appeared for the defence.

Weeks of legal preamble concerning Josie's co-defendants had tied up the court, much of it listing charges relating to a string of long-standing serious offences: deception, fraud, forgery and burglary, primarily carried out by George Davis, delivered to the court in the sonorous tones of Inspector Yandell of the Yard. The long, drawn out statement, read parrot fashion from his regulation Metropolitan Police black notebook, referred to the past records and careers of the key defendants going back six or seven years.

Apologetically asking: 'Might I refer to my notebook m'Lord,' he also appraised the court of further offences to be taken into consideration. These included assault and similar misdemeanours committed in the city of Hereford and carried out in the names of Captain St. Hillier, DSO, Lord St. Hillier and Captain Danvers. Inspector Yandell also confirmed that Davis was the son of respectable working-class parents in Hereford and was educated locally at Lord Scudamore School, until 1912.

'On leaving school, he obtained employment in the office of a Mr. Britton and, true to form, absconded with his employer's motorbike. He remained unemployed until conscripted into the Machine Gun Corps during World War I and, in 1919, he was demobilised as being of very good character and said to have returned to Hereford to live with the defendant O'Dare. I immediately.....'

Intervening to address the jury, Sir Ernest Wilde said: 'At this the point you should be aware that Miss O'Dare has already pleaded guilty to the charge of fraud and deception at an earlier hearing and is currently on remand in His Majesty's Prison Holloway awaiting sentence. The court looks forward to hearing her evidence later in the proceedings. Please continue, Inspector.'

'Thank you, m'Lord. During my investigations into the Docker fraud, I received a 'tip-off ' that the accused, Davis had scarpered back to Hereford and I was obliged to inform the local constabulary who advised him to return to London. Detective Constable Bishop spotted him in Russell Square, arrested him, and he told him he was to be charged with O'Dare of conspiring in the forging and uttering of a will. Bail was refused and he was remanded in custody.'

His sleep-inducing evidence over, Inspector Yandell trooped from the witness box, sat down and mopped his sweating brow with a large, metropolitan blue handkerchief run up by his wife on her new-fangled sewing machine at their police house in Putney.

Noticing that the jury was as weary as he, Sir Ernest Wilde called for a thirty-minute recess to 'stretch one's legs' and made signs to his clerk that refreshments would be welcome.

After the break, the prosecution called Detective Constable Bishop to the stand for his first major trial; far from looking apprehensive, he was positively bubbling with enthusiasm. Taking the oath in his stride he gripped the Bible, holding it aloft like a Methodist preacher in full flow.

Sir Travers Humphries lumbered to his feet, paused and invited the constable to describe the arrest of Davis.

He responded with the consummate ease of well-practised Hyde Park corner speaker: 'At about 12.30pm I was cutting through Russell Square on my way to the High Holborn public convenience when I saw the prisoner approaching from Bernard's Street. I asked him if he was William George

Davis and he replied he was not. I told him I believed he was and informed him he was under arrest for the forgery of a cheque. Claiming he knew nothing about it, he told me to carry on, so I took him into custody at the nearest police station where he confirmed his name, gave an address in Hereford and said he was twenty-nine and journalist. When charged with the forgery of the cheque, he again asserted he knew nothing about it but, after a search at the police station, Davis had upon him a cheque book order form from Barclay's bank, a slip of paper with the names of banks upon it and other memoranda.'

Questioned on a second arrest the following day, D.C. Bishop revealed that Adrian Morton, a company director, was arrested in Upper Gloucester Place. When told the charge, conspiring with Davis and O'Dare, he replied: 'There is no truth in it. I have already given you evidence and I stick to that evidence throughout.'

He was released on bail set at £250. After the lunch adjournment, further deliberation between prosecution and defence took up most of the afternoon session and being Friday, much to the relief of the court, the Recorder brought the hammer down on the week's proceedings.

Back in the remand wing at Holloway, Josie had been on edge for most of the weekend. Irritated by prison gossip naming her witness-in-chief for the prosecution and, as 'grasses' were the lowest of the low in criminal circles, she had been involved in a barney or two in the exercise yard. A few long-term offenders wing, intent on unnerving her before her trial, warned her about being a grass; she gave as good as she got.

Despite her worries for the outcome, she kept her spirits up by reassuring her contemporaries: 'I have already pleaded guilty to fraud and my solicitor has told me that the charges against my former partners in the crime had little to do with me, except as a witness.'

To bolster her confidence, she gave a little twirl of bravado, but, underneath it, was an all-or-nothing situation for the Hereford adventuress. Her day of defiance was nigh and she was nervously aware that very soon she will face her public, the press and more important, her dangerous enemies.

Come Monday morning, Josie lightly painted her lips, powdered her face and carefully dressed to kill; escorted by Mavis Buck, her cheerful, cockney wardress, she waved goodbye to her prison companions and walked the long walk to the main gate. After an optimistic chat with Mavis, she took a moment to enjoy the fresh air that promised a touch of spring. The Black Maria was parked at the Gatehouse; she turned for a last wave at the faces peering out of the barred windows. Urging her towards the vehicle, Mavis announced: 'Your carriage awaits Miss O'Dare. All spick and span with just a splash of the Governor's Chanel No.5; it makes a change from Prison Pee No.2.'

Josie responded with her trademark hearty laugh and, in an overtly posh accent replied: 'I should be so lucky, Miss. Best we get this over with and be on our way; kindly ask the driver to pick us up after tea.'

Settled into her booth, Mavis leaned over and strapped her into her seat; Josie took her silver locket from the pocket of her dress. Handing it to her, she asked: 'Please, Miss, could you fix it around my neck? It's just a little trinket and it would mean so much if I could wear it in court.'

Mavis was surprised. 'How did you manage to hang on to this? All valuables should have been handed in at reception when you were booked in.'

'Ask no questions and you'll hear no lies, Miss. It is a simple keepsake, a charm sewn into the hem of this dress, just in case. Of course you haven't seen it?' and seductively slipped it inside her dress top.

'You're a cunning little blighter, O'Dare, I will give you that. You very well know I won't snitch. Now settle down and let's get under way, otherwise we'll be late for court.'

Slumped against the wooden wall of her booth, for the first time in her life, she felt alone. No sister to laugh and cry with, no mother to praise her, no Lady Constance to flirt with and, more importantly, no special companion to share her bed. Just silent guilt to grapple with.

As the secure double gates opened up she heard the Gatekeeper shout 'Good luck Miss' and the Black Maria with its solitary prisoner and friendly escort slipped slowly into the busy London traffic. When it eventually pulled up at the gates leading to the rear of the Old Bailey, the waiting crowd of curious sightseers and photographers forced the van to stop. Eager to catch a glimpse of society girl turned bad, they called out her name, drummed on the side of the van and aimed their cameras at the barred windows. Undeterred by the intrusion, Josie held her head down until the gates opened to allow the van to edge forward into the secure courtyard. When it came to a standstill,

Mavis unstrapped her, helped her out of the vehicle and handed her over to the custody officer to be booked into the detained cellblock. She wished her popular charge good fortune and promised to be back at closing time. Aware that Josie was trembling slightly, she took her by the shoulders and gave her a stern, chin-up hug before locking her into the lonely holding cell below the dock.

After a brief visit from her solicitor, Josie sat silently listening to the muttering of officialdom drifting down from the courtroom above her head. The Clerk to the Court called for order and asked the usher to bring the twelve good men and true into the jury box for yet another week of boring legal banter, or so they thought, but things were about to change.

It was the moment the entire court had been waiting for, the prime witness for the prosecution and the third defendant in the Edwin Docker affair was about to be called to the bar.

On the order, 'please be upstanding for Judge Sir Ernest Wilde' the packed courtroom stood as one; below stairs, the shuffling of feet told an anxious Josie that his Lordship had arrived. The once-noisy assembly settled down, the clerk announced 'this court is in session' and with a stern nod, the judge brought his hammer down and 'bring up the prisoner' echoed around the marbled halls and corridors and all eyes turned towards the dock.

Heart beating like a drum and the adrenalin pumping, Josie, accompanied by two prison officers, climbed the stone staircase to the dock and gripped the highly polished brass rail until her knuckles went white... Adjusting her dark red dress just enough to expose her fulsome cleavage, she casually rearranged her hair to show off her handsome features, highlighted by just a hint of make-up, and deliberately played with the silver locket around her neck. Taking a deep breath, she paused and looked directly into the sea of unrecognisable faces below, pointedly ignoring her co-defendants straining to catch a glimpse of her and hissing threats of 'grass' in her direction.

In the body of the court, anybody required to be there was either shuffling papers, conspiring with associates, examining the architecture or pacing the floor in preference to being caught staring at the charismatic young woman in the dock. Behind her, the public gallery, filled to the gunnels with high and low curiosity seekers, eagerly awaited the star performer. It took some time before Josie spotted Fanny sitting quietly in the furthest corner of the backbenches. Fearful that any acknowledgement would draw attention to her sister, she redirected her gaze to the rest of the expectant crowd. However, she failed to spot Francine her much-loved, former intimate companion carefully protected by her dog-collared father in the seats reserved for the clergy. She also failed to see the handsomely ageing Constance Radcliffe part hidden by shadows in a reserved box usually set aside for visiting Magistrates.

The first hour or so of the morning session confirmed the various charges against Davis and his associates, but matters were not moving along fast enough for Josie and she drummed her fingers on the bar surrounding the dock.

Deliberations between opposing barristers in the Docker case appeared to be annoying the Judge too and he spoke to his clerk before proceeding further. Referring to his papers, he announced that it was time to push ahead with the charges against O'Dare and, on instruction of the clerk, stood up and faced the judge. From the corner of her eye, she could see Davis watching her and, without a hint of hesitation, she confirmed her earlier guilty plea. Her co-defendants pleaded not guilty and, before sitting down, Josie turned to the press box and winked.

Outlining the case for the prosecution, Mr. Cassels informed the jury that Miss O'Dare was a young woman brought up in Herefordshire by a farm labourer named Skyrme. 'Five or six years ago she came to London, since when she has followed no formal occupation yet appears to have lived in style in Park Street, Mayfair, a most sought-after area of London. Among her acquaintances were the defendants and Edwin Docker, an elderly solicitor from Birmingham who has since died. Over the course of this trial, the court will hear how three days after his death in April this year, the defendant Davis and Miss O'Dare discussed with others at her home in Park Street whether Mr. Docker had left anything to her in his will. The defendant Morton suggested if not, she should make certain of the matter and production of a will in her favour was discussed. The sum of £20,000 was proposed but natural modesty prevailed and the figure was altered to £15,000. After forging the will, the defendants systematically swindled banks in London and the Home Counties.'

Detailing the facts as to the forging and uttering of the will, he called Josie to the witness box. The atmosphere was electric; it was he moment the court had been waiting for, the prime witness was about to take to the legal stage and present her version of events to the all-male jury.

Leaving the dock, she glanced confidently back at Davis and Marriot and mouthed bastards at their frightened faces. A gentleman usher led her to the witness stand, helped her up the steps and handed her the Bible for the oath. Dramatically clutching the Bible to her daring cleavage, she delivered the oath in a clear and convincing voice and then turned to face her examiner.

Asked for her full name and address, she gave her current residence as His Majesty's Prison Holloway, agreed she had earlier pleaded guilty to offences connected to the forging of Edwin's last will and testament and was waiting to be sentenced. Pressed by prosecuting counsel, she confessed to her part in the plot and, straight-faced, confirmed that in the best interests of justice, she had agreed to co-operate as a witness. A humorous snigger rippled through the public gallery and the press box, earning stern 'silence in court' from the clerk. With most of the morning gone, the Judge announced a suitable moment to adjourn for lunch and Josie returned to her cell to feast on a Fortnum and Mason picnic hamper sent in by an admirer.

Lunch adjournment over, Josie took a final swig of champagne, wiped her mouth with a linen napkin and returned to the witness box for further questioning.

Reminded that she was still under oath, she surprised the court by asking to make a personal statement. Smiling at the bemused Recorder, she said: 'There is one point I am most anxious to clear up before proceeding with my evidence, your Lordship.'

A rustle of excitement filtered through the airless courtroom; bored by the morning session and dulled by a few drinks at the Wig and Pen, the collective clatter of writing material hitting the press box floor roused the heaviest of dozers. Uninvited personal statements were as rare as carrots in criminal proceedings and, to the astonishment of the court, Sir Ernest ruled the request valid.

Clearing her tight throat, she asked for a glass of water and the gentleman usher almost tripped in his rush to produce it. Using the delay to gather her thoughts, she sipped it slowly and somewhat seductively between her dry lips until prompted by an unusually agitated Judge, to get on with it. Choosing her words carefully she announced:

'Suggestions were made at my hearing in the Police Court that I was the mistress of many men. I wish emphatically to state that I have never been any man's mistress and the prison doctor at Holloway could give evidence to prove my statement.'

Gasps of disbelief escaped from the public gallery but, strangely enough, George Davis seemed to nod in agreement. Josie glanced at Francine and gently smiled before directing her attention at a stunned Sir Ernest Wilde. Politely lowering his eyes, he made heavy weather of recording her statement.

Wide-eyed journalists broke records for note taking and, at the back of the court, Constance Radcliffe hid a secret smile behind her expensive silk scarf.

Momentarily lost for words, the startling admission had completely wrong-footed J.D. Cassels KC and he paused long enough for the wily old Judge to complete his notes.

Warning Josie that she was still under oath, Sir Ernest asked the bewildered King's Counsel if he wished to continue questioning the witness. After further preamble, Cassels sat down, handed over to Sir Travers Humphries and watched Josie return to the dock.

The clerk called Detective Inspector Yandell. Shoes polished, good conduct medal pinned to his regulation uniform jacket and helmet under his left arm, he marched across the courtroom, stumbling over the extended leg of a solicitor's clerk on his way to give evidence. Raising the Bible in his right hand, he solemnly took the oath, adjusted his dress uniform belt and tie, smoothed his well-greased hair and presented himself ready for his second appearance in the high profile trial.

Asked by counsel if O'Dare could be described as a clever criminal, he cleared his throat: 'Yes. Whilst I do not know what her social standard was in respect of the upper portion of her Park Street premises, the lower portion was nothing more than a thieves' kitchen travelled around a Daimler car driven by a convicted thief and brothel-keeper.' Pressed further he declared: 'Miss O'Dare had acquired at least £20,000 from her adventures in London, only the sum of £1825 obtained by her from Mr. Docker, was alone obtained by fraudulent representation. There was no evidence to support any suggestion against him (Docker) and nothing to show that he was on good terms with O'Dare.'

Confirming Davis as 'an exceedingly clever forger without equal in the country and sometimes known as the Captain', he also had evidence to show the witness was really Theresa Agnes Skyrme, born at Holmer Cottage, Wellington in Herefordshire.

'About twelve years ago, she left the family home and took her mother and sister to live at Barton Manor in Hereford city, a place said to be not as pretentious as the name might imply. There she associated with undesirable companions until, early in 1922, she left for London where she associated with convicted thieves eventually becoming a moneylender's agent.'

His evidence over for the day, Yandell waited for permission to step down and left the witness box.

After briefly conferring with Sir Travers Humphries, Josie's counsel Laurence Vine asked permission from the Judge to call William Poole, Miss O'Dare's former chauffeur, to substantiate that his client went in fear of Davis. The Recorder agreed and the court waited for the appearance of the so-called brothel keeper; he turned out to be a well-dressed middle-aged man who quietly swore to tell the truth, the whole truth and nothing but the truth and looked across at his former employer.

Referring to the night of the alleged conspiracy Poole said: 'At eleven o'clock at night, Davis came to Park Street and demanded to see Miss O'Dare. I called out to her and, when she came down from her bedroom, Davis flew at her and smacked her face saying: 'I will murder you if you do not do as I tell you'. He flourished a revolver and threatened me when I interfered.'

Cross-examined by Edward Peregrine, counsel for Davis, Poole acknowledged that he did have suspicions that certain cheques were being forged but was not party to any criminal acts. New Scotland Yard can confirm this.

Asked if Miss O'Dare was a good employer, Poole explained: 'Fairly satisfactory. I was a mere general servant and did practically everything in the house. I also lent her £2400, which I had expected to get it back but I now have nothing left. I was not charmed by her but felt sorry for her but soon realised that Miss O'Dare was a lady who never showed irritation in any shape or form.'

After he stood down, Mr Vine told the court: 'Davis was the boss of the show and his client, Miss O'Dare had first met him when she was young girl at the May Fair in Hereford. She bumped into him again when she was selling roses and flags near a hotel in High Town and he was wearing the military uniform. They became acquainted and for some time walked out together. Afterwards he started on his career of forgery and, as they say, he has never looked back.'

Further discussion regarding the antecedence of Davis and his associates ended the day's session and the Judge adjourned the court for the weekend. Miss O'Dare would undergo further questioning by both the prosecution and the defence, on Monday morning.

It was back to Holloway for the tired adventuress; Mavis was waiting to collect her and she made an effort to enjoy the ride through North London. Asked how it went, Josie replied: 'I suppose it went well so far but Mr. Vine tells me tomorrow could be a long and difficult day, the prosecution will keep on at me and I can expect a hard time from George's legal team, particularly Roland Oliver, KC. They say he is a bit of stickler and my legal lot have stressed that whatever I do, I must not lose my head or he will have it off. So, as me old Gran from Canon Pyon would say, it's up the wooden hill early tonight me girl.'

'Not before you've had a proper meal,' Mavis advised. 'Cook has kept you a warm a plateful to help keep your pecker up. No-one will bother you tonight, the night staff will make sure of that, they all know what you are going through, even the hard nuts. I've seen a good few come a cropper trying to be too clever in court; these lawyer chaps can be a shifty bunch.'

'You don't have to tell me that. Between you and me, when it comes to women and greed, there have been a good few rich suckers, lawyers or not, that have fallen into my trap.'

As she stepped from the van onto the cobbled prison courtyard, she heard the old familiar raised voices of welcome as the double doors creaked open to receive her.

'Let's get you checked back; someone will bring you supper and its bob's yer uncle for a quiet night in.'

Josie grinned: 'It's like coming home to the family, Mavis.'

'Of course it is dear, good girl or bad, that's what we're here for until the jury decides. Now when you've taken off your best dress we can hang it up and brush it down ready for Monday but for now tuck that locket away before anyone sees it otherwise I'm for the bloody high jump.'

CHAPTER SIXTEEN

Dawn brought a drizzle of a wet Monday to London, leaving Holloway prison draped in a murky mist. The familiar sound of distant foghorns from laden Thames barges heading for the estuary and the coastal waters of Essex, rarely kept prisoners from sleep, but not Josephine O'Dare. She tossed and turned for most of the night, her usually clear head filled with questions, questions and more questions from bewigged, pinstriped, puffed out men determined to bring her down.

Despite her worries, she had a relaxing weekend and on Saturday night she performed a light-hearted number or two from the music hall. To please the Chaplain, she went to chapel on Sunday morning; after lunch Lady Mary Carter and her actress friend Sybil Thorndike, came to apologise for not being at the final day of the trial; they had tickets for the All England Lawn Tennis Championships at Wimbledon and later in the week they were off to Kennington Oval to watch New Zealand on their first international cricket tour.

However, this morning she had the jitters; her sleepless night had not helped her stay calm. It was almost five am and time for night staff to boost up the hot water system in the communal showers before going off duty at six am. Aware of Josie's final court appearance, the night officer checked out the ablution room, handed her a large, striped prison towel and, left to herself, she lingered under the hot shower for more than the regulation three minutes. Vigorously towelling herself, she took advantage of a rare moment of silence and quietly contemplated her future.

Hurriedly reminded by her escort that it was time for the 'rise and shine' call and the race for first place in the shower queue, she wrapped herself in her towel and slipped silently into her cell before the day staff came on duty.

Feeling more relaxed, she dressed in freshly laundered underwear and her prison uniform and she joined the noisy line in the refectory for ham, eggs, toast, marmalade and coffee, ordered on her account the night before. She also ordered a batch of hot sausages for the table she shared with some of her mates and, determined not to show her true feelings, she tucked in and enjoyed the last decent breakfast for some time. Back in her cell, Mavis brushed up her clothes for court and, apart from her make-up, she was ready for the ride to Central Criminal Court.

It was the same routine drive through Highbury and Islington but this time she was tenser than ever as the Black Maria approached the back entrance to the Old Bailey.

She caught a brief glimpse of the Scales of Justice balanced above the old building and quietly hoped they would fall in her favour. Mavis formally handed her charge to the court custody officer and gave Josie a brief, stiff upper lip hug before she left. Today she faced cross-examinations from both the prosecution and defence counsels and needed to be on her guard. Her own man, Lawrence Vane, was waiting to brief her on her statement warning her that although she had pleaded guilty to the charges against her, Sir Travers Humphrey for the prosecution, was unlikely to let her completely off the hook. He also warned her that Roland Oliver, Morton's counsel, was a clever bastard with words but if he edged towards character assassination, then Sir Ernest would step in.

When Josie stepped into the dock, her co-defendants were ready and waiting for her and she shivered in anticipation of what was to come. Looking around for just a hint of support, she found it in a short-lived smile from her sister seated in the public gallery and, surprisingly, a fleeting glance at Francine, this time alone in the clergy box.

She was about to turn away and face the bench when she noticed Kristy Potts dressed in her Salvation Army uniform, complete with bonnet and bow. It was a poignant moment; they had not seen or heard from each other since her acquittal and Josie was delighted to see her again, whatever the circumstances. Adjusting the neckline of her dress enough to expose a little more of her cleavage, she turned and looked directly at the eager gentlemen of the press and smiled 'you ain't seen nothing yet chaps'.

As if by magic, Sir Ernest Wilde appeared and the clerk called in the jury; it was curtain up for the second act of the Crown versus the Hereford adventuress. Reminded by the Judge that she was still under oath she stoically faced up to Mr. Cassels, KC. After corroborating the facts outlined by Mr.

Cassels, Sir Ernest reminded her that 'she was not obliged to give evidence unless she desired to do so and, having already pleaded guilty in a lower court, she must not assume her evidence for the prosecution would in any way help her when he (Sir Ernest) passed sentence'.

Acknowledging the warning, Josie prepared for further questioning, this time by Sir Travers Humphries for the prosecution; he asked her about her relationship with George Davis. 'I lost touch with him until three years ago when he was living in Victoria and I was residing at 58 Park Street, Mayfair. Two years later, he began writing libellous articles about me in a Scottish newspaper and when I went to his address in Highbury to protest, the articles ceased.'

Admitting to knowing Edwin Docker very well and, from time to time, receiving amounts of money from him, she went on to explain the business of his will.

'When Edwin died in April, Morton suggested, in the presence of witnesses, the making of a new will in my favour. I told him perhaps Mr. Docker had already left me something but he said I was not to be silly. He persuaded me we should prepare a new will, purporting to be Edwin Docker's leaving me £15000 and George Davis should be the forger.'

Afterwards, I met Mr. Davis at Kettners Restaurant in Soho to give him a will form and a letter written to me from Mr. Docker. I suggested it should be used to copy his signature and told him to get on with it. The following day he called Park Street with Mr. Docker's signature; Morton and a Miss Holbrook, who was not a willing party, signed and witnessed it. The will was dated 29th January 1926 at the Centaur Club, St. James, Piccadilly and stated 'I give and bequeath to Miss Josephine O'Dare the sum of £15000 as a token of the deepest esteem I hold for her and her many kindnesses. The remainder of my estate, I bequeath to my two sons, to be equally divided'.

Sir Humphrey told the court: 'Following Mr. Docker's demise, O'Dare consulted a solicitor in an attempt to prove the will. There were, however, some difficulties, one being that on April 21st, nine days before his death, Edwin Docker made a will leaving his entire estate, valued at £25000, to his family. In consequence, the forged will fell.'

Continuing his condemnation of Josie, counsel suggested: 'Despite the problems over the forged will, Miss O'Dare had not been idle and on the strength of it arranged to borrow some £500 in cash from a moneylender in expectation of her forthcoming inheritance. The money was used in part to meet her mounting bills and the remainder was sidelined for a proposed scam to flood outer London banks with forged cheques. It is also alleged she conspired with Davis to sign a cheque for £600 purporting to come from Viscount Curzon, a former acquaintance of the witness. She had arranged for it to be presented to his bank but it was held up pending enquiries and needless to say was not cashed.'

Picking up from where his co-prosecutor left off, Mr. Cassels adjusted his slightly skewed wig, gripped the lapels of his gown and addressed the court: 'I submit my Lord that in the matter of Edward Docker, to a large extent the case against Davis rests on the evidence of Miss O'Dare who has admitted to being an accomplice in the transaction. Whilst it might be dangerous to convict on the evidence of the accomplice, there is other evidence of corroboration, especially of the man Poole.'

Turning to the dock, he also pointed out: 'In February 1926, Davis did an extraordinary thing. He arranged with the London editor of the 'Glasgow Weekly Record' to sell articles featuring the life of this witness. A synopsis headed 'The Story of Josephine's Life' recalled her adventures, criminalities, her impressions of society and so on. A further feature told 'How I drugged the Prince and secured his cheque book'.'

A titter of amusement drifted through the courtroom but the witness continued to play at looking bored and, with an exaggerated muffled yawn, she put her head in her hands as counsel droned on.

Although Cassels was a bright, intelligent prosecuting lawyer, his verbal delivery was lacking in action or emotion. Nevertheless, when it came to cross examination of a witness turned King's Evidence, he was keener than most.

Josie was not the only one looking bored, so was the Judge. He was almost asleep when she stifled a yawn and, with a pleading smile, looked at him for support. It worked.

Pulling himself together, Sir Ernest addressed counsel: 'The witness has been questioned for long enough. To rid the court, Miss O'Dare and indeed myself of the soporific atmosphere I suggest we adjourn for lunch and get on with cross examining the witness this afternoon.'

That said Sir Ernest Wilde, swiftly followed by his clerk, made a hasty exit and headed to the Judges' Chamber to enjoy a fine lunch in the palatial dining room. As the door closed behind him, the jury officer escorted his charges into the jury room for a not-so-lavish meal.

Grouped on the steps of the Bailey, legal eagles and court officials reviewed the morning's manoeuvres as they stretched their legs and limbered up for an hour or two of critical analysis on the morning session. Fully aware that Sir Ernest was prone to a wine induced catnap before returning to the bench, they made the most of the adjournment. Other groups, keen to escape from the claustrophobic atmosphere of the public gallery, congregated in the nearby Lyons Corner House for a bit of hot gossip.

One shady looking meeting of criminal minds turned out to be associates of George Davis and were loudly cursing 'that cow of a woman O'Dare for grassing him up'.

Sitting alone at a table in the window eating a Chelsea bun and nursing a cup of tea, Fanny Skyrme thoughtfully contemplated the outcome for her sister. When she saw and heard the conclave of crooks that had already made their noisy mark in the public gallery, she quickly ate the bun, gulped down the tea and beckoned to a passing 'nippy', unsteadily juggling a loaded tea tray.

After paying the bill at the glass-fronted booth, she covered her head with a rough scarf and, unable to take much more of the loud and provocative gossiping, slipped quietly out into the street where she settled for the safety of a nearby tram shelter. A few minutes later, a pleasant young woman in Salvation Army uniform unexpectedly joined her.

Meanwhile back in the holding cell at the Central Criminal Court, her sister delighted in yet another good lunch, this time delivered by a courier from Harrods. Tucking into the delicacies, including fresh Herefordshire strawberries, she smiled at the card in the bottom of the basket. The inscription read 'there is no place like home, be it Hereford, London or even Shanghai. Enjoy'.

Constance was never far from Harrods; the lunch adjournment over, Josie tucked the card under her sleeve. It went unnoticed by the officer as he helped her up the steps leading to the dock; his hawk-like eyes focused on her cleavage and he blushed to maiden pink when she caught his wandering eye.

Standing in the dock, she scanned the VIP box for her lunchtime benefactor but she was not there. Instead two over-dressed 'toffs' more suited to the late Oscar Wilde's trial than hers sat in her place. Acknowledging Josie with a brief wave, she knew the gift had come from Lady Constance; Harrods Food Hall was her playground and the witty comment on the card confirmed this. Just before the afternoon began, she noticed Kristy Potts helping Fanny into her seat in the public gallery but, before she was able to attract her attention, the usher escorted her into the witness box. Reminded by the Recorder that she was still under oath, she calmly faced up to counsel for the prosecution.

Questioning her over allegations about her association with a foreign prince in Nottingham and the other nasty articles about her, she stoutly replied: 'I deny claims that I posed as a youth at the Victoria Hotel in Nottingham or the part I was supposed to have played in doping the Prince, or inducing him to let me purchase racehorses for him by giving me a cheque for £10000. I can assure your Lordship, had he given me an open cheque for £10000, would I be here now? No, I would not.'

Taking the point, Sir Ernest quietly smiled before asking the witness to move on.

'I certainly will, Your Lordship. If there is any person before this court to show that I authorised these articles, where is it? It is nothing but imaginative rubbish and lies from the prisoner in the dock.'

Looking somewhat defeated Mr. Cassels invited Mr. Peregrine, counsel for Adrian Morton to cross-examine Josie. Forewarned by Mavis Buck, her all-knowing prison escort officer, that Mr. Peregrine was a clever bastard with words, Josie cleared her mind and concentrated on his expected attack upon her character.

'Do I understand that you have always been friendly with Davis?'

'Yes. I bear him no animosity whatsoever and never have.'

'Have you always been known as Josephine O'Dare?'

'Not always, my birth name is Skyrme.'

'Have you ever stayed at a Lancaster Gate Hotel with Davis as his wife?' Counsel asked.

Josie emphatically answered: 'No, never.'

'Have you ever lived with this man as his wife?'

'No. But once, when I lived in Hereford, I ran away to a place called Riversdale where Davis was also staying.'

'Have you ever lived in Saville Row, Piccadilly or any other place in the West End as Mrs Louise Millet or as the wife of George Davis?'

Exasperated, Josie was about to say 'Bloody No' when his Lordship intervened from the bench.

'Mr. Peregrine, is this an attack upon character? If so, be warned not to take this much further.'

Counsel paused. 'No, My Lord, it is not. It is to show the relations existing between these two persons, Davis and O'Dare, and I suggest this is all about jealousy.'

Josie angrily retorted: 'That is not so.'

The tension was rising in the courtroom; it was cat and mouse as witness and counsel continued to argue. Warming to his line of questioning, Peregrine persisted: 'Would it be true to say that you number among your friends some forgers?'

Josie rebutted vehemently: 'No, it would not be true.'

'Do you suggest that Davis is a forger?'

'He can forge, yes.'

'Do you know a forger named Guy and have you ever in your life visited Wormwood Scrubs prison?

'I may have done. So what?'

'And did you give the name of Louise Millet?'

'I may have done. So?'

His Lordship intervened again. Mr. Peregrine, if this is not an attack on character, has it anything to do with this case? If so, pray tell where we are heading.'

'Yes, My Lord it does. It is designed to show that, although these cheques may have been forged, the witness had other friends to assist her and she may have applied to them.'

'That is not so, Sir,' Josie said.

The Judge paused and consulted his clerk before ruling: 'If this is an entirely different line of cross-examination and is relevant to the case, you may continue Mr. Peregrine.

'It is m'Lord. I will try again. Did you ever see Guy in Wormwood Scrubs?'

'Yes. He was charged with Davis.'

'So was Guy convicted of forgery?'

'I don't think so,' she replied.

'But you did visit Guy in prison?'

'No. It was Davis I visited.'

'Did you make an application to visit Guy when you were there?'

'I think both.'

'Then the answer to the question would be yes. I ask you again Miss O'Dare. Was Guy convicted of forgery?'

'No. I believe it was over some cheque affair. He is no forger.'

Questioned on the matter of Edwin Docker's generosity, Josie confirmed: 'Mr. Docker had promised me that during his life time he would settle upon me £20000.'

'But when you went to see him at the nursing home is it not so that his relatives refused you permission to talk with him?'

'Not true,' she replied. 'They thought it better not to see him because he was sleeping.'

Unconvinced by the answers, Mr. Peregrine changed tack.

'Now, about the butler, Poole. As I understand it, he has been in your employ for three years. Was he a poor man?'

'He was not a rich man,' Josie answered. 'But he did lend me £2000.'

Sir Ernest raised his eyes. 'A very valuable butler indeed. Have you paid him back?'

'Not yet M'Lord.'

A ripple of laughter echoed through the courtroom. Asked about her relationship with Poole she explained: 'Whenever we had a tiff he usually left my employ; he always came back again and he is still with me. I had borrowed money from and used the loan to pay off moneylenders.'

Satisfied with the butler situation, Mr. Peregrine returned to the estate of Edwin Docker.

'Miss O'Dare we turn again to the forged will. Would you please tell the court just who played the leading part in the whole forgery business?'

'Morton,' she replied.

'Yet it is alleged the important part in this forgery business was played by Davis at your request?'

'Yes.'

'And not one penny of the proceeds of the money obtained under the forged will was received by Davis?'

'No.'

His Lordship intervened again: 'When was Davis to be paid?'

174

'When I had won my case.'

'You mean when you had got the bogus legacy?' the Judge suggested with another wry smile and began writing up his notes.

Ignoring the Judge's quip, Mr. Peregrine looked quizzically at Josie and thoughtfully posed his next question.

'Is it true Davis and Morton threatened to inform Scotland Yard if you did not give them cash from the forged cheques.'

'It is true. They were blackmailing me and threatening me what they would do if I did not go to the bank with the forged cheque.'

'So you say, but if your story is true were you really afraid that they would go to Scotland Yard?'

'Yes, I was afraid of Morton. He did mention the matter before a third party and it would have been foolish to have ignored it, would it not Mr. Peregrine?'

Follow-up questions centred on cash payments she had received from Edwin Docker and, after further formal evidence, Josie returned to the dock.

The courtroom clock was ticking towards the end of day when Sir Irvine Wilde announced: 'We have heard much to digest in this case and it is my opinion that the witness and jury have had enough for one day. If both counsels agree, I intend adjourning proceedings until Wednesday when defence counsel for Morton can begin his cross-examination of the witness.'

'And he has a day's fishing on the Hampshire Teste booked for Tuesday,' Cassels muttered sarcastically to his opposing counsel.

Reminding the jury of their duty not to discuss the case with anyone and to avoid lurking members of the press, Sir Ernest expressed his hope that summing up could begin on Thursday.

It had been a long day for Josie and she was tired. Her mind was in a whirl, her head was aching and, as she journeyed back to Holloway, she longed for the peace and quiet of her prison cell. Although she wanted the trial over and done with, she was looking forward to a day off on Tuesday to relax with her cellmates. Mavis tried to bolster her mood.

'From all accounts you appear to have stood up to that old bastard Peregrine.'

'Appeared is the right word. Underneath all the bravado, I am struggling to survive, just as I always do when the going gets tough. Now I've got one hell of a headache.'

'It's the adrenalin winding down my dear, that's all; a good night's sleep and a free day tomorrow will soon cure that. You've got a couple of visitors booked in for the afternoon and that should cheer you up.'

'How come and who are they?' Josie asked.

'You remember young Kristy Potts, remanded for GBH and acquitted at the Bailey earlier this year; when she was cleared she joined the Salvation Army.'

'Of course I do. We were good pals inside. Funnily enough, she was in court today and it was so nice to see her again, if only from a distance. Is she coming?'

'Yes. When she heard the trial had been adjourned for a day, she applied for a visitor pass to see you and a few of the others still on remand. She's bringing a friend for company.'

'Blimey! That's nice. Let's hope she's not bringing a hymn sheet and tambourine for a revival sing-song.'

Laughing their way into the prison yard, they were still chuckling when the van went through the Gatehouse.

'Must have been a good day in court, Miss,' the cheerful gatekeeper said as he signed them back in.

Pleased to back in Holloway, she grinned and said: 'All I need now is a good supper, a warm bed and sleep, glorious sleep without thinking about an early start tomorrow. I'm back in the family again.'

As she made her way to her room, she felt a collective ripple of feel-good coming from the other cells. Sleeping through the wake-up call, she had missed breakfast but someone had left bread, jam and tea on the table. Rousing herself, she nibbled at her breakfast and waited for the ablution block to empty. Watched from a dignified distance by her corridor officer, she took a long soak in the bath and, lingering in the hot fragrant water, she washed her hair and scrubbed her body until it tingled.

For a short while she drifted back to the hop yards and hills of North Herefordshire and the days of innocence shared with the farmer's boys, by now grown-up with families of their own. Nevertheless, she could not allow herself to dwell on her Wellington days, the May Fair and the awful reasons why she left home with her mother and sister. She was no longer Trixie Skyrme but Josephine O'Dare and, whatever happens, must not lose her grip in court.

176

It was mid-morning when she finally appeared in the exercise yard. The day was warm and sunny and she strolled round the yard before deciding to sit on a part occupied bench.

'Budge up and make room for a little one. I need to rest for a bit before we have a game of softball. You get stiff hanging about in the witness box for days and I need to loosen up before court tomorrow. Anyone up for it?' she invited.

'Bloody hell, you're keen,' said a sporty prisoner from the main wing. 'You're right, though, you do need to flex the muscles for a long session at the Bailey.'

The athletic-looking woman called to the nearest guard: 'Got a bat and ball Miss, we're training for the summer Olympics next year. Did you know that women can take part in athletics for the first time?'

The guard laughed: 'That's next year Tew, in Amsterdam. With your record, you will be lucky if you make it to Berlin in 1936 but keep on with the training.'

'I asked for a bat and ball, not an opinion on my running potential thank you, Miss. Now, are we playing or not? What's it to be Remand versus Lifers or what? Will you be umpiring, Miss? We would not want you knocked over would we teams?' she grinned. Josie captained one team, Tew the other and the game continued until the dinner bell; after the meal she was back in her cell reading about her exploits in some old magazines given to the library by a the Prison Visitor Service. Disturbed by the tinny sound of a loudspeaker calling 'visitors in reception', she quickly pulled herself together.

Splashing her face with water and lightly touching up her make-up, she adjusted her prison clothing and made her way to the remand wing visiting room.

Kristy was waiting at the far end of the open-plan type room with tables and benches for visitors. Watched over by two or three wardresses, the room was light and every effort had been made to make it a comfortable, welcoming environment for families. Small bowls of summer flowers, grown in the prison garden, rested on the ledges of the barred windows and a free refreshment bar, organised by volunteers from prison welfare organisations, was open during visiting hours.

Quietly chatting to her friend, Kristy stood up to introduce Josie her companion. She need not have bothered; she recognised the boot under the long, dark blue Salvation Army skirt and almost shrieked in surprise. Anxious to keep the situation light, Josie whispered: 'Still got that decent boot I bought you, our Fanny. Don't cry for God's sake or you will give the game away, it's been hard enough keeping you and Ma out of this bloody place. When did you two meet up?'

Overwhelmed at seeing Josie, she left it to Kristy to explain.

'In Lyons Corner House during the lunch adjournment yesterday. I was in court for the morning session and when I saw her limping, I remembered you told me about her. I followed her out of the Bailey, caught up with her and we had a chat over a cup of tea.'

Josie could see her sister was puzzled and held her hand.

'Don't worry Fan, I met Kristy inside and we had something in common. Just like our father, her father was bashing her mother about too; she belted him over the head with a heavy chair and was charged with grievous bodily harm. A couple of months ago, she was acquitted at the Bailey, thank God, but her father and brothers threatened to find her so I got in touch with my prisoner visitor to see what she could do to help her.'

Kristy took over: 'When I came out, the Salvation Army found me and mother a couple of rooms at a hostel in Denmark Hill; I play in the band and that helped too. When I read in the papers that your sister was appearing at the Central Criminal Court, I was determined not to let her down.

'She stood by me and I am standing by her and you Fanny. Now I am sure you two have plenty to say to each other so I will find a cup of tea and a couple of other prisoners to chat too. Would you like me to bring you a cup?'

Josie quickly realised Fanny had something on her mind.

'Now what's up our Fanny? It's clear you have something on your mind. Out with it.'

'It's Ma, Trix, she's not good. Her memory is addled, she can't remember who you are and all she talks about is her old stomping grounds in Hereford. I am very worried about her.'

'Are you still coping in Westbourne Park? I feel so helpless in here but you must use the 'rainy day' fund if you need help with her.'

'Yes, I'm managing. Now and again she does recognise me, neighbours sit with her to give me a break and the local doctor is very good with her; I clean the surgery to help pay his bill and we have a tabby tom cat to chase the mice away. She never stops talking to him and he keeps her company when I go out.'

'No need for you to work, Fanny, I left you with enough cash to take care of you both and there's plenty more.'

'But that's your 'rainy day' fund Trix and I'm saving it for when you come out of prison. Anyhow the trial must be costing you a small fortune.'

'That's taken care of. I pleaded guilty to the Docker conspiracy, turned King's Evidence and my court costs are paid by the Crown and other charges shelved. I expect to go down for my part in the conspiracy. Outstanding charges for forgery, bank frauds, theft and burglary are down to George and the rest of his gang and they have pleaded not guilty.

'The prosecution can't pin any of that on to me and although I might have to do two or three years, I reckon George will do at least thirteen years hard labour.'

Shaken at the news, Fanny was more worried about future threats to her sister after the trial.

'Yes, but what happens to you when he gets out? Knowing him, he will be after you like a dog after a bitch.'

'He always was our Fanny, but like all the rest of 'em, he never got as much of a sniff of the real thing.'

The two sisters laughed and chatted until Kristy came back.

'How are you two doing? It will soon be time to go and Josie needs a quiet rest of the day and a good night's sleep before she goes to court tomorrow. Fanny and I will sort out a few family matters over a cup of tea on the way home, so please don't worry. If things get difficult at home, I can arrange for a couple of women from Denmark Hill to help out with your mother until we have a bed in our nursing home. Until then your mother can live with us at the hostel.'

Josie was apprehensive and concerned for her sister's well-being but Kristy soon reassured her.

'Fanny has a big living cum bedroom, a tiny kitchen with cooking facilities and a shared bathroom on the landing. She will be able to see your mother every day; I have already put in a word at Headquarters and they will place her on the standby list.'

Fanny almost broke down in tears and Josie gave her a hug. 'It's for the best Fan and a very kind and generous offer. Thank you, Kristy.'

'Yes, Josie, but your generous donation to our cause when I was acquitted went down well at Denmark Hill and we don't forget. I expect to see you in court tomorrow but I doubt it will do you any good Fanny but I will keep in touch over plans for your mother.'

Taking Fanny's arm and assuring Josie all will be well, she scurried towards the exit, bonnet ribbons flowing and issuing blessings all round as she passed through the corridor to the exit.

After supper, Josie played a game or two of rummy with a couple of warders, and then it was lock-up for the night. Before lights out, she made herself a mug of cocoa, thought about her mother and wondered if she would ever see her again. Tomorrow is another day.

CHAPTER SEVENTEEN

It definitely was. Having slept quite well, Josie took an early morning shower before dressing for breakfast. She toyed with her food, passing much of it to her table companions and returned to her cell to change for the court. Dressing less provocatively, she applied a simple covering of make-up to her clearly-worried face. She didn't quite know why she had made changes to her usual appearance and, for some reason, she had also decided to hand in her silver locket and chain for safe keeping in her personal effects locker.

Accepting it could be her final appearance at the Bailey, she waved goodbye to her closest prison chums and made her way to the waiting area to meet up with Mavis, but Mavis Buck was not around. The wardress in charge explained that the remand unit governor had insisted on changing the rota and taken Mavis off escort duty. Josie was not happy with her replacement, a virtual newcomer from the long-term wing and, from that moment on, the day went pear-shaped.

Shocked and angry, Josie yelled at her new escort: 'Why the bloody hell has she done that?'

'Don't ask me. I didn't ask for escort duties. I'm supposed to be supervising the sewing brigade in the work section, not taking guilty pleas for sentencing.'

'Why not?' Josie asked.

'Because when they come back weeping and wailing, they are banged up on suicide watch until they calm down, that's what. As I always say, do the crime, do the punishment, so there you are?' If there was such a moment of explosive silence, Josie managed to control it but the blue touch paper was smoking. Her pale face deepened to an angry flush and, in three strides of her laced-up, booted feet, she pushed her way through the small group of bystanders and reached out for the offending officer.

'If I want a poxy opinion on crime and punishment, I will ask the bloody Lord Chancellor not you,' she said, poking the escort towards the door. 'Now will one of you call for the silly cow who made this stupid decision and ask her to come and sort it out, otherwise neither I nor anyone else will be going to the Bailey today.'

Josie sat down on a chair and, catching her breath, she announced: 'I haven't even been sentenced yet so give me a bit of respect until I have. And, as for suicide watch, you can shove that idea up your snooty hooter.'

A muffled titter brought a hint of a smile to the speechless group huddled in the reception area. In the adjacent toilet block, the cleaner removed her ear from the flimsy wall and headed for the exercise yard to break the news of Josie's semi-mutiny to any prisoners hanging around. In her eagerness to make haste, she dropped her bucket and mop and, giving the game away, she had been eavesdropping on the whole charade. News of the one-woman mutiny whipped through the wing and, among the loud cheers, a lone voice yelled: 'Go for it O'Dare. See you when you get back.'

The collective laughter of the heavy mob in the penal wing said it all but, despite her colourful language, the remand governor would not be over-ruled and bundled both prisoner and escort into the waiting Paddy wagon.

With a derisive wave, she sarcastically called out: 'See you later, at least one of you.'

When the van passed through the Gatehouse, she looked through her barred window to see Mavis giving her a sign of encouragement but the usually friendly gatekeeper was missing.

With Mavis no longer on board, there was an eerie silence inside the prison van. There was little supportive chatter from her companions, just an occasional sigh from the bored, tight-lipped escort, keen to get back to her cushy number in the sewing room.

Apart from wanting to pee, Josie cared little for her escort's attitude and, in a deliberate attempt to annoy her, asked if she could relieve herself in the piss-pot. She could have hung on until she reached the detained cell but, much to the officer's disgust she lifted her skirts, peed into the bucket and, to make a final point, kicked it over. Josie mockingly apologised and wished her a stinking return trip to Holloway.

The rear yard at the Old Bailey was flooded with early morning sunshine and, once again, the golden Scales of Justice caught her eye, but this time she imagined them tilted against her.

The custody officer was waiting to receive her.

'Glad you're on time, O'Dare. His Lordship hopes to sum up and sentence today which means an early start for the court.'

Looking around he was surprised not to see Mavis.

'Where is Officer Buck? I thought she'd be here for the finale. Is she not coming today?'

'No. They have kicked her off the run and replaced her with the po-faced, jumped up cow, hanging onto my coat tails. I can't seem to shake her off.'

'Well, chin-up, Miss, it won't be long now. It could be the start of your new life!'

'Yes, and it could be the start of bloody awful one if I go down,' Josie said as he locked her in the holding cell.

'Oh yes. I'm to remind you that if you are to be sentenced today, duty Matron must sit with you at all times. I know you won't like it, but rules are rules Miss, so don't give her a hard time, she's only doing her job. Anyway, who knows what will happen? Good luck.'

The elderly uniformed Matron took over and tried to make light conversation but Josie wasn't keen; nevertheless, she tried to keep up with the chitchat and was relieved when she heard her name called. On cue, both women stood up, adjusted their very different outfits and waited for the custody officer to unlock the cell. At the bottom of the staircase leading to the dock, Josie tried to shake off her escort but Matron was having none of it.

'I have to come with you just in case you faint or something dear,' Matron explained. Josie laughed nervously.

'Faint! Trixie Skyrme faint at adversity. Hereford girls are made of stronger stuff, Matron.'

Yet she knew she was on a sticky wicket and nervously waited for the Judge and his clerk to appear and the jury be called.

Today, it was a subdued courtroom; same old faces, same old scene but much quieter and it felt as if the stage was set for an inquest rather than a high profile trial and she imagined a feeling of pity and excitement as she waited for the court to settle down. Alongside her, part-hidden behind the screen, George Davis grinned and, before the guard could restrain him, poked his head around the corner and winked the 'special girl' wink she knew so well.

Before coming into court, counsel had warned her she could expect a morning of intense questioning on her relationship with George, from his counsel Albert Davis as well as Roland Oliver, counsel for Adrian Morton. She could also expect further cross-examination from Edwin Docker's family solicitor, but not necessarily in that order.

After a short delay, she was shepherded to the witness box by a court usher, the sturdy Matron remaining at the rear of the dock with the custody officer. A further announcement from the court clerk that a juryman was feeling unwell and proceedings were to be delayed, gave the star witness an opportunity to seek out a friendly face or two, and she did.

Francine and her father sat in the clergy pews; Fanny and Kristy huddled together in the corner of the public gallery amid the gossip-mongering associates of George Davis; and the VIP seats overflowed with the high and the mighty of Mayfair society, eager to witness her downfall.

Just as the jury was about to be called, the door at the rear of the court was noisily pushed open by a uniformed usher and, to Josie's utter surprise, a slightly over-dressed Constance, wearing a stout rather than stylish hat to shield her face, took her place in the VIP box.

She was accompanied by pseudo socialite, the Honourable Nicholas J. Evans, bon viveur and party organiser and his chum, Sir Michael Cottering, more often seen accompanying her to the opera, ballet and the occasional Henry Wood concert at the Queen's Hall; not the Central Criminal Court.

It was a comic moment in the sombre atmosphere of the Old Bailey. The two foppish gents, one exceptionally tall, dressed in a lemon and grey plus four suit, sporting a red, white and blue cravat; the other, an eccentric Professor of Latin Literature and Music from Cambridge University, more known for his obsession with Antonio Vivaldi. Both gentlemen were prolonging the proceedings even further until his Lordship insisted they settle down or leave the VIP enclosure.

It was more restoration comedy than serious crime proceedings and, like the rest of the court, Josie appreciated the light relief they had brought to the gloomy atmosphere. During the unexpected chaos, she also noted the carefully concealed nod of recognition from Lady Constance.

The humorous buzz ended when Sir Ernest Wilde reminded her yet again that she was under oath and Albert Davis prepared for cross-examination.

Explaining he was unrelated to his client, he pressed ahead with his questioning. Confirming she had known his client for seven years, he asked her: 'It is a fact that you lived with my client as his mistress?'

'Never,' she replied and the game was set.

'Did you ever live with him?'

'No, I did not.'

'I suggest you did, at Hereford,' counsel insisted.

'I went away with him but never lived with him.'

'I suggest you did live with him at Riversdale in Hereford?'

'I stayed there but never lived with him.'

'Not even as Mr. and Mrs. Houghton?'

'I may have called myself Houghton at sometime but I never lived with George Davis.'

'But did he ever call himself Mr. Houghton?'

'He may have. But I am not sure; it was such a long time ago.'

'Did you stay with him at the Lancaster Gate Hotel in London?'

'I do not remember.'

Undeterred by her controlled responses, Albert Davis reviewed his notes and changed direction.

'For sometime before the affair of Mr. Docker's will, you say you had not seen him.'

'That is correct. I did not see him for a long time.'

'And it was only through some newspaper articles that you were able to ascertain his address?'

'That is quite right. I have already explained this.'

'And these articles appeared in the 'Weekly Record of Glasgow'?'

'Yes, and they were absolute lies and that is the reason why I sought him out.'

'In one article he was not very kind to you.'

'Most unkind I would say,' she replied with some irritation.

Pausing to review his notes again counsel suggested: 'In those articles he described you as a decoy for wealthy pigeons on the social scene?'

'Yes.'

'And was that true?'

'It is not and I intend suing him and the newspaper for libel.'

Albert Davis paused again and adjusted his reading glasses.

'Miss O'Dare, from what I am reading I suggest, at the time of the will, you did not know where Davis was and his address was given to you subsequent to the fabrication of Edwin Docker's last will and testament?'

'No, it was before my arrest. I eventually found he was living in Highbury in North London; he was an Arsenal supporter and he had found rooms near the ground. I went to him to complain about the articles. At the time, my relations with the accused were not friendly and, although he had some knowledge of the will, he was not present at any meetings with Adrian Morton.'

Vigorously refuting the prosecutor's suggestion that Davis had not the foggiest idea who Edwin Docker was, she confirmed: 'None of the money raised from the will went to Davis but he received £70 for forging the will.'

'But he was not promised anything at the time,' counsel insisted.

'Yes he was. Two or three days after he made out the will he asked me what his share might be.'

'And what did you reply?'

'I asked him if he would be satisfied with £2000 but he thought he was worth a little more. I told him it was a very fair figure and he said he would leave it to me. I gave some money to Morton but not to Davis and, although I had thought about bringing in a third party to forge the will, I am absolutely resolute that George was the man who did it.'

Leaning on the brass rail on the front of the dock, both defendants looked accusingly at each other and then at Josie, each shrugging to come to terms with her betrayal. In one last push to break her evidence down, Albert Davis put it to her: 'It is my contention that your evidence against my client is a tissue of lies from start to finish.'

'I do not see why I should lie against Mr. Davis.'

'And that you have given this evidence out of spite,' he added.

'Not at all. Why should I?'

'Because my client refused to have anything to do with you?'

'That's not true. He wanted me romantically but I have never wanted him. Quite frankly Mr. Davis, he wasn't at all my type.'

Realising that there was little chance of breaking her down, counsel shrugged his shoulders, stuffed his paper work into a rather shabby Gladstone bag case and snapped it shut.

'No rebuttal Mr. Cassels. Have you finished with the witness?' Sir Ernest Irvine asked.

'I fear so m'Lud,' he replied and despairingly sat down.

Satisfied the cross-examination was over and believing the witness needed a break before the next confrontation, Sir Ernest called for a thirty minute recess. Josie returned to the quiet of her below stairs cell and prepared herself for further questioning from Eric Sachs, counsel for Adrian Morton.

Speculation was rife in the marbled corridors leading from number one court. The public gallery emptied into the main foyer for a quick smoke and gossip but Fanny and Kristy kept their distance and settled for a small bench part hidden by a pillar supporting the balcony.

The short break from proceedings was just what they needed and allowed little time for finding refreshments but Kristy, like all good Salvationists, was prepared. Her serviceable shoulder bag, normally used for sheet music, hymn sheets and copies of the 'War Cry', contained a packed lunch and a well-used thermos flask.

Handing out a few rich tea biscuits, she poured hot, milky, camp coffee into small tin cups and, for a brief moment, Fanny seemed to relax. So much so that she was able to laugh out loud at the two theatrically dressed gentlemen inviting the 'riff-raff' to make way for Lady Constance, on route to the Ladies Cloakroom. As she passed below the balcony, she glanced at the two women and nodded towards Fanny and Kristy. A surprised Kristy asked: 'Who on earth is that. Do you know her and what is she doing here with those peculiar gents?'

'I'm not sure. I think I have seen a picture of her somewhere, perhaps in one of my sister's magazines.'

'But how would she know you?'

'No idea, Kristy. She may have something to do with the case. Best we go to the cloakroom and then to our seats.'

The unexpected strange encounter had disturbed Fanny and she was left thinking about the part the well-to-do woman might have played in Josie's society life. A slight skirmish between an usher and the melee scrambling their way into the public seating was silenced by the announcement that proceedings were about to commence. Legal eagles headed for the courtroom, smokers extinguished cigars and cigarettes in the nearest sand buckets and, in the last minute dash for the gents, fly buttons were adjusted on the run.

Ten minutes later Josie was back in the witness box, this time facing Mr. Roland Oliver, counsel for Adrian Morton. He began his cross-examination by asking her: 'Was the forged will your first venture into crime?'

'Yes, it was my first,' she confidently replied.

'And you are asking the jury to believe that it was the defendant Morton who tempted you into it?'

'Yes.'

'And you are to be pitied and he is to blame?'

She looked him in the eye and thought carefully before answering: 'No, I am not asking for that because I am equally guilty but it was his suggestion. He was at the police court but I cannot recall if he was witness for the prosecution or the defence. In any case, he has told an awful lot of lies.'

Roland Oliver carefully phrased the next question.

'Miss O'Dare, do you consider yourself to be a very clever criminal?'

Lowering her eyes, she faced the Judge and coyly answered: 'I'm very much afraid I shall never be a clever criminal, my Lord.'

A collective snigger burst from the public gallery; George Davis leaned back in his chair, looked to the heavens and then stared hard at the witness and alone in the public gallery said it all: 'Can't say fairer than that George can she; you said she was bloody useless most of the time.'

The interruption triggered hoots of laughter and almost threw Mr. Oliver's questioning off course. Josie shrugged her shoulders, waited for the next question and grinned at the amused press gallery.

Irritated by the disturbance, Sir Ernest brought his mallet down and ordered the anonymous speaker to stand up. At least ten rough looking men responded, causing even more loose laughter and His Lordship was forced to address the entire public gallery.

'This is a court of law, not a back street entertainment for the lower classes. Any more interruptions of this nature and I shall hear the rest of the case in closed court. Are you ready to carry on Mr. Oliver?'

'Indeed I am m'Lud,' and obsessively shuffling his paper work into a neat pile, turned to Josie.

'Now where were we Miss O'Dare?'

'I don't know where you are, Sir, but I'm in the witness box at the Bailey and I have just told the court that I am not a clever criminal.'

Ignoring her flippant answer, he pointed directly at her.

'So you say and under oath too. Nevertheless you have pleaded guilty to a good many crimes, have you not?'

'No, I have not but I have pleaded guilty to many of which I was not really guilty,' she replied.

Turning the pages of his notes again and again, counsel tried a different route to the truth.

'I want you to clearly understand what I am suggesting too. I am suggesting you are a criminal and a liar upon oath and I intend to enlighten the court of these facts.'

What until now had a rustle of interest in the court was blowing into a storm of a story but Josie took it all in her stride. Turning to face the VIP enclosure, she caught the amused expression of Lady Constance, eyes wide open, nudging her two gentleman friends. Josie tried not to catch her eye as she waited for counsel to continue.

'At previous cases against you, including bankruptcy, did you not claim to have been born in Shanghai and that your father, an Irish peer was connected with banking.'

'That was absolutely true.'

'Is it though? In a previous interview did you not state you were born there and your father sent you to Ireland when you were three years old?'

'Yes, I was sent to school in Ireland and lived with an aunt but, when I was old enough, I went back to China to work for him. From time to time I returned to the land of unhappy memories but eventually settled in England when he died about ten years ago.'

Feigning utter amazement and disbelief counsel suggested. 'Really, I suggest that the only thing you knew about Ireland was your grandmother's name O'Reilly and for the past eight years you have certainly lived the life of Riley.'

Smirking at his own joke and then at the jury, he said: 'I suggest it is a pack of lies and you are the daughter of a farm labourer, John Skyrme, and born in the village of Wellington, in North Herefordshire?'

'That is not so Mr. Oliver.'

Holding up a sheet of paper, counsel replied: 'Oh, isn't it. According to the birth certificate I have in my hand, your real name is Theresa Agnes Skyrme and you were born in 1899 at Holmer Cottage, Wellington in the county of Herefordshire.'

'That is not so. Mrs. Skyrme was actually my aunt, she took me with her to England where she met Mr. Skyrme and they looked after us as family but he was very cruel to us.'

'Well if that's not a cock and bull story then pray tell me what is? However, shall I move on. Were you called Trixie Skyrme and until 1921 you lived on your own?'

'No. I have always had a chaperone.'

Her answer brought even more laughter from the upper gallery and another warning from Sir Ernest: 'Cross-examination is a severe enough ordeal for the witness to face, without having people laughing at her. Any more interruptions and I will instruct the usher to remove the offenders; now can we continue?'

Confirming she had lived in London in comfort but not in luxury since 1921 in her new persona Josephine O'Dare, she also agreed she occasionally entertained her guests at Berkeley's, the Ritz and Claridge's as well as at her Mayfair home. Roland Oliver smiled.

'And very nice people came to see you?'

'Yes they did, some of the nicest people in England.'

'Absolutely respectable people knew you?'

Josie looked towards the VIP seats. 'Absolutely! It has never been disreputable to know me Mr. Oliver and I can assure you of that. I have entertained peers of the realm and their ladies, a theatrical knight or two, actors, fashion models and successful businessmen. I was often seen riding in Rotten Row and have occasionally visited Monte Carlo.'

'So we are led to believe, but what about your household and income? Tell us about that.'

'Now let me see if I can remember, Mr. Oliver. As you very well know I have been away for some time but as I recall I had a very adaptable butler, three competent servants and a very loyal housekeeper; my foster-mother Mrs. Skyrme lived with us too, but I was never extravagant.'

'Really! And how were you able to keep up with the expense and maintenance of such a large property in Belgravia as well as supporting such a large household?' counsel asked.

'I was receiving an allowance of £2000 per year.'

'Who from?.'

'I am unable to say but if his Lordship wishes I will write it down for him.'

Interrupting the intense dialogue Sir Ernest asked. 'Is this relevant Mr Oliver?'

'It is m'Lud. My colleague Mr. Sachs will be pressing the point this afternoon.'

'Then I think it's time to adjourn for lunch and when Mr. Sachs has finished with this witness I hope to deliver a speedy summing up, prior to sentencing. If all goes well today, Davis and Morton will be put to the jury tomorrow and remain in custody until the verdict is returned.'

After the hectic morning session, Fanny and Kristy needed a breath of fresh air and a few minutes of peace and quiet. St. Paul's Cathedral was a short stroll away but with Fanny handicapped by her foot it took a bit longer. In the calm surroundings of the Cathedral graveyard, the two friends enjoyed a simple picnic and discussed the morning session.

'All those questions and answers and you don't know what to believe; it must be especially hard for you Fanny?'

'It is, but she's my little sister and I know her so well. Whatever she might or might not have done she's family and I will always be there for just as she always was for Ma and me. Ever since I can remember, she promised us she would look out us, find us somewhere to live together and get me a proper fitted boot; she kept her word. She brought the money in and without it Ma would be in an early grave and me a poor, lonely cripple for the rest of my life.

'My sister gave my life back to me, I don't care how she did it, but she did. She always said that God had given her a clever brain and a big personality and she knew how to use them. Every day I thank him for it.'

'And you must go on believing that Fanny. Whatever happens today you and your Ma will be safe, I will make sure of that. Remember Fanny, your sister changed my life too.'

In the distance Big Ben chimed the three quarter hour. Gathering up the remains of the picnic, Kristy helped Fanny to her feet.

'We'd better get a move on Fanny or we'll be late for court and lose our seats. Shall I go on ahead?'

'Not blooming likely. My sister didn't fork out for this hand-made boot to slow me down; with a bit of help from you Kristy we'll make it with five minutes to spare.'

It took a while for the court to settle down; the Judge was in place and Josie about to be escorted to the witness box when, at the request of the defence, the Judge agreed that Adrian Morton could be recalled to the witness box for further questioning.

Roland asked him: 'In the interests of fairness, would you explain when and how you first met the witness?'

'Yes, Sir. I first met her in June 1924 when she lived in Park Mansions, Knightsbridge. She wanted to buy a car and I sold her an Armstrong-Siddeley Coupe for £500.'

'Did you regard her as a very wealthy woman and did she invite you to her entertainments.'

'She did sir.'

'Did you take up her invitations and, if so, and what sort of people did you meet?'

'Miss O'Dare entertained only the very best class of people, sometimes at home and at the Ritz or Claridge's, but chiefly it was at the Princes Hotel. I never went alone and always took my wife,' he guiltily stressed.

'And when did you first meet George Davis?'

'That was two years later in September 1926.'

'You had never before met him or Miss O'Dare, perhaps in Hereford under different names.'

'No sir. Never.'

'And you have never conspired with them to forge the late Edwin Docker's will?'

'No sir, I might be many things but I am not a forger.'

That said, Roland Oliver confirmed: 'I have no further questions for the witness and ask that Miss O'Dare is recalled for final cross-examination by my learned colleague, Eric Sachs.'

Before he could question the witness, the Judge interrupted proceedings: 'I must remind the witness you are still under oath. As to you Mr. Sachs, I sincerely hope you will not be going over matters already touched upon in three previous cross examinations of this witness.'

'In some part, my Lord? However, I am authorised by my client, the defendant Morton, to challenge the witness over some points and I am obliged to defer to him.'

'And to me, Mr. Sachs, you are also obliged to defer to me and to this court. Now if the witness is ready you may continue.'

Sachs looked at his senior partner who shrugged his shoulders and whispered: 'Best get on with it Eric.'

It was a hesitant start from both parties. Josie seemed paler than ever and counsel, red-faced with irritation at the Judge's rebuke, fiddled with his wedding ring before asking: 'Is it not so that upon your arrest you were described by Scotland Yard as the most skilful and unscrupulous adventuress they had ever set out to capture?'

'They may have done but I assure you I am not.'

'And by using your obvious charm and strength of personality, you were able to wheedle your way into London society intent on draining wealthy young men of every penny as well as their pride?'

'You are mistaking me with someone else Mr. Sachs, I am a much maligned woman with enemies and I refute what you say.'

'You may say that now but the longer story tells it differently. Now, could you confirm for us how and when you first met the man we know as George Davis and how the alleged will came into being?'

Before she could answer Sir Ernest intervened again: 'No, Mr. Sachs. Don't go there. We have heard it all before in a variety of fashions and I ask you again, do not pursue this line of questioning and move on.'

'Noted m'Lud. Now Miss O'Dare, you have heard the witness, Morton, comment on your London life. Do you still insist that you did not live in luxury in Mayfair, a very smart area of London?'

'As I have said before, I do not think so.'

'Yet you purchased an expensive motor car from Morton at a cost of £500, entertained lavishly the very best class of people at your magnificent Park Street home and from all accounts wined and dined strings of guests at the smart establishments and night clubs in Belgravia. Is that not so?'

'On special occasions, that is true. I was a much sought-after hostess.'

'I bet you were,' counsel implied.

'Word of warning Mr. Sachs, I will not tell you again. Now stick to the facts or I shall officially caution you,' Sir Ernest promised.

'M'Lud. Can you tell the court how much were you spending at that time?'

Josie was ready for the question

'Not off the cuff. Can you Mr. Sachs?'

'That's beside the point but did you not say earlier that you had an allowance?'

'Yes. I have already explained this in previous questioning. I have been receiving a mere £2000 per year since I was twenty one but due to my arrest it has since stopped.'

Turning to his senior, Sachs said: 'When my colleague asked you before the lunch adjournment where the allowance came from you declined to answer verbally and offered to write the name down. Did you do so?'

'Yes I did. I wrote the name and address on a slip of paper; he was a gentleman from Birmingham.'

Shuffling through his papers, counsel pulled it out, and examined it closely. 'This is not an address in this country at all.'

'I didn't say it was. The gentleman in question spent a good deal of time overseas but on his return frequently stayed in Birmingham. My allowance was paid to me quarterly in bank notes and sometimes he sent me extra cash by courier or registered post should I need it. He was most kind to me and I was very fond of him.'

Questioned on the extent of her involvement in the conspiracy, Josie directed her eyes at the bench and apologised to the court.

'I did not realise the serious side of what had been done by my co-defendants until I found myself in the police court at Marlborough Street. That is why I have pleaded guilty and I hope that you my Lord and the court will take this into consideration.'

Loud hissing from the public gallery blotted out the ripple of applause from the body of the court forcing Mr. Sachs to end his examination.

Calling for order, Sir Ernest Wilde informed the court: 'In the interests of expediency, I will commence my summing up in this case after a short break after which I shall invite both counsels to present submissions prior to sentence.'

Gathering up his paperwork, he retired to his chamber.

There was some relief in the courtroom, particularly for Josie, now back in the holding cell considering her position. Although a long sentence was a possibility, she had expected to be back on remand wing for another 24 hours, giving her more time to sort out her personal affairs before sentencing. However, with a large part of the afternoon session remaining, it looked doubtful.

Whatever the outcome, Josie knew she could rely on Kristy and the Salvation Army to look out for her mother and sister. Lady Carter would also ensure regular liaison.

It looked even more doubtful when, fifteen minutes later, Sir Ernest reappeared, this time accompanied by two visiting Magistrates; the stipendiary from Marlborough Street Police and the other from West End Central and Josie returned to the dock.

She noticed that Inspector Yandell and his team had slipped quietly into court for the sentencing and it was difficult to hide the fear in Josie's pale face as she twisted her silk handkerchief into a crumpled knot. Gazing down onto the scene below, she was tempted to shout 'bring in the Christians', and she silently thanked God she was not on a murder charge.

When Lady Carter and Sybil appeared in the VIP enclosure, Josie was reassured that should she go down for a long time they were there for her and her family. Feeling more relaxed, she blanked out the aggressive whispers from her co-defendants in the dock, the atmosphere was electric and she faced up to the bench.

Fazed by her brief look of hope, Sir Ernest coughed, cleared his throat and calmed himself with a glass of water before commencing his summing up.

'Before I deliver my pre-sentence address, I have taken advice from my clerk and in fairness to the not guilty pleas of the other defendants I have stood the jury down. I shall recall them tomorrow. I shall now address the guilty plea.

'Josephine O'Dare, you have pleaded guilty to conspiracy to defraud, forgery and deception at a lower court, since when you have remained in custody at Holloway Prison on remand. You are the prime witness in the prosecution of your co-conspirators who have pleaded not guilty to this particular charge and, because of your co-operation, I am optimistic we shall soon see the end of this long, drawn-out case against you.

'However, this does not mitigate the circumstances that you find yourself in but it is fair to say that notwithstanding this long, newsworthy and public trial you have handled your situation well, despite the lurid headlines we have been forced to read.

'We have heard from both the police and the prosecution the bones of this affair and your part in it. We have also been told that it is common among the criminal fraternity that George Davis was and, perhaps still is, an exceedingly clever forger and we can assume he was much of an influence in the forging of the Edwin Docker's will.

'We also heard that your real name is Theresa Agnes Skyrme and you were born and brought up in the village of Wellington in Herefordshire where perhaps you may have known the defendant Davis, but that's as maybe.

'Nevertheless, it is fair to say that your life then is not your life now and has not been so for the past eight years. Today I find myself considering the case against Miss O'Dare, not Teresa Agnes Skyrme and I must consider this before sentencing.

'It seems to me that apart from living a profligate, carefree and cunning existence in London, you are also a woman of shrewd determination and, apart from several appearances at debtors' courts, this is the first time you have been caught, and I emphasise caught, at a criminal offence. You claim to have been influenced into criminal ways by Davis and his gang of villains and I am assured on good authority that there is no official record of any other court proceedings to this effect. However, bearing in mind that in the case against Davis and Morton there is another side to this argument which will be put to the jury tomorrow, I can say no more than that at this stage.'

Pausing to scrutinise his notes, he addressed his comments to the court in general and not the defendant.

'I shall now remark upon the long time spent by counsels on the lengthy and vigorous cross-examinations of Miss O'Dare, particularly from the prosecution standpoint and one is reminded of the old line 'thrice he slew the slain' and one might think her accomplishments have been somewhat exaggerated.

'For example, did the defence really believe that Morton, a full man with a young wife was, as has been suggested, in love with O'Dare. If so, would he go into this thing without hope that he was going to make something for himself out of it. After all was it not Morton she discussed the question of the will with. Was it he who told her not to be a silly girl and think about herself, and was it not he who promoted the idea that a man called Davis should forge the will for her? He evidently did and the plot fell.

'Regardless of this information, the fact of the matter is that it was O'Dare who provided the letter signed by Edwin Docker from which Davis was able to forge the signature and, if that is not conspiring with others, pray tell me what is?'

The wily judge looked at his notes again and thought for a while before continuing. Stroking his long chin, he said: 'What we have before us is a clear case of conspiracy to fraud, deception and forgery to which Miss O'Dare has pleaded guilty and in doing so has co-operated with the police in every way, having admitted her part in it.'

The yell of 'grass in court' was followed by a scuffle in the public gallery and the anonymous orator was dragged from his seat. Annoyed and angry at the unwanted interruption, Sir Ernest ordered: 'Take him down, I will deal with his contempt for this court later', and quickly advanced his summary.

'Suffice it to say, this devious and clever young woman had the audacity to contest the will favouring the family but that fell through too and she was arrested.

'Over the weeks and months of this trial, counsel for Davis and Morton, her co-conspirators, clearly accept that Miss O'Dare was and remains a very cunning swindler and a greedy, criminal careerist and today, a woman out of time.

'We have also heard of her alleged links to other criminal practices in this particular case, evidenced by her inconsistent defence to other charges, including obtaining sums of money from financial sources including the noble

Lord Curzon from whom she scooped £800 on the prospect of her substantial inheritance. Like so many others, he has refused to give evidence against her.

'However, I am mindful a good deal has been rumoured as to Miss O'Dare's reckless and decadent lifestyle and I would need convincing as to why I should take it into consideration, although I suspect prosecuting counsel will refer to it when advocating sentence. That said I also intend to reflect upon her early years in Herefordshire and contemplate the part William George Davis might have played in grooming her into criminal ways.

'To allow me time to digest the written information in front of me, I intend to adjourn for ten minutes after which I shall invite Sir Travers Humphries for the Crown to address the court on sentence. Having no formal representation Miss O'Dare will mitigate on her own behalf and, time permitting, I will endeavour to pass sentence today.'

Anticipating more character assassination from the leading prosecutor, Josie pondered on the summing up with mixed feelings; nevertheless, she knew it would be uncomfortable for her loyal band of supporters.

She was also well aware of the threatening comments from Davis should her shady double-dealing become an open book. Life was catching up with her and she shivered in anticipation.

Sir Ernest and his intense looking clerk returned to the bench and calling the court to order he announced: 'Sir Travers Humphries are you ready to proceed?

'I am indeed m'Lud,' and adjusted his wig.

'Since the start of the year, month after month, police proceedings against O'Dare and her accomplices have dragged their weary way to this lengthy trial at the Old Bailey. At each step, the police made new and sensational discoveries until it seemed there would be no end to the manifold crimes of O'Dare and her satellites. This long investigation completed, Scotland Yard were ready and eager to present the prisoners in the dock in their true colours. Without doubt, it has been a combination of lies, deception, theft and fraud rarely seen in the Metropolis and it is down to the dedication and steadfastness of Detective Inspector Yandell and his team that we are at the pinnacle of the British Justice System today.'

He droned on: 'Over the weeks, we have observed and listened to a woman of unexplained means, a woman who made money her God, greed a necessity and luxury an unashamed way of life. Commencing her career in theft, forgery and much worse, when she was just sixteen years of age, ten years on and with little education other than at her rural school, she was able to sustain a place in London society and become the most notorious swindler and trickster of her day. Yes, we have seen her portraits in illustrated magazines and have heard witnesses describe her vulgar extravagances, scheming ways and outrageous behaviour. By day, she was the indolent, carefree, money-to-burn girl about town, by night the unscrupulous leader of a villainous gang of thieves planning more criminal activity than the Metropolitan Police could ever have imagined. When it wasn't burglary, it was blackmail, deception and fraud, raising much-needed cash to keep up appearances. It had to come from somewhere and she always found a way but not without leaving a trail of broken, dispirited and ruined young men in her wake. That was m'Lud until she took to sniffing cocaine.'

Sir Ernest interrupted again: 'This is all very well Sir Humphrey but we are here to deliberate on the charges in forging Edwin Docker's will and I question your slide towards antecedence?'

'Point taken m'Lud but I fear character in this case is valid.'

'Maybe, Sir Humphrey but we are here to sentence a guilty plea, not to provide a route to appeal against sentence. However, on reflection I will take your remarks on board with a warning to move on and consider winding down your eloquent submission to avoid falling into the obvious legal trap.'

'Thank you, m'Lud, I have noted your guidance and will push on. Suffice it to say when her criminal earnings had dried up, she sought various ways of securing ready cash and foolishly teamed up again with William George Davis, the man who had groomed her at an early age, known then as Theresa Agnes Skyrme. The same fellow who stood alongside her in the dock at Hereford when she was just seventeen. The charges were dropped because prosecution witness statements could not, for legal reasons, be given in evidence and without the statements needed to convict, *Nolle prosequi* (un-willing to prosecute) was entered.

'It was a narrow escape from justice and she left the court with a warning from the Magistrate to stop the life she was leading and put her talents to other sources.'

Raising one eyebrow Sir Ernest audibly muttered: 'It's a great pity she ignored his advice, it would have saved this court a great deal of time and money. Now, where are we going with this Sir Humphrey? What we want to know is how Mr. Davis eventually located O'Dare?,' the Judge asked with more than a touch of impatience.

'I am coming to that m'Lud. On his release from prison, he learned of her exploits from reports and pictures of her extravagant lifestyle and eventually tracked her down. He was welcomed into the fold with open arms and was soon up to his old tricks, setting up pigeons for her to pluck but, as always, she kept him at a safe distance when it came to her private goings-on.

'The concluding chapters of her extraordinary society career belong to long-term friendships with certain noble Earls, including the Earl of March and a list of wealthy businesspersons. It was the late Andrew Carlisle, confidante of the ex-Kaiser, who, it is said, eventually saw through her.'

By now, Sir Ernest Irvine was openly irritated with the long, drawn-out statement.

'Yes, yes Sir Humphrey. We know all that but I am anxious to conclude today. Just tell the court how and when she met the deceased victim.'

'Again my apologies, m'Lud. A certain Duchess, who wishes to remain anonymous, introduced her to Docker at Sandown Park races. A meeting destined to plant the first steps to her inevitable downfall.'

Surprised at the statement, Josie looked at Constance who purposefully dipped her eyes beneath her wide brimmed hat.

Taking a sip of water, counsel pressed on regardless.

'Dazzled by the attentions of such a charismatic, much-younger woman, Docker positioned her 'an old man's darling' and happily contributed to her every financial whim. It was the beginning and today, hopefully the end, of the unscrupulous adventuress before you. She may not be all reported of her in the press, or indeed what has been said of her during this trial. That is a matter for you to decide, m'Lud. The crime she has admitted to is, without doubt, a very serious indictment served only by a custodial sentence. Thus, I conclude the degree of guilt in this case is not deserving of special consideration for her co-operation but more worthy of a long term of imprisonment. I leave it in your hands, m'Lud.'

His submission over, Sir Travers Humphries KC tossed his brief onto the lectern and, with a flourish of indignation, sat down and wiped his sweating brow. Satisfied it was a job well done, he accepted a hearty handshake or two from his impressed colleagues.

Josie turned as white as a sheet when a grim-faced George Davis mouthed 'Bitch' and was about to add more threats of violence were it not for the firm intervention of Matron and the custody officer. Sir Ernest broke the silence. 'Thank you, Sir Travers, having no defence counsel to mitigate for her, I will invite the accused to speak for herself if she so wishes.'

Lady Constance took a deep breath and looked up at the dock. Encouraged by her two eccentric escorts, she tried hard to communicate with her former close companion but Josie was deep in thought. Suddenly she jumped up and, with a supportive thumbs up from Lady Carter, she gripped the bar of the dock and geared herself for the speech of her life.

Looking directly at Travers Humphries, the Judge pronounced: 'Before you begin Miss O'Dare, I wish to refer to the matter of Viscount Curzon.

'In my closing statement, I referred to the noble Lord's alleged loan of £800. Let me make it quite clear. I am advised by my learned colleague, the visiting stipendiary from Marlborough Street Police Court, that the noble Lord did not simply refuse to give evidence in the matter, Viscount Curzon went into the witness box and, under oath, denied any knowledge of a £800 cheque to the accused and I am happy to put the record straight.'

Travers Humphries appeared unmoved by the inference and, after a moment or two, Josie nervously began her own mitigation.

'I have no wish to waste the court's time. Like you, my Lord, I would like to get home tonight, wherever it happens to be.'

The court rocked with laughter at the quick-witted response; the Judge simply nodded and with a sardonic smile muttered 'touché' in her direction.

'Despite what you have heard today, I am a much-maligned woman unfairly described as leading a wicked, evil, unscrupulous way of life. That is not so. I have been fortunate to have many men, young and old, thinking they were or might be in love, or, should I say, besotted with me. I could not, in all honesty return their affections and flatly refused to have affairs or any romantic dealings with them. I was, however, able to help them financially and tried to point them in the right direction and to the right people. Am I not the victim here? Am I a wronged woman simply because foolish men chose to exaggerate my intentions towards them? Would it not be grossly unfair, my Lord, if you failed to consider this when sentencing. After all, is it not one's sacred duty to do the best for oneself and for one's family? As my old granny once said, cast your bread on the waters and with a bit of luck it will come back buttered.'

She let the ripple of amusement settle down before continuing.

'Today I stand guilty of conspiracy and all that goes with it and, for the record, had I known it was serious enough to earn a prison sentence I would not have allowed myself to be influenced into colluding with my co-defendants. Having done so, and realising the error of my ways, I was persuaded to turn King's Evidence and become chief witness for the Crown purely in the interests of justice for my old friend Edwin Docker's family.'

The loud guffaw from the press box was met with a firm rebuke from the bench: 'Enough is enough. As I have said before, this is not a music hall. Give the defendant a fair hearing, otherwise I shall clear the court. Please continue Miss O'Dare.'

'I do not expect to escape punishment for my transgressions, all I ask is for due consideration for my honest admission of guilt and my acceptance to take what is coming to me. I am aware that the world and his wife will be expecting a long sentence for my misdemeanours but not my mother struggling with a feeble mind in a nursing home far away from all this. My dearest wish is to be there at her end. That is all I have to say in my defence, my Lord, and I leave my fate in your hands.'

A moment of sadness settled over the court and Josie used it to search the room for some sort of response but the sea of faces remained unmoved except, that is, for her friends and supporters.

Expecting a positive result, the Crown prosecuting team went into silent conclave; in the dock, her anxious co-conspirators were wondering if their fate could double hers.

Closing his portfolio of documents, Sir Ernest conferred with his clerk before addressing Josie: 'I am grateful for your brevity. I shall not leave you a moment longer before pronouncing sentence; as you suggest, we all wish to be home early; thus I will leave your co-defendants to the safe hands of the jury and pronounce on them tomorrow.'

He nervously cleared his throat, sipped a glass of water and adopted a sombre tone.

'I have taken account of what you have said and made allowances for your bad upbringing and unfortunate association with William George Davis. It has been very clear from the start that you are a treacherous, dishonest and dangerous young woman who, over the years, has amassed large sums of money by means into which it is better not to enquire. You lived beyond your income and sought to make up your losses in whatever way you could, leaving your victims at rock bottom without a penny to their name. I congratulate Inspector Yandell and his officers for their dedication into bringing you to justice.

'I have no alternative but to send you to penal servitude for four and a half years and I am pleased to confirm that the world in general, and London society in particular, is now rid of the most remarkable and dangerous young woman of this, or any other century. Take her down.'

Josie looked straight ahead, the colour slowly draining from her face as she realised the hopelessness of her position.

She would have stumbled had not Matron taken her arm to lead her down the steps to her cell. It was all different now, she was to be a prisoner for the next four and a half years and she knew it would be a long haul. As she disappeared from view, the temporary politeness from the press was overtaken by a rugby-type scramble in the press box as excited reporters dashed for the exit in an effort to be first to file the news with their editors. Intrepid as ever, the 'Hereford Times' reporter, urged on by threats from his news editor to not miss sentencing, had stayed on with his reliable sister in Kilburn. Unable to meet the regular weekly deadline, he had ample time to write up his copy on the homeward bound train.

Outside the court room, all was confusion. Shocked at the sentence, Fanny and Kristy trudged down the staircase into the main foyer, pushed and shoved by Davis' supporters until they found respite on an isolated bench adjacent to the Ladies Cloakroom. Before they could leave the building, Lady Carter and her friend Sybil approached them with instructions from Josie to make themselves known. Josie had written her sister a letter during the lunch adjournment, explaining that Lady Carter was the welfare and family's visitor and that she and Kristy will take care of things.

The four women went to Lyons Corner House to arrange a plan of action for visiting Josie in Holloway and Lady Carter agreed to liaise with Miss Potts should Fanny and her mother move into the Salvation Army hostel in Denmark Hill. Sybil, kindly as ever, said: 'Not to worry my dears. We have cars and good, strong men available to help when the time is right. We will keep in touch with your sister until visiting orders are available. Now we are happy to see you home and help explain to your mother what has happened to Josie.'

Too upset to reply, Kristy accepted on her behalf and they left the Corner House together. As they passed the Bailey, the Black Maria had arrived at the rear entrance gates for the return journey back to Holloway.

CHAPTER EIGHTEEN

When Josie reached the bottom of the steps, the custody officer was waiting for her. He said very little except that transport was on the way to collect her. Almost apologetically, he led his prisoner to the more secure convicted cell and, knowing her place in the order of legal propriety, Matron followed a step or two behind. Should her charge faint, she carried the regulation bottle of smelling salts inside her apron pocket just in case. However, she knew from experience, that her last confrontation with the prisoner confirmed that she was dealing with a stoical young woman and silently admired her for it. Seated with Matron in the secure cell, Josie tried to blot out her racing emotions. Aware of how she was feeling, the custody officer brought in three cups of strong, sweet tea on a tray, passed them round and encouraged Josie 'to drink it while it is hot, it's good for shock'. She was about to utter a sarcastic response but the wise old Matron, aware of her anger, nodded her disapproval and instead Josie muttered her thanks. The trio had nothing to say to each other and concentrated on sipping the hot tea until transport arrived to take Josie back to Holloway.

'Here we go, Miss,' Matron said. 'Drink up and you'll soon be on your way.'

For a moment or two, Josie did not move; shocked by the harsh sentence, she had been expecting a token eighteen months at the most for turning King's Evidence. The custody officer, more gentle than usual, took her arm and helped her to her feet. 'Come on love, time for you to go. There's a few papers to sign before you can leave,' he said and handed her a clipboard and a pen. She did as instructed and signed the documents with a flourish.

Handing them back, she said: 'Not many folk can say they have my autograph, except on a few dud cheques,' she said with a laugh.

'You'll do girl,' Matron said. 'If you can keep your spirits up for the first couple of months, you'll survive in Holloway.'

'Count on it, Matron. They say I'm as tough as old boots where I come from,' she optimistically replied.

'That's what they all say, luv. Be lucky,' and the custody officer signed her over to the escort from Holloway.

Outside in the yard, the noise of six o'clock London was at a peak; the June sun was still shining brightly, reminding Josie that for the next four and a half years she will be living in its shadow. She shaded her eyes in an attempt to block it, and so many other, worries out.

As she boarded the Black Maria for the final journey to Holloway, she could hear the newsvendor on the corner belting out: "Evening News', read all about it. Forgery case ends, O'Dare gets four and a half years.'

As she tried to plug her ears with her fingers, she contemplated how a girl from Wellington had finally made the banner headlines but for all the wrong reasons. What she needed to hear was the verdict on George, but that was tomorrow's headlines. However, daily newspapers were not available at Holloway and she would have to wait until her first visitor, hopefully Lady Carter, brought her the news.

As she settled into the old familiar prison van, she noted that this time she had two escorts as company.

'I don't intend to a runner. I'm looking forward to three good meals a day and regular sleep so you won't lose your jobs on my account.'

There was no response from her escorts and they quietly seated her in a cubicle, buckled her down and thumped on the driver's cab for him to move off. It took almost an hour to reach Holloway; the journey dragged along in silence until she heard the gatehouse doors swing open and the familiar voice of the gatekeeper asking: 'She's back then?'

'Yes, I'm back and going to make the best of it,' she muttered under her breath and once again Josie found herself in the reception office but this time she was a long-term offender; the kid glove treatment of the remand wing reception was finished. Deprived of all her smart clothes, personal belongings and possessions, she was stripped naked, her clothing sent to be laundered and stored until release. Showered, soaped and dried off, she dressed in a clean set of second-hand prison clothing and was allocated an overnight reception cell until her formal induction into prison life the following day. After supper and a good night's sleep she woke early, ate a bland breakfast and made ready for the penal system.

The first interview was with the Prisoner's Aid Society welfare assistant who offered to visit the family home to make sure children or elderly parents were not alone.

Knowing that Lady Carter and Kristy Potts would care for her mother and sister, Josie declined the kind offer, insisting other prisoners were more in need of help than she was.

Then it was through the glass doors and into the convicted wing for the new prisoner tour and she was not expecting Thomas Cook to show her round.

It is behind these doors that the inner life of Holloway begins and she was more than surprised to see the well-kept English and Catholic churches and a small non-conformist chapel. With expectation rather than fear, she climbed the great staircase to a well-lit upper hall painted in cream and pale blue and a maze of polished corridors leading to God knows where. At the top of the staircase, a wide landing led to the Governor's office, a smaller adjoining office for the Deputy-Governor and a large boardroom for meetings and private interviews with inmates. Secretaries and clerks shared a central office alongside the medical stores and the dental treatment surgery. From there, Josie came face-to-face with the thick, secure glass doors opening onto high rising landings and row upon rows of cells.

Seated behind a solid oak desk, the duty keeper of the keys stood up and unlocked the glass doors; passing through the security check, Josie was surprised to see a large jug of flowers. Her guide explained: 'We call this the centre point of the building. Prisoners are encouraged to grow flowers from seed in the prison gardens; some are blown in on the wind and grow wild.' Josie was impressed.

'Who would have thought it? I suppose in prison you have time on your hands to do other things and not just sit around twiddling your thumbs.'

'Let me remind you O'Dare, this is penal servitude. You will be assessed for work and, before you know it, you will be glad of a good night's sleep. Work, education and rehabilitation, that's what you are here for and if you like to read we have a good library stocked with books and outdated magazines. Now dinner is up soon; it is brought to your cell, let me take you there and settle you in.'

Her single occupancy cell was not much bigger than on remand but in some circumstances, high profile prisoners had larger rooms, with barred, high windows. At first sight Josie thought it rather bare; a corner washstand and a wooden water closet with flush provided for day-to-day ablutions and table and chair for eating and writing. Bedding was stored in a corner cupboard with two drawers for clothing and three shelves above were for cutlery, plates, crockery, sugar and space for books, photographs and personal effects on the top shelf. The bed had a fixed light for reading until lights out at nine o'clock and, tucked underneath, a small wicker laundry basket. To provide more space during the day, the bed folded against the wall; after closer inspection, Josie agreed it was reasonably comfortable, if somewhat impersonal.

Leading from the streets of cells, a metal staircase dropped down to a wide landing set aside for women needing medical treatment or special diets. It also housed a nursing station, rest room for recovering and sick patients and a secure waiting zone for visitors to the adjacent infirmary.

At the nursing station, Josie looked at the landings rising above her like tenements and shuddered at the thought of losing her freedom for such a long time. She tried light conversation with two or three tearful women sitting on a bench outside the infirmary and looked to her escort for support but all she got was a disinterested shrug indicating don't bother. Idly thumbing through a glossy magazine, she tried to concentrate on pruning roses.

Called into a side room for a thorough inside and out physical investigation into her health and fitness, the woman doctor raised a quizzical eyebrow at the unsuspected result of her vaginal examination and made notes. After a short lecture on prison hygiene, she received a weekly supply of soap and tooth powder, a toothbrush and flannel for her own use and a warning not to share them with other prisoners.

After a busy morning, Josie was ready to eat. Dinner time was 12.30pm on the dot and the food was brought to each floor in heated trays on wheels and trundled along the corridors by a couple of strong women lifers. Depending upon diet, it was usually stewed or roasted meat in thick gravy plated up on a round tin plate with an upside down lid for the potatoes and a second vegetable.

Every two weeks was pudding day when steamed ginger or golden syrup pudding with custard was served in lieu of vegetables and raised a cheer when it arrived.

A diet sheet listing the daily amounts of food by weight was allocated to her and, if she needed more, she could ask for it. She noted that Sunday dinner is always corned beef and potatoes because the cooks needed a break. Josie enjoyed the meal and complimented the chef as if she were dining at the Ritz. When her tour guide returned, she explained: 'You can fetch a big jug of hot water from the bathrooms and use it to freshen up and perhaps wash your hair before you meet the Governor this afternoon.'

Josie trotted off to the bathrooms to collect her jug; a short queue on the same mission explained the 'afternoon splash' as they called it, a daily habit to make sure workers stayed awake after dinner, especially in the sewing rooms where accidents with needles can easily happen.

For the first time since she left the Old Bailey, Josie began to feel more at ease with herself, but it was early days. The unexpected friendliness from serious offenders and from the officers eased her worries and she was ready to face the next long interview in better spirit.

She took her time washing and grooming and waited patiently for the interview with the prison Governor. He seemed a decent enough man and invited Josie to sit down, listen carefully and take note of what he had to say. Like most men meeting her for the first time, he appreciated her appearance and personality and opening the conversation with a smile, told her: 'Your reputation precedes you O'Dare but I am not here to judge; I see my work primarily custodial and hopefully rehabilitation, carried out in an atmosphere of discipline administered with fairness.

'Each day must run like clockwork and I expect my officers to try to understand each case, even those of the worst kind, and must not in any way bully or terrorise offenders under our care. However, I can tell you that much is achievable while you are here and for your own sake and my advice is that you settle in quickly and plan towards a future as a changed woman. Having studied the report of your time on remand and talking to the Chaplain, I am recommending you for relocation to a larger room on C floor near to the infirmary.

'Your work placement is the kitchens and during association and before lock-up you have the opportunity to mix with women worse off than yourself and learn from it. You are an intelligent young woman and if you follow the rules, an asset to this prison. Dismissing her with a courteous nod, she progressed to the Deputy Governor for a rundown of work placements, feeding times, exercise, association, disciplinary procedure and visiting rights. She also informed Josie of her statutory rights.

'Any prisoner with a grievance can request to see the Governor or the Board of Prison Visitors at any time and when visiting Justices come for the monthly inspection, any woman with a complaint can ask to be seen alone. It that clear O'Dare?'

'Seems fair to me ma'am but just one request. Will Lady Carter be my prison and welfare visitor?'

'Yes, she will. At Holloway we believe in continuity and you will be registered with her for the duration of your sentence.' 'Thank you, Ma'am,' she replied with a grin and went for a cosy chat with the Chaplain, her old friend the Reverend Seymour King. He welcomed her warmly.

'I'm sorry to see you back in here, Josephine, although, if I am honest, we all expected it. The Governor, impressed by your efforts on remand and with the Kristy Potts situation, is persuaded to let you transfer your valuable work to the convicted wing. I shall speak to Lady Carter about it and I'm sure she will agree, if you are still keen.'

'As mustard Reverend, keen as mustard. It could be the redeeming feature in my long sentence. I shall keep my fingers crossed.'

'And I shall pray for you, my dear. Now, I hope to see you in chapel on Sunday?'

The kindly parson pottered along the corridor humming his favourite hymn 'Lead kindly light amid the encircling gloom'.

Josie smiled to herself and watched him disappear through the glass doors to freedom; something she was going to miss until her release, but she had to play his game if she was going to make it through until 1932.

After long days in court, the first few first nights on the penal wing can be a desolate place for the newly-convicted prisoner. Most prisoners and officers do their best to help settle newcomers but, even in her darkest hour, Josie preferred to be alone. It had been a long first day of induction and she was also feeling hungry.

Tea at six o'clock is the last meal of the day in Holloway and, like dinner, delivered to the door by kitchen workers. To avoid rumbles of discontent, it was getting food to the cells hot and quickly. Josie had no complaint with her enamel bowl of good vegetable soup, bread and a lump of tasty cheese, followed by a mug of tea. Drinking water was on tap and, if you were lucky to have a mate working in the infirmary kitchen, you might get a steaming mug of delicious cocoa before lock-up at seven o'clock.

Josie was working on it. She also learned the importance of human contact and no prisoner was completely left alone. Throughout the night, each landing had a duty officer on call, each inmate a bell to press if things got tough; after lights out, the quiet call 'Are you alright?' became the watchword for prison life in Holloway and for many inmates it was a welcome relief. Josie's first night on the penal wing ended with a loud clang at six o'clock, the noisy wake-up bell reminding all and sundry that it was time to clean out the cell, stow away the bedding and carry out daily ablutions.

On the remand wing, meals were served in the canteen or sent in from outside for those willing to pay but today breakfast arrived dead on 7.30am. This time it was tea, bread, margarine and porridge on a tray, not her favourite coddled or poached eggs, toast and marmalade, but there was plenty of it.

'It's not the remand wing so you best get used to it,' the friendly server reminded her and, taking her at her word, Josie tucked in. Afterwards she was sent to the sewing room and measured up for her prison uniform, an ordinary dark blue dress with a red star indicating a first offender. At the clothing store, she collected underclothing, stockings and stout shoes, a dark blue-buttoned cardigan for winter and two pairs of standard overalls for kitchen work and outdoor jobs. Returning to her room, she saw her uniform dresses laid on the bed with a note reminding her laundry day is Wednesday. The note also reminded her that her weekly, thirty-minute bath was on Fridays in one of twelve bathrooms on the wing; an officer would oversee the queue to make sure the women took their turn. Older, frail and long-term inmates, some with disabilities, could also use the hospital ablution rooms.

In the afternoon, she attended a lecture on visiting rights, family arrangements and mail. Supervised monthly visits required advanced clearance, incoming letters were limited to one in eight weeks and read by officials before distribution and replies, in pencil only, were censored before posting. Warned that punishment for misconduct, particularly after spot searches during visits, could affect early release, Josie was determined to keep her nose clean and never lose a day of remission. Whether she had the discipline to sustain four years or so of good conduct was a different matter.

The meeting ended with an encouraging, 'do your time, stay clean and you will be out before you know it' speech and the mixed group of nervous first offenders shuffled off for thirty minutes in the exercise yard before tea. Josie went with them and waited for the expected catcalls from the heavy mob keen to unsettle her from day one but she was in for her first surprise; Tew was waiting for her.

'Glad to see you back O'Dare. Fancy a quick game of softball, it keeps you fit in here,' and tossed the ball at her.

'I hear on the grapevine Davis got twelve years hard labour in Brixton. Don't fancy your chances when he gets out, grasses don't prosper.' She grinned and patted her on the head.

Josie went as white as a sheet and blustered: 'Who in here says I'm a grass? He led me up the garden path and I was not going down for him. What did Morton get?'

'I'm not sure on that one, I was only told about Davis but I think he got about four years.'

'In a place like this how do you find out these things?' Josie asked her.

'Prison rumour train love, it doesn't stop until it hits the buffers but in this place it's not what you hear, it's who you know inside that counts.'
'Meaning what?'
'People are in and out of here every working day, if you know what I mean? I will soon be out of this place and, before I leave, I'll put a good word in with the 'swell mob' and they might let you join the club.'

'Who the bleedin' hell are they?' Josie snapped backed.

'You'll be surprised but they will find you if and when they need to,' Tew replied.

It took a good few months for Josie to settle into prison life. She made friends, some closer than others, and an enemy or two as she worked her way through the daily routine of being locked up. Her first work placement was in the spotless kitchens cleaning the huge soup cauldrons and polishing the pots and pans until they shone. Kitchen work did have a few benefits and Josie made the most of them. She enjoyed swapping leftovers from the Governor and the officer's dining room with an older woman keen to clean her cell or make curtains and covers for her in the sewing workshops. Later she graduated to cooking and often baked cakes for someone's birthday. What spare time she had she spent reading, choosing her two books a week allocation from the impressive range in the library; library jobs were much sought-after and usually went to the better educated inmates. During the association hour before lock-up, Tew kept her in touch with the outside world but, a month later, Tew was released earlier than expected and promised she would keep in touch but Josie missed her.

In the run-up to autumn, Lady Carter and Kristy were frequent visitors but not Fanny. Fearing the press might pick up on her, Josie insisted her sister was kept away from the prison and relied on her friends for updates on her mother's condition. Well settled into their new accommodation in Denmark Hill, Lady Carter had also arranged for a doctor she knew at King's College Hospital to take care of Mrs. Skyrme. Apart from her confused memory, she was reasonable happy and Fanny was kept busy with her domestic duties at the hostel and the local Citadel.

It was about ten months into her sentence when the unexpected happened. Josie, now an assistant cook, was looking forward to cooking Christmas dinner when, much to her surprise, Prison Officer Mavis Buck arrived on the wing. She had been on a course since the trial and was now Senior Officer on the long-term offender's wing.

When she walked into Josie's room an hour before lock-up, it was poignant moment for both of them. The two women had built up a warm relationship on the remand wing, more so during the Old Bailey trial, and Josie was devastated when she failed to show up for sentencing and she often wondered why. Over a year had passed since they last met and Josie was deep into a book when she appeared in the doorway.

'Got yourself a cushy number have you O'Dare? Word has it you're the Mrs Beaton of the prison service.'

Josie looked up and could hardly speak. Stunned by the sudden appearance of her favoured warder, she instinctively threw her library book at her. Dodging the throw, Mavis picked it up, looked at it and said: 'That's no way to treat Thomas Hardy.'

Shocked at seeing her after a long absence, she tossed it back yelling: 'And where the hell have you been since you buggered off after my trial.'

'I'm sorry about that but I'm here now and just in time for Christmas. I will tell you all about it over a cup of tea.'

Producing a packet of Mazawattee, she went to the wing kitchen, brought back two mugs of tea and sat on the bed. Passing Josie a mug, she explained: 'It was out of my control. The day before you were sentenced the Governor had me in and gave me an ear wigging for getting a bit too close to a high-profile prisoner.

'He was worried in case the press got wind of it and agreed with the prison board to find me a place at the senior officer's training school and promotion afterwards.'

Still shocked at seeing Mavis again, Josie was not convinced. 'It didn't last twelve blooming months though, did it? No-one told me, not even that snotty officer who took over, so I tried to forget you. Where have you been and why are you back here now?'

'I was sent overseas on secondment to the Indiana Department of Correction in America; a brand new women's prison had opened and the Governor required an experienced, female officer from England to help set it up.'

'And you jumped at it did you?' Josie insisted.

'It was more like being pushed into it. I only agreed on condition I could return to Holloway to see you through your sentence. It was obvious you were going down and I wanted to be around for you.'

'And here you are, senior officer and on the wing of your star prisoner?'

'No. It is not like that. I do not have favourites but I do have valuable experience in the prison work and I recognised your people skills on remand. You were so good with Kristy Potts and I believe you could help prisoners on long-term just as well; I wrote and explained to the Governor why I needed to come back and he agreed. If that is okay with you O'Dare,' she said sarcastically.

For a moment Josie felt ashamed for doubting the situation, nevertheless she was no pushover.

'It took you long enough, didn't it? But thanks for not giving up on me, Miss.'

'I never stopped. When I heard you had gone down, I was bothered about you and wondered how well you were coping. I was banned from contacting you myself but a couple of old colleagues kept in touch and I was grateful for that.'

The two women drank their tea in silence until Josie asked: 'Where do we go from here, Miss?'

'Who knows, O'Dare. I have a large wing and some two hundred prisoners to oversee and until I have a set routine, I will be here, there and everywhere. You have at least another three years to do, you know I will always do my best for you but no promises,' she declared with little conviction.

'Now it will soon be lock-up and I have to supervise the landing closedown.'

She picked up Josie's book, looked it over and handed it back to her. ''Tess of the d'Urbervilles' is one of my favourites. How are you finding it?'

'I'm only just getting into it. What happened to her could happen to anyone, all those rich bastards trying to get into your drawers would drive any woman to murder. That reminds me, Miss, Kristy told me about Rose; she should have been hanged years ago for killing her employer, a rich and important businessman with a mansion in Surrey. Kristy said she was just a seventeen year old companion/maid employed to befriend his daughter but when he tried to take advantage of her, she refused him. He forced himself on her and brutally raped her but I don't know all the details but I was told she is still in here?'

'Yes, she is but it happened about twenty years ago, long before I joined the service. It was rumoured that the servants heard her screams but were too frightened to give evidence against such an important man. Hundreds of women raised a petition for an appeal against sentence and sent it to Herbert Gladstone, the Home Secretary, but it took a long time and the poor soul was tossed between life and death for weeks on end. After fresh evidence from the household staff, she was eventually reprieved and given a life sentence.'

'Does she have any family or friends?'

'Not as far as we know. What we do know is that she went into service at fourteen and, apart from the prison visitors and Kristy, all the friends she has are in here.'

'And she's still got a lump growing in her,' Josie asked quietly.

'Yes, she has and it's getting bigger. She has good days, some very good and bad days when the pain gets her down, but, with a little help, she sleeps. We will always take care of Rose until she leaves us, probably in a wooden box.'

Josie was clearly upset. 'Same old story, just like the music hall song Ma used to sing: It's the rich what gets the money, it's the poor what gets the blame. Blimey. No wonder Kristy asked me to take an interest in her. How old is she now?'

'Somewhere in her early forties, I think. We don't talk about age in here especially when your days are numbered; most of the others in here don't know how to handle their own feelings let alone hers and tend to keep their distance.'

'So she's alone?' Josie asked.

'Totally, by choice I think, she tends to keep herself to herself. She has a very comfortable room in the infirmary, good facilities, day and night nursing care and Kristy Potts drops in when she can with treats and reading material. If you would like me to, I could pull a few strings for you to see her. That's if she wants to see you.'

'Please try, Miss. I did promise Kristy I would try to help her but I'm still coping with my own loneliness at the moment.'

'I'll see what I can do. In the long-run, it could be good for both of you. Now it's time for lock-down for the night, I'll take the mugs back and you can get your nose in to 'Tess' until lights out.'

Closing the heavy door behind her, Senior Officer Buck called out 'start lock-up' followed by a clatter of heavy doors and the routine 'are you alright' from the duty officer.

Back in her cell, Josie couldn't concentrate on her book; her head was full of thoughts and concerns about Rose, quietly admitting she would have done the same if any rich bastard had done that to her.

CHAPER NINETEEN

Winter, spring, summer or autumn, the weeks and months went by and daily life in Holloway continued its disciplined routine; work, meal times and lock-up followed by an hour of association. Playing games or going round in circles in the exercise yard helped keep mind and body fit and, despite the weather, Josie made the effort. She was halfway through her second year in Holloway when she discovered the pleasures of Sunday afternoon in the chapel when celebrated entertainers and musicians volunteered to give concerts, dramatic performances and poetry readings; for prisoners cut off from social and cultural activity, the effect was magical. In the days after these popular events, the prison hummed with the sound of music and laughter and the daily round was awash with smiling faces. Inspired by the performances and her memories of the music hall, Josie quietly made a few plans of her own.

Occasionally she went to the infirmary to sit with Rose but her health was deteriorating and she suffered a relapse; unable to visit her, Josie was at a loose end and, with her second Christmas in Holloway approaching and always looking on the bright side, she was hopeful Rose might still be around. After a discussion with the Wing Governor, she arranged a seasonal concert and perhaps a carol service on Christmas Eve. Deciding it was good for morale, the Governor gave the go-ahead and referred Josie to the Chaplain. He was so enthusiastic, he had a rush of blood to the head and immediately contacted the Choir Master at the City of London Boys School 'whom he knew well' to help him plan the event. Lady Carter persuaded her actress friend, Sybil Thorndike, to chair the Christmas Concert Committee and, after contacting her theatrical associates, she arranged for a carol service on Christmas Eve and a variety concert on Boxing Day afternoon. When news leaked out, musicians and singers from inside the prison wanted to take part, and it was agreed that the concert should feature inside talent backed by professional guest artists.

This suited Josie, all she wanted was an opportunity to sing a couple of her favourite Marie Lloyd songs and keep it a secret until the performance.

Her prison credibility on the up, Josie was invited into the 'Swell Mob'; the well-to-do women thieves generally convicted for robbing passengers on train journeys when the carriages were in dark tunnels. These classy female crooks also practised the art of quietly dipping into expensive handbags for money, jewels and cheque books and for conning mink coats from not-so-bright cloakroom attendants in posh London hotels. When Josie heard details of their daring escapades, she reminded herself that was her speciality, when she first started out on the road to ruin in Hereford, and still could be when she is released. Even more keen to join the elite group of offenders, she befriended Lou, an attractive, well-educated and amazingly brave new prisoner from a noble background. Like many of the better-educated prisoners, she worked in the library and Josie became her prison mentor; it took just a few weeks to unwind the terror her new friend had gone through.

At a very young age Lou ran off with a good-looking rotter and her wealthy family disowned her; later, she made a bad marriage and her unhappy parents bought him out of it, paid him off and kept their daughter in funds.

As their friendship grew, Josie learned a great deal about Lou and her early life.

Utterly devoted to her grandmother, when her family finally gave up on her, she went to live with her at the ancestral retreat in the countryside. There, she enjoyed the outdoor life with no restrictions, ran wild with the farm hands and had little teaching of what was good and what was evil. Far too restless to earn a living, Lou simply thought everyone was out to get the best for themselves so why not have a good time and make the most of it and she did. By the time she was twenty-six and living on her wits, she was caught out in a fraud on a smart hotel in Sussex. Arrested, tried and sentenced to fifteen months in prison, her reputation went before her and she was welcomed into the 'Swell Mob'. Yet, thanks to her father's influence in high places, she gained early release for good behaviour and for while kept in touch with Josie. Eventually, she married a University man, set up home in Essex and became pregnant; Josie never heard from her again. Apart from the wealthy parents and aristocratic background, Josie had had much in common with Lou and she missed her company but life goes on in prison and, by November, Rose had improved enough for a visit.

Josie approached the infirmary with some caution. Taken to her room by a kindly nurse she was delighted to see Rose out of bed and in a chair. Kristy had already arrived with fruit and out-of-date magazines and the two were deep in conversation. Apart from medical needs and assorted equipment, the room was comfortable and, despite the cold outside, it was always warm inside.

Leading the conversation Kristy said: 'It's bitter cold out there, I wish we had this sort of heating in our hostels during the winter; it might save a few lives.'

'Not mine,' Rose said. 'There's not much left of it to cling onto but now I'm feeling better. I'm glad to see you, Josie, and hear a bit more about your life in Herefordshire.'

'And you can tell me what it has been like locked up in this place for years on end,' Josie replied.

The three women chatted easily for about an hour until Rose showed signs of tiredness which seemed to upset her; when they encouraged her to rest, she asked them to sit with her until she fell asleep. After a few minutes, Kristy whispered: 'This might not be the time and place, Josie, but I think you should know that your mother is not good. She has been laid up with a bad bout of influenza and Fanny is very worried.'

'And so am I, Kristy. Has the doctor been called? It could be serious at this time of the year and she must be kept warm. Fanny knows not to spare the expense; we do have a nest egg for emergencies. Who is treating her and is she well cared for?'

'The doctor at our nursing home. He is more worried about her memory, she has little idea of what is happening but she is in good hands.'

Josie asked quizzically: 'Does she ask about me, Kristy?'

'Not really but when Fanny shows her a picture of you, she sometimes smiles. Now shall we change the subject? How are you coping, you never let it show?'

'Ticking the days off the calendar but there is still a long way to go. I'm not even halfway through my sentence and I do miss Fanny.'

'I know, Josie, and she misses you too but she does have a lot on her plate dealing with her mother. Perhaps I could find a way to bring her in with the band for the carol service; you do know we have been asked to play and she could carry the sheet music.'

'If only it could happen it will be the best Christmas ever, Kristy, it really would.'

'Just remember that God moves in a mysterious way, his wonders to perform. We shall have to see,' Kristy warned.

Rose was coming out of a doze when the nurse hinted it was time for her medication and they should leave. The visitors gently kissed their sick friend goodbye and left the room.

Before leaving the infirmary, Kristy said: 'Please keep seeing Rose, when she's more lucid she is good company and you can help keep her chin up. I will be in touch about your mother; meanwhile I will give some thought to a visit from Fanny. Until next time then?'

Rehearsals for the Christmas show were progressing well; feelings of boredom switched to excitement as music floated through the wing. The Hackney Music Hall Company delivered a large selection of unwanted costumes, sending the sewing room into a hive of industry cutting, shaping and adjusting suitable outfits for the performers; Josie took the pick of the bunch and went for secret fittings to avoid rumours that she was making an appearance. Sunday mornings were dedicated to carol practice and, in the week before Christmas, kitchen staff were up to their eyes baking mince pies, steaming up puddings and stuffing the turkeys generously donated by Lady Carter from the family estate near Chelmsford.

It all went well on the day, particularly for Josie. Kristy kept her word and delivered Fanny in full Salvation Army uniform to the Chapel where she dished out sheet music to the band and hymnbooks to the mixed congregation of prisoners, staff and VIP guests. Senior Officer Buck permitting, over hot sausage rolls, mince pies, chocolate biscuits and tea, Josie was able to reassure her sister, without giving the game away, for about fifteen minutes and, after wishing her a Merry Christmas, Kristy took her back to the band.

Christmas Day lunch was at one o'clock and served by prison staff, the Governor risking bouts of indigestion as he dashed from wing to wing. Josie had permission to have hers in the infirmary with Rose who was sitting in an armchair near her bed; she had a table in front and chair opposite for Josie. Wearing a chef's hat, Lady Carter carried in a light lunch for Rose, the full works for Josie and a couple of crackers to pull.

'No booze I'm afraid, only lemon barley water. As our young Salvationist would say, enjoy, happy Christmas and blessings all round.'

Expectations for the Boxing Day concert were high. The morning had been busy and, by the time Josie arrived, trusted prisoners from nearby Pentonville had laid out benches for the audience and erected a raised platform for the performers. The meeting room served as the main dressing room, the guest artists, a compere, comedian, magician and a couple of soft shoe dancers used the Governor's office. Customers from the local pub in Camden Road had wheeled over a slightly out of tune piano and the pub pianist offered to play for Josie, the surprise item on the programme. She was meeting him for a run-through before the rest of the performers arrived and, ready for anything, she knew her stuff when it came to music hall. What she did not know was that Rose would be at the concert with Mavis Buck.

It all got off to the rollicking start expected from people cut off from day-to-day culture. The slightly risqué comic brought a good few belly laughs and the magician did his best not to disappear in a cloud of over-confidence; to riotous applause, the two hysterical soft shoe dancers almost shuffled of the end of the stage. The audience was on the edge of restlessness when the compere announced: 'To end the show, the concert committee has acquired, at enormous expense, an entertainer appearing at this or any other of His Majesty's Prisons for the very first time.'

The audience, silent now, waited and waited until encouraged by a loud 'get on with it', the compere bellowed: 'I give you the amazing voice of the Canary of Holloway prison, the one, the only, Miss Josephine O'Dare.'

The moment the pub pianist played her on stage, the audience gasped and then exploded into cheers and whistling from the heavy bunch at the back of the hall.

'Show them what you've got O'Dare, do it for Rose and Tew.' The cheers almost lifted the chapel roof.

The Governor, guests from the Prison Service and senior officers in the front seats did simultaneous double takes when their charismatic prisoner appeared.

Dressed in a pale blue dress with a plunging neckline and carrying an empty birdcage, she nodded to the piano player.

Josie belted out 'My Old Man Said Follow The Van' and, encouraging her audience to join in the chorus, prisoners, staff and guests responded with gusto.

In a side aisle Rose, propped up in a bath chair, laughed louder than most, bringing many of the hard, longer serving prisoners and staff who knew her well, almost to tears. The reception was electric and the inevitable encore was called for; being the good trouper she is Josie exchanged her birdcage for a parasol and did a provocative rendering of Miss Marie Lloyd's 'When I Takes My Morning Promenade', the song which so offended Queen Victoria.

The applause hit the roof again; Holloway had never seen anything like it; they gave her a standing ovation and called for another encore. She declined, left the stage, and walked off to speak with her friend. 'Don't forget, Rose, whatever you do or where you are going, always leave them wanting more. That's my motto,' she said with a poignant smile.

Exhilarated by the performance, her usual pallor had a pink flush to it, so much so, her nurse asked her if she was feeling all right.

'Yes I am, Miss, I really am. I have been locked up in here since I was seventeen and never seen anything like it in my life. It was marvellous, Josie, and I know you did it for me.'

'Don't mention it. It will give us plenty to talk about when I visit you. Now I expect the nurse needs to get you back to the infirmary and if I'm allowed I will drop in for cocoa.'

In an effort to get the landing cleared quickly, the Governor made a welcome announcement. 'To allow you to settle down after this wonderful show, I have extended lock-up by an hour. No need to say Merry Christmas everybody, it jolly well has been.'

Leaving the platform, he caught up with Josie.

'I don't know how you do it O'Dare, but you do. You have made Christmas in this prison a happy event and perhaps extended a few months of life for Rosie. Well done and if you are available for next year?' he laughingly said. Walking towards his office with Mavis Buck, Josie heard him say: 'You were right Buck, she's getting to be a habit around here and it's good for us all. Long may it last?'

The turn of the New Year brought with it dull weather conditions and the occasional light snowfall. A cool, wet spring soon followed and the first hint of a severe economic depression was beginning to tell and a general election was on the cards. After years of hectic campaigning and public disorder from determined suffragettes, women were able to vote for the first time. Nevertheless, whatever was going on beyond the stout walls of Holloway, made little difference to the residents. Prisoners of either sex could not vote.

In April, the Governor announced the annual inspection by His Majesty's Prison Inspectorate. Spring cleaning was under way on most of the wings, extra duties were in order and it was all hands to the mops, buckets, brushes and dusters. Working together in teams was good for prison morale but, now and again, a row broke out over rumours and idle gossip and the possibility of redecoration, new furnishings and upgrading on the wings spurred on even the slowest worker and there was no slacking.

Lady Carter and Sybil continued to deliver the latest news from the outside world, particularly the arrival in Southampton of Don Bradman and the Australian cricket team for the forthcoming Ashes matches. Excited at the prospect of an England win, Mary Carter managed to get tickets for the final Test at the Kennington Oval. Reminded she knew little of the game until she met Lady Constance, Josie laughed with them at the prospects of the England team winning the series. Visits from the two old friends were occasions to treasure but did not last long.

Bad news hit Josie in June. Kristy came to tell her that her mother had died in her sleep at the nursing home, leaving Fanny distraught. It was natural causes and no need for an inquest; the Salvation Army offered to make the arrangements and Lady Carter informed the Prisoners Aid Society and the Governor. Despite her mother's long illness, it was a terrible shock for Josie and, for twenty-four hours, she cursed, swore and refused to see anyone or leave her cell. It was a difficult situation for Mavis Buck; she waited until Josie had calmed down and tried to talk her through it.

'Nothing will stop me from going to her funeral. She is my mother and it's my right to be there. So please don't tell me that in here I have no rights. I will break out if I have to.'

'You won't have to, Josie. When the arrangements are confirmed, I will take you there under escort. Meanwhile, if you would like to see your sister, I can arrange a private visit.'

'I don't want to do anything, anyway I can't face her now, and it's all too much. I feel bloody awful leaving her to cope on her own.'

Mavis was more than sympathetic and reassured her: 'If you change your mind or need to see anyone else let me know. I will leave you to think about it and come back later.'

She paused in the doorway and then turned back. Breaking the rules, she put her arms around Josie and said: 'I'm so sorry Josephine, I really am. It's tough being locked up at a time like this. Keeping your mother away from this place was the right thing to do and we are all thinking of you.'

For the rest of the day and night, a strange silence clouded the usual comings and goings on the landing; there was very little chatter during evening association, lock-up came and went and, without so much of a jangle of keys, the officers trotted about on tip-toe. If anything, it was a mark of respect, a quiet reminder from the mothers and daughters locked away from their own family and Josie was grateful for the silence. The peace and quiet gave her time to remember her childhood and her hard-working mother; a mother who, back in Herefordshire, took regular beatings from a drunken husband to bring up her daughters as best she could with little to show for it except unconditional love, returned in full until the end of her days. Although Mary Skyrme may have suspected that her youngest child, Trixie, was living dangerously, she did not know her daughter was locked up in jail. Despite her confused state of mind, her mother's final years were reasonably comfortable and Josie was grateful to the Salvation Army for caring for her until the end.

Sleep did not come easy that night; her thoughts were a mess of guilt and regret and she tossed and turned until dawn. Whatever the outcome of her past criminality, Josie had never looked back or shed a tear but by dawn's early light, she had sobbed herself dry.

Never one to say 'let it be', by breakfast she had determined to let things take their course, at least until after the funeral.

From then on she would try to get through the rest of her sentence trouble-free and ease Rose through her pain in any way she could. In between, she quietly planned for a future beyond Holloway and working on ways to pursue her idol, money. Intent on getting through the next week without too many tears, she asked Mavis Buck to set up a visit with her sister and Kristy to discuss the arrangements for the burial. Lady Carter had already been to see the Governor and Sybil offered to drive them from Denmark Hill to Holloway next day. The Governor allowed the visit to take place in the small meeting room on the administration landing; Officer Buck agreed to provide refreshments in her office next door.

They all arrived together, each wearing the obligatory black armband of mourning and accompanied by a sympathetic warder. Quietly entering the comfortable meeting room, they sat down to wait for Josie and her escort, Senior Officer Buck. Prison protocol was tossed aside when Josie saw her grief-stricken sister. Mavis Buck relaxed the basic rule of no contact and allowed, indeed encouraged, her charge to hug her sister.

'Come on our Fan, Ma wouldn't have wanted this. She's best off where she is now and what she needs is a proper Herefordshire send-off and we are here to sort it out.'

From her quivering lip, it was clear to the others, including Mavis Buck, that Josie was close to the edge and, keeping her own pecker up, Fanny struck the right note: 'You mean a proper job, our Trixie? A real proper job.'

It broke the moment, giving Josie time to explain to her friends: 'Ma always said that when she wanted a job done well. It's a well-known saying in Herefordshire.'

When Officer Buck slipped out for refreshments, Lady Carter detailed the funeral arrangements: 'We spoke to the Salvation Army and, subject to your agreement, Fanny would like the service to be at Denmark Hill Citadel followed by interment at Nunhead Cemetery, in Peckham, both well in reach of the hostel where Fanny will continue to live.'

'If that is alright with you, Fan, then I'm happy with that. After all you will be visiting the grave for the next couple years until I come out.'

'As long as you can get there for the service I'll be alright. Honest, Trix. God willing I will be content to stay at the hostel until you come home.'

Mavis returned with a large tray with sandwiches, cake and a regulation pot of tea.

'I shall need to know when, where and what time the funeral is. We require Home Office permission to take Josie.'

Lady Carter rustled through her notebook.

'Monday afternoon at 2pm at the Citadel; Kristy is organising things at her end and she will confirm the details. Fanny thought your mother might have been brought up a Catholic but there is nothing to confirm this.'

Josie thought a moment, looked at her sister and asked: 'I'm not sure Fanny? As far as I know, she never went near the Catholic Church in Hereford; if she did go to church it was for harvest festival at the Methodist chapel. Anyway, in the end the Sally Army took care of her so let's keep it simple.'

Kristy was pleased and explained the procedure: 'It's custom for the band to play for the hymns and I expect her neighbours in the hostel will come to the service.'

She paused for a moment and blushed before adding: 'I have been walking out with Captain Anthony Bramwell from the Citadel; he's a little older than me and has offered to take the funeral service and the burial, if that suits everyone?'

'Seems the perfect solution all round,' Sybil said.
'I'll order flowers on my account at Constance Spry, it will be my pleasure.'
'Thank you Sybil but please take Fanny to choose ours. She knows what Ma liked and what to write on the card and, while you are at it our Fan, polish up that boot.'

For the first time Fanny smiled. Losing her mother after a long illness was a bombshell but seeing her sister at almost her former, amusing self, restored her hope for the future.

Details done and dusted, Mavis Buck called time on the visit and, promising to make sure her charge would be there, she opened the door and asked a waiting officer to escort the visitors to the Gatehouse.

Fanny took one last look at her sister and hugged her again.
'See you then, our Trixie?'

'You will and more often until I get out of this place. Thank you everyone and you too Officer Buck. What would I do without you?'

'Indeed. What would you?' she replied and, with a wry smile, closed the door and walked her charge to her cell.

'I can't stay and chat, I have to sort things out with the Governor about transport for Monday.'

Still on edge over the arrangements, Josie pleaded: 'Please, Miss, not the Paddy wagon; I cannot go to Ma's funeral in a Black Maria.'

Mavis Buck chuckled and before she locked the door added: 'Who do you think you are, Eliza bloody Doolittle? You'll do well to remember your place O'Dare!' and headed for the Governor's office.

Two days before the funeral, Rose asked to see Josie. It was a difficult decision for the dying woman and even more for her friend; nevertheless she went for an hour or two and it turned out to be more positive than she expected.

Assuming Rose would be feeling low at her loss, Josie cautioned herself not to be overly upset when she saw her sick friend; she was surprised to see her up and about in her room, feeling better and able to walk slowly to the door to greet.

'Well! You do look better Rose. What has brought this on?'

'You have, Josie. When I heard about your mother, for a couple of days I felt bad not being there for you at such a sad time and I took to my bed.'

'But why, Rose? You need all your strength for your own recovery not mine and I need you around to get me through these dark days.'

'Exactly. The hazy relapse induced by my treatments did confuse me but, after sleeping it off for a few of days, it suddenly shifted and I wanted to help you.'

'But how can you? I suspect I am not the first woman in here to have survived a family tragedy or indeed the last. What is killing me inside me, if you'll pardon the expression, is that I wasn't there for her at the end.'

'Perhaps it was better for you both you were not. She was very frail and confused and it is unlikely she would have known who you where. What you must do now is always remember the good-hearted mother who kept you safe and brought you up a strong woman able to handle all that life throws at you. You should also be glad she didn't see you locked up behind bars, just feel blessed to have had her in your life. My family deserted me when I was arrested and I never saw my mother again,' she added, her sad eyes struggling against the tears.

Shocked by the disclosure Josie took her hands.
'Does anyone else know this truth?'

'Not really. I was too ashamed at what I had done but it did not matter. I was going to be hanged and you're a long time dead, so I stuffed it to the back of my mind until I heard your sad news and realised how I would be feeling in your shoes.'

Josie was dumbstruck and found it hard to understand how any mother was capable of leaving her seventeen-year-old daughter to rot in jail.

'Tell you what, Rose. When all this is over and I get back to normal, I'll share my mother with you and tell you all about my life in Herefordshire.'

'And, if the good Lord allows, I will tell you about my family home - Holloway prison- and how the suffragettes became my mother and took me under their wings. It is thanks to them I managed to get through the first years of hell in this place and you will be able vote. So use it Josie, don't abuse it, I won't get the chance.'

Despite reassurances from Lady Carter that all was well, the days before the funeral were slow and anxious. The Home Office finally approved Josie's day release and Mavis Buck would escort her to the cemetery. To prevent possible leaks to the press, details of the route were limited and, on the sad day, two plain cars left Holloway; one a decoy, the other drove Josie and Officer Buck directly to Nunhead cemetery for the interment.

The day went well. To provide cover for the plain prison vehicle and its passengers, the band arrived well ahead of the hearse. Josie wore a stylish, long black coat over a simple black cotton dress run up for her in the sewing room; a wide-brimmed matching hat shaded her face from curious bystanders. Determined to look the part of a grieving daughter, she unashamedly held her head high when Captain Bramwell delivered the final prayers and when the band played 'Nearer my God to Thee', she joined hands with Fanny and laid a wreath of wild flowers, lightly bound with a single strand of Herefordshire hops, beside the open grave. The card read 'Our Ma. You always did a proper job! Never forgotten, remembered forever. All our love, Fanny and Trixie'.

The Church Warden kept his promise to leave the vestry open for an hour for refreshments provided by the Salvation Army Emergency Refreshment van parked outside. After tea and a chat, Josie thanked the mourners for coming and Captain Bramwell and the band for all the help. She also arranged for Fanny to dip into the 'rainy day' fund for a donation to Denmark Hill College.

'No need, Trixie; Ma still had a few valuable pieces of jewellery which you had given her over the years; she kept them in what she called her 'Box of Trix'. Lady Carter is taking care of them for now and believes they will bring in a tidy sum at auction. That's unless you want them, Trix?'

'I don't want them or the money. You do what you like with it, it's all yours; you will need a few bob to tide you over until I get out.'

Interrupting the conversation, Lady Carter pointed out: 'We are not talking pennies here Josie, these items are valuable and I have been advised they could fetch a bundle in the right auction house, certainly enough to provide for Fanny's upkeep at the hostel and a donation to Salvation Army funds; if she so wished she could also give up her cleaning job.'

'But I don't want to. I enjoy my little job at the chapel and I meet lots of good people; now Ma has gone, I shall have no-one to look after and I can earn more money. When you get out of prison it's you who will need the 'rainy day' fund not me.'

Grabbing her in a bear hug, Josie announced: 'You really are the best big sister in the world, our Fanny. Now, be brave until I see you again, hopefully on regular visits.'

Fanny beamed. 'You mean I can come on the bus and see you on a proper visit?'

'You can, can't she Officer Buck?'

'Once we have sorted out the paperwork, your sister will be on the visiting roll, but only once a month. Now come on O'Dare, it really is time we made a move.'

Saying goodbye to Kristy, Lady Carter and Sybil was hard enough, but leaving her sister to fend alone was very difficult; as she walked to the waiting car, she shed a few tears.

Concerned she would breakdown, Officer Buck took her arm. 'Don't worry Josie, she'll be fine. It will take time but with all those good folk to watch out for her it won't be long before she is standing on her own two feet and waiting for you to come home.'

'I know she will, Miss, but times like this make you realise it's hard being locked up. Anyway, thanks for bringing me, I could not have coped without you and I can't wait to get back and tell Rose how it went. Oh yes! Thanks for the flowers from the wing. It was good of you.'

Mavis affectionally smiled. 'Away with you, O'Dare. It's part of the job. Now driver, don't spare the horse-power and get us home in time for tea.'

It took many months for Josie to come to terms with her mother's death; she preferred her own company and instead of association with the rest of the wing, she remained in her cell with her books. In many ways reading empowered her; apart from society and fashion magazines she had little time for literary pursuits but, being imprisoned with a library full of stories, she soon became the wing bookworm. It was an interest she shared with Rose, often reading to her until she fell asleep but it was clear to Josie she had little time left. However, in her more lucid periods, Rose steadfastly insisted on listening to Josie's adventures in exchange for hers.

Thumbing through some magazines provided by the Prisoners Aid Society, Rose was about to ask her nurse to take them away when she noticed a folded old newspaper caught up in a copy of 'Picture Post'. Pulling it free, she studied it, gasped aloud and dropped it to the floor.

Thinking her patient was about to have an attack of breathlessness, the nurse offered her oxygen but it was weakly brushed aside. Pointing to the floor Rose explained: 'Sorry, I'm quite all right. I thought I saw a familiar face in that old newspaper, could you take the magazines away and leave the paper on the bed.'

Making sure Rose was comfortable, the nurse gathered it up, briefly looked at it and with a patronising smile and suggested: 'It must be your imagination dear. It's an American paper and you won't know anyone from there, do you?'

Too sleepy to read, the newspaper remained open on the pillows until tea time and, when she woke up, Josie was reading it.

'Well, well, well. I have made the headlines in a few newspapers as well as the good old 'Hereford Times' but blimey, pictures on the front page of the 'Milwaukee Journal' in America, is the dizzy heights where I come from!'

'And are you the 'Daring O'Dare' in the pictures and when are you going to tell me all about it?'

'Yes Rose I will, but, as they say, it is a long story.'

'And I'm on short time, so you best get on with it.'

Between bouts of enforced sleep and increased treatment, Josie slipped in and out of the infirmary like a travelling raconteur as she narrated her story to her dying friend. The farmer's boys in the hop yards at Wellington, May

Fair in High Town, the mist over the River Wye and her criminal escapades with George 'bloody' Davis and, when she had the strength, Rose questioned her on her high life in London society; she was rewarded with laughter-filled stories of rich men and women falling over themselves for her favours.

As the stories continued, Rose was mesmerized enough to ask why; Josie told her the truth as she saw it.

'For me it was about money; clever scams, bouncing cheques and the occasional fraud and I can honestly say I have never physically hurt anyone in my life, except my father, to stop him beating Ma and Fanny. If I did hurt people it was in the pocket or perhaps emotionally and now and again a badly broken heart.'

'And you never fell in love?'

There was a long pause before Josie felt able to answer: 'What is love, Rose, but a passing stranger in our lives; in mine at least because I simply could not afford it. True, many men and some women have fallen at my feet but for me they were a route to riches and I never once succumbed to their sexual advances or pleasures.'

Puzzled by the answer, Rose asked her to explain.

'Because I saw how my boozed-up father and brothers treated us, especially Ma, beating and bullying us whenever they felt like it. I was determined not to fall into the same trap and had to find us a new home so I used my wits and womanly wiles to make a living and soon realised I could have any man in the palm of my hand. Many declared their love for me but all I wanted was cash for nothing, not for love. You see love can make a woman weak not strong and I needed to be strong for so many reasons; being locked away in here with so many lost souls, confirms that.'

Stage by stage, the story unfolded and Rose's room became more a confessional than a sick room and the two women bonded in friendship. After careful thought, Rose asked the inevitable question: 'And would you do it all again?'

'That, dear friend is for another day. You're tired and nurse Kelly keeps giving me a time check. You must wait until tomorrow for the final instalment. Sleep well my friend and, don't forget, when you are ready I want to hear your story too.'

Josie kissed her softly on the forehead and, on her way out, Kelly handed her a mug of hot cocoa.

'She has really bucked up since you've been coming, we all thought she would be done and dusted by now but she's clinging on because of you. You cannot give her hope O'Dare because there isn't any but you are the tonic she needs at this stage of her life and it's working, at least for now.'

Josie had just about finished her cocoa when Officer Buck came through the doors.

'It's almost lock-up Josie, time you were back in your room. You have a book to finish before lights out.'

As Josie walked away, Mavis turned to Kelly and asked: 'How's Rose doing. I hope O'Dare is not keeping her up?'

'Not at all, ma'am. It's time to keep up her spirits and O'Dare is certainly doing that but it will not be long now. It's been a good friendship for both of them and it's going to hit O'Dare very hard when her time comes. You will need to watch her ma'am.'

Making a mental note of the last comment, Mavis Buck headed for the landing to lock up the wing. It seemed more quiet than usual and, after a few minutes of key jangling, the wing settled down and waited for lights out. Alone in her cell, Josie pondered on her friend's unexpected question and, knowing she would insist on honesty, it took her most of the night to work it out.

Next morning, workplace gossip centred on the increasing depression in the outside world. A million people were out of work and on the dole, including the bread winners of some of the women in Holloway. Josie was concerned that Fanny, who was due a visit that afternoon, may be struggling to get by but Lady Carter confirmed all was well and she looked forward to seeing her sister again.

An hour before visiting time, Josie was called to the Deputy Governor's office. Officer Buck met her at the door; believing she was in some sort of trouble, after a short, nervous wait, she was given the good news that, with remission, she could look forward to early release.

Somewhat bewildered, Josie had become so conditioned to prison time, she had little idea that she was into her final year.

Senior Officer Buck clarified the situation for her.

'You have been in Holloway since June 1928, O'Dare, that's about three years and a half on my calendar and we have to think about preparing you for the outside world.'

Josie was unexpectedly adamant.

'I'm not leaving here until I'm good and ready, Rose needs me and I'm staying put until her time is up, not mine.'

Sensing her dilemma, the Wing Governor sympathetically told her: 'Of course not, O'Dare. Whatever happens, we are looking twelve months ahead less your remission but we do need to plan for your future employment.'

'Don't bother too much about that. If needs be I can plan for myself,' she told them.

'Yes. We are aware of your personal skills O'Dare but there is a laid-down procedure for release and rehabilitation and we do not allow prisoners into a changing world, before they are ready. If you don't agree then you can stay put.'

'What do I have to do then?'

'Join a few classes for sewing and beading, toy making, and knitting soft woollen animals; believe it or not we have a big market for them and our retail shop in Holbein Place, Sloane Square, takes orders from the public and we have other outlets too. What we need is a woman with a sharp financial mind to organise and manage it for us and Officer Buck thinks that could be you.'

'It will be good experience O'Dare and very worthwhile. Just give it some thought, we need to get some sort of ball rolling soon and you might even end up working at Harrods!' Buck added with a loud laugh.

Ignoring the comment, the Deputy Governor took a more serious view. 'As for Rose, what you do for her is very important but we must be realistic. You must except that she cannot go on for much longer but at least she has a friend to support her through it. Time to move on O'Dare and, I repeat, please give it some thought.'

Mavis Buck took her cue and escorted her charge to the visiting suite where Fanny and Kristy were waiting for her. On the way, she advised Josie to think carefully about her future. 'Surely you want to be out of here as soon as you can. Talk it through with your family and friends; you owe it them and to yourself, to get it right.'

'Oh, I will get it right, Miss, you can be sure of that; I'm already making plans in my head,' she said with her usual 'I'm up to something' grin.

The visit went well, most of it spent chatting over domestic matters and Fanny's new job offer as housekeeper to a comfortably-off widower and his son. Josie was concerned about the arrangement and told her so.

'I'm not keen on you living in a house with two blokes. Never know what they might get up to.'

Fanny, slightly embarrassed by her sister's remarks, asked Kristy to explain the situation.

'As you know, Josie, Fanny has been working as cleaner cum caretaker at a church hall nearby and has been recommended by the vicar.'

'Where is it and who for? I hope you have checked it out Kristy. It could be a doss house or something.'

Excited by the prospect of proper employment for the first time in her life, Fanny proudly added: 'Of course it isn't Trix, Kristy wouldn't do that. It's a proper job in a big house in Lillian Road, Barnes, that posh area the other side of Hammersmith Bridge. We have been to see it, he is a real gent, and his son is too. I get a couple of attic rooms, furnished real smart and a bit of a washroom under the eaves. I will get a small wage, full board and lodging and no bills to pay. The river is a ten-minute walk away and buses into the West End pass the end of the road; for the first time in my life I can stand on me own two feet. Ma will be proud of me, Trix,' she added.

'I'm not too sure about this Fan, being a gent means nothing these days.'

'We have to let her do it,' Kristy said. ' It is what she wants and needs. We, Captain Bramwell and I, will help with the move and she can take her own bits and bobs with her. Don't worry Josie, it's not too far from Peckham and Denmark Hill, it's on a regular bus route and she can visit us. We will of course visit her but the hostel will miss her cheerful good nature.'

Josie seemed convinced and after some thought said: 'Seems a proper job, our Fanny; if you're happy I am too. If not I will not send for you sister, I may be around sooner than you think.'

Kristy and Fanny looked at each other more in shock than surprise. Her sister spoke first.

'What do you mean, are you coming out soon? Please tell us when will it be?'

'It's a bit of a maybe at the moment. I have done more than a third of my time and maybe, just maybe, I might get some remission but I am not banking on it yet. So don't start getting your hopes up.'

'You can and live with me in Barnes when you do.'

'We'll have to wait and see, Fanny. Now take her home Kristy before she pees her pants with excitement and look after her when she moves.'

After the visit, Josie went to the infirmary to see Rose, she was sleeping heavily so she went to stretch her legs in the exercise yard. A softball game was in play, she joined in and was about to take a swipe at the ball when a loud voice interrupted her concentration.

'Watch out O'Dare, I'm back. I hope you have been keeping my bunk warm?'

It was Tew, returning this time on remand for God knows what. Josie dropped the bat and went over to greet her.

'Blow me down, it's been ages. What went wrong this time? I will meet you for association after tea and you can tell all.'

When she got there, Tew was waiting for her at a corner table in the quiet area. She was her usual jolly self and eager to relate her latest misdemeanours.

'Well, I knew you couldn't survive in this place without me so I blagged my way into a posh Ladies Night at the Turkish Bath House in Portobello Road. I had already visited a couple, one in Chancery Lane the other in The Strand, pickings were good, made a bit of a killing and decided to go upmarket.'

'Doing what?'

'Handbags, purses, jewellery, a bit of this and that from the best hotels and spas. I tried the Kensington Spa and nearly got copped but when an old school chum from Henrietta Barnett told me her mother once took her to the Turkish Baths in Portobello Road, I thought I'd try it out.'

'You went to Dame Henrietta Barnett College in Hampstead? I never would have thought it.'

'Just because I don't use a snooty voice, it doesn't mean I'm not educated. Don't be deceived by my small talk, O'Dare, I had private elocution lessons and variety of voice and pitch goes a long way in my line of work.'

'So your parents paid for your education at a public school. When did it start?' Josie asked.

'Two years after it opened just before the war. We lived in Muswell Hill and father insisted I had a decent education but much good it has done me. Anyway, you are not the only one to change the spots, I dropped down and you went above your station. You can't blag a blagger, O'Dare?'

'So, if you are that good how did you end up behind bars this time?'

'Bit of bad luck I suppose. While my partner in crime, and a few other things, waited by the bus stop outside I slipped through a side door and waited for the women to get under steam, if you will pardon the expression. It's more than a little friendly in the steam room on ladies nights so I waited until they were up to their tits in steam and nipped in the changing room. I had more time than usual to root through the pockets and bags lying around the locker rooms, with easy pickings, cash, purses and jewellery everywhere. I grabbed what I could and was about to leave when a big woman in her birthday suit bounced in, yelled 'stop thief' and I was off on my toes to the foyer exit. Slipping on the wet tiles, I hit my head and woke up to a sea of bosoms hanging over me. I thought I was dreaming but it was a nightmare when the police arrived. Fortunately, my partner heard the rumpus, dashed in to help and pretended to check for identification; with a swift sleight of hand she cleared my poacher's pockets of loot before the police woman had time to search me. Feeling rather shaken from the fall and dazed by the collection of tits, I was cuffed, charged and carted off to Paddington Green nick. Next morning, I was up before the bench, remanded in custody and well worth it just to see the Swell Mob and you again O'Dare.'

Chatting away like old friends, catching up on the Holloway gossip and swapping stories was always good value and, with her friendship with Tew cemented, Josie found the next few weeks easier.

The following day she dropped in to see Rose and found her looking much better. Outwardly refreshed by long periods of morphine-induced sleep, it was clear there was little defence against the powerful cancer. She had twice refused invasive radiation treatment at the nearby Elizabeth Garret Anderson. Instead, and thanks to Lady Carter's generosity, she agreed to mistletoe infusions at the Homeopathic Hospital in Great Ormond Street for respite care.

Nevertheless, she was on reasonable form and teasing her friend on the question 'would she do it all again?' Josie pulled up a chair. 'I had hoped to hear your story this afternoon, not a repeat of mine. Come on, Rose, shall we start at the very beginning?'

'Not until you honestly answer that question. It really is important for me to know you trust me with the truth, Josie. I don't want to take lies to my grave; surely we mean more to each other than that.'

It was a big moment for Josie, too. Knowing she must be true to her dying friend she said: 'You're right Rose. These past few years have been special and I cannot betray your memory. Now, please ask me again?'

'All things considered would you do it all again?'

'Yes, I would Rose, once a bad girl, always a bad girl and under the same circumstances I would do it all again. It is so hard to explain it to an unworldly woman like you but when I think about my past escapades, the excitement and the adrenalin surges in my head, I am back on the criminal roundabout.

'By the time I get out of here, I will be heading towards thirty-five years old and ready for a second roll of life's dice. How, when, where and what, God, or maybe the devil, knows; I am what I am, and ready to use my wits to survive. Where I get it from I don't know, but it's there in the blood and that blood keeps circulating.'

Josie relaxed her hand but Rose continued to cling to it.

'And who am I to challenge that? Since I was seventeen, my life has been fear and pain but the end is in sight and I cannot help but welcome it. I once had a family who loved me but it all came to a sudden end when I was raped and you know the rest. Sometimes I wish it had ended then, at the gallows, not thirty years on with a savage disease raging through my bones but I might not have met you had you not been a bad girl.'

'A very bad girl indeed, Rose. Meanwhile you must rest and I need some exercise and a catch-up with Tew in the yard; if you're awake I'll come back and you can tell me about the suffragettes.'

'I'll try to and if you're playing catch-up on memories with the irascible Tew, beware the adrenalin rush,' she murmured, her tired eyes fixed on Josie until medication claimed her undivided attention.

On the way back from the exercise yard she bumped into Mavis Buck; she was on her way to supper in the officer's mess and stopped to ask.

'How is Rose? I understand that it's down to you she is holding her own. She is agitating to see you again tonight and she has not finished telling you some story or other. She's expecting you after tea and has promised to keep awake.'

'Right, Miss. I'll have my tea and get down there. Are you on the wing tonight?'

'Yes, I'm on duty until lights out. Don't worry, I'll be around if you need me,' she quietly replied.

Back in her cell, Josie played with her food; she was feeling well but didn't have much of an appetite so she pottered about her cell until the whistle blew for association.

Taking her time, she arrived at the infirmary to find Rose sitting up in anticipation of her visit. Freshly washed and brushed up, she wore a clean white night shift and a knitted woollen shawl to keep her warm. More animated than usual, she was ready to start where she had left off yesterday, nevertheless Josie noticed her friend was more distant than she had expected and for the first time she saw how deeply blue her eyes were.

Normally shaded by tiredness, they were wide open and shining and her ageing skin had a smooth, waxy look about it.

Aware that Nurse Kelly was hovering in the background, Josie did not notice Senior Officer Buck was quietly conversing with the Deputy Governor on the landing. Her thoughts were suddenly broken when Rose leaned closer to her and insisted.

'Listen up then, Josie, I haven't got much time. Do you want to hear my story or what?'

It seemed an abrupt request; almost as if she was being reprimanded for not paying attention.

'You bet I do. I've been waiting a long time to get to this stage and I'm ready for anything,' she said with a laugh.

'So have I, dear friend. Apart from a few years in the execution suite, I have many good memories from this long imprisonment, more so since I became ill. People have been kind and mostly caring and in many ways, being in here has opened my eyes to the bigger picture, albeit through rose-tinted glasses of my own making. Yes, I have seen many changes, most of them good; before I came here, it was a mixed prison with male warders but living conditions have since been updated and we have more female officers.'

'Good God. It's bad enough now, it must have been hell then. What was it really like, I wonder? I don't suppose anyone knows unless they were there?'

'Thankfully I wasn't either but one old lag I got to know was. She had been inside for years before being packed off to Bedlam, but she did tell me a bit about it before she left. It was a bit addled and it might not be true but she did remember Holloway as a dirty, poorly-lit building with overcrowded cells, little sanitation, rotten food and rats as big as cats. Although the women were separated from the men, it didn't stop them from being abused by the guards in exchange for extra food and water.'

Rose paused and almost slipped into doze; Josie watched over her for a while and Nurse Kelly brought her a mug of tea. 'Strong woman, isn't she? I have seen them come and seen them out of this world but this one has a stronger will and from what I'm overhearing she hasn't finished telling you her story yet, a story she needs to tell. Thank God you turned up. I don't know how you cope with her O'Dare, despite all my training I'd find it tough, never mind those two out there.'

'What two, out where?'

'The Governor's team; they have been on watch since you arrived. There is not much they can do but in prison, times like this can affect the whole wing and we must be prepared. Look, I'm right she isn't finished yet, I think she is waking up again.'

Looking slightly bewildered, Rose blinked and then briefly rubbed her eyes. Seeing Josie looking at her, she sleepily muttered: 'Still here are you. You must be a sucker for bedtime stories?'

'It depends on the storyteller so I'm sitting comfortably ready to listen.'

She waited for Kelly to plump up the pillows and together they lifted Rose into a more comfortable position; Kelly gave her another injection. Josie was curious.

'Morphine and that's as good as it gets for Rose.'

'Not cocaine then?'

'No, but what do you know about cocaine O'Dare.? Come on be honest with me.'

'I got into a bit of a habit a few years back; it was all the go in London society but after treatment at a clinic I kicked it,' Josie admitted.

'And make sure you don't get hooked again when you leave here. Whatever the pressure, it's not worth it.'

Anxious to get her story on track again, Rose was getting more restless than ever and she began gesticulating irrationally at her companions. A surprised Josie asked: 'What's that all about Kelly?'

'Side effects from the morphine, she should calm down in a couple of minutes.'

She did, and insisted on concluding her story.

'When I arrived changes were already under way but I never expected to survive long enough to see them. For two years, I was isolated in the execution unit waiting for the drop but it never happened.'

Her tiny hand gripped Josie's as she paused to control her laboured breathing.

'No need to rush, old girl, take your time; let's start with how the suffragettes became your family?'

'Yes they did; they were in and out of here like clockwork and seemed to enjoy causing a rumpus and upsetting the government. We had no idea why they were in prison until someone explained they were fighting for our rights. They were mainly toffs, with rich husbands to bail them out but once we got to know them, they were jolly good fun. Their supporters kept yelling encouraging messages over the wall, some even chained themselves to the railings around Parliament and one poor soul was so upset she threw herself in front of the King's horse at the Derby. When they all went on hunger strike and were force-fed, we thought they were crackers, and when they gagged and screamed we cheered them on to hide the noise.'

Pausing only for more breath, Rose was determined to continue. 'Even then they found time to take on my troubles and told all their posh friends about me; it caused a heck of a stink in high places. Hundreds of women up and down the country signed a petition to the Home Secretary and I was allowed association with other prisoners, including the suffragists.

'Mrs. Pankhurst was so kind to me and fought hard for a stay of my execution and one funny old girl called Ethel Smythe, dressed a bit like a bloke in tweeds and a collar and tie. She never gave up the fight for votes for women and believed it would happen one day. She was in here for two months and wrote a song 'March of the Women' for the campaigners. One afternoon

240

during association, she organised a sing-song in the exercise yard; all the suffragettes and most of the prisoners and staff turned out and, using her toothbrush as a baton, she leaned out of her cell window and conducted us in a rousing chorus. Everyone joined in, some threw their bonnets in the air and somehow it got to the newspapers and caused another stink.'

Rose unexpectedly burst into laughter, giving Josie just a hint of what her young life might have been; the laughter quickly tuned in to a severe attack of coughing soothed only by more medication. Kelly warned Josie: 'Not much longer O'Dare, she's getting very, very tired and you must leave soon.'

Ignoring her and despite her breathlessness, Rose pleaded with Josie to carry on for just a little while longer at least until she fell asleep.

Josie looked at Nurse Kelly who simply shrugged her shoulder. 'So, you eventually got a reprieve?'

'Yes, but some people saw it as getting away with murder but they didn't know the truth, not even the officers and when it finally got around I did get some sympathy but not from my family, they left me to rot.'

'Why?' Josie asked.

'Because the man I was accused of killing was a member of my father's club and he blamed me for tempting him when I was working at his house. He had promised me clerical work but I ended as companion to his bitchy wife and daughters; when I refused him, he forced me so I hit him hard and he fell into the fireplace. It is all in the past now and I settled down as a lifer. I discovered a lump in my breast about fifteen years ago but I would not let them cut it away. They tried hard to persuade me but I knew it would not cure me so I kept on with the mistletoe infusions until I had little strength left. Since then I have been slowly rotting away in here and, even now, some of the old lags think its retribution for my sins. In their eyes, what the noose failed to do, the good Lord has, but I cannot grumble. From the moment I arrived in the condemned cell, Holloway has looked kindly on me; it has been my home and the staff my kin. Nurse Kelly, she is my angel of mercy and I shall miss her.'

Kelly was clearly moved and so was Josie when Rose pulled her closer and whispered: 'I wish I had known you for longer; our friendship may have been short and sweet, but for me it has been more precious than gold. Live long and enjoy what life brings you and one day we can catch up again.'

Not knowing it would be the last goodbye, Josie kissed her friend on the forehead, as she did so she felt Rose's limp hand slip from hers; not wanting to let her go, she held it more tightly than ever. Kelly knew better and, carefully untwining the joined up fingers, she felt for a pulse and after a long pause murmured: 'She's gone O'Dare, I'll give you a moment with her and then we must leave it to the Governor.'

Josie stood alone beside the bed until Mavis Buck arrived.

'How peaceful she looks, she has you to thank for that; all has been said and done and you made it easy for her to let go. She has reached her final peace and we must leave.'

After a few more silent moments, Mavis led Josie into the corridor and explained to her: 'This is where the system takes over. Rose made it clear she wanted no family involvement and no fuss, except to be buried in the prison garden, as she would have been if she not been reprieved. When the Chaplain arrives, I will walk you to your room and remind you of the brave soul who chose to share her last hours with you. Be comforted by it.'

Back in her room, Josie was a mess of wretchedness and deep sorrow. Lock-up was later than usual and kindly Nurse Kelly brought her cocoa; she sipped it slowly until lights out and in the darkness silently shed her tears.

By morning, word that Rose had died circulated beyond the wing and a rare, uneasy silence hung over Holloway.

Laid up in the non-conformist chapel, Lady Carter, Kristy and Josie paid last respects; two days later she was buried in the shadow of the prison walls, a simple spray of wild flowers from the prison garden marked her grave.

The exercise yard was unusually quiet that day; Josie sat alone on a bench inwardly counting the days to her possible release. Emerging from a cluster of women deep in conversation, Tew trotted across the yard, sat down beside her and placed a comforting arm around her shoulder.

'The girls were saying it must have been tough handling all that. I'm not sure if I could have sat through it.'

Shrugging her shoulder, Josie tried to hide her true feelings.

'Yeah, well. You get used to kicking the bucket where I come from. It wasn't so far back that I had to bury my Ma.'

Trying a more rational approach, Tew advised: 'We all have to face it at sometime but it's best have to move on; you will be out of this place soon so keep your mind on that. It's what the Rose we all knew would want for you, getting out and getting on with it.'

'I know and I will, so let's change the subject. You must be due at the Bailey soon. What's the charge this time?' Josie asked.

'Theft with all the trimmings, I suppose. My brief is going for a couple of similar offences to be taken into consideration in return for a non-custodial. Can't say it will work but I'm keeping my fingers crossed but hearings at the Bailey are slow and I could be out at the same time as you. Could be fun, though,' she said with a laugh. It wasn't far from the truth. Three months later Tew was back inside again, this time for twelve months, less three on remand.

Meanwhile, Josie's commitment to the Sloane Square craft shop had brought her six months remission instead of the anticipated three. Her release was imminent and she was given a release date.

As her leaving date approached, Lady Carter accompanied Josie to a meeting with Friday Committee, to discuss her future. The Chairman considered her employment potential with the Governor and Wing Governor and Senior Officer Buck confirmed preparations for release were in hand. Well aware of her own potential and prospects, she carefully kept them to herself. Next day she met the Discharged Prisoner's Sub-Committee and agreed a cash grant for new clothes, transport to the station and a ticket home.

Explaining that nobody leaves Holloway without board and lodging, the ebullient woman in charge suggested she might prefer to stay at the 'Fanny Hobson Hostel for released Female prisoners' to help her adjust to her new life. It was ten shillings a week for board and lodging, paid for by the Discharged Prisoners Agency and she was told she had forty-eight hours to prepare for release. Thanking the committee for their help, she asked them to inform Lady Carter of her coming release and went to her room to think it through.

Word of Josie's early release rattled around the wing and Tew was waiting for her in the exercise yard.

'So you've done your bird and are about to fly away into the big bad world outside. Are you going for the Fanny Hobson route or under your own steam?'

'Now that would be telling,' Josie insisted and tapped the side of her nose. 'But how will we stay in touch if I don't have an address?' Tew asked.

'I'll just have to contact Henrietta Barnet Old Girls Association, won't I,' and the two chums laughed all the way to tea.

Leaving day was always an early start; the prison hierarchy preferred a quiet undercover discharge rather than the lively farewell often accorded to a popular inmate. The night before had been something of a humdinger; cakes were baked, hooch was secretly bottled and shaded eyes ignored suspicious goings on. After much cheering, Josie was persuaded to perform one last Marie Lloyd song.

Quickly realising that party-time could get out of hand, the duty officers clamped down on the noise and eventually the wing calmed down. In the darkness after lights out, mystery voices whispered good luck messages to their most colourful co-habitee.

CHAPTER TWENTY

The morning after Bonfire Night was wet and misty. For most of the night, rain had drizzled on the final embers of the community bonfires, leaving the remains of a Guy Fawkes dummy or two to lie among the hot cinders. The smell of gunpowder and smoke lingered in the early morning air and an occasional firework exploded in the street. In the precincts of Holloway prison, there was no sign of celebration and, apart from inmates with windows on the top floor, Bonfire Night had passed most of them by.

A soft red dawn flooded the London skyline, casting an eerie light through the bars of Josie's cell and reminded her of her mother's cautionary threat 'red sky at morning, shepherds warning' to her father and brothers as they set out for a day's work in the hop yards. She hoped it was not an omen for the future. Her sentence at an end, she had been awake for hours and was looking forward to a long soak in the bath before the inevitable pre-breakfast dash to the ablution block.

As the wing slowly came to life, she carefully dressed in the made-to-measure, going-away outfit made for her in the sewing room and applied a light touch of make-up to her pale face. Pulling her greying hair into a fashionable bun, she adjusted the prison issue spectacles framing her face. The poor quality of light for reading in her cell had weakened her eyesight and, today, she looked more like a schoolteacher than an ex-con society hostess and she was well pleased with her new look.

Enjoying her last prison breakfast, porridge, bread, jam and tea, the hand-made good luck notes from chums on the wing, including a special card from Kelly, on the breakfast tray, touched her emotions and she quickly stuffed them into her battered Gladstone bag.

Mavis Buck kept her promise to see her off the premises and, as escort and prisoner walked the wing to the infamous glass doors, orchestrated clapping broke out. At the top of the staircase, she paused to acknowledge the fond farewell with a confident smile and a majestic curtsey but, behind the round, wired prison glasses she was filling up with tears.

At this time of day, the reception area was more a departure lounge; release papers had to be to signed, personal effects checked and wages for prison work paid in full inside a brown envelope. Rummaging through her storage box, she shook out her glamorous Old Bailey outfit and donated it to the prison entertainment group set up after her first Christmas show. More important, she removed the silver locket and chain from its little box and asked Officer Buck to fix it around her neck.

'Thanks, Miss. It's my good luck charm and back where it belongs; I thought it might have been nicked,' she cynically suggested. Mavis chuckled and edged her towards the doors.

'Time you were on your way O'Dare. Keep out of trouble and if you need help at anytime, call me.'

'Yeah! And you will come running, Miss? Pigs might fly?

'They might indeed Josephine but it's up to you to find out,' Mavis replied with a touch of sadness.

Silenced by the warm, friendly comment, Josie gave her escort an affectionate goodbye hug.

'Fair play, Miss, you've been good to me and I won't ever forget it. Just one thing before you go, could you tell Tew Fanny Hobson is not for the likes of me, I'm going south of the river this time.'

Unlocking the heavy bolts on the main doors, Mavis gave a last few words of advice: 'Remember O'Dare; look back on this place once and only once. The world outside is yours, give it your very best shot and it will reward you.'

'You can bet on it, Miss,' Josie said with a grin.

Picking up the battered Gladstone bag, she stumbled over the threshold and waited until the door closed behind her; this time shutting her out instead of in. At the Gatehouse she put bag down, breathed in the fresh morning air and turned for one last look at the place she had called home for almost four years; a lone, loud voice spoke for all inside 'Good luck O'Dare we will keep your porridge warm just in case'.

Ignoring the gentle shower of rain, Josie stretched out her arms in an all-embracing, symbolic hug for all those inside the grey prison walls and allowed the water to trickle like tears from her upturned face. Blowing a farewell kiss to the prison, she shook hands with the elderly gatekeeper, picked up her baggage and almost skipped along Parkhurst Road.

At the junction with Camden Road, she spotted her sister limping towards her and waved at her. Surprised to see her using a walking stick, it was an emotional reunion for the two women and they clung to each other in silence. Josie spoke first.

'How long have you needed a stick. You never had one when you came to visit me?'

'They called it an offensive weapon at the Gatehouse and I had to leave it behind. It was Ma's stick and I like to use it; it helps balance my boot and I feel comfortable with it. Look if we stand any longer we'll get soaked, I'll call a taxi cab to take us Barnes,' Fanny suggested.

'Not likely. If we take the bus to Liverpool Street, we can pick up the number nine bus to Mortlake; a ride through my old patch is just what I need and on the way you can tell me all the news. So where is the house?'

'Down by the river, it's very nice. Since Ma died having a proper job has kept me busy and I am very good at housekeeping. You can live with me until you decide what to do and where to go.'

During the journey, they talked about their mother and discussed future plans, Josie reminding her sister: 'All we have now is each other Fanny and I really want to stay with you until I sort myself out, if that's alright? I won't get in your way but after living in prison for the past four years I need peace and quiet to make plans for my future. I have a three-month lodging grant and prison wages in my pocket, so I can pay my way.'

'No need for all that. I have been preparing your room for weeks and you can stay for as long as you need to. I am earning a good wage and the 'rainy day' fund is safely tucked away. You can stay forever if you like?'

Parked along side Liverpool Street station, the number nine bus was ready and waiting for the last few passengers. The sisters dashed through the drizzle, climbed on board, paid the cheery conductor for two single tickets to Barnes; with a double ring on the bell and a call for 'any more fares please', the bus moved off. Pointing out familiar places along the route, the Aldwych, the Strand, Piccadilly Circus and Regent Street, Josie was almost childlike in her excitement; when her former haunts, the Cafe Royal and the Ritz caught her eye, she laughed and waved.

Passing through Belgravia, Knightsbridge and Kensington brought even more memories for Josie and when the bus stopped outside Park Mansions, she thudded on the window and announced to the amused passengers: 'When we were on the up, that's where we lived with Ma.'

She was about to expand on the subject when the bus jerked forward, throwing her back into her seat. A relieved Fanny calmed her down and it wasn't long before the happy pair were crossing Hammersmith Bridge into Barnes, alighting at the first stop over the bridge. Crossing over into Lonsdale Road, Fanny said: 'I live in a big house, Trix, down by the river; we take the next right into St. Hilda's Road, walk to the end and turn left at the bottom into Lillian Road. It doesn't take long from the bus stop, about ten minutes at my speed; you will do it far quicker and there are plenty of buses into town.'

Walking down Lillian Road, Fanny paused and turned into a wide drive leading to a substantial double-fronted villa part hidden by trees. Josie gasped in surprise.

'Is this it? Blimey, our Fanny, Kristy said it was big, but not this big. It's a little palace.'

Pointing up at two large attic windows, one with a small balcony her sister said: 'That's where I live, Trix, I can see all the boats and barges through those windows and it's lovely. Come on I'll take you up. We have to use the back stairs, it's a bit of a climb but I'll go up first and you follow with your bag.'

The large, comfortable and surprisingly well-furnished sitting room at the head of the staircase was bright and airy with large sash windows to let in the light; outside each window a small balcony supported a variety of potted plants.

A well-stuffed horsehair couch, large enough to double up as a spare bed was positioned below the sloping ceiling between the windows and a sturdy and well-polished oak table and two matching chairs stood against the opposite wall. A sturdy dresser with shelves divided the room from the small kitchen and off the wide passage cum landing, a door led to a small, narrow bathroom and WC.

The main bedroom at the end of the passage was about the same size as the sitting room but with hanging cupboards under the eaves for clothes and storage. It was furnished with two beds, a dressing table with three mirrors, two chairs, and a small bedside table with a lamp. Electricity was connected and the living room and bedroom had coal fires.

Back in the sitting room, Fanny brewed a pot of tea and set out a tray with pretty cups and saucers and a plate of assorted biscuits and the sisters sat down on the bulky sofa.

Josie was more than pleasantly surprised to see how well her sister had done for herself.

'I never expected the likes of this. It's really comfortable and all mod-cons; was it all done up when you first came here?'

'It was nicely decorated but a bit sparse. Kristy helped me out with crockery and odds and ends for the kitchen and my employer, Mr. Duncan, supplied the material for curtains. Lady Carter helped me make them and I made the cushions from the off cuts; the rugs were our Ma's, including the one you bought her from Heals.'

'And was there electricity and a proper bathroom?'

'No, but it was already in the house when I came but not in here. I used oil lamps until Mr. Duncan had the electric brought up last year; he also employed a builder to change a store room into a little bathroom for me. He is a very kind man and when I told him you might be coming to stay he ordered another bed and bedding and Kristy helped me make a patchwork quilt from the Chinese curtains I took from the Park Street house.'

Touched by her sister's good nature, Josie was pleased to find many of her own personal items, including much of the expensive jewellery she had acquired in her heyday, stored by Fanny in the attic cupboards.

'What a clever sister I have; I'm amazed at what you have done and you have kept all my clothes for me too. I'm much slimmer these days and hope they still fit me?'

'You can try them on later; I have been taking sewing lessons and can make and mend anything these days, I can even do alterations, but that's not all. Come with me and I will show you.'

Taking her sister's arm, Fanny led her to the bedroom; opening a store cupboard behind the bed, she carefully lifted a few loose floorboards. Dragging out a dusty, battered leather suitcase, she passed it to her sister; it was stuffed to bursting with banknotes of all denominations.

'Blimey, o'Riley, our Fanny! What's all this. Where did all this come from. Have you robbed the Bank Of England or something?'

Grabbing the cash, she went wild with pleasure as hundreds of high denomination bank notes flew through the air and fell like rain onto Josie's head.

'Hang on, Trix. Wait until I close the windows or it will be floating down the Thames to South End pier.'

'It's a small fortune, but where's it all come from Fanny?'

'The 'rainy day' fund and I haven't spent a farthing of it. When you were arrested, I took your advice and managed to sell most of the furniture and fittings from the Park Street house and it raised enough to move to the house you rented for Ma and me and pay for Ma's nurse. You had already paid the rent for a year and when I got work I earned enough for our day-to-day expenses until we went to live in the hostel.'

'But there's still a few thousand quid in this suitcase. Where did that come from?'

'Most of it from your earnings. You told me to save it up in case things went pear-shape, and they did. After you went down I kept it as safe as I could, under the floorboards, just as we did at Barton Manor.'

'Haven't you spent anything on yourself?'

'No need, Ma's bits and pieces of jewellery did very well at auction and more than enough for her funeral costs and a good donation to the Salvation Army. I did keep quite a bit in her knitting bag and it's still there if you need it.'

Josie was amazed and quickly changed the subject.

'And you're happy living here, Fanny.'

'Very. Since becoming Mr. Duncan's housekeeper I am very comfortable. They are both Christian gentlemen and I sometimes go to All Saints with them on Sunday morning. Mr. Duncan is a Church Warden and helps with cleaning. Sometimes, I decorate the church for weddings and at Christmas. I am also walking out with Bobby and very content, more so now that you are out.'

Taken by surprise at her sister's news and worried she might be in the way, Josie was curious to know if her sister had disclosed any private information to Mr. Duncan.

'I don't want to spoil things for you Fanny but what do they know about me?'

'Not much except that you have been suffering from a tropical illness since you came back from Central Africa and have been recovering in a sanatorium in the countryside.'

'And my name is?'

'Cousin Teresa Anne,' she replied with a laugh.

Full of admiration, her sister laughed too.

'Clever girl. You must have had a very good teacher?'

'Yes I did. You taught me how to use my brain but no more lessons, though, not while you live here. Now, you must have been up very early so have a bit of a sleep while I potter about the house and then I'll make us a late breakfast.'

Sleep was not easy; nevertheless, she catnapped between thoughts until she heard her sister clumping along the passage to wake her. For the rest of the day they chatted over cups of tea, enjoyed a short walk along the riverbank and watched the world go by from the sitting room window.

Asked what she wanted for supper, Josie asked for a plate of fish and chips and Fanny trotted off to the parade of shops near The Bridge Tavern to the best chip shop in Barnes; afterwards they shared the dish washing.

Explaining she had to do the final chores downstairs before bed time, Fanny suggested: 'Don't wait up. I'll be an hour or so locking up the house and laying the fires for the morning and you need your beauty sleep. I'll be up and about early in the morning getting breakfast for Mr. Duncan and Bobby so you can have a long lie-in.'

'That will be a treat, our Fan, it was up with the lark and no excuses in Holloway.' Unable to believe her good fortune, she closed the door behind her and went to the window to look at the river; it was still there.

For a while, she watched the port and starboard lamps on the boats manoeuvring up and down stream and then wandered off to the bedroom to explore the cupboards under the eaves. In the first one, she discovered the chest of drawers last seen in her lavish bedroom in Mayfair; pulling out a lower drawer, she carefully removed an oriental silk robe, held it to her cheek and was almost overcome by the smell of mothballs. Undressing slowly, she stepped out of her day clothes and slipped into the soft silky material just as Fanny came into her room.

'Just popped back to show you the workings of the hot water supply in the bathroom. It's what they call a gas geezer; turn it on, light it with a long taper and wallah! instant hot water, if you're lucky. I'll leave you to it.'

In the small bathroom, thick towels brought from Park Street hung from a rail and assorted bottles of sweet smelling oils and soaps, also salvaged from her former home, rested on a narrow shelf above the deep bath. Carefully following her sister's instructions, she lit the geezer and waited for the anticipated explosion which, for Josie, was something akin to the Royal salute in St. James's Park. Waiting for the window to stop rattling, she tipped a few drops of Penhaligon's Hamman Bouquet into the steaming water. The scent, named after the man who established many Turkish bath houses London, was Josie's favourite fragrance and reminded her of Tew's exploits. Delighted it had been rescued, she allowed the rising steam to drift over her and ,slipping into the comforting water, she recalled the noisy arguments in the primitive ablution block in Holloway on bath day. No scented soaps or baths oils to indulge in, only carbolic soap and rough towels for drying.

Snapping back into the present, she hummed a few strains of Marie Lloyd songs, bathed in the bubbles and dried herself on the soft white towels. Dressed in the soft, silk nightdress laid out for her, she folded back the freshly laundered sheets and climbed into her new bed. Lying back on the pillow, she removed her eyeglasses and the last thing she saw through her slightly blurred vision was the framed embroidery of a Hereford Bull and the words 'Home Sweet Home' worked by Fanny at school. She smiled herself to sleep, leaving the flask of hot cocoa left by her sister untouched.

There was no bell to wake her up next morning and, by the time she opened her eyes, the bright rays of the morning sunlight lit up the room and dazzled her. Fanny had remade her bed and was pottering about in the kitchen; the appetizing aroma of a cooked breakfast was enough to tempt Josie out of hers and into her dressing gown.

In the kitchen, her sister was scrambling eggs and frying bacon just how Josie liked it, to a crisp; coffee was on the boil, the toast was warming nicely by the fire and the table was set for two.

Picking up a photograph of herself, her mother and sister at a garden party, she squinted at it. 'I have left my specs in the bedroom but I'm sure this wasn't on the sideboard last night, Fanny.'

'No. It was in the drawer. It was taken at a charity do we had in the garden at Park Street and I have been keeping it for you.'

Josie laughed. 'And, as Ma used, to say, charity always begins at home our Fanny,' and sat down at the table for breakfast.

The days and weeks went by in similar vein. Fanny went about her domestic routine and in her spare time altering her sister's clothes on her sewing machine and laughing at her plans for respectability. In quiet moments, Josie caught up with her reading, enjoyed walks along the riverside and found her way around Barnes and Hammersmith.

Eventually, it was time for formal introductions to Mr. Duncan and Bobby which took place over afternoon tea; both gentlemen went out of the way to make their 'housekeeper's cousin' welcome, giving Josie the opportunity to practice suburban respectability. As expected Josie charmed everyone, including George, the gardener / handyman, he was quite a character and most amusing when she chatted to him in the garden and when he delivered coal and wood for the fires. More important, he kept her up-to-date on the local gossip and brought her the 'London Evening News' when he had finished with it. A dedicated Chelsea supporter; he went to Saturday home games at Stamford Bridge and over the weekend studied all the football news on the printed page before passing it on. George lived alone in an artisan's cottage in Hammersmith peddling to and from Lillian Road on a rusty old bike towing a small wooden trailer. When not mowing lawns, he pottered among the flowerbeds whatever the weather, preferring to be kept himself to himself in the bothy at the bottom of the garden.

At first, Lady Carter and Kristy kept a low profile and for a while preferred to meet up in the Tea Rooms on the Green at Barnes followed by a stroll round the pond to feed the ducks.

However, in the winter, they came for lunch or tea and sometimes supper and, if it was dark, Captain Bramwell came too. Nevertheless, Josie was restless for change and excitement.

It was approaching spring and Fanny was working her way through her sister's wardrobe and altering her summer clothes. Since leaving prison, Josie had put weight on and her once designer outfits no longer hung loosely on her slim frame; a nip and tuck here and there proved the point and, with a fit of the giggles, Josie tried them on and added them to her fashionable collection. After stowing away the sewing machine and tidying up the reels of cotton and bits and pieces of material, it was time for Fanny to go about her household duties and make supper for Mr. Duncan and son. Josie made a cup of tea and read the classified pages of advertisements in the 'Evening News'.

Eventually her sister arrived with the leftovers from the evening meal, explaining that Mr. Duncan had been called to an unexpected business meeting and was in a rush and Bobby was going with him. Half a home-made chicken pie and vegetables followed by the remains of a trifle provided a pleasant supper for two after which Josie announced it was time to take a job.

'Whiteley's in Queensway are looking for a counter assistant in the haberdashery department and I'm going to apply. It's not much but it's a new start and with a bit of help over references I might get it.'

Taken by surprise, Fanny exclaimed: 'Blimey! Whiteley's in Bayswater. Now that is a bit posh. Mr. Duncan has an account there and orders goods by phone for same-day delivery, otherwise, he sends me in a taxi to choose what I want.'

'So you know where it is and how to get there.'

'I know my way around the store like the back of my hand and like to chat to the counter assistants while I am waiting for my goods to be wrapped. Did you know that the staff live in a hostel owned by the store and sleep in dormitories; there is a theatre on the top floor and a staff golf course on the roof? Blimey! Bet you did not know about that, did you?'

'No, I didn't but I'm not sleeping in any dormitory, I had enough of that inside. It will take some thinking about but I'm going to have a go; anyway it's time I did a bit of earning and I need to move on.'

When the letter offering Josie an interview with the personnel department arrived on Saturday morning, her adrenalin was up and she kept it from her sister until the following day.

Lillian Road on Sunday was a quiet place; Mr. Duncan respected the Sabbath and took his Church Warden duties seriously. After morning service, he usually lunched with the Rector and Bobby, a keen horticulturalist, preferred to lunch with his cousin, a curator at Kew Gardens. After a stroll through the tropical glasshouses, he arrived home in time for evensong. Fanny and Josie enjoyed having the house and garden to themselves and, in the light of Josie's work plans, there was much to talk about. Settling for the peace and quiet of the shaded rose garden overlooking the river, Fanny had prepared a light picnic.

'How are you going to explain who you are?' Fanny asked.

'You know me. I was a teacher at a Scottish Mission School in Natal and returned home to the Shetland Islands to care for my ailing parents. They both passed away within a few months of each other and, after settling the rather complicated estate, I came to live in Barnes with my married cousin and her family.'

'Will you need references?' Fanny asked.

'I expect so. I have forged a good few cheques in my time and the 'Swell Mob' in Holloway taught me a few tricks too so I'm sure I can manage a couple of references. I may need to use this address.'

'Why not? I'm up in the mornings to pick up the first post and I watch out for later deliveries, all you need to do now is prepare for the interview next week and polish up your voice.'

Slipping into a soft Scottish accent, Josie dropped her new, steel-rimmed spectacles to the end of her nose and mimicked: 'If I can be of any assistance, Madam? I can arrange for a floor walker to help you choose and carry your packages to a taxi cab.'

Helpless with laughter, the two sisters played customer and sales assistant until Bobby appeared, heard them laughing and came to see what was amusing them. Fanny offered him tea and cake.

'You are early, Bobby. It is so peaceful in the garden, and we've been gossiping all afternoon.'

Blushing profusely, Bobby said shyly: 'My apologies ladies for interrupting but if I may remind you Fanny it will soon be time for evening song at Holy Trinity; I would welcome your company and perhaps your cousin will join us?'

'I'm so sorry Bobby, Josephine has an interview for work later this week and we have been making plans. Please excuse us this evening and, if you don't mind, I shall leave a cold supper in the pantry for you and Mr. Duncan.'

'Of course, my dear. I won't detain you any longer,' Bobby said and, looking somewhat embarrassed, he waved to Fanny, and wandered back to the house.

Clearing up the remains of the picnic, Josie collected the tea tray and took it to the kitchen. Halfway up the back stairs, Josie faked shock. 'Me, at evensong? Not likely. I did enough God-dodging in Holloway to last me a lifetime; the prison Chaplain invited me to his services but I told him christenings, weddings and funerals were enough to cope with and you did not get many of those inside. You go with Bobby, he does seem rather fond of you and I shall be busy all evening brushing up the accent and working on my references.'

The interview had gone better than expected. Dressed in a manner befitting a returning missionary, Josie wore a small crucifix on the lapel of her navy blue two-piece tailored costume bought in a jumble sale in East Sheen and comfortable lace-up shoes and dark silk stockings bought from the same source. Determined not to look flighty, her crisp white blouse buttoned securely, her hair drawn into a light bun, rested in the nape of her neck. She carried a leather handbag containing a purse, reading glasses and a manila envelope with two forged references. The first from a fictitious Church Missionary School in Natal, the other confirmed her retail experience in a woollen goods shop in Aberdeen; both carefully forged by a prisoner at the Sloane Square craft shop.

Impressed by her references, sharp mind and pleasing personality, the Personnel Manager took her to meet the manager of the haberdashery department for a brief test on pricing. This included cash balancing, billing and minor accounting, which she passed with flying colours.

Taken to view the staff facilities and dormitories, she explained she would not need accommodation as she lived in Barnes with a married cousin and buses were plentiful. The interview over, she was handed a list of staff rules, promotion prospects and rates of pay and, if successful, she would be fitted with a uniform.

Leaving by the staff entrance, she winked at the uniformed doorman and he touched his cap. Confident the job was hers, she looked at the famous shop and mouthed: 'God Bless you, Mr. Whiteley, I'm back on the road again'.

Haberdashery was a very busy department and, as well as the manager, there were four female counter assistants, a handyman in the stockroom and a boy messenger and it took Josie some time to find her way around.

A quick learner; within six months she had risen to senior stock control assistant with accounting responsibilities for haberdashery and lingerie. Both departments shared the same stock room and the Paragon overhead rail loop, an ingenious accounting system linking to the accounts department. After a sale, the counter assistant placed the customer's cash and bill into a tube attached to a pulley and, propelled by gravity or catapult action, it whizzed to the department cashier and returned a few minutes later with a receipt and any change. However, being new, it had a few technical problems and often broke down, sometimes to a standstill and Josie was bright enough to see how she could cash in.

Jim Bates, the stockroom handyman, was smitten with Josie; a bit of a dab hand with the electrics, he was easily persuaded to divert the odd tube or two into the stockroom where she often removed some of the cash. The shortfall was put down to breakdowns, dishonest staff in the cashier's office and the occasional customer helping themselves when the system stopped. It was a workable arrangement; Jim pocketed his share and Josie, aware of spot checks on staff, hid the greater proportion in an old cane chest with a false bottom, covering it with off cuts of material, just in case. It was a good way for quietly topping up the 'rainy day' fund but, when the auditors stepped in, Josie ended it and Jim removed the extension rail during his night shift.

A month later, poor old Jim suffered a stroke and was retired on grounds of ill health. He finished up very confused in the staff nursing home at Eastbourne and because he had no relatives to speak of, 'kindly' Josie, at the firm's expense, offered to oversee his welfare and visit him, at least until she was sure his memory had fully lapsed.

Keeping herself fit and healthy was as vital as looking her best, and when she was offered to become floorwalker in the lingerie department, she jumped at it.

The position required discretion, particularly when it came to the gentlemen customers. Realising that the gift-wrapped lingerie purchased for the lady wife, was destined for a mistress; for a clever woman like Josie, it was a perfect short-term swindle. Simple and straightforward, it was easy money; when a gentleman account customer made an expensive purchase, Josie made a point of noting if the postal address differed from that of the account holder and queried it with an obvious wink.

Blustering his way into an explanation, Josie quietly suggested he paid her twenty per cent in cash, which she pocketed, leaving the relieved customer to sign the full amount to his account. If any of her victims, and there were some, became disgruntled with the arrangement, she threatened to expose him, but it rarely came to that.

A few near misses, a snap stock take and an external audit postponed at the last moment, boosted her adrenalin but when she recognised Lord Curzon entering the department, Josie feigned an attack of the vapours, called an assistant to take over and made a swift retreat to the staff toilets. Unsettled by the incident, she decided to call it a day.

Josie had been with Whiteley's for almost fifteen months and it was time to return to Natal and follow the path the good Lord had set out for her. Stunned, yet full of admiration at her decision, her co-workers promised a good send-off and a farewell sherry party, hosted by her floor manager in the senior staff room.

In an atmosphere tinged with genuine sadness and warmth for the dedicated woman, tributes praised her exceptional work overseas and her dedication, honesty and kindness to colleagues who gave her a variety of gifts including a serviceable watch suited to African conditions. Her speech of thanks was moving enough to draw a few tears from the older women in the department after which Josie charmed management into donating the chest of unwanted material in the stock room to the Mission School children. As a mark of respect for her good works, management agreed and arranged for the company Daimler to take her to Barnes.

Waving a last goodbye to her gullible workmates, Josie had difficulty concealing her amusement when the porter stowed the chest in the boot for the journey to Barnes.

Little did he know that beneath the false bottom of the old chest the fruit from her in-store frauds; some £1500 in cash and a collection of high-class lingerie?

Gliding through Notting Hill, the chauffer-driven limo cut through South Kensington to Hammersmith; crossing the bridge into Barnes, Josie finally relaxed, sat back and enjoyed the view.

Fanny was setting the table for supper when her sister heard the car; moving across to the window she was amazed to see a chauffer-driven Daimler turning into the driveway. She was even more amazed when her sister stepped out carrying a clutch of monogrammed carrier bags from the popular department store. Hearing the car horn, the gardener dashed from his potting shed; Josie called him over, asked him to deliver the chest to her sister's rooms and in her soft Scottish accent thanked the chauffer. George was puzzled when he wished her well on her overseas travels and called for the bothy boy to help him haul it to the top of the house. Watched by a surprised Mr. Duncan and son, the Daimler turned into Lillian Road, leaving Josie to explain she had left her employment at Whiteley's and the chest was a going-away present.

Upstairs in the flat, Fanny insisted on seeing the contents of the chest. Ferreting through the cotton reels and colourful materials, she lifted the loose bottom, took out a thick, brown paper parcel and laughed again. Amused at her sister's reaction, Josie suggested: 'Can you manage to count it before I stuff it in the 'rainy day' bag until I have decided how to spend it? Now, shall we have supper first and then you can me what you have been up to,' Josie said and sat down at the table to read her post.

Noticing her sister was unusually quiet, Fanny asked if she was troubled.

'Nothing at all for you to worry your head about our Fan, I have to go to court next week, that's all.'

'What about?'

'It's the damn libel case against 'Reynolds Illustrated News'. When I was in prison, George fed them a pack of lies about me and my society goings on and my solicitor advised me to sue. The case comes up next week in Edinburgh and I have to be there.'

Supper was almost over when Fanny blushed and blurted out: 'Bobby wants to marry me. We have been courting for a long time and he thinks we should settle down. He won't wait forever.'

Josie she was not too surprised at the news and had already given it some thought.

'If that is what you truly want then you have my blessing. After all, I shall be moving on myself and leaving you in safe hands will make us both happy. Have you told Kristy?'

'Yes she knows how I feel about Bobby and so does Lady Carter but I need your approval. Mr. Duncan wants to buy us a home of our own but we want to stay here and take care of him.'

'Well, that seems a very good solution for both of us and you do not need mine or anyone's approval. It is a lovely house with plenty of room for my visits; as long as you are happy and Bobby treats you well, I am pleased for you both. Have you set a date?'

Fanny looked surprised.

'No. I wanted to tell you first but perhaps next summer would suit? Anyway Kristy is getting married to Captain Bramwell soon.'

Josie threw her arms into the air.

'Praise be! She's taken long enough to make up her mind hasn't she?'

'Not really. They have been making plans since she joined the band and started courting Captain Bramwell.'

'So why take so long before getting married?'

'Because it couldn't happen until Kristy finished her training. In the Salvation Army, an officer can only marry another officer and not a foot soldier. Six months ago she was promoted to Lieutenant and all is well for an autumn wedding.'

Josie was delighted at the news and, picking up the photo of her mother on the sideboard, she said: 'Ma will be so proud of you, Fanny. Now, let's sort this chest; we are going to need a wedding fund and there is some classy lingerie fit for a honeymoon underneath this lot. When I get back from Scotland we can start planning for the big day.'

'But Mr. Duncan wants to pay for all of it,' Fanny said.

'Not for my sister he doesn't. He can front up for the wedding do afterwards but when it comes to the best for my sister, I'm splashing out, big time.'

Some weeks later at the High Court of Justice in Edinburgh, the jury was about to return. Self-assured and well-turned out, Josie sat alongside her counsel; the defendants, 'Reynolds Illustrated News', appeared agitated and anxious. As she looked around the packed courtroom, she noticed a flashy young man in the public gallery staring at her. When she caught his eye, he shaded his face with his arm and looked away.

The Judge recorded a verdict in favour of the plaintiff and Josie and her counsel were delighted but badly shaken when awarded damages of just one farthing. Costs were set against the newspaper and Josie had nothing to pay. Shaking hands with her legal team, she turned down counsel's eager invitation to dinner and left the court convinced she had dashed his hopes of an overnight promise.

Accompanied by her legal team, she walked through the foyer and noticed the man from the public gallery staring at her again. Gripping her solicitor's arm, he dutifully escorted his client across the main marbled hall to the doorway; at the bottom of the steps, he called for a taxi to take her to Waverley station for the London train.

An hour later, she was ready to board the first-class night sleeper to King's Cross but failed to notice the same flashy young man wedged in a telephone kiosk making a call. After a good dinner in the club car, she retired to her small but comfortable carriage; the bed was made up and she settled down to read 'The Scotsman' for news of her trial. Lulled into sleep by the rocking motion of the carriage, she woke up to tea and a shortbread delivered by the sleeping car attendant. An hour later, she was enjoying breakfast in the dining car and, over her final cup of coffee, nervously considered how George Davis, currently residing in Wormwood Scrubs, would take the news of her latest victory.

CHAPTER TWENTY-ONE

Despite the autumn nip, it was a lovely day for a wedding. The trees in Ruskin Park had changed colour and above Demark Hill, the one hundred sixty feet high tower of the William Booth Training College built in 1929 by British architect Giles Gilbert-Scott, stood memorial to the founder of the Salvation Army.

Lady Carter had arranged for her chauffer to take her, Fanny, Josie and Sybil Thorndike to Kristy's wedding at the Citadel and a feeling of happiness and goodwill was evident. Newly promoted to Major, the handsome groom, resplendent in full uniform and sporting a cream rose in his buttonhole awaited his wife-to-be. The bride chose not to wear customary white, she preferred the traditional dark blue and maroon uniform and matching bonnet worn by women officers.

Excited by the occasion, Fanny pointed out: 'Kristy is a Major too. She was only given her badges last week and I had to sew them on for her.'

'How come she's a Major as well?' Josie asked.

Lady Carter was on edge. 'She'll be here soon and we haven't much time for questions so I'll be brief. As I understand it, when a marriage takes place between officers in the Salvation Army, both parties must be equal in rank, meaning promotion for the lower rank, at least I think that is how it works. Is that clear enough for you Josephine?'

'I should say so. Now, that is what I call fair play for women. Does Mrs Pankhurst know about this?'

'Hush Josephine, a little decorum please. Kristy is about to arrive and Fanny and I must do our duty.'

Lady Carter did not believe in 'giving a woman away' but agreed to walk Kristy down the aisle with Fanny.

Circumstances had prevented her own family being there but it was clear to everyone present, she had a worldwide family behind her.

To the strains of the wedding march played by a section of musicians from the college, the bridal party moved off and smiling happily at her friends, Kristy greeted her husband-to-be with the sunniest smile of all.

The Salvation Army Corps flag provided the backdrop for the simple wedding ceremony conducted by a senior officer from the college and the local Registrar. Appropriate prayers delivered the Salvationist tradition of music and hymn singing hit a very high note. Vows taken, prayers said and rings exchanged, the service ended with Kristy and Anthony adding 'and this I declare upon my honour as a true soldier of Jesus Christ'.

Josie nudged Sybil Thorndike and said: 'It's my sister next. I hope she knows what she is letting herself in for Sybil?' and laughed.

After signing the register, Major and Major Bramwell left the Citadel under an archway of tambourines trailing ribbons. The ceremony over, photographs were taken in the college garden and afterwards guests, including Major Bramwell's parents, both active Salvationists, enjoyed a substantial, alcohol-free wedding breakfast, the gift of the college. After a brief honeymoon in Worthing, they set up home in Denmark Hill.

It was coming up to Christmas 1935 and Josie had been free for over two years; nevertheless, she was becoming edgy, restless and unusually touchy. Feeling trapped in a boring way of life she needed to escape, not only her habitat but her personality too. She loved her sister dearly and wanted to see her happy and if that was with Bobby, then so be it.

Fanny was a year older than her sister and she secretly hoped for a family; the wedding was set for June and with nothing much to do but grow older, Josie was becoming prickly and difficult to live with.   The adrenalin was missing and she needed to get back into the swing of society again; now in her mid-thirties, she felt more like a woman of means and not the daring adventuress she used to be.

Keen to launch a fresh challenge while she was fit and healthy, she was at the end of her tether; eager to keep up her pretence status it was necessary to make important changes as she approached her middle years.

It came through the pages of 'The Lady' magazine, a weekly journal for gentlewomen. Concerned that she would have little to read in darkest Africa, the girls in haberdashery at Whiteley's had a collection to pay for a twelve-month subscription to the popular magazine. Her sister promised to forward it to her and, although it was not quite Josie's style and she preferred 'The Tatler', she was thumbing through it in Barnes, not Africa.

Domestic tips for housewives, cooking for Christmas, needlepoint for beginners and making your own rag rug, did little for Josie's wellbeing but today, grooming for the middle-aged, hiding your wrinkles and preparing for the 'change of life' brought her attention to advertisements for sea holidays. A special feature recommending the Tendring Peninsular on the Essex coast as the finest seaside holiday resort in England for the well-off, was just the ticket; sun, sand and sea in peaceful and luxurious surroundings for the discerning visitor. Offering special rates for long-term bookings, it was the perfect opportunity to improve her standing and she was excited at the prospects of a couple of months by the sea. Reading the details to her sister, she announced: 'Well, I'm definitely up for some of that, our Fanny. I can well afford it and it will surely put a bit of colour back into my prison-dulled cheeks.'

On a chilly morning in late October, Josie waited at the bus stop for the No 9 bus to Liverpool Street station. Apart from the journey from Holloway to Barnes, she avoided passing through Mayfair. It brought on too many emotions but today, her natural enthusiasm was simmering and, eyes wide open instead of hidden behind dark glasses, she wanted more than a glimpse of her heydays.

Alighting at the station, she headed for the bookstall and purchased a copy of 'East Coast Joys', a sixpenny booklet full of information on seaside resorts and a timetable for trains from Liverpool Street. In the steam-filled buffet on platform one, she ordered a cup of piping hot chocolate and a Chelsea bun and sat down to study the times of trains to Frinton-on-Sea.

Christmas and New Year over and done with and wedding plans safe in the hands of Mr. Duncan, Josie decided to announce her long-awaited trip to the east coast. Fanny was well aware of her plans, but she told Kristy, Lady Carter and Sybil Thorndike during lunch at Richmond-on-Thames. It came out of the blue.

'Look, you have all been so good to me but I need a change and what better place to start than a quiet and peaceful seaside town well away from London. I shall be going out of season and expect to be away for some months but never fear our Fanny, come what may, I shall be back for your nuptials. I wouldn't miss it for the world and that's a promise.' Fanny was about to cry. 'But I want you to walk me down the aisle like Lady Carter did for Kristy?'

'And I shall,' she said and hugged her sister. 'You have good friends and Bobby to take care of you and you did very well on your own when I was in prison. Now wipe your tears away and wish me well.'

Ever the mediator Lady Carter sympathized with both sides. 'It's best she starts a new life of her own Fanny but that doesn't mean she will disappear. Next June you are going to marry Bobby and your life will change too; Josie will always be there for you, just as she has always been and I do have a sneaking feeling she will not be too far away from you. Like you, she may be Herefordian at heart but both of you have lived here long enough to call yourself Londoners and I suspect whatever she chooses to do with her life, London is where she will end her days. So buck up Fanny, we have a wedding to look forward to and good friends are with us always.'

For four weeks, Josie carefully planned a wardrobe for all occasions; evening dresses, smart outdoor clothes and footwear and, more important, a collection of jewellery worthy of a well-secured deposit box at Coutts bank. To give her a more mature look, Miss Bignell from a highly rated hair salon in Church Street, Kensington, restyled her hair into a fashionable modern 'bob'. It suited her natural features and, while she was under the dryer, she had her nails manicured and polished and a facial. Mr. Duncan arranged for his driver to take her to Liverpool Street station and George, the gardener, loaded her collection of matching suitcases into the boot.

Josie emerged from the main entrance wearing a smart, soft grey woollen top coat with turned back button down cuffs and patch pockets for tickets and small change; a chic, peacock blue, wide-brimmed trilby added a touch of mystery. As Fanny walked her to the car, George said: 'You look a real corker girl. The tide will be sure to turn when you get there and so will the toffs, so mind how you go miss?'

'Tell me something I don't know,' she whispered to her sister and laughed as the limo drew away.

On platform one, the midday train was ready for boarding; the porter escorted her to a reserved compartment in the First Class carriage and stacked her luggage in the rack above her head. The small dressing case containing her jewels never left her side. Thirty minutes later, first sitting for lunch was called and taking her 'Marie Claire' magazine with her, she strolled to the restaurant car, ordered a full lunch, a half bottle of champagne and settled down for the journey to somewhere.

Chugging through the East End of London to the Thames Estuary offered little interest but beyond South End and Clacton-on-Sea, the sandy coast of Essex offered much to catch the eye, but picturesque Frinton-on-Sea was, without doubt, the jewel in the crown of English coastal seaside resorts. The train slowly approached the level crossing on the edge of town, allowing Josie time to take in the smart, architect-designed homes on the Frinton Park estate. The green lawns along the promenade stretched the length of the seafront and tropical palm trees shaded the white and blue Lido. Rows of pastel painted, wooden beach huts decorating the golden sands, finally convinced Josie she had made the right choice for her renaissance.

The Grand Hotel, overlooking the sea, lived up to its name.

Comfortable, spacious apartments furnished by Waring and Gillow had sea view balconies and en-suite bathrooms with a lavish supply of soft towels and assorted Chanel toiletries. Afternoon tea dancing in the Palm Court ballroom and the black-tie dinner-dance on Saturday night were open to all who could afford it and, despite the town's temperance image, the well-stocked cocktail bar was available for guests.

A chauffer-driven limousine collected Josie from the railway station and at her request took the long route to the Grand Hotel. Drawing up at the main entrance, she waited for the uniformed doorman to help her from the car; a porter took her luggage into the reception area. Thanking the driver with a large tip, the impressed doorman accompanied her to the reception area where the attentive owner/manager and his staff greeted the wealthy guest. She signed the register with a single stroke of her hand. Calling for the bellhop, the manager announced: 'Kindly escort the Hon. Mrs Templeton-Austin to the penthouse suite and ensure she has everything she needs, including afternoon tea.'

Well aware she was attracting considerable interest, she responded with a pleasant but coy smile and disappeared into the marbled lift. A fawning waiter served tea in her room and, after dismissing him with a generous tip, she kicked off her shoes, settled into a comfortable armchair and polished off the cream tea.

Rested and refreshed from the journey, Josie dressed carefully for her first dinner at the hotel; seated at a window table reserved in her name, the waiter presented the menu and left her to ponder on her choices. Much to his surprise, she ordered in French and accepted a complimentary jug of elderflower cordial in preference to a flute of champagne. Determined to practise her cover story she sipped her drink and casually watched the mannerisms and sedate behaviour of the other, mainly middle-aged guests. The meal over, she took coffee in the women-only lounge and after an hour retired to her room.

The first month was more familiarisation than a restful holiday. Josie enjoyed daily walks along the promenade, joined in croquet games on the lawn and was soon in demand as a fourth player for early evening bridge. Twice a week she took gentle exercise with the local branch of the Woman's League of Health and Beauty, and inspected the dancing in the Palm Court ballroom; more important she was building useful relationships with the hotel staff.

On the fourth weekend of her stay, Josie made her first useful discovery; a much older, well-dressed gentleman dining with an attractive young man. There was a hint of mystery about him and, according to odd snippets of staff gossip, she knew him to be Arthur Brooks, an important civil servant from London and regular weekend guest at the hotel.

Pleasant, courteous and friendly, particularly with the young waiters in the dining room, he mixed well in company, rarely left the hotel and generally kept himself to himself, except on Saturday afternoons when he liked to walk the long promenade.

On one such occasion, Josie decided to follow him; it was a cold day and the March wind was more bracing than ever. Unconcerned by the weather conditions and well wrapped up in her grey top coat with the patch pockets, she pulled a woollen hat over her ears and tied a thick scarf around her neck. She also wore gloves, carried a small leather handbag and waited in the reception lounge until the mysterious Mr. Brooks arrived in the foyer.

He too was dressed for the weather and Josie waited a few minutes before following him on his customary walk along the seafront. Normally a popular afternoon stroll for visitors and locals, today high seas had discouraged most people and rather than be exposed to the elements she dogged his footsteps at a safe distance.

Noticing he lingered outside the men's lavatories before going inside and curious to know what he was up to, she sat on a nearby bench to keep a subtle watch; he reappeared later followed by a fair-haired, lithe young man who walked in the opposite direction. Surprised to see anyone seated on the bench, he instantly recognised Josie as a guest at the Grand and was clearly relieved to see her wave to him and smile warmly.

Formally introducing himself as Arthur Brookes, he walked her back to the hotel and invited her to take tea with him in the ballroom and she readily agreed.

The Regimental Band of the 44th of Foot, (The Old East Essex) was in concert and well into Ivor Novello's 'Careless Rapture' and they waited for a suitable interval before entering the ballroom.

During afternoon tea, they chatted amicably about the very public love affair between King Edward and the twice-married American divorcee Wallis Warfield-Simpson, the hovering dark clouds of war and less importantly, the continuing depression and the economic state of the nation.

Arthur Brooks took to Josie, he found her an interesting companion and invited her to join him and his young companion for cocktails before dinner but she declined; she had arranged to dine in her suite that evening and he was clearly disappointed.

The following week, it was back to the old routine for Josie; bridge, croquet, walks and exercise and, for a change, a trip to the local amateur theatre club for a 'whodunit?' It wasn't up to much but in a way, she did enjoy the outing and was looking forward to sharing her amusement with Arthur Brooks on Friday. Arriving on Saturday morning, he apologised to the staff claiming, 'something had come up at the Home Office'.

Soon after his arrival, he took a short stroll along the prom and for most of the afternoon stayed in his room to work on his government bag. Joining

Josie for a brief afternoon tea, he hoped he would see her again during the evening.

The last Saturday of the month was always Gala Dinner and Dance night at the Grand; with the extra guests to accommodate, the dining room had been extended into the Palm Court Ball Room. The stage set for resident band, 'Dave Witherstone and the Blue Notes' and their popular vocalist Suzi Quine; catching the end of their rehearsal, she reserved a table discretely hidden behind the potted palms adjacent to the stage.

It had taken Josie a good two hours to change; it was well worth the effort. Wearing a pale pink and mauve drop-waisted flapper dress with a calf length hem trimmed with lace accompanied by a midnight blue boa and matching soft, leather dancing shoes, her entrance was greeted with gasps of approval by the astonished guests. She might not be invited to dance but was certainly going to dress the part and, by George, she did. The effect overwhelmed the Blue Notes almost bringing them to a slow stop had not Dave Witherstone gripped his baton.

The menu offered the customary five-course dinner with a wide variety of choices; waiting to be served, Josie whiled away the time people-watching until the wine-waiter arrived with a glass of champagne. He directed her attention to Arthur Brooks seated at a nearby table; he cut quite a dash in his dark blue velvet dinner jacket and pink bow tie and she smiled at him, took a sip and he smiled back. Dinner almost over, she ordered a pot of coffee and watched couples glide across the ballroom room as if competing to become the Ginger and Fred of the Essex coast.

Amused by their efforts, she giggled behind her well-manicured hand, reminding herself just how good she had been on the dance floor in her younger days.

At the table to her left, Arthur Brooks seemed deep in thought. Keen to learn more of his business and personal life, she asked the waiter to bring more coffee and invite Mr. Brooks to join her. At first, the conversation was fairly general but, aware of his embarrassment, she told her own, fictitious story.

'My late husband, a much older man, was a Brigadier in the Indian Army; he passed away two years ago and quite simply I could not bear living in India without him and came home to England, where I have family.'

'So what brings you to Frinton? Have you retired to the area or is it the sea, sand and fresh air of our bracing Essex coast that brings you here?'

'The latter, I'm afraid; since arriving home late last year I have been laid low with a rather stubborn bout of jaundice and I came here to convalesce. There may be plenty of sand and buckets of sea but not a lot of sun this time of the year; nevertheless, I'm beginning to feel better. Mind you, arriving in England in mid-winter didn't help but I am glad to be back.'

'And where are you based at the moment?'

'Temporarily with a cousin in Surbiton; she has been most kind to me but I cannot put upon her forever. I do have a sister in London but lost touch when I went to India to join my late husband. London is my natural home and, as soon as I find suitable accommodation, I shall make the move.'

Josie paused for a moment or two and then smiled.

'Now Arthur, if I might call you that, tell me all about yourself, I suspect we may have much a common? Shall we dance? I am rather good at the Tango.'

For the next ten minutes, the couple swayed to the pulsating rhythm of the Blue Notes and enjoyed the spontaneous applause from other dancers. Exhausted, they flopped out at the table and, refreshed by chilled champagne, continued what was to be a very open conversation.

Confirming his rumoured position in the Home Office, Arthur explained: 'I have always lived with my parents; we had a very large family home in Wimbledon Park, my parents were very keen on lawn tennis, and we never missed the All England Championships.'

'Are you still in Wimbledon?' she enquired.

'Not any more. Father died seven years ago and two years later mother had a stroke and took to her bed. With the help of a private nurse, I took care of her until she died last year.'

Sympathetically patting his arm and tactful pointing out that she had lost her mother too, Josie said: 'With so many sad memories, it's best to move on. I know what it is like to lose a parent, it does take a long time to get over it. May I ask where you are living now?'

'It does indeed. I live in central London; my father was a very successful executive in the city and, to avoid the daily train journey from Wimbledon, he purchased a very generous apartment in Chesterfield Gardens, Mayfair, that I duly inherited. After mother died, I sold the house in Wimbledon and moved to Mayfair, a pleasant walk through the parks to my work at the Home Office, and parks are good for meeting friends.'

At the mention of Mayfair, Josie went into adrenalin mode.

'What a coincidence, the Brigadier and I had many friends in Mayfair, we particularly enjoyed dining at the Ritz and the Café Royal when he took his annual sabbatical.

Pausing, she added: 'Now, may I speak freely? Living alone can be difficult at any age and one's friends are most important, whoever they are, including those special friendships you seem to be are engaged in.'

Arthur blushed and turned his head away; Josie touched his arm and continued. 'Believe me I do understand and you may confide in me whatever your little peccadilloes.'

Lowering her voice to spare his deeper blushes, she quietly added: 'After all, my dear late husband and I were very much aware of his long, lonely months patrolling the Khyber Pass with the young Subalterns. I never questioned his intentions, we army wives preferred to take it as read.'

Brooks fell for it, hook, line and sinker and thanking her for her clarity and sensitive understanding of his 'delicate' situation, he suggested: 'I may have known you only a short time Lady Templeton-Austin, but I do feel we have much in common as companions, purely platonic, of course. Perhaps we should meet up in London and I can show you my apartment. After all, we both lack partners, so to speak, and in many ways we could provide each other with social acceptability.'

'What an excellent idea, Arthur, but away with formality, please do call me May. Now if you will kindly excuse me, I will retire to my suite, give it some thought and perhaps we can discuss it further at lunch tomorrow. Good night.'

Five weeks later she was surprised to find Arthur Brooks had settled her final monthly account with the Grand and, thanking the staff for their kind care and attention, she handed out generous financial rewards to all the staff. At the front entrance, the hotel limousine was waiting to take her to the railway station. The manager presented her with a handsome bouquet of spring flowers and wished her good fortune on behalf of the staff; helping her into the car he whispered with a grin: 'Done yourself well then, yer Ladyship,' and winked at her.

Turning to his staff he muttered: 'Lady Templeton-Austin be damned. We may not see the likes of her again but give the woman her dues, she pulled it off in some style.'

'We mustn't grumble boss, she left us all a few quid better off and can't say fairer than that,' the doorman added and saluted in the direction of the railway station.

Arthur Brooks was waiting for her at Liverpool Street and Josie was delighted to see him again. Greeting him affectionately, he called for a porter with a barrow large enough for her luggage and, openly at ease with each other, the couple strolled along the platform to the taxi rank.

The substantial apartment in Chesterfield Gardens was very impressive. Arthur's manservant had moved on and two large rooms and a bathroom, refurbished by Heals, pleased Josie.

More than anything, she wanted to see her sister and, unbeknown to Arthur, the following day she took a taxi to Barnes to collect her personal effects. Fanny was overjoyed to see her back in London and, after a hug and a few tears, she asked George to bring her boxed-up belongings downstairs and into the taxi cab. After discussing wedding plans, the sisters arranged to meet up for tea in town once she had settled in and promised to stay in touch but wanted to keep her return secret for a while.

Since her release from prison, living south of the river with her sister had provided the perfect hideaway and, although she had made an occasional foray into her old hunting ground in Mayfair, until now she had kept a low profile.

Keeping her criminal past from Arthur, she carefully reflected on how his position at the Home Office might affect her status. Earlier suspicions as to his sexual behaviour turned up trumps and, if needs be, his shady lifestyle might be exploited for her own ends.

The following day she purchased a little black notebook from a local stationery shop.

Settling into life at Chesterfield Gardens did not come easy for both of them and she was shocked when, to protect his professional reputation, he suggested she drop the pseudonym, Lady Temple-Austin, she had used at Frinton-on-Sea and take his mother's name, Joan. Readily agreeing to his terms, thus began the slow progress of carefully establishing her new persona among the great and the good of Belgravia.

On the surface, much of the old Josie had changed but a glance into a mirror confirmed that her years in prison had affected her features, her body weight and her demeanour. She was also ten years older, grey haired and wore spectacles and this, coupled with a radically changed hairstyle, revealed little of her past. Her new look protected her identity; she hoped she would go unnoticed but, beneath the top coating, she was still the scandalous swindler with an eye for the main chance.

Apart from the occasional beggar, the worldwide depression made little difference to day-to-day life in London's rich quarter. Nightclubs, restaurants and cafes, and flourished theatre tickets were like gold dust and the overpriced departmental stores bustled with indiscriminate buyers; in the East End, trouble was brewing.

Unemployment and poverty was rife, petty crime out of control and desperate people were looking for desperate measures to help them survive. Targeted by Sir Oswald Moseley's black-shirted fascists and, despite the unrest in Nazi Germany, nobody cared.

Neither did Josie. Untouched by the plight of the poor East Enders she was hell bent on launching her new life as Joan Brooks, long-lost goddaughter of Arthur Brooks, whom, despite her age, he hoped to adopt. Consulting with his associates, he sensibly postponed the adoption process until he knew more about her.

In many ways, their unlikely meeting at Frinton-on-Sea mirrored Josie's chance meeting with George Davis at the May Fair in Hereford, each planning to use the other for their own ends. The high-ranking Civil Servant needed cover for his suspicious sexuality and Josie wanted a suitable playground for her scams, swindles and similar misdemeanours. Gradually bonding into a plausible couple on the social scene, Arthur's secret trysts allowed Josie opportunities to meet and plan her financial escapades. Sometimes she sensed people in and around Belgravia staring at her but, generally, the relationship worked.

Arthur continued with outings to the opera and ballet accompanied by a variety of youngish men; most of his associates believing they were visiting nephews, not ballet dancers from Sadler's Wells, and there was very little gossip. Nevertheless, each outing was carefully detailed in Josie's little black book.

In 1935, Josie celebrated three years of freedom from prison and it was time to give more thought to her future earnings. Arthur continued to pay the domestic finances and for anything else needed to make her life comfortable; despite her protests, he provided a generous allowance for her personal use and added her new name to the register of voters. Nonetheless, she felt a kept woman and to take her mind off her plans, she invited Arthur to accompany her to her sister's wedding at Holy Trinity Church Barnes, in June. Aware of her sister and late mother, he knew little of their Herefordshire background and when Josie explained friends she had not seen for sometime would be at the wedding, he agreed to keep a low profile.

Nonetheless, wanting to be part of such an important family event, he hired a fancy car for the journey to the church.

Josie dressed in a light cream linen costume with a corsage of pink roses and wore a soft pink, wide brimmed hat; her handsome partner chose a grey double-breasted suit with a pink rose pinned to the lapel, white shirt and a pink polka dotted tie. Causing more than a stir, the striking couple joined the small crowd of relatives, friends and casual onlookers to await the arrival of the bride.

A few minutes later, Fanny, wearing a full-length white dress and carrying a bouquet of pink roses and wild flowers, stepped from the horse-drawn carriage and almost burst into tears when she saw her sister. Lady Carter escorted her to the church and Kristy, wearing her best Salvationist uniform, was maid of honour. Greeting her sister with great affection, Josie turned to Lady Carter.

'If you will allow me, your Ladyship, this is my duty and my pleasure.'

'Indeed it is and I shall be delighted to pass it on,' and the wedding party moved into the porch. Inside the church, the organist took the cue and the beaming bride took her sister's arm. 'Here we go, our Fanny. Ma would be so proud of you,' and walked her to a smiling Bobby.

The service over. the happy couple stepped into the sunshine to walk through an archway of Salvation Army tambourines. Carefully pulling her wide-brimmed hat over her face, Josie linked arms with Arthur for the obligatory photograph with Bobby's father and aunt and, after a good luck kiss from the local chimney sweep, the wedding party moved on to The Boleau Arms Hotel for a traditional wedding breakfast generously paid for by Mr. Duncan.

Later that evening Josie and Arthur had been listening to the end of a play on the BBC Home Service. Switching off the radio, Arthur suggested: 'Coffee and a nightcap, Josie?'

Disappearing into the kitchen, he returned with a tray set with two glasses and a bottle of whisky; he went back to the kitchen to brew the coffee.

Popping her head through the serving hatch, Josie said: 'It has been such a lovely day and thanks to your generosity my sister and her husband will be enjoying a pleasant honeymoon in Frinton; it was so kind of you to make all the arrangements with the manager at such short notice.'

'It was a pleasure, she is your family and it solved my problem of a wedding gift,' he said.

Responding with a smile, Josie said: 'It was strange how we met there and I am grateful we did. Here I am living in a smart part of Mayfair with a true gentleman, my sister is happily married and I suppose, in a way, I am too.'

'And so am I, my dear Joan. It has been a rather special day for us all and I am grateful to you for allowing me to share it.' Pausing he added: 'Since we joined forces, you have brought so much into this lonely life of mine and I truly hope you are happy with the situation we find ourselves in.'

'Of course I am Arthur and your little secrets are safe with me,' she jokingly reminded, but there was more than a hint of the old Josie in her laughter.

Draining her coffee, she yawned and suggested: 'It has been a very long day Arthur and I shall retire to my room. I expect you will take your usual walk to Green Park and I shall see you in the morning.'

'Yes I do need to stretch my legs and I wish you a good night of sleep. Thanks again for a most pleasurable day,' and went to fetch his topcoat and hat. It was a familiar scene and getting her nowhere, but changes were looming.

If she was good enough as partner for an important government officer, she was good enough for his friends and colleagues; mature and ready to play the part, she felt comfortable in a role she could eventually use to forward her clandestine career and her earning potential. Making the good works brigade her next target for a scam, she set her cap at the Belgravia community but was Mayfair ready for her. Unknown to his partner, Arthur was calmly persevering with his enquiries into her background.

Autumn arrived promising a general election and a new government and on November 4th 1935, Josie was able to vote for the very first time. She strolled to the Polling Station in Berkley Square, humming Ethel Smyth's 'March of the Women' and reminded the duty Police Constable that it is all down to Mrs. Pankhurst and the Suffragettes that I can vote today.

Enjoying their first Christmas Day together, Josie and Arthur spent Boxing Day with the Duncans in Barnes and celebrated New Year's Eve in Trafalgar Square. Other than that, they lived quietly until gossip over the King's relationship with a divorced woman took over Arthur's working life. It was clear that the King and the Government were at loggerheads over his demand to marry his mistress and the newspapers, hell bent on feeding gossip to the nation, were having a field day. Thus began a constitutional crisis destined to split country and commonwealth, divided in their loyalty, leaving the Royal family in disarray and the Duke of York on standby to take over the throne.

Day and night Arthur was in and out of the Home Office like clockwork and unable to discuss the state of the nation with Josie. It was difficult trying to keep the details out of their conversations. It all came to a sad end on December 12th when, in broadcast to a world on tenterhooks, the King announced he was giving up the throne of England to marry the woman he loved.

Stunned by the news, Josie quietly waited for Arthur to come home. Like most people, she had heard the announcement on the wireless and wanted to know more from her secretive partner.

'Bloody hell Arthur, he's gone and done it. Did you know it was going to happen? You must have done, trotting across Green Park to the office at all hours of the day and night. Why didn't you tell me what was going on?'

'You know I could not, state secrets, I'm afraid. It is all part of the job I do and that is all I can say except, I can keep secrets too if I have to,' he added with a smile.

Josie changed the subject. 'I feel sorry for the new King and Queen, thrown into the deep end with the two young Princesses and the threat of war on the horizon. Poor bloke, that's what I say.'

'It's a bad time for us all and there was little choice for the Government. What with no jobs for the workers, an army to assemble, a Coronation to organise and not a lot of cash in the kitty to pay for it, I suppose we should be thankful that Edward was never crowned; at least we can use the same arrangements for King George.'

He paused for a moment. 'I can tell you, Joan, it will take some patching up if the country can't reconcile itself with what has happened.'

New Year 1937 brought a mild January and a dry spring to London and the Home Counties but, despite warnings that Adolf Hitler was on the rise in Germany, the promise of a May Coronation excited the whole the country. It was business as usual on the social scene and Josie and Arthur continued to wine and dine at weekends with the right people in the right places but preparations for the Coronation of George the Sixth were at fever pitch; matters of state, security for the overseas guests and ensuring the Metropolitan Police was ready for the big day, kept Arthur very busy.

After work Arthur liked to stay at home in the evenings, enjoying a light supper, reading and listening to the radio with Josie but today she had been to a matinee with her sister followed by high tea at Rumplemayer's Tea Rooms.

Noticing that she was knitting, Arthur teased: 'I never, ever thought I would hear the click of knitting needles in my home. Bit early for baby clothes, isn't it?'

Josie threw a ball of wool at him, he caught it like the sharp slip fielder he used to be. 'For your information, Mr. Brooks, I have joined the afternoon knitting group at St. George's, Hanover Square; we are knitting socks for soldiers just in case war breaks out. Is that alright with you?'

'Of course it is. Now I'm off on my evening stroll around Berkeley Square and I may call in at the club, so don't wait up'.

Josie knew the signs and started clearing the table and, when Arthur reappeared, dressed in his dandyish suit, he asked Josie to tie his bow. 'Have an early night and leave the clearing up for the maid in the morning,' he said, closed the door wished her a goodnight.

Smiling to herself, she continued with her knitting and tuned into the wireless; there was much talk on the news about Edward and Mrs Simpson, she listened intently and afterwards muttered: 'Now there's a woman with ambition, she manages to trap the bloody King of England that's all, and he gives up everything, including the Crown of England, for the love of an American divorcee. Good on you girl, go for broke. What's love got to do with it, anyway?'

Two weeks later, she invited her sister for tea at Rumpelmayer's; it was full and Fanny was late but Josie had reserved a window table. Spotting her sister crossing the park from the bus stop, she thought how well she looked since her marriage and, despite her crippled foot, walked more easily. They chatted and caught up with each other's news and Josie was surprised to learn her sister had enrolled with the Workers' Education Association for a course in typewriting at the Community Hall in Hammersmith. Reminding each other how they occasionally enjoyed afternoon tea with their mother when she first came to London, they asked for the tea menu.

'It's changed a lot since then,' Josie explained. 'Not quite so posh but lots more visitors with plenty of money to spend.'

'But the tea looks just as good and, like me, our Ma always enjoyed afternoon tea here. Oh, by the way I picked up the latest 'Evening News'; I buy it for Bobby when I'm passing a news stand. Do you want to have a quick look before we go?'

For a few moments Josie glanced through the pages until she stopped at one particular page; shocked at the headline she gasped out loud, her face turned very pale and, hands shaking, she poured out another cup of tea.

After a short while, she pulled herself together and passed the newspaper to her sister calmly waiting for her reaction to a report. Hastily scanning the page, Fanny dropped it onto an empty chair and comforted her sister with words of assurance. It was then she noticed a woman staring at her. Unnerved by her presence, she turned away in case she caught her eye. 'Keep talking, Fanny, and don't look round, just hide your foot under the table.'

Fanny obeyed and the woman left but not before giving them a long, inquiring last look. Convinced she might have seen her somewhere before, after a suitable interval Josie called for the bill, paid it at the kiosk and walked her sister to Green Park to catch the bus to Barnes. In the tearooms, the two waitresses, hopeful of finding a tip, quickly cleared the empty table. Noticing the discarded newspaper, the older women picked it up and read it out: 'George Davies, London's most notorious villain about to be released from Wormwood Scrubs.'

With a casual shrug of her shoulders, her colleague replied: 'So what?'

So what indeed.

CHAPTER TWENTY-TWO

With Arthur up to his eyes in Coronation planning, Josie made the most of her temporary freedom. Between her 'charitable' good works she took time out to familiarise herself with the popular visitor attractions laid on for the celebrations. Carefully working out the best for a few scams and a bit of pick-pocketing, she practised her dormant skills in the street markets in Soho and Paddington. She had just completed a successful morning picking a few pockets in Portobello Road when she heard a familiar mocking voice coming from a pavement café: 'Hallo, hallo, hallo, what have we here, Miss?' A firm hand gripped her shoulder. 'You've been nicked O'Dare by your 1929 classmate at Holloway.'

Josie froze in her tracks. The tone was familiar enough and she gave a sigh of relief when she recognised Tew, her ex-prison chum. In a strange way, she was delighted to see her again and the pair went into a nearby cafe for coffee and a catch-up chat.

'How are you doing old friend, still stalking the ladies-only Turkish bath circuit or, like most 'old girls' from Dame Henrietta's, going up in the world.'

Tew laughed. 'Not quite but I have stayed out of trouble.'

'How come? I thought you of all people would never change her spots?'

'It was inevitable, I suppose. I'm back home with the parents now; Dad, like many other businessmen lost quite a bit of cash when his investments went pear-shaped during the depression and mother had a heart attack forcing her to live quietly. We sold the Muswell Hill house and went to live in the family pile in Saffron Walden with the grandparents and dear old aunt Daisy.'

'And you are happy there living with the oldies?'

'As far as it goes, I suppose I am. I get a generous allowance from Grandpa, a couple of Bedlington terriers to keep me fit, a Siamese cat to keep me company and a dotty aunt to keep me amused with tales from the family archive. Now and again, when I'm a bit down, she slips me a few quid to get away and enjoy myself in London.'

'But you do have your own space, Tew? It's important when you leave prison life.'

'You bet I do. It was part of the deal for moving to the country; I have my own flat above the coach house with a sort of working studio below. To keep me out of mischief, I write a few articles for women's magazines.'

'Not about tits in Turkish baths, I hope?'

'No. That was my defiant period and I'm over it now but something like tales from the Turkish baths in the right format might make a series.'

Josie laughed. 'I don't know about that Tew, something like that in 'The Lady' magazine and your writing career could end tits up. Just like your ladies in the bath houses.'

The old friends rocked with laughter and, to calm down the situation, Tew explained: 'I usually come to town a couple of days a months for a bit of shopping and to watch the world go by, and look who I find in Portobello, dangerous O'Dare, my old sparring partner from Holloway. What are you up to these days O'Dare, I can see you have changed?'

Not wanting to give the game away, Josie thought carefully before answering: 'I had to, for my sister's sake. She has recently married and, after all she went through with our mother and me, I try to support her by being a better sister. Fanny lives in Barnes and we keep in touch and sometimes we go shopping and to the music hall; she's happy enough.'

'But what about you, Josie. Are you happy?'

'Yes and no. I share a very comfortable home with a gentleman companion, and I mean companion. He leads a very busy life and I keep house; I also serve on various charitable committees helping hard-pressed families in the East End to cope and that's about it.'

'Blimey, you have changed!' Tew said. 'I am sorry we did not keep in touch. Have you heard anything from Kristy? I heard she married into the Salvation Army but I never hear from her now, do you?'

'Yes, I do. After my release I lived with my sister; we meet her now and again and believe it or not with good old Lady Carter and we all went to Kristy's wedding.'

Tew went quiet and Josie wondered why.

'What's up? Was it something I said?'

'So you don't get news from Holloway then. I thought you would have heard by now.'

'Heard what?' Josie questioned.

'About Mavis, Mavis Buck, our former senior officer?'

'What about Mavis, I don't hear from her these days.'

'Two years ago she had a severe stroke while she was on duty and never really recovered.'

Josie was shocked to the core. 'Mavis dead. I can't believe it. When and where did it happen?'

'I don't know all the details but, as I understand it, when you were released she threw herself into her work, volunteering for extra duties and refusing ever again to take a prisoner to the Old Bailey. One evening during association, she collapsed on the wing, lingered for a couple of days at the Garrett-Anderson then passed away peacefully. They said she had lost the will to live, but in my opinion that was not her style, she simply missed you.'

Deeply affected by the news, Josie tentatively agreed to meet up again and noted her old friend's address before saying goodbye. Giving her a last wave, she caught the bus to Marble Arch and from there crossed Park Lane into Curzon Street. Approaching Chesterfield Gardens, she watched a tired-looking Arthur walking towards her; pulling herself together, she caught up with him, took his arm and headed for Chesterfield Mansions. It was back to the old routine; supper, the wireless and a nightcap before Arthur set out on his nocturnal stroll through the parks.

The thrill of easy pickings in Portobello Road and the possibility for more during Coronation Week had stimulated Josie's immoral appetites but the sad news of Mavis Buck had dampened her natural enthusiasm.

Listening to Arthur's concerns over security, night after night, was driving her mad, particularly when he drivelled on during supper. If it was not about Metropolitan Police Commissioner's final fitting for his ceremonial dress uniform, the next night it was clearing up the horse shit before the State Coach arrives at Westminster Abbey.

Just about ready to nod off Josie muttered: 'You can't be in control of the horse shit Arthur, that's not your job, is it?'

'According to the Home Secretary's personal, private assistant it is and I can expect to take flack for the whole constitutional department, not just security and policing.'

With just a hint of amusement, Josie said: 'Look on the bright side dear, this time next week it will all be over bar the cheering and back to civil service slow time for everyone.' Arthur chuckled. 'Take your point my dear. Talking about time, I best be off for my stroll before it gets too dark. Oh yes that reminds me, if you would like to watch the procession from my office in Whitehall, you will need a pass and security clearance. A bit of a celebration party has been arranged too.'

Josie's heart sank. The last thing she needed was police clearance and she had to think quickly.

'Oh dear, when I realised it was a busy time for you, I promised to share the day with Fanny and Bobby in Barnes. Mr. Duncan has bought the latest HMV 900 combined television and radio set to watch the outside broadcast and invited the neighbours over for a bit of a do.'

'That's fine Joan, dear, but you do understand for security reasons, I shall be sleeping in my emergency room at the office on Coronation Eve and won't be home for at least twenty four hours. Will you be alright?'

'Of course I will. If the buses are not running, I shall stay with Fanny.'

The overnight arrangements suited her and she was able to plan an early start for a bit of thieving on Coronation morning.

The weather forecast for London on May 12th was dry; the promised April frosts had come and gone and all was well for a grand day. Josie, dressed for the occasion in red white and blue, carried a basket full of small union flags for the children before swiftly dipping into the bag or pocket of a grateful but distracted parent. Compared to the money she picked up, the flags were well worth the outlay and, by the time she caught the train out of Waterloo to Barnes, she had thoroughly worked the processional route, doing very good 'business' along the way.

Arriving at Lillian Road just in time for the televised broadcast, Josie tucked into the delicious buffet her sister had laid out for the visitors but the new television proved the main attraction. The walnut case featured a small screen in the lift-up lid and a radio and speaker below; despite the occasional muzzy black and white images, the televised pictures were a great success.

After the loyal toast, the neighbours went home and Mr. Duncan took the family for dinner at The Dove Inn on the riverside at Hammersmith.

As expected, Josie stayed overnight and, after a good breakfast, she sat by the river idly chatting to her sister.

'I couldn't resist a bit of business on the way here yesterday, that's why I was late.'

'What sort of bit of business.'

'You don't want to know?'

'Then why tell me?'

'You know me and crowds, Fan, when the harvest is plentiful I go out and reap. I get an urge to dip into a few pockets and bags and I just can't help myself.'

'But surely you don't need the money, Trix? The 'rainy day' fund is safe and sound and Arthur looks after you well enough.'

'Yes he does but at a price. But it's not the cash; it's the kick I get from doing it. It never goes away. Anyway, it was scary reading about George and I might need a quick getaway. Now I best be on my way or Arthur may be worried that I didn't come home last night and call the plods. We don't want that, do we? On second thoughts, I doubt if he went home either?'

Fanny was puzzled. 'And what does that mean?'

'Well, between you and me, he likes to play with the boys in the park, and I leave it at that. I keep a little black book on his nocturnal visits to the park; it might come in useful some day?' Worried her sister was troubled, Fanny assured: 'That report on George getting out was weeks ago Trix and we don't even know if he has been released. If he has, he could be back in Hereford by now.'

'Maybe,' Josie said and handed her a package.

'Put yesterday's takings with the rest of the cash and take what you need, there's plenty in the pot.'

'You're a good one, our Trix, and we sticks together like what?'

'Glue,' Josie said and laughed all the way to the bus stop.

Less than a month after the Coronation, the Duke of Windsor married his mistress in a quiet ceremony at Chateau de Cande in France. The King banned any members of the Royal Family, including his brothers, from being present and, when Arthur returned from another bad day at the Home Office, he was incandescent with rage.

Pouring a large whisky, he paced the room and yelled at Josie: 'What did the bloody man expect? He ditched the throne for a three-time divorcee, sulked over a title for his wife, packed his bags and leaves the country with war on the horizon. If that's loyalty to his brother, it's no wonder the Prime Minister is at his wits' end.'

Josie tried to calm him down. 'If you go on like this Arthur, you will have a heart attack. What's done is done and he's not worth it.'

'Yes, but you do not know what I know my dear?'

'And what's that?'

'I'm not supposed to tell anyone. If the papers get hold of it, it's an early pension and a minor ambassadorship somewhere like Central Africa for me.'

Josie pushed him further. 'You must get all of this worry off your chest Arthur, I can keep a secret but it's up to you?'

Pouring another large whisky, Arthur gulped it down.

'Look he's buggered off to France and thinks he can still have a say in matters of state. He is not the King any more; he is a resentful bastard and relinquished any power when he abdicated. Now he's upset because his wife is not an HRH.'

He paused, took another long gulp of his whisky, and blurted out: 'Would you believe that against all the advice from the Foreign Office he wants to meet Adolf 'bloody' Hitler? There I've said it, so for God's sake keep it to yourself Joan,' and stormed off to his room.

For the rest of the year, Josie kept herself busy with charity work, impressing Arthur with her fund-raising and communication skills. He introduced her to people in the right places, particularly the city moneymen, and she built up the relationships with the sole intention of calling in a few favours when the time was right. Occasionally she suspected someone from her past was following her but it was more suspicion than reality.

While Josie concentrated on her good works, Arthur was up to his eyes at the Home Office. Public anger over the abdication and the subsequent marriage of the Duke and Duchess of Windsor had left Britain and the Empire feeling betrayed and the Home Secretary was expecting trouble on the streets during the State Opening of Parliament in October. Arthur was on standby again but it was not the only problem facing the government; Europe was coming under serious threat from Germany.

Working with the church welfare group kept Josie busy and she rarely saw Arthur; the possibility of war with Germany meant late nights working on plans with the War Committee at the Home Office and they had almost become ships passing in the night.

During the Christmas break, they did manage a few days together in Brighton before Arthur set out for the Cinque Ports to inspect sea defence plans in case of invasion.

When the cat went away Josie went out to play at picking a few pockets and donating a proportion of the spoils to the Church Welfare Committee for East End Children in Need. The unexpected generosity boosted her credibility as a good woman, who did good things, lifting her way up the charity ladder and opening many more doors.

When possible, Josie and Arthur entertained friends at their home in Chesterfield Gardens where they enjoyed catching up on gossip and the latest news; sometimes they went to the theatre or the cinema. To keep his partner entertained while he was out, Arthur installed a television set in the sitting room; it did not prevent his late-night strolls in park.

The changing face of England came with an announcement for all children to have gas masks and calls went out for volunteers to take on Air Raid Protection duties. Prime Minister Neville Chamberlain continued to 'make peace' with Germany and life in London went on as normal. Out of the blue, little known English Actress Vivien Leigh was chosen to star as Scarlett O'Hara in Hollywood blockbuster 'Gone With the Wind' and in the final Ashes match of the series played at Kennington Oval, England opening bat Len Hutton took 364 runs off the Australian bowlers. When world-weary Arthur unexpectedly arrived home early from the Home Office, Josie was engrossed in Daphne Du Maurier's latest novel 'Rebecca'.

Noticing his worried brow she asked: 'Surely not another government crisis? What's the PM been up to now? I thought he was meeting the German Chancellor for more talks?'

Arthur sighed deeply. 'That was last month when he promised 'peace for our time' and I, like many others, don't believe a bloody word of it. Poland and the rest of Europe are living on the edge and I fear we could soon see the start of a second world war.'

Casting her book aside, Josie sighed. 'Crikey Moses Arthur! Not another one. The last one was bad enough, let's hope we are better prepared this time?'

'Just about my dear, that's why I have been working all hours God sends on poster campaigns for civilian safety, air raid protection and emergency rationing. Our regular forces are on standby, conscription is on the cards and we are recruiting from across the Commonwealth; whatever happens, we must be ready on the Home Front too.'

'Why Arthur I thought Europe was in trouble not us. We don't need protection, do we?'

'I am afraid so, my dear. The military believes London will be the first target from the air and we must be ready to evacuate the children to places of safety. Air raid shelters are being erected in parks and gardens across the capital and underground tube stations may have to be designated shelters too but this requires government approval.'

Alarmed at his nervous demeanour, Josie said: 'You look worried sick Arthur, sit down and I'll pour us both a stiff whisky and you can tell me more,' and pottered off to the kitchen.

Keeping the conversation going, she suggested: 'According to the daily papers, rumours have it that Churchill may be joining the government and we must all pull together and make the most of what could be our last Christmas together,' optimistically adding, 'until then we must carry on as normal.'

Making the most of it was right up Josie's street.

Immediately after Christmas, she called a meeting of the Church Welfare Group, set up a sub-committee for fund-raising and food supplies and offered her experience as Voluntary Organiser of Fund-raising and Food Distribution.

The Women's Voluntary Service took on responsibility for the evacuation of children from central London and Josie volunteered to arrange billeting and transport. Her associates, impressed with her ability and enthusiasm, immediately agreed to underwrite the first stages of funding and Arthur offered the apartment for regular meetings of her committee. One evening he returned from the office early and, apologising for the intrusion, explained he was working late again and needed a quick meal in case he had to sleep at the office. Quickly closing the meeting, the women went home and Josie went to the kitchen to check the oven; she was pot-roasting a joint of beef for dinner just in case and she called for Arthur to come to the table.

Looking very tired, it was clear to Josie that with a full-scale war pending, his heavy workload was taking its toll. After dinner she updated him on WVS plans for evacuating children from the Westminster area. Encouraged by her commitment, he suggested nominating her for the London Committee for Evacuees and promised to arrange it with the Home Office civil servant in charge.

At last Josie had the insider contact she needed and Arthur had unwittingly helped set up her next fraud. Fetching his hat and coat from the hall, she saw him off the premises with a smile. She was about to clear the table and make notes when the telephone rang; it was an anxious Fanny eager to tell her that she had heard Davies was back in Hereford and asking about her. Calming her down, she told her Hereford is a long way from London but to be on the safe side keep a low profile, avoid inquisitive strangers and do not talk about it to anyone, not even family. After further encouraging chat she replaced the receiver, manically paced the floor and picked up her handbag. Carefully unzipping a small pocket in the lining, she took out a folded envelope containing white powder, sniffed it, pulled away quickly and walked to the mirror over the fireplace. Addressing her image, she smiled and said: 'Is this the moment to use it or shall I keep it for the storm to come?' After a brief moment, she put it back where she found it.

On September 29th, Poland was defeated and war with Germany was inevitable. Preparations had been in hand for some months; young men trained with the reserved forces and as soon as war broke out all males aged nineteen to forty became liable for military action. Women replaced them in the workplace as truck drivers, ammunition workers and agricultural labourers and the reality of war came into focus when friends and colleagues simply vanished from the home or workplaces. Merchant ships bringing supplies of food from across the Atlantic came under heavy attack from German U-Boats, leaving the country short on food, clothing, and fuel and rationing came in. So did Josie's survivor instinct; she kept her spirits up, made sure her sister and friends had what they needed and carried on with a bit business on the side.

CHAPTER TWENTY THREE

For twenty-six consecutive nights, the Luftwaffe bombarded London; searchlights straddled the night sky, sirens wailed countless warnings and bulbous anti-aircraft balloons floated above the city. It was red sky night and day as incendiary bombs hit their targets, leaving the dead and injured buried under tons of rubble. A complete blackout of buildings, homes and street lighting caused chaos and panic on the streets. To meet the demand for places of safety, air raid shelters sprang up like mushrooms and the War Committee sanctioned the use of the underground tube stations. Throughout the entire Blitz, Londoners took it on the chin and carried on regardless.

Arthur had warned Josie to take care walking home at night; deaths from accidents caused by lack of street and vehicle lights, almost equalled those from the bombing but, for Josie, life was a challenge. After all a scam was a scam in any situation and, with tightly controlled rationing, the black market was ripe for the picking.

Unable to get home on a regular basis, Arthur stayed at the Home Office. It suited Josie very well, giving her carte blanche to fleece out-of-town punters and think up new swindles, if only for the thrill of it. She also had more time to visit her sister in Barnes and stay until the late evening if she wished; it was on one such occasion that the first seeds of a classy fiddle began to germinate.

The number nine bus stopped outside Hammersmith Palais de Danse in Shepherd's Bush Road; the pavement was buzzing with young women and soldiers keen to dance the night away before leaving for Europe. Without a second thought, Josie hopped off the bus, queued for a ticket and stepped into a dance hall full of atmosphere.

A swing band was belting out the latest hits and couples were jitterbugging as if it were their last chance of the good life. Before Josie could take it all in, a Squadron Leader whisked her off her feet and spun her around the dance floor until she was giddy. He thanked her as if he would never see her again and, catching her breath, she escaped into the night air and waited for the next bus. She did like dancing but she was more a tea dancer these days. Nevertheless, she felt an emotional urgency among the dancers on the crowded dance floor and noted it for future use.

It was dark when she stepped from the bus at Hyde Park Corner. Carefully manoeuvring through the piles of sand bags, she relied on a passing police officer to guide her to her front door in Chesterfield Gardens. Arthur was more or less living at the Home Office, giving her more time and space to think about what the future might hold.

Two weeks later, she received a delirious telephone call from her sister announcing she and Bobby were expecting a baby. Delighted at becoming an aunt, Josie offered to arrange evacuation to Herefordshire for her and the family but Fanny declined. Six months into the pregnancy, Bobby joined the Royal Navy and, after basic training at the Supplies Division in Chatham, he joined a frigate on escort duty in the North Atlantic sent to protect merchant ships bringing food and supplies from America.

Fanny was distraught and, after consulting with her father-in-law, went to stay with Lady Carter at the family estate in Essex. Kristy Bramwell, also pregnant, had been living there since her husband volunteered for active service with the Medical Corps. It was the perfect place of safety for her sister. Josie had plenty to do in London but agreed to visit now and again, particularly when baby Teresa arrived.

With Arthur tied up at the office and her sister out of London, it was the right time for Josie to stretch her wings and make a few business plans.

Using her connections in the war office and respected by her many committees, she manipulated her way through the devastated Dockland and East End, collecting imported food and supplies for distribution by the Red Cross.

Keeping a third of the supplies back for home use, she sold most of it to small cafés and shops for ready cash.

There was no end to her unscrupulous behaviour. When wealthy families offered her money for decent billets for their evacuated children, a financial arrangement was quietly agreed and a chancy scam with a West Ham garage owner keen on forged petrol coupons, worked well until police arrested the printer.

It was a near miss and, for a while, Josie kept a low profile. Working alone and keeping in with her committees kept her on business but she had not bargained on bumping into George Davis in Shepherd Street market.

On a shopping trip to London, Fanny, Kristy and Lady Carter had arranged to meet Josie for lunch and, for a brief moment, George Davis failed to recognise his former partner in crime but he did recognise Fanny's booted foot.

Josie ordered her sister to stall him and then dashed off in the direction of Berkeley Square and the Red Cross Hall. Catching up with Fanny, George demanded to know: 'It is you, Fanny? I would know that pretty face anywhere and pregnant too. What are you doing in London town?'

'Shopping with my friends. I am living with them in the countryside until the war is over and my husband comes home.'

Pressing her further, he asked: 'And where has your sister been living since she came out of jail? Come on, you must know where she lives?'

'If I did, I wouldn't tell you. These days she is a changed woman leading a quiet life somewhere in Sussex. When she feels up to it, we meet up in London.'

Noticing Fanny was shaking like a leaf, Lady Carter turned on George: 'Kindly leave us alone. She is pregnant and very tired and we need to get her home.'

Ignoring Lady Carter, he grabbed Fanny's arm.

'I want to know where your sister is. She grassed me up and I need to talk to her now.'

'Then I suggest you leave a contact number with Fanny and she can pass it on, otherwise leave her alone or I shall call a policeman.'

Rebuking Lady Carter's threat with snarl, he thrust a card with a handwritten phone number at Fanny.

'I have ways of tracking her down, so do not forget to give it to her or you will both regret it,' and scuttled towards Hyde Park tube station.

Lady Carter looked aghast. 'Whatever was all that about Fanny, you really don't need this in your condition? Do you know him, Kristy?'

'I know of him but never expected to see him and that's all we need to know. Well done Fanny for sticking up for Josie, best you tell her about it straightaway and I'll try and explain to Lady Carter.'

As the three friends walked away, they spotted Josie heading towards St James's.

'She's off to Rumplemayer's. It is her favourite teashop; she usually goes there when troubled. We must catch up with her and have tea before we go home?' Fanny suggested.

Later that evening Josie telephoned the number on the card and was surprised to find it was The Railway Hotel, Upminster. She asked to speak to George Davis, and after a while, he came on the line.

'George Davis here and who wants him?'

'Same old voice, same old George. This is Trixie. I understand you want to talk to me. How can I help you?'

'By meeting and telling me why you grassed me up. Are you in London, if so I can come to your place?'

'Not possible George, my life is different now but I shall be pleased to meet you anywhere you like, within reason of course.'

He hesitated. 'And you'll come alone. No cops or anything?'

'Of course I will. You have to trust me on that, I am a changed woman now,' she assured him.

'Yes well I did that once too often and it got me thirteen years. Where do you want to meet? I am in Epping and use this place for business. It's easy for getting in and of the East End and I can book a table for lunch or something, if that suits.'

'Very nicely, George, thank you! If it is on the tube, I shall come by train. What with the blackout, I shall feel safer going out in the daytime. Shall we say Saturday?'

'Done. I'll look out for you about noon, we have a lot to talk about,' and hung up.

It was a warm spring day in London and what trees were left standing after the bombing were surprisingly in bud.

Josie explained to Arthur she was taking a small group of East End children for a picnic in Epping Forrest and hoped the fresh air would clear the smoke from their little lungs. She gratefully accepted his money for treats and, wearing tweeds and shoes, she carried a wicker basket, a walking cane and, to complete her disguise, she added a plain hat, gloves and glasses for effect.

At St James's underground station she boarded the Metropolitan and District line train to Upminster and settled down to read the 'Church Times'. Most of the journey was overland and she was shocked to see the devastated communities, many raised to the ground by bombs from the Luftwaffe. Despite her work with the Red Cross and other committees, the reality of war had not brought home the suffering and hardship among the working classes and she felt a moment of guilt but today guilt was not on the agenda. Today she had to go through some difficult hoops to get out of George's clutches and that was that.

The Railway Hotel was definitely not her cup of tea; it was like going stepping backwards into the Market Tavern in Hereford but without the smell of livestock.

The large saloon bar was filled with American servicemen from nearby airfields dining on black market beef and English ale before heading for the bright lights of the West End, the Windmill girls and a bit of casual sex in exchange for a couple of pairs of nylon stockings.

George Davis was at the bar chatting to the landlord and keeping a close eye on the door; more flashy than ever in his pinstriped suit, wide lapels and gaudy tie, he looked, despite his years in jail, reasonably fit for his age. When Josie arrived, he was drinking whisky; spotting Josie in the doorway, he quickly pointed to the dining area in the lounge bar. In an attempt to look frumpy, she had dressed down and deliberately peered at him through the round prison spectacles chosen for the occasion. Taken aback at her unexpected appearance he exchanged a polite word or two and escorted her to a laid-up table in the dining room.

Surprised at the number of American soldiers with plenty of money to spend, George explained: 'Around here Yanks are big business. Paid in dollars, their USA rations are worth a small fortune on the black market and I am doing ok buying and selling this and that. I am also making a fair amount on a petrol fiddle with a couple of aircrew from the local US Air Force base in Essex. Now, Trix, I promised you a good lunch and you shall have it, I have a special arrangement with the landlord so let's make the most of it?'

Josie played it low key and, during a good lunch edged uncomfortably around their criminal past, the cross-examination began.

'So what's your game these days, Trixie? You must have something up your sleeve to fall back on?'

'Not really. Prison life has taken its toll, body and soul and I have never felt well enough to adjust to life outside my cell, so to speak.'

George laughed. 'I don't believe it, I really don't. You grassed me up and expect me to believe what you say. Don't pull that one, Trixie, I know you too well. At the time I could have happily killed you for sending me down.'

'And do you want to kill me now George?'

'Sometimes, yes. I have thought about it but I soon realised you are not worth swinging for; but have you really changed!'

'I have changed my ways, George, these days I really am a reformed woman and live a good Christian life with my sister and brother-in-law in Kent. I earn my living as a seamstress, a trade I learned in Holloway and I am reasonable happy I suppose.'

Ever the cynic, George laughed wickedly and challenged her to come clean, but Josie held her own.

'Think what you like George Davis. I am who I am now, not who I used to be; those days are dead and gone. I do regret them, particularly when my mother died during my sentence.'

George softened a little. 'I'm sorry about that ,Trix, Mary was a true, Herefordian woman, a good sort; it must have been tough for you and Fanny. Did you get to the funeral?'

'Yes, under escort, but at least I could say goodbye and support our Fanny for a couple of hours.'

George changed the mood. 'I did thirteen years hard labour for you Trix and I got through it by thinking sweet revenge, I still do but I am doing well for myself these days and I won't mess up again, not for anyone.'

His chilling stare unnerved her but she played him well. Taking his arm, she said: 'Truly George I have never forgiven myself for what I did to you. I did try to pluck up courage to see you but my dear late mother felt I should let it lie, as time is a great healer. I hope she is right.'

George raised his voice enough to stop all conversation in the room. 'Yes, it might heal your bloody four years in 'make yourself at home' Holloway but not my thirteen years locked up in Dartmoor and the Scrubs.'

He thumped the table with such force that the plates almost jumped off the table; she tried to calm him down with a plea for forgiveness.

'After all George, the Lord tells us 'to err is human, to forgive is divine'.'

Her unexpected burst of religious fervour failed to impress George; picking up her copy of the 'Church Times', he suggested: 'So this is where you get your religious claptrap from. If I didn't know how old you are I would put it down to your change of life.'

Nevertheless he was puzzled by the new, whiter than white Trixie and half agreed with what she said.

Quick as a flash she decided to quit while she was ahead. Looking at the watch conveniently pinned to the lapel of her tweed jacket, she stood up.

'My goodness George, how time flies; my brother-in-law is meeting my train from Victoria and I must dash if I am to make the connection.'

On the platform, she smiled and kissed a bemused George Davis on the cheek; over his shoulder, she made a mental note of the high number of servicemen piling into the train. Climbing aboard, she pressed a small printed card into his hand. Slipping it into his top pocket, he closed the carriage door, returned to the bar and ordered a large whisky.

It took a minute of two to realise he had no idea where she lived, where she was going or who she really was; assuming the card she had given him contained her address, his quizzical expression turned to anger. It was a religious tract taken from the 'Church Times': 'The Love of God is Broader than the Measure of Man's Mind'.

Rushing to the door, he watched the train pull away from the platform; as it moved slowly past him she smiled. Tearing up the card, he yelled at the landlord: 'She's done it again. She has bloody well done it again,' and ordered another large whisky. Gulping it down in one go, for a split second he pictured her laughing all the way home, and silently admired her impudence and downright bravery.

Moreover, he was right. No longer the fake, frumpy spinster, she discarded the hat and gloves, removed her spectacles and pinched her cheeks to improve the colour; as she walked through the carriage to find a seat, her smile said it all. Observing a small gathering of American servicemen seated at the end of carriage, a young officer stood up and offered her his seat. Thanking him politely, her polished upper class accent and Englishness captivated the young officers and they struck up an easy conversation.

During the journey, she discovered they were from respectable, wealthy New England families and keen to taste the bright lights of London before leaving for Europe. Impressed by the kind-hearted middle-aged English woman, they asked if she knew of a quiet club or hotel in a pleasant part of central London suitable for clean living American officers on regular weekend leave.

Josie's heart missed a beat; she listened to all their ideas and suggestions and told them that by sheer coincidence she had put forward similar proposals to a Fair Play for Servicemen committee she had recently set up. If all went well, she could send them more information and suggested they keep in touch. Most of the servicemen left the train at Tower Hill, and the last to leave, the chatty young officer, handed her a card with details of the Officer Commanding at their United States base in Suffolk.

The seed planted, Josie scribbled a few pointers on the back of the card, left the train at Westminster and strolled home through the parks deep in thought for perhaps, a lucrative, final rip-off.

By1943 the American Embassy in Grosvenor Square was the nerve centre for all American Armed Forces serving in the United Kingdom, the most popular place for a leave pass. GIs occupied most of the West End and just about every decent hotel, guest house, club and private residence in central London housed officers. The Embassy Ballroom became a very grand Officers Mess, other ranks, billeted in private homes in and around the suburbs, socialised in the Allied Forces Club, the Nuffield Centres or the Navy Army and Air Force Institutes for non-commissioned officers.

However, the popular Rainbow Club on the corner of Piccadilly Circus and Shaftsbury Avenue was open to all ranks, day and night. Very soon it became Josie's target project; membership was free for women and girls and unknown to Arthur she became a regular at club events. To give her proposed project respectability, she occasionally invited members of her Church Welfare Group but mainly it provided essential research for her latest swindle. When it finally came together, she knew she was on a winner.

It happened by chance on Curzon Street, close to her home. The recently refurbished Washington Hotel served as the American Red Cross Club and she made it her duty to drop in for coffee and doughnuts. The visits consolidated her plans for running a smaller, more personal and even private establishment for the discerning officers from good American families. Convincing her associates to back her plans for private membership club, she tentatively suggested a voluntary donation to help with initial expenses, and it worked.

Arthur was so impressed he organised a start-up grant from the Home Office and persuaded his counterpart at the American Embassy to match it.

They did more, offering to supply American style home comforts and food, but did not want to be involved in the day-to-day administration.

It was the arrangement Josie needed and readily agreed to find suitable premises for dances, social events and whatever else it took to keep the troops happy during their duties in London.

After taking her advice, the committee recommended the club should be in a quiet area away from the temptations of the West End. When the former vicarage at the Camden end of Regent's Park became available, the committee approached the Church Commissioners; subject to restrictions on alcohol consumption, they agreed a short-term lease until the war ended. A cleaning party went in and within the month 'The Connecticut Club for the Sons of New England' was up and running. The rules were simple, the membership private and the club billed as 'home from home' for serving United States officers of good standing. Food supplied by the US Embassy was plentiful, regular and not adverse to the English palate. To meet with the no-alcohol clause, beer and spirits were sold on to local pubs and clubs, the income shared unequally between the committee and Josie's back pocket; a handsome, if illegal profit.

The club was off to a flying start; membership quickly grew and, for a fee, Josie provided intimate home comforts for married men missing family life. She also encouraged members to meet 'friendly' local women and invite them to the weekly dances and socials.

The comings and goings of service members brought a fair share of problems for Josie including the inevitable close relationships developing in the club between consenting couples but, as usual, Josie helped solve them, at a price.

Late one autumn afternoon, an older Lieutenant in a state of agitation, left his seat in the foyer and for the third time confronted the receptionist, demanding to see Mrs. Brooks. Told she was still in a meeting, he sat down, lit up another cigarette, took three puffs and stubbed it out in the already filled ashtray.

Inside the committee room, Lady Winter-Green had been praising 'dear Joan' for her good works, particularly 'The Connecticut Club' and, after a unanimous vote, appointed her Honourable Treasurer for another three years.

Showered with compliments from the well-heeled committee, she modestly accepted. Lady Gwendolyn Tingey called for sherry to toast the marvellous

Mrs. Brooks and the meeting broke up. Making her excuses, Josie swiftly left the room, went to her office and was about to leave the building when her attention was drawn to the troubled officer, seated with his head in his hands, and she invited him into her office.

She was aware of his dilemma and offered him a drink but he refused; invited to sit down, he explained yet again his dilemma. His lady friend, one of the girls from the club, was pregnant and he was about to be shipped to Europe. It was of course untrue; the financial sting was about to bear fruit for the third time.

Overcome with guilt and distraught at the news, he begged Josie for help. 'What am I to do Mrs. Brooks? I come from a good Christian family and engaged to be married; my parents and Kay's too, will be as shocked and distressed over this, as of course I am,' and he broke down in tears.

Offering her condolences, she took him to a settee, sat beside him and gently explained her position: 'I shall, of course, keep this matter in strictest confidence but I must be impartial. I am very proud of the women who come to the club to welcome and befriend our American allies and sad to say this is not the first instance of this kind. I understand how emotions can spin out of control, especially in wartime, nevertheless, taking advantage of inexperienced young girls is irresponsible and matters can often get out of hand. As for me, I am fond of the young woman in question and will do all I can to help, you will both have my trust, but the club must remain sacrosanct.'

The officer recovered his composure. 'But you can help me? I am so sorry for the young woman involved and would like to meet and tell her how sorry I am.'

'It's a little late for that Lieutenant, she has gone home to her family to think matters over and make a decision.'

Panic-stricken he asked: 'What kind of decision? Is she going to report me to my Commanding Officer? It could end my promotions if she does. My grandfather was a General and Kay's father is a Naval Flag Officer in Washington and questions will be asked back home. You have to help me Mrs. Brooks, you really do.'

'As I said before, I have to be impartial and if I can I will help both of you. It is, of course, an expensive business and I shall require a substantial donation to the club welfare fund, in cash of course.'

'Whatever it takes but we have to arrange it today. I knew I was in trouble when I last saw you so I brought cash with me just in case. What will it take to hush it up?'

'Yes, I can arrange things here but I must telephone the young woman for instructions, she might have had a change of heart and insist on keeping her baby. Wait in the lobby, I won't be a moment,' and escorted him to the door.

Shortly after, she called him back and he waited for her to finish writing down a few notes; fearing the result of the non-existent telephone call, he took a deep breath.

Calming him down, Josie explained: 'As you Americans like to say Lieutenant, I'll give it to you straight; she wants to abort the pregnancy before it's too late. This means a private clinic, an operation and post medical care; she will also expect compensation for loss of earnings.'

White as a sheet he said: 'You mean she intends to kill my child?'

'In a manner of speaking, yes; it's the way of the world in these troubled times. What did you expect?'

'Well I supposed she would keep it if I promised financial support. This really is a shock Mrs. Brooks, I'm a good Christian, say my prayers and obey the commandments but this?'

Josie tried to reassure him. 'How can you make such a promise, you could be sent to France, killed in action and what would she do then. She is very sorry about it but she is at her wits' end; it is a termination or public exposure should you die. Would you like to go away and think about it?'

Overwhelmed, the gullible officer was sweating profusely. Josie poured him a brandy and this time he took it and gulped it down. It was a scary moment, she had pulled out the stops for this one and the price was right.

Watching him struggle with his conscience, she drummed her fingers on the desk; in case the scam went pear-shaped she had organised for a bogus telephone call and, after five minutes of waiting, the sudden ring brought the officer to attention.

He nervously waited for Josie to answer it. 'Do calm down, my dear. He has not yet made up his mind. I know it is difficult with your mother listening over your shoulder but I hope to have some news soon. I will, I promise. Just think of the child and keep your fingers crossed, I will let you have any news, hopefully this evening.'

Replacing the phone she waited for his response, she got what she wanted to hear.

'Is she alright ma'am? I do not want to make this difficult for her; I have caused her enough distress. I'll pay whatever it costs.'

Relieved at the outcome Josie smiled. 'Good man and well done, you're a credit to your family and your country; in England, a true gent. I'll tot up the figures and we can settle the account now.'

It did not take her long. 'Shall we say £1000 for medical expenses and a further £500 for hurt feelings, in cash of course; I will give it to her once the unfortunate matter is over and done with. In return she will give an undertaking; neither she nor her family will pursue the matter.'

The officer handed her a large envelope containing £2000 in cash. After carefully counting it, she queried an extra £500.

'It is a donation to the club for services rendered and to thank you ma'am for your kindness.'

Josie put an arm around him in a motherly fashion and showed him the door; he squeezed her hand, smiled and left the 'Connecticut Club' a much-relieved man.

Returning to her desk she sat back, threw the money in the air and rang the bell on the desk; an attractive young woman came into the room. Giving her £100 and a train ticket to Brighton, Josie told her to stay away for a few weeks adding: 'What a mug, what a blooming mug. You okay with that love. Next month I will find us another sucker.'

Pocketing the cash and waving the ticket at her boss, the young woman left the room with a broad smile.

Pouring herself a stiff whisky, Josie raised a glass and laughingly announced to the empty room: 'Another damn Yankee bites the dust; let's drink to the rest of the suckers.'

She never saw him at the club again. Six months later, he lost his life during the Normandy landings and he was not the only one. Her brother-in-law Bobby was missing at sea, leaving Fanny a widow and a little girl fatherless.

CHAPTER TWENTY FOUR

The aftermath of the war brought severe austerity to parts of London but not in Mayfair and Belgravia where VE Day celebrations carried on regardless of cost. Street parties continued for days and the pubs, clubs and hotels hardly ever closed.

Comfortably entrenched in Chesterfield Gardens, Josie yearned to be earning again; she missed the excitement and the personal benefits of war and was itching to find new ways of making money. Her charitable committees disbanded, Josie had lost her position and her perks, leaving her at a loose end. To fill her time, she continued to update her little black notebook with more details of Arthur's nocturnal wanderings and kept a closer eye on her sister.

Six months after he went missing, Bobby was officially declared 'lost at sea' and, apart from her daughter Terri, all Fanny could look forward to was a war pension and keeping house for her ageing father-in-law. More than happy to support her sister financially and help her sort out Bobby's effects and paperwork, she enjoyed pushing her niece Terri around Barnes pond.

On one particular Sunday morning, Josie arrived to find her sister out of mourning and looking and feeling much better.

Bobby's father had discovered a will, made by his son when he volunteered for the Royal Navy, leaving his share of Lillian Road to Fanny and their daughter. A year later Lillian Road was sold, Mr. Duncan went into a private retirement hotel in Chiswick and Fanny bought a pleasant cottage by the river in Mortlake, close enough for a daily visit to her father-in-law. Mother and daughter settled down to a comfortable lifestyle and invited Aunty Trixie to live with them.

However, Belgravia remained her playground and, promising to visit her family more often, Josie, concerned for her own safety, explained that in future she would travel to Mortlake by train from Waterloo. Convinced George Davis was having her watched, she took sporadic sniffs of cocaine, relied on her wits and got on with life.

War or no war, Arthur was still very busy at the Home Office. In the first general election in ten years, war-time leader Winston Churchill lost out to Clement Attlee's Labour Party in a landslide victory based on a promise of full employment and cradle to grave welfare for everyone. A positive transition of government was paramount and Arthur was under pressure to consider his position in the new Civil Service sanctioned by new Home Secretary James Chuter Ede.

Unhappy with his future prospects, he was not easy to live with, his moods making domestic life at Chesterfield Gardens even more difficult for Josie. With fewer committees to build on, apart from a few dealings in forged ration books, clothing coupons and petrol vouchers, most of her frauds were running out of steam and, apart from keeping house, she had little to occupy her day.

With her earnings slipping away and her relationship floundering, petty squabbles, usually over money, unsettled both partners. Knowing little about her income or the secret 'rainy day' fund, Arthur was concerned for her financial wellbeing should he be retired early. On the other hand, he was close to retirement age and it might suit them both to take advantage of a promised financial package.

Josie refused to listen; she was more bothered about government plans calling for skilled women who replaced men in the workplace during the war, to go home, clean the house, and be good wives and give their jobs to returning servicemen.

Riled by the suggestion, she argued the case with Arthur.

'Let me remind you it was Mrs. Pankhurst and the suffragettes who fought tooth and nail for the rights of working women. They were good enough to take on the skilled jobs in the factories, shipyards and steelworks when the men folk left for war but now it seems they are only good enough for bedding and housekeeping. The government should be ashamed.'

Arthur had never seen her so angry. 'Don't take it out on me Joan, I don't make the rules.'

'I know, but you must have been expecting it. Did you know about it Arthur?'

He defiantly stood his ground. 'I was Home Office, not Work and Employment. This government is so bloody chaotic and what they are doing is beyond me, I might as well retire gracefully.'

Again, Josie refused to discuss the idea and it took Arthur more than a year to take the plunge but when he proposed retiring to Frinton-on-Sea to enjoy the fruits of his labours, Josie hit the ceiling.

'Good God Arthur, I'm certainly not ready to put my feet up, I do accept we have a sizable age gap but I'm only forty seven with much more socialising to do before we settle for slippers. What about the young men from the ballet? They adore you and you enjoy meeting up with them, you won't find such nice boys in Frinton, not in the public toilets anyway.'

Arthur blushed. 'They might adore me but they also adore my bank account but it is fun and perhaps now is not the right time to discuss it. Unless I am pushed, we can think again and leave it for a year or two but I do take your point on having a good time. Why don't we do the rounds of our old haunts, it will do us both good and you can dust down your best togs?'

Josie gave him a hug. 'That's the ticket Arthur, we've been through a hell of a lot since we got together, shall we start with the Ritz?' and left the room to check her wardrobe for moths.

She was her high society self again but a small, quiet voice warned: 'Steady the Buffs, mind how you go and watch your step. These days, you do not know who may be watching and waiting.'

For over a year Josie and Arthur played the society field, enjoying the theatre or the latest film, dining out in the best restaurants and drinking with old friends in the Lord Curzon Arms. Eventually it was clear Arthur was slowing down and he knew it; it was back to the old routine of a light supper at home and a drama on the radio or television but Josie was missing the social whirl.

One quiet wet afternoon, Arthur decided to sort out the desk and cupboards in his room and when Josie asked him what he was up to, he shouted: 'It's time I tidied up this mess of paperwork and old newspapers in the cupboards. It's been around for years, much of it when father was here; the bin men come tomorrow and they can cart it way at one go. It will take a good while to sort out so put your feet up old girl and have a catnap for an hour or so.'

Busy making notes in her black book, she took little notice of his comings ad goings and, after a while, she curled up with her latest library book.

She had been reading quietly for two hours when a red-faced Arthur burst into the sitting room; he was carrying a battered, civil service issue, attaché case lined with a fading newspaper. He took it out and threw it at Josie, hitting her full in the face.

'If you want a cup of tea Arthur, you only need to ask?'
and carefully picked it up. 'Are you trying to tell me something or do you want me to bin it?'

'No. It is an old copy of that awful rag, 'The News of the World', look at it and tell me if you recognise anyone, and no lies?'

Seeing herself on the front page of the faded copy, Josie trembled from head to toe.

'It is you, isn't it, the notorious Josephine O'Dare, sent down for four and a half years at The Old Bailey for conspiracy and fraud. You may be twenty years older now but I can see it is you. For God's sake woman, why didn't you tell me who you were and me a senior civil servant at the Home Office?'

Head in hands, he sat down and waited for an explanation.

Thinking on her feet and believing attack was the best form of defence, she argued: 'What would be the point of telling you, Arthur, what's done is done. I did my time and started a new life with you; anyway, you're not so squeaky clean.'

Surprised at her attack on him Arthur challenged: 'Meaning what may I ask?'

'Meaning, you break the law every time you make a pick-up in a public urinal, meet a guardsman in the park or when you rent a boy from the ballet. Believe me I know what you are up to and don't come the innocent with me Arthur Brooks; I have it all here, in my notes.'

'What bloody notes. Have you been keeping notes on me?'

'Have you had me watched? Someone has?'

'No not at all. I had an idea you might not have been whom you say, but having you watched is not my style. You may be my companion but I was lonely for my own kind.'

'And I the daughter of a drunken farm labourer who beat his wife and crippled daughter, as well as me and I got in with the wrong 'un. All I wanted to do was protect my Ma and sister and that took money, but I never dropped my drawers for anyone, not even George Davis,' she said and pointed to his picture also on the front page.

Arthur remained distraught. 'I was a senior civil servant in the bloody Home Office. It could have cost me my job, pension and my credibility had my bosses found out and where would we have been then?'

'The same situation had they discovered your peccadilloes but they haven't, anyway it's all in the past now. What I worry about is Davis. I grassed him up; he went down for thirteen years and wants revenge.'

'And how do you know that?' Arthur challenged.

'Because I met him and he told me he wanted to kill me for setting him up.'

'And where is he now?'

'I have no idea. We arranged to meet at Upminster five years ago and I was able to put him off the track. I have never heard of him since.'

Arthur blustered on: 'If he is somewhere in London, pray tell me where and maybe I can have him removed.'

But before she could answer he broke down in a fit of coughing and had difficulty in breathing.

Josie quickly calmed him saying: 'What good will that do except draw attention to us. Anyway, after the war he went back to Herefordshire and has no idea where I am or live so let's be practical and forget about it until something does happen. Now, I suggest you rest before you go out tonight, forget differences and try to get along.'

Josie made supper and waited until he left for his walk through the park before burning the evidence of her criminal past in the kitchen sink. It was almost midnight when she heard his key in the front door. He had been drinking heavily and stumbled into the hall muttering: 'Sorry, Joan, I am so sorry,' and went to bed.

Next morning it was all sweetness and light; over breakfast, he apologised for his disgraceful behaviour. Josie smiled and gently patted his head. Still bothered about the secret notebook and alarmed by his companion's criminal past, he pondered over whether to pursue the matter or stretch it out for a little longer.

Unlike Josie, keeping secrets did not come easy for Arthur excluding, perhaps, his sexual orientation. Fully aware he had used his female companion as cover for his indiscretions, he was not ready to give up on his private life and for that reason alone he liked to keep domestic life companionable. Nonetheless, he continued his nocturnal rambling around the Royal parks but failed to notice Josie doggedly following him at a safe distance. Mostly he picked up guardsmen from Knightsbridge barracks, paying them for their services; the more interesting liaisons, a noted actor or politician, she carefully logged in her pocket book.

Although they had agreed to rub along amicably, beneath the surface trouble was brewing. After a couple of large gin and tonics, Josie liked to tease him about his sexual persuasion, mischievously warning him to be careful whom he meets in the dark. Each time, more in shame than anger, he verbally threatened her with more disclosures and public exposure about her past.

In between the increasing bouts of drinking, hostilities ceased and the odd couple got along quite well until money problems intervened. The apartment was looking shabby, running repairs to the fabric of the building had become a priority and, as well as a jobbing builder, Arthur brought in close friend Placido Vincenti, an elderly designer from Italy, to advise on interior decoration and soft furnishings but Josie had other plans.

'Surely I have a say on furnishing and decorating my own room and bathroom as well as the kitchen?'

Arthur was not keen on her involvement, neither was his friend and the bickering began.

'This is my apartment and I just about pay for everything including you. As I shall also be paying for the refurbishment, my say is final.'

Placido gleefully clapped his hands and nodded furiously in agreement but Josie was quick on the rebound.

'Yes, you old shirt-lifter and no doubt you will do very nicely out of it. So I suggest you keep your nose out of this please.'

Affronted at her rudeness, Arthur took a 'high horse' attitude.

'How dare you speak to my friend like that. He is from a fine Italian family in Venice and his father once worked at the Consulate. I have high hopes for him.'

'I bet you have, old boy,' she replied with a wry smile. 'If you won't stump up for my rooms, I shall use my savings and commission myself to design my own rooms; it will be cheaper in the long run.'

That said she collected her coat and bag and called for a cab. Still on his 'high horse', Arthur asked: 'And where do you think you are going madam?'

'To Heals, where I shall choose my own furnishings and pay for them with my own money, on delivery; I shall also buy a lock to keep you out.'

Slamming the door behind her, hands on hips, Placido shouted: 'Bloody bitch. Who does she think she is?'

Arthur reprimanded him. 'That was rude and uncalled for. Despite our difficulties, she has been my companion for many years and I will not have her treated this way. It was supposed to be my surprise for her 50th birthday in January and we have ruined everything; I think we should leave it for now and hope she comes round after I have explained the situation to her. Now to lunch at Giovanni's in the Italian Arcade.' Like a spoilt child, Placido sulked all the way to Southampton Row.

A month before Christmas, Heals delivered Josie's furniture. She was out when it arrived, leaving Arthur to take delivery of her bedroom suite, occasional tables, a comfortable armchair and reading lamps. Charging them to his account, he asked the deliverymen to remove and replace the old furniture, tipped them well and waited for Josie's reaction.

Although he had apologised for his and Placido's behaviour, apart from meal times, she kept him at a distance, occasional speaking out of necessity rather than socially. When she saw the new furniture in her rooms, she could not hide her feelings and she smiled her Josie smile again. Asking him for the account, she was surprised to find it stamped, paid in full. 'This is most unexpected Arthur, I had no idea they would arrive today; I shall reimburse you tomorrow when I can get to the bank.'

'But do you like it, Joan? I asked the delivery porters to arrange it like this, it suits the room this way round, don't you think?' he said hopefully.

'It does indeed and we didn't require your friend's input. He hasn't been around lately, where is he?'

'Back with his family in Venice; if he changes his ways his father has promised to find him a studio to play in.'

'So he will not be back to sway you?'

'It's unlikely but I believe there are plenty more fish in the sea for an old 'un like me. I never wanted to fall out with you Josephine, I had intended to spruce up the apartment and refurbish your rooms for your 50th birthday in January. I could not think of anything else to give you and if you are pleased then I am too. I have also arranged for a celebration party at the Café Royal on your birthday so make a list of guests and we will start the New Year with a smile.'

The peace and quiet ended at Arthur's appointment as Chief Tour Guide for the great Festival of Britain. Recognised for his experience and wide knowledge of London streets, transport routes and places of interest, part of his retirement package from the Home Office required him to be available for state occasions including the huge festival on the South Bank of the Thames. His well-paid duties also included showing VIP visitors around the impressive site, providing entertainment and hosting various official functions. Much of the capital was still in ruins and a national festival was the road to recovery and a tonic, not only for London but also for the whole nation, after years of war-time austerity.

The festival opened to great public acclaim in May 1951 with something for everyone regardless of age; roundabouts and swings, a splendid concert hall, an amazing Dome of Discovery and an awesome, cigar-shaped Skylon rising three hundred feet above ground, coincidently made in Hereford.

For Josie, it was Hereford May Fair all over again but this time bigger, better and more colourful than ever and she was excited at being a part of it all, but it did not happen.

Reminded by his superiors his partner was not a wife and therefore could not be accorded the privilege of spouse rights, Arthur was quietly relieved. Unable to understand why she could not accompany him, she spiralled into depression, refused to eat and spent most evenings drinking heavily in The Curzon Arms. Shocked at her condition, Arthur called in her physician, Dr. Michael Creighton and, taking his advice, she finally accepted medication; he also encouraged her to get back to her old, familiar self again but it did not help.

Not knowing who she really was, she decided to stay with Fanny in Mortlake. Arthur confessed to missing her and begged her to come home and, before leaving, she handed the small black notebook to her sister.

'Keep this safe and if anything happens to me, use it as you see fit. I was going to sell it to a national newspaper in case I needed some cash; keep it in the shoebox with the 'rainy day' fund and don't tell a soul about it.'

Fanny was shocked at the strange request and, for the first time in her life, she questioned her sister's motives.

'What's going on, our Trix? This is not like you, for years you could not care a fig about anyone except your family. You have been looking so worried, almost scared, and you are drinking far too much. Please tell me what's wrong?'

Josie sighed. 'Life is no longer a bowl of cherries. The fun has gone out of it and I am bored half to death with Arthur and his bloody moods. I have had enough Fanny and there are days when I would gladly go back to where it all began in Barton Road with you, Ma, Doris and the girls.'

'And I suspect George Davis. Despite everything you miss him, don't you?' Fanny asked.

'Sometimes, yes. I know he is around and desperate to get even with me and I think he is having me watched; we keep getting telephone calls asking for Josephine O'Dare. Arthur is just as bad; whenever I go out he checks up on me, it's like having the Gestapo on the doorstep and I can't take much more.'

'Then come and live with us for a while, at least until you find your feet again. Teresa would love it too. There's still a good few quid in the kitty and we have two spare rooms.'

Josie was touched. 'I know that, Fan, but it's not about George, it's about me. My sense of adventure has shifted, the tingle of excitement is dead and these days I feel a bit of a nobody.'

'You'll never be a nobody. Crikey, Trix, you bluffed your way into high society, gave Ma and me a damn good life, hit the headlines and did a proper job. One day someone will tell your story but until then you are still my little sister and I will always love you.'

She burst into tears and the two sisters hugged each other, as if for the last time.

Soon after the visit, Josie took to wearing her silver locket again; it was in the corner of her jewellery box and she wore it with pride. It reminded her of 'the good old days' in Hereford, with the Davis gang and the girls in Barton Road and she began to wonder where it all went wrong.

Life in Chesterfield Gardens was driving her to drink and rows with Arthur went on and on until he finally told her: 'You must stop drinking and gossiping about me over the bar at the Curzon or you'll find yourself homeless.'

Josie brazened it out. 'May I remind you I still have my notes and you can't afford a scandal so I suggest you withdraw that last remark?'

Before he could reply the telephone rang, he picked it up and waited before speaking: 'I have already told you, Josephine O'Dare does not live here,' and, fixing her with a cold stare, he added: 'At least I don't think she does?'

Replacing the receiver, he turned to Josie and after a long, thoughtful silence told her: 'That's the sixth inquiry this week and a reminder that life does have a habit of catching up with you, Joan. Quite frankly it can't go on like this?'

'It certainly does dear boy, for both of us but who is going to crack first I wonder?' and walked to the drinks cupboard, taking out two glasses and a bottle of champagne and laughed at him. 'Let's drink to the past Arthur and to my future. I prefer to drink to that.' He said nothing.

Raising her glass with a flourish she said: 'All right then, let's drink to your future, the boys in blue and your hefty pension. As to my future, I have nothing to lose. You, old boy, have it all to lose.'

Later that evening they called a truce and went for a few drinks at the Curzon but it did not end there. The few drinks turned into a few niggles and then into a full-blown row with verbal aggression unlike any other row witnessed in the lounge bar. Friends and fellow drinkers tried to laugh it off, it was no use; turning their backs on them, the unhappy pair went home. The row over his lifestyle rumbled on into the lift and along the hallways and corridors, making it clear to all and sundry that two months into the South Bank Festival she was still incensed over her rejection as spouse. Accusations were flying around and it was plain enough she believed he had arranged it.

'You are having the time of your life, chaperoning important people around London, wining and dining them in the House of Lords and enjoying concerts in the Festival Hall and at Covent Garden. Be honest, Arthur, you are more than happy mixing with your own kind, wherever they come from. These days you are looking younger than your years, dying your hair and dressing down helps, yet still refuse to accept who you really are but I do and cannot ignore it.'

Shocked at her words, most of them heard by the neighbours, he pleaded with her to keep her voice down but she persisted with threats to expose him, this time for cash. It finally came to a head in July; they had just about finished supper when Josie jokingly suggested: 'Now that you're mixing with the bigwigs I'm thinking of cashing you in. I have seen you in the park with a certain Lord of the Realm, some politicians and a couple of well-known actors and me and my little journal may tell all to the 'News of the World'.'

Snatching the bottle of champagne from the table, she tucked it under her arm, defiantly strolled to her room and closed the door with a click.

Arthur's normally mild manner had turned to pent-up anger. Striking the table with his fist, he flung the champagne flute into the kitchen sink and shook like a leaf. Trying to control his anger, he gripped the table until his knuckles distorted and changed to white; after a few minutes, he went to the bathroom, removed a small bottle of pills from the medicine cabinet and slipped it into his pocket. Shutting the mirrored door, he stared at his image until his eyes filled with tears and could look no more.

Leaving the bathroom, he paused outside Josie's door and, tempted to knock and try the handle, he decided against it and continued along the corridor to his own bedroom.

Safely in her room, Josie, dressed in satin pyjamas, was ferreting through a drawer in her dressing table, catching a finger on a pin and it began to bleed. Wrapping a white hankie around the small wound, she continued with the hunt until she found what she was looking for, her cheap silver locket and chain. Wrapped around a small box, she carried both of them to her bedside table, unravelled the chain and went for a hot soak in her private bathroom.

Returning to her bed, she smoothed out the fresh silk sheets, plumped up the matching pillows and settled against them; for a moment or two she played with the locket.

The small box contained a fine white powder and, fighting her feelings, she took a tiny dip, touched her nostrils and sniffed; it was a mistake and she knew it. Dashing to the bathroom, she blew her nose on the bloodied white hankie and emptied the powder into the lavatory, the handkerchief with it.

'Sod that Arthur Brooks, I'm done with yer, you ain't bleedin' worth it' and brought the lavatory seat down hard.

She was still a Herefordshire a girl at heart and acting as if she was taking everything out on George Davis twenty years ago. Back in her bed, her muddled thoughts drifted back to Wellington, the farmer's boys, May Fair and the Davis gang. She was almost asleep when Arthur when tapped lightly at the door and interrupted her dreams.

'Sorry to disturb you, Joan, I have some warm milk, it might help you sleep. I shall leave at your door with your tablets. Do not forget to take it dear. Goodnight.'

'Good night. I shall drink it later,' she murmured sleepily, her dreams at an end.

Next morning Arthur was suffering from lack of sleep; normally up with the birds and bustling about the kitchen making breakfast, today it was

312

different. Today he was sitting on a kitchen stool watching the kettle boil its self silly, steam filling the kitchen almost to the ceiling.

Confirming his sleepless night, dark rings circled his eyes and he appeared confused and somewhat bewildered and could not be bothered with the steaming kettle. When the morning paper dropped through the letter box, he dragged himself into the hall, collected it and on the way back casually turned off the kettle, switched on the wireless and sat awhile and stared into space.

Generally, he took Josie tea and toast, but this time, there was no tea, no call, just an abrupt knock on her bedroom door. He waited, listened and then returned to the kitchen to make a single cup of tea and sat down to read the paper; it was eight o'clock and another hour passed before he tried again.

Again no response and, agitated, he pottered about the kitchen in his nightclothes tidying up this and that and repeatedly wiped down the same surfaces. Eventually he boiled himself an egg, made toast and percolated a pot of strong coffee; gathering himself together, he made a third attempt at waking his companion; this time opening the unlocked door.

Strangely, he appeared unsurprised at finding her in a deep sleep; there was evidence of spittle on her lips and she was partly covered with a silk sheet deep sleep. She was barely breathing and, without the slightest hint emotion or panic, Arthur bent over her and whispered her name two or three times. When her eyelids began to flicker, he quietly left the room, went for a shower and carelessly failed to pick up the tablets on the floor; he did, however, remove the empty cup of milk on her dressing table.

An hour later, he emerged from his bedroom washed, shaved, refreshed and fully dressed. In the kitchen, the radio was still chattering away, he turned it off and made one final check on the unconscious Josie. There was little sign of life and, to be sure, he took a hand mirror from the dressing table and held it in front of her mouth and nose but she had not breathed her last. Wiping it clear with a small towel, he returned it to the dressing table and, nervously picking up the telephone beside her bed, called Dr. Creighton. Instructed to leave the still body on the bed, he hurriedly checked the room and waited for the Doctor; the tablets were no longer on the floor but beside her on the pillow.

The doorbell raised the first moment of panic. Ignoring Arthur Brooks, Creighton went directly to his patient and immediately called for an ambulance. Ordering a fretful Arthur to wait outside on the pavement until it arrived, he checked his patient. Out on the street, Arthur was himself again, his future had not changed but behind a door in Chesterfield Gardens the future of a Hereford adventuress had come to a final, wretched end.

CHAPTER TWENTY- FIVE

St. George's Hospital, Hyde Park Corner, is a short walk from Chesterfield Gardens and Arthur Brooks was first to arrive at the casualty department. Claiming Joan Brooks as his adopted daughter, he was desperate to present his version of events before Fanny arrived but he was too late. Dr. Creighton and the ambulance team were already conversing with a senior police officer and, believing he was under suspicion, he tried to intervene; the police officer waved him away.

Ten minutes later Fanny arrived with Lady Carter; fortunately she was at her London home when Fanny broke the shocking news and instructed her to take a taxi and meet her at the hospital. Advising her to speak to no-one until she arrived, she also promised to contact Kristy.

Catching sight of Arthur reminded Fanny of her sister's doubts about him but it was not the time or the place to fall out but, after hearing details of Josie's sudden death, the colour drained from her face. When Arthur suggested he should identify Joan, her sister politely refused and, unnerved by her response, he insisted it was his right to identify his 'adopted' daughter. Before a minor argument turned into a humdinger of a row, Fanny saved the situation by announcing to hospital staff: 'I am here to identify Theresa Agnes Skyrme; Mr. Brooks can identify whoever he likes.'

The bickering ended when the Coroner's Officer arrived to take witness statements. Names and addresses exchanged, the police officer explained because of sudden death an inquest would determine the cause and, being the legitimate next of kin, Mrs. Duncan (Fanny) will be required to identify her sister. It did not take long and afterwards the tearful friends comforted each other at Rumplemayer's Tea Rooms. Meanwhile, Arthur insisted on seeing his late companion and the Corner's Officer escorted him to the mortuary; later he made a statement and, pending further enquiries, went home.

For two or three days the residents of Chesterfield Gardens and confused regulars at the Curzon Arms tried to untangle gossip from fact and mumbled rumours of suspicious circumstances grew when Arthur Brooks was taken in for questioning. The formal interview took place at Scotland Yard and Arthur was a bundle of nerves; he was about to be questioned over Joan's death and asked for his legal representative Dennis Sandleson to be present. He was not available.

Alone in the Flying Squad, he suspiciously scuffed his shoes across the floorboards under the desk. When two CID officers arrived, one of them holding a brown envelope, he shiftily stood up as if he had something to hide. Suspicious of his actions the younger officer intentionally dropped the envelope onto the floor. Keen to discover what Brooks was trying to conceal, Senior Investigating Officer, Detective Sgt. Hewitt picked it up and at the same time scooped up the remains of crushed tablets. After showing them to Arthur, he carefully slipped them into a small envelope, sealed and signed it and placed it in his file.

Officially introducing himself, Hewitt explained: 'You have not been arrested, you are here to help us with our enquiries into the sudden death of Joan Brooks. I understand your legal representative is not available but you can request a duty solicitor. Do you understand?'

As befitting a retired Home Office official, Brooks knew his rights and nodded. Asked to turn out his pockets, he produced various small, personal items including a handkerchief and pieces of white tablets; he also handed over some letters and a leather wallet from a pocket inside his top coat. The writing in the letters matched the envelopes brought in by the junior police officer and, after examining them closely, Detective Sgt. Hewitt added them to his file.

Questioned about his relationship with the deceased and how and when he discovered her body, the rest of the interview centred on his attempt to hide evidence. He was then cautioned to be available for the Coroner's inquest and warned he would be expected to give evidence under oath. The interview completed, Green Park was a welcome respite from the confines of the depressing police station but it was not over yet. The inquest hung over him like the shadow of doom and he was not looking forward to the outcome.

News that the mystery woman found unconscious at her flat in Chesterfield Gardens on August 16th could be the notorious adventuress Miss Josephine O'Dare, caused a stir in the press. The inquest, adjourned until September 11th was reported in the late editions of the evening papers; it did not go unnoticed.

Seated at her usual table at the Savoy Hotel, the elderly Lady Constance Radcliffe, widow of Lord Henry, was quietly sipping a brandy and soda when she noticed the report tucked away on the page three. Now some twenty years older, her wrinkled face could not hide her handsome features or dignified manner. She spluttered, coughed and her eyes filled with tears as she read the news for a second time, her heart almost burst with sadness. She showed it to her younger companion.

'I knew her once. She was a delightful young woman but very, very naughty and I had to drop her from my circle. I often wondered what happened to her, such a terrible end for a lovely young woman. I am heartbroken, Sarah, and I must go home, alone. Be a good secretary, find out when and where the funeral might be and bring the car to the side entrance.'

The inquest, conducted by Mr. H. Neville Stafford at Westminster Coroner's Court was a mix of family and friends, curious observers and the police investigation team desperate to discover what really happened to Miss Joan Brooks at her home in Chesterfield Gardens on August 15th.

In the front seats, set aside for principal witnesses, Fanny distanced herself from Arthur Brooks and sat with Lady Carter and Kristy; they were joined by ex-prisoner Tew.

She was on a trip to London when the news broke in the café in Portobello Road where she occasionally met up with ex con chum. Josie had given her Fanny's telephone number and, shocked to hear the rumour was true, she promised to be at the inquest and funeral service.

As expected, Arthur was called first and confirmed.

'I adopted Joan about twenty years ago and for some time she had been a martyr to nerves and insomnia. On August 15th, I found her lying on her back in her bed with her head slightly inclined to the right, as if she were sleeping. I had often seen her like that and it did not occur to me that she may have taken an overdose of sleeping tablets.'

The Coroner interrupted: 'Was she under the care of her General Practitioner, Dr. Creighton, at the time of her death and did he prescribe sleeping tablets for her?'

'Yes she was but the tablets were not strong enough, in fact I think she said they were rubbish so she also drank quite a lot to make her sleep.'

'But did she say she did not want to live?'

'She did, many times.'

'Did you take her seriously?' Mr. Stafford asked.

'No,' Brooks replied. 'She would be like that for a few days and then she would be bright and happy again.'

Recalling what happened on August 14th, the day before the incident, Brooks told the inquest: 'We went to a hotel in the West End where she had three double whiskies before returning home to the flat; it is difficult to say if she was influenced by drink because she rarely showed signs of it. We had a meal and went to bed before midnight, there was no quarrel and we parted on the best of terms. Next morning I went to her room about nine o'clock, she did not respond to my knock and I left it for an hour or so. I went back again and tried her door; it was not locked so I went in and, as I said before, found her lying on her bed as if she was sleeping. She was breathing heavily and there was a light hint of saliva at the corner of her mouth; I shook her and said Joan wake up but I came to the conclusion that she was more or less unconscious and left her there to recover.'

The Coroner was puzzled. 'I am not clear as to why you did not call the doctor at once if, as you say, she was unconscious. Unconsciousness is a very serious condition and a doctor should have been called.'

Looking worried, Arthur glanced at his solicitor before replying and after a moment to think, answered: 'I had seen her like that on several occasions and she soon recovered, I did not realise she was so ill but I did call him later and he arrived shortly after 11.00am.'

The Coroner suggested: 'Better late than never, I suppose, but I'm not entirely convinced. I presume we shall hear Dr. Creighton's version in due course.'

Adjusting his spectacles, Neville Stafford shuffled through his papers, paused to record his notes and then handed Brooks an open letter.

'Can you confirm if this is the hand writing of Miss Brooks and where and when did you find it?' he asked.

'It was in a registered packet sent to me from somewhere in Gloucester; it arrived around the weekend after she had died.'

Arthur was beginning to sweat but the Coroner persisted with his line of questioning and handed him a matching envelope. 'Where did you first notice them Mr. Brooks?'

He squirmed before replying: 'I found them on the morning of August 27th; hidden in the silk lining of a suitcase belonging to Joan.'

'And why were you searching inside her belongs and what did you expect to find?'

Realising his client was under pressure, Dennis Sanderson intervened: 'Can you tell us Mr. Brooks was there a reason to suggest any immediate financial threat hanging over the deceased?'

'I believe that was the case, Sir, but I thought it was being dealt with.'

Satisfied with the answer, Neville Stafford adjourned the inquest until after lunch, leaving an already restless court somewhat confused. Fanny went outside with her friends but, fearing unwanted contact with Arthur Brooks in front of the waiting press, she returned to the safety of the courtroom to eat Christie's well-prepared packed lunch.

In the afternoon session, Dr. Creighton presented well. Confirming his address as Charles Street, a short distance from Chesterfield Gardens, he told the inquest: 'I occasionally gave my patient, Joan Brooks, prescriptions for depression, the last one on July 15th for twenty four capsules. When I arrived on the scene, I checked the bottle to find very few had been used.'

Looking directly at Brooks he added: 'If I might say so, Sir, Miss Brooks was fully conversant with the danger of overdosing and knew how and when to take the tablets. She had never once threatened to take her own life and I would be knocked for six if she did.'

Home Office analyst Dr. John Henry Ryffel admitted to recognising Arthur Brooks but he could not be sure where he had seen him before. However, in his professional opinion, actual death must have been due to other causes, secondary to the taking of barbiturates and cabitrol which I found in her body. An amount grossly in excess of a medical dose had been taken.'

Dr. J.F. Taylor, pathologist at St George's hospital confirmed: 'I found recent needle punctures in her arm but no evidence of previous puncture marks. It is my belief the immediate cause of death was hypostatic pneumonia and acute respiratory problems which appeared to be due to some sort of narcotic poisoning.'

Mr. Stafford thanked both doctors for their evidence and invited Detective Sgt. Hewitt, the investigating officer, to present his evidence.

'On August 27th at Scotland Yard, I found the letter produced in court earlier; it was in the right-hand coat pocket of a jacket worn by Mr. Arthur Brooks, the envelope was in his left-hand trouser pocket.'

Passing him a small envelope, the Coroner asked him: 'And where did you find these tablets?'

'I was in the process of interviewing Mr. Brooks and I noticed him rubbing his foot underneath the desk and I stopped him.'

Impatience was setting in. 'We already know that, all I want to know is where you found the tablets?'

'On the floor, in the Flying Squad office, at Scotland Yard,' he replied.

'Did he give you an explanation of what they were and where he got them from and were you satisfied with his reply?'

'Yes, Sir.'

'Are you satisfied you have completed your enquiries?'

'Certain enquiries I am making in this case are not yet complete but in relation to the death of Miss Brooks my inquiries are ended and I do not wish the inquest adjourned further.'

'And as a result of these enquiries are you satisfied there are no suspicious circumstances?'

'Yes, I am Sir.'

'And you don't need any more time to investigate?'

'Not into the death but for other matters in this case, I will need more time.'

Summing up, the Coroner referred to the undated letter addressed by Miss Brooks to a person in North Gloucester. 'That the letter appeared to be of a suicidal nature means I will need time to consider this and all other matters relating to the untimely death of Miss Brooks, in particular the evidence of handwriting. Only one witness was able to recognise it, her companion Mr. Brooks, and I must consider this before reaching my conclusion. I will record a written verdict for the next of kin in due course. Thank you all for attending this inquest and send the condolences of the court to the deceased's sister Mrs. Duncan.'

Clearly relieved at the verdict, Arthur shook hands with his solicitor but before leaving the court offered his heartfelt condolences to Fanny and promised to pay for the arrangements.

She gracefully replied: 'Not now Arthur, it is too soon and far too painful. She was my only, much-loved sister and I will never let you into her life again. You do have a right to be at her burial and, when the body is released, I shall let you know details, other than that I want nothing from you.'

Later that night, George Davis emerged from Piccadilly underground station; helped to the nearest public house by dubious associates and lifted onto a barstool. He had aged enough to go unrecognised in his home town of Hereford and was clutching a rolled up copy of the late edition of the 'Evening News' in his shaking hands. Unrolling it, he exposed the headline to his pals: "Unexplained Suicide of Mayfair Woman. Verdict.'

'Did you know her, George?' the landlord asked.

'I did once. I would have taken a bullet for her and nearly did in the Somme, but she grassed me up years ago and I wanted revenge.'

'Did you get it mate?'

'Sort of, I suppose,' and dropped to a heap on the floor.

Five days later, the Westminster Coroner announced his verdict: 'Joan Brookes came to her death through hypostatic pneumonia and acute bronchitis consequent upon barbiturate poisoning administered in circumstances not fully disclosed by the evidence.'

Two days later, he released the body for burial.

It was a sunny afternoon and a surprising number of mourners had gathered for the funeral at Nunhead Cemetery, Peckham. Trixie wished to be reunited with her mother and for the Salvation Army to conduct the graveside service and internment. Fanny had made all the arrangements and for some reason, had placed an obituary notice in 'The Times' and the 'London Evening News'; she had also contacted the few named friends in her sister's meagre address book, more in hope than anything else. At the last minute, a frail and distraught Lady Constance arrived with her secretary but preferred to sit in the car rather than be seen by all and sundry. Her arrival did not go unnoticed by Fanny who, surrounded by her loyal friends and members of the Salvation Army, had spotted the chauffer-driven Rolls-Royce.

A smartly dressed youngish man, said to be his nephew, accompanied Arthur Brooks to the graveside and a few former colleagues from the Home Office and regulars from the Curzon Arms, joined the mourners. In the shadow of the church, part hidden by an ancient oak tree, a presentable George Davis waited in the wings for the final rites.

After a brief service delivered by a heavily pregnant Kristy, familiar faces from the past assembled at the graveside, some from the Park Street days; Fanny shook hands with each one and offered them a handful of earth to drop into the grave. It was a poignant moment when she recognised a much older

Albert Marriot leaving a wreath of summer blooms; he nodded to her and then walked away alone.

The funeral party was about to break up when Fanny noticed a distraught Arthur silently gazing into the grave; he had lost much of his usual arrogant demeanour and she went to stand with him. Loud enough for everyone to hear, he read the simple inscription on the shiny brass plate on the coffin: 'Theresa Agnes Skyrme, 1899-1951, Rest in Peace.'

'After the life she led, will she ever get it, Fanny?'

'She will now, Arthur,' and he walked away.

As the first shovel of earth hit the coffin, he hesitated and walked back to Fanny. Lady Carter, who was waiting to take her to the car, had invited everyone to the wake at the Curzon Arms and reminded Fanny it was time to go but she wanted to see the flowers and took Arthur with her.

Standing over the grave, she opened her handbag, took out the black notebook and gave it to him.

'My sister gave this to me a time ago, to do with as I wished. I know what it contains and why she kept it; it is of no use to me, she is gone and that is that. The matter is now closed.'

Walking to the car with Lady Carter, she looked back and noticed he was crying as he read the contents; aware people were watching his tears fall on the open pages, he choked back his final goodbye. Fanny caught up with him again, took the notebook and, to his surprise, dropped it into the grave. From his inside coat pocket, Arthur removed Josie's silver locket and chain and showed Fanny the photos inside.

'That's George Davis,' she told him. 'He won it for her on the hoopla stall at Hereford May Fair when she was sixteen; best place for it now is in there with her.'

Leaving him to his thoughts, she walked away again.

Arthur waited for the next two shovels of earth to fall and then dangled the locket and chain over the grave; when the coffin was suitably covered, he tossed the locket into the air, waited for it to drop onto the soft earth and, accompanied by his nephew, walked to his car.

Beneath the oak tree, George Davis raised his trilby hat and in the silent graveyard laid his own floral tribute, a single red rose, at the head of the finished grave.

Generously tipping the gravedigger, he said: 'Keep it nice and tidy and I'll see you right but not a word to anyone.'

The after-show party, as Josie would have called it, was organised by regulars at the various licensed premises around Chesterfield Gardens. They knew little of her colourful past and a few drinks on the house could loosen tongues and revive many more memories for some of the outsiders. The Curzon Arms had a particularly large function room and agreed to lay on food to match the drink donated by the other licensees.

By six o'clock, the place was buzzing; people had settled into small groups each questioning the others' right to be there. Alcohol was flowing freely, matched by gossip and hearsay and familiar faces lingered until Fanny dutifully made their acquaintance. Many of them had aged over the years, particularly Lady Constance Radcliffe, deep in conversation with Francine, the Bishop's daughter from White Water Hall and Tew, lately of Holloway.

A couple of waitresses from Rumplemayer's Tea Shop in St. James's shared a table with the few remaining volunteers from the Church Poverty Action Group and the rest were associates of Arthur Brooks. Amid the rights and wrongs of Trixie's former life and her sudden death, the landlord of the Curzon Arms called for order and invited Arthur to say a few words. Stepping up to the small dais in a corner of the room, for a moment or two, he could not speak; encouraged by his friends he said: 'Joan was my best friend. We met at Frinton-on-Sea about fifteen years ago and I invited her to share my London home.'

'I trust not your bed as well,' said the anonymous voice at the rear of the room. Arthur blushed and carried on regardless.

'Yes, she liked a drink, she liked to laugh and, as you all know, she did good works during the Blitz but whatever the past may say about her, as far as I'm concerned she never hurt a living soul and those who knew her well will surely agree. Her death is a great loss to young Teresa, her much-loved niece and her sister Fanny and me; we are all going to miss her. What's done is done and it's time to raise a farewell glass to Joan Brooks, confidante, companion and friend to so many.'

To much applause, he sat down and hoped that was that. It would have been had not Constance Radcliffe enjoyed more than enough gin and tonic. Assisted by her companion and part hidden in a haze of cigarette smoke, she staggered to her feet sweeping all before her.

'She was a corking little filly and I knew her well in her heyday. She could charm the birds from the trees and she knew the men from the boys when it came to claiming their assets. According to the newspapers, she was only a farm labourer's daughter, but in London society, she was nothing short of a 'swell' and carried it off in style. She did me proud I can tell you and I was one of the many ready to fall at her feet. But she let me down and I never got over it.'

She was about to cry when her secretary suggested she had said enough, but to loud cheers she insisted: 'Remember this, we may never see the likes of her again; I invite you all to toast the most daring and delightful adventuress Scotland Yard ever set out to capture, the silly sods! She fell into her chair and sobbed into her Chanel hat. Fanny, who had taken more than her fair share of sherry, decided to end the day.

'Thank you all for coming. Trixie was my sister and if it wasn't for her, Ma and me would have sunk under the fists of our brother and father years ago. Back in Herefordshire we would have been done for, but Trixie did us proud and got us out of the hellhole for good. She was no angel but what she did, she did in her own crazy way and we must respect every moment of her memory. One day we may read about her but for now let's raise a final glass to Theresa Agnes Skyrme and go home.'

Smiling up at the ceiling, she quietly proposed: 'A proper job our Trixie, a right proper job.'

EPILOGUE

Throughout her life of crime and deception, Trixie Skyrme made a good many enemies; peers of the realm, rejected lovers, bankrupted wealthy suitors, betrayed thieves and most of all George Davis, who, on the evidence of his one time prodigy and partner in crime, went down for thirteen years hard labour. A betrayal he could not forget and he wanted revenge. Arthur Brooks also felt betrayed by his long-term, platonic partner, a woman he later claimed to be his adopted daughter. Why, after trying to wake her at her usual time, did he wait two hours before trying again and calling a doctor? Did he also write the alleged suicide letter supposedly written by Trixie to a person in Gloucester and discovered a week after her death in the lining of her suitcase? Brooks alone identified the handwriting but the supposed recipient was not named at the inquest. What was he hiding when he was caught destroying tablets said to have caused the death of his companion? Finally, why did Detective Sgt. Hewitt turn down an offer from the Coroner of more time to investigate the death, yet admitted on-going enquiries were continuing into other aspects of the case.

What really did happen to Trixie Skyrme could lie in the little black book used to record the illicit secret life of Arthur Brooks? Perhaps not. Maybe the adrenaline of living dangerously had simply stopped pumping and at fifty-two years of age she could not accept it was all over. Yet under oath her long-serving doctor was not convinced she was suicidal at any time.

Young Trixie Skyrme took life by the scruff of the neck, shook it out at every turn and never looked back and, for a woman described by Scotland Yard as 'the most remarkable and dangerous adventuress they had ever set out to capture', suicide would have been an unlikely choice. Destiny had carried her from the hop-fields of Herefordshire to the Mansions of Mayfair without pausing for breath and it is worth noting that she never physically hurt anyone except in the pocket. Did she carelessly fail to tie up a few loose ends or did someone do it for her?

BOOKS BY JEN (JENNIFER) GREEN.

THE MORNING OF HER DAY

Tells the story of a woman who saw a gravestone and became a writer. From then on she became obsessed with the death and life of a seventeen year old servant girl hanged early in 19th century for the murder of her bastard child. There was no escape from the historical web that the myth, hearsay and fact weaved around her and the great change it brought about as she approached the middle years of her life. She took on the pain of a town that had carried a secret for over two hundred years; a town still divided in its loyalties to the dead girl even today. It would have been so easy to give up the search for the truth but the possibilities of a gross miscarriage of justice, albeit over 200 years ago, confirmed her beliefs that fair play should be available to all regardless of class.
First Published by Divine Books (1987) Second edition Darf Books Ltd (1990)
277, West End Lane, West Hampstead London NW6 1QS. Tel. 0207 4317009
ISBN 1 85077 221 5

REVIEWS
"It is a haunting story which feminists have adopted as metaphor for the guilt imposed upon woman for the crimes of men". She Magazine.

"A marvellously strange little book, vivid and moving"
Duncan Fallowell. Novelist and Travel writer.

~~~~

"TRAVELS OF A BOTHY BOY"
Foreword by Mayor of London Ken Livingston,

This beautifully produced autobiography of RJ Corbin, Horticulturist and Gardener extraordinaire, written with Jen Green follows the life and career of man described by his peers as one of natures gentlemen. Currently in his ninth decade, this is a visual and written record of a well-travelled and popular horticulturalist favoured by HM The Queen. From childhood days in the New Forest until present day London's Royal Parks, Estates and Gardens, it is a life dedicated to gardening, horticulture and grounds-manship across the world. One of the last remaining pre-war old boys from the Royal Horticultural Society college at Wisley, Robert Corbin served the London County Council for thirty-five years and played a major part in restoration of the Royal Parks after the blitz. He remains an active member of the RHS, served the Institute of Ground-manship as President and a Judge at Chelsea Flower Show.
As well as a gardeners string of stories and glories, the book has a stunning collection of photographs taken by RJ Corbin his journey's across the world.
Travels of a Bothy Boy is published by Potting Shed Publications (2007)
ISBN 978-0-9528956-0-2.

"CHANGING SCENES"

foreword by

Sir Roy Strong, Historian
and former Director of the National Portrait Gallery
and the Victoria and Albert Museum

Changing Scenes is a written and pictorial history of Tenbury Wells, Queen Victoria's
'Little Town in the Orchard" in Worcestershire. Commissioned by Tenbury Agricultural
Society, one of the longest remaining Agricultural Show organisers in the UK, to
celebrate 150 years of rural life, the book is a kaleidoscope of social history told through
the life and times of a small market town and it farming community.
Filled with a collection of rural and farming memories and old photographs from the
past, it is a must for researchers, readers and students of country life and all those who
care about traditional farming. Told in a non-academic style, "Changing Scenes" is a
delightful and amusing meander through English social and rural history, long forgotten
today.
Written, compiled and produced by Jen Green, "Changing Scenes" is published by
Tenbury Wells Agricultural Society Ltd (2008), ISBN 978-0-9559373-089.

COMMENTS

*"It is absolutely stunning and tells of the history of Tenbury Wells and rural life quite
beautifully - the pictures are absolutely captivating. Tenbury Agricultural Society is very
lucky indeed to have found someone to record its history with such sensitivity and
historical rigour."* HRH the Prince of Wales.

*"I love its pell-mell character; one minute we read of the impact of the First World War,
the next about Bill Dipper whose role was to kill the farm pig and joint it up for the
family. This book will bring a great deal of delight to farming communities and is a
testament to the resilience and enterprise of Jen Green, Tenbury Wells and the Teme
Valley"* Sir Roy Strong.

POETRY

EARLY MORNING CATS
Illustrated by Nina Moores

Early morning cats belong to us all or do we belong to them?
In the cold light of dawn look around and you'll see them....
Somewhere!
A narrative poem with twelve watercolour illustrations, written after observing the same cats, in the same places, on early autumn mornings in North Herefordshire.

Published by Jenina Books (1996) ISBN 0-9528956-0-9.

~~~~

ALZABAR THE CYBER CAT
Illustrated by Pauline Vincent.

Jen's second narrative poem was inspired by her own cat, Morgan, who occasional slept on the mouse mat while she was working. The twenty-four verses tell the tale of Alzabar, a cyber cat, who is log onto a computer by a friendly mouse and travels across the world on the mouse mat to seek the lady cat he met while surfing on the internet. Quirky, colourful illustration by London based artist Pauline Vincent, bring the story to life, a story Jen Green told to her great niece during hospital visits. The book was written for and in memory of Megan Rose Tanner who died for want of a new heart when she was four years old.

Published by Angel Works (1999) ISBN 0-9537534-0-9.

Jen Green is currently editing "The Salopian Connection" a series of short stories featuring Shropshire characters from history written as if she was reporting their story at the time. Her second novel "Fallout" an amusing, satirical tale of a Welsh Border Community ordered to carry out a Nuclear Defence Exercise in 1981 and based on her experiences as a district councillor at the time is work in progress. She is also planning to publish a collection of her 'occasional' poems, written since she was 16 years old covering events and happenings during her lifetime.